A

Laura Martin w
adventurous under
her time working a
she lives with her h
loves to lose hers
to read from cover to cover in a sing
story is particularly gripping. She also loves to travel –
especially to visit historical sites and far-flung shores.

Regency Scandals

Regency Scandal:

Benefits of a Betrothal

LAURA MARTIN

MILLS & BOON

First Published in Great Britain 2021
by Mills & Boon, an imprint of HarperCollins*Publishers* Ltd,
1 London Bridge Street, London, SE1 9GF

www.harpercollins.co.uk

HarperCollins*Publishers*
1st Floor, Watermarque Building,
Ringsend Road, Dublin 4, Ireland

REGENCY SCANDAL: BENEFITS OF A BETROTHAL
© 2021 Harlequin Books S.A.

An Earl to Save Her Reputation © 2018 Laura Martin
A Ring for the Pregnant Debutante © 2017 Laura Martin

ISBN: 978-0-263-30045-1

MIX
Paper from
responsible sources
FSC˚ C007454

This book is produced from independently certified FSC™ paper to ensure responsible forest management.

For more information visit: www.harpercollins.co.uk/green

Printed and bound in Spain
by CPI, Barcelona

AN EARL TO SAVE
HER REPUTATION

For my family, all of you.
Together you make me stronger.

Chapter One

'Three husbands in six years. If I didn't know it to be true, I wouldn't think it possible.'

'And the rumours of how those poor men died…'

'She might have a pretty face, but I wouldn't want any relative of mine becoming embroiled with her. One can only guess what will happen to husband number four.'

'It's nothing short of scandalous how she's swanning around this ballroom. Hardly out of mourning and she's all smiles and laughter.'

'And insisting she continue to run that grubby little business of her second husband. It's not ladylike and it's not proper.'

Anna closed her eyes for a moment before pressing herself further into the recess of the ballroom. The two women who were gossiping openly and maliciously were shielded from view by a tall, lush potted plant. But one of them only needed to move a few inches to their right or left and they would catch sight of Anna desperately trying to avoid them.

The words themselves didn't hurt. She had been married three times and all three husbands had died within a year of their marriage. Anna was well aware of the less-than-complimentary names she was called by the spiteful matrons and wide-eyed debutantes. *Murderer, husband killer, black widow.* It didn't seem to matter to them that it just wasn't true and Anna had learnt long ago that it was better to let people speculate than to fuel the gossip with denials and pleas to be left alone.

Despite becoming hardened to the infamy, Anna hated the sort of situation she found herself in right now. She wished she could just slink away without anyone noticing her presence.

'Lady Fortescue, how pleasant to see you again after so long,' a man Anna vaguely recognised called out in a voice that seemed to echo off the walls. From her position behind the plant pot Anna saw the two gossips turning to look her way. There was no escaping their line of sight.

Straightening her back, dropping her shoulders and lifting her chin, adopting the posture that made her look more confident even if she didn't feel it, Anna stepped out of the recess and into the ballroom. She acknowledged the man with a polite incline of her head, then turned to fix the two women with a glacial stare.

'Give my regards to your brother, Mrs Weston. Such a darling man,' Anna said, before gliding away as if she didn't have a care in the world. Anna wasn't sure if Mrs Weston even had a brother, they'd certainly never been introduced, but the small deception was worth it for the look of abject horror on both women's faces.

Anna needed to get away. With a quick glance across the ballroom she saw Beatrice, her young cousin who she had agreed to chaperon for the Season, dancing a lively cotillion, her face lit up by a sunny smile and her chest heaving from the exertion. Beatrice would be unlikely to require Anna's attention for a few minutes at least, so quickly Anna slipped out of the ballroom.

It was noticeably cooler in the hallway and there was a scent of freshly cut flowers mixed with the smell of hundreds of burning candles. Even out here small groups gathered, glad to be away from the heat and crowds in the ballroom for a few minutes, and Anna had to force herself to walk calmly past them rather than pick up her skirts and run. She just wanted some privacy, or even better anonymity, to be able to enjoy the music and dancing without everyone talking about her behind their hands.

As she ventured further from the ballroom the hallway became quieter. Anna felt her heart beginning to slow and the panic that had seized her only moments before start to subside. She tried one door handle, then another, finding an unlocked door on her third attempt. Quickly she slipped into the room, closing the door softly behind her.

It took a few minutes for her eyes to adjust to the darkness after the brilliantly lit hallway, but after a while Anna could make out the lines of bookshelves against the walls and the shapes of a few comfortable chairs with a desk at one end. This was some sort of study or library, the perfect retreat for a few moments' peace. Before long she would have to steel herself for another round of sideways looks and malicious gossip in the ballroom, but right now she would just enjoy the solitude.

Anna lowered herself into a high-backed chair, her posture rigid even though no one else would see her. Her late husband, her *latest* late husband, had been a stickler for good posture and impeccable manners. Anna had learnt quickly to glide slowly around the house, sit with a straight back and never let any emotion show on her face. The punishment for breaking these rules was unmerciful, like many of Lord Fortescue's whims.

Closing her eyes, she listened to the distant hum of conversation from the ballroom and the first faint notes of a waltz. Even through the background noise Anna noticed the sound of hurried footsteps getting closer, but before she could move the door to the study opened and two people slipped inside. It was apparent immediately that Anna's unwanted companions were a man and a woman, and by the excited whispers and scent of champagne she could only assume they were here for some secret assignation.

'Your husband won't miss you?' the man said, as Anna heard the rustle of silk.

'Old fool is at the gaming tables—he wouldn't notice a stampede of wild horses.'

Anna wondered if she should stand and make her presence known. The last thing she wanted was to become embroiled in this couple's illicit affair, but she didn't much desire to be witness to their intimacy either.

She'd just gripped the armrests, ready to push herself up, when the door opened for a second time. Anna heard the couple freeze, then spring apart in a rustle of fabric and clatter of shoes. The light of a candle illuminated the room, causing the shadows to lengthen around her. She sank back into the chair, fervently hoping that the new guest would scare away the couple and then leave her in peace.

'My apologies,' a deep, slightly amused voice said. Anna analysed the tone and intonation, but was sure she had never met this newcomer before. Even after being removed from society for the past couple of years she

still was familiar with most of the aristocratic gentlemen who frequented these balls, but this man she did
not think she recognised.

The young woman gasped theatrically and ran from
the room.

'Edgerton.'

'Wilbraham.'

The two men greeted each other with just a single
word which suggested they knew one another at least
passably well. The silence stretched out uncomfortably as Anna in her hidden position held her breath and
willed both men to leave.

'You won't say anything, old chap?'

'No. Not my place.'

Footsteps and the closing of the door followed, but
the candlelight still illuminated the room and Anna
could hear the light breathing of one of the gentlemen.

Wondering whether to make a dash for the door,
Anna shifted in her chair just as the newcomer came
into view.

'Good evening,' he said, no trace of surprise at finding her sitting in the high-back chair evident in either
his face or his voice.

'Good evening.' Despite her thumping heart Anna
managed to sound poised and calm. Years of practice at
maintaining a serene façade came in useful sometimes.

'Looking for a little peace?'

'Yes.' Anna kept her voice clipped and icy, hoping
the gentleman would understand she wanted to be left
alone.

She watched as he sauntered around the study, opening cupboards and cabinets until he came across what
he was looking for: a bottle of whisky and two short
glasses.

'Can't abide champagne,' the gentleman said, pouring out two generous measures of the caramel-coloured liquid. 'And punch is even worse.'

He held out one of the glasses, waiting for Anna to take it before he sat down in the chair next to hers. Taking a gulp, he examined the liquid thoughtfully before chuckling softly.

'What's so funny?' Anna asked, regretting the question as soon as it passed her lips. She knew better than to engage.

'Prendy's servants are watering down his whisky,' he said, raising the glass to his lips for another taste.

'Prendy's?'

'Lord Prenderson. Our host.'

'You know him well?'

'Doesn't everyone know everyone else?'

Anna was just about to bid her companion farewell when he fixed her with a penetrating stare.

'Although I don't think we've ever met.' He regarded her, letting his eyes sweep from the top of her head, across her features and down over her body. 'I'm sure I'd remember.'

The polite thing would be to introduce herself, yet Anna stood abruptly, set her untouched glass on the table and took a step towards the door.

'I wouldn't go out there just yet if I were you.'

She took another step forward.

'Bad idea.'

Two more steps. In another few seconds she would be out of the study and heading back towards the crowds.

'It's your choice, of course, but the gossips would be delighted to find you in here unchaperoned.'

Anna stiffened, closing her eyes for a brief few seconds before turning slowly and facing her companion.

'Gossips?'

'A group of middle-aged matrons are recovering from the heat of the ballroom out in the hall. I'm sure it would not escape their notice that you were in here with Lord Wilbraham and Mrs Featherstone.' He frowned as if something had just occurred to him. 'What were you planning on doing if they'd decided to further their intimacy?'

'In the study? So close to the ballroom? I hardly think that was likely,' Anna said, her voice dry and her face serene.

'I understand some people find the danger exciting.'

Anna knew he was teasing her now, but instead of rising to the bait she changed the subject.

'When will it be safe to exit, Mr Edgerton?'

'Lord Edgerton,' he corrected absently. 'And now you have me at a disadvantage.'

'Lady Fortescue,' Anna supplied reluctantly.

He fixed her with a curious gaze that told her he'd heard the rumours. *All* the rumours.

'The notorious Lady Fortescue,' he murmured.

'You're not meant to say that,' Anna said, adding under her breath, 'At least not to my face.'

'It is a pleasure to meet you, Lady Fortescue,' Edgerton said, standing and taking her hand, bringing it to his lips after a few seconds.

This close Anna could appreciate his physical size. He was at least a foot taller than her and sported broad shoulders that filled his jacket perfectly. For the first time since he'd entered, Anna realised the folly of being alone with this man. It wasn't just the scandal that could occur if they were discovered, but the risk he might take advantage. Slowly she stepped back. He didn't look as though he were about to pounce on her, but history had shown her to be a poor judge of character. Kind eyes and a relaxed manner didn't mean a man was trustworthy.

Harry saw the flash of fear in Lady Fortescue's eyes before the stony façade once again concealed her emotions. Quickly he stepped back, realising it was him she was afraid of. That had never been his intention, to scare the poor woman—he'd been called many things in his life, but frightening was not one of them.

'Let me check the hallway,' he said, summoning his friendliest smile.

Crossing to the doorway, he opened the door a crack and peered out. The group of meddling matrons still stood fanning themselves and chattering ten feet away. There was no way past them, at least not without being seen.

'Still there. I'm sure they will return to the ballroom shortly.'

Harry returned to his chair and sat, watching Lady Fortescue out of the corner of his eye. When she'd introduced herself he'd been unable to stop from staring. Normally so in control of his reactions, he'd been thrown by her identity. She was notorious, perhaps the most notorious widow in society at the present time. Married three times before the age of twenty-five, her latest husband, Lord Fortescue, in the ground for twelve months now. He'd expected her to look different somehow, perhaps more exotic. Instead a perfectly pleasant-looking young woman stood before him. She was pretty, but not any more so than most of the young debutantes. He couldn't deny she had poise and grace, but there was a coolness about her that hinted at a reserved character and a tendency to shun company. Her most intriguing feature were her eyes. Cool and grey, they seemed impenetrable. Normally a young woman's eyes gave away her emotions, but not Lady Fortescue's. If eyes were the window to the soul, then Lady Fortescue's were shuttered and barred against intruders.

They remained silent for some minutes, Harry reclining in the armchair, Lady Fortescue standing in the middle of the room, her hands folded together in front of her abdomen, the perfect picture of demure womanhood.

'So tell me,' Harry said when he could bear the silence no longer, 'are the rumours true?'

His companion sighed, a deep and heartfelt sound that hinted that she'd rather be anywhere but here.

'I find rumours rarely are,' she said evasively.

'Very true,' Harry murmured. He knew better than most the damage malicious gossip could cause. 'How do you bear it? People talking about you, speculating?'

Lady Fortescue shrugged, an instinctive movement that she seemed to try to suppress at the last moment. 'People will always talk. It doesn't matter what they say if you don't listen.'

Although she was younger than he, and undoubtedly hadn't been exposed to as much of the world as he, she had a quiet wisdom about her that suggested she'd had more important things to cope with than a little gossip in her time.

'Most women would not feel comfortable leaving the ballroom on their own, let alone wandering about a strange house,' Harry said, changing the focus of the conversation. He was curious as to why she had put herself in this position in the first place. Although the *ton* were meant to be respectable, the cream of society, some of the men still got uncontrollably drunk at functions such as this and thought it their right to take advantage of any unchaperoned woman. From a young age the future debutantes were cautioned about wandering away from crowds if they wanted to keep their virtue intact. A necessary requirement Harry was painfully aware of.

Again that almost imperceptible shrug. Lady Fortescue might be intriguing, but she certainly wasn't the easiest woman to make conversation with.

'Sometimes a little peace is worth a considered risk.' Moving gracefully, as if she were gliding across the floor instead of walking, Lady Fortescue crossed to the window. 'This leads out on to the terrace,' she said, turning her neck to look in one direction and then the other. 'It would be an easy way back to the ballroom.'

'Surely my company isn't so intolerable you have to contemplate climbing out a window?'

A grimace and then a reluctant smile flitted across Lady Fortescue's face. Although the smile was barely more than an upturning of the corner of her lips, it transformed her face and Harry caught a glimpse of what her three husbands must have been so enamoured with.

'I am supposed to be chaperoning my young cousin,' she said by way of explanation, still eyeing up the window as if it were a valid option.

'You're far too young to be relegated to the role of chaperon,' Harry said, without thinking the words through. It was a compliment, in a roundabout way, and he had the feeling Lady Fortescue was not comfortable with receiving compliments.

'Three times a widow,' Lady Fortescue said, adding so quietly Harry was sure he wasn't meant to hear, 'and happy to never have to dance a waltz again.'

She'd just stepped away from the window when the faint hum of voices out in the hallway became a little louder. Both Harry and his companion stiffened, and

Harry realised he was holding his breath waiting to see if the doorknob started to turn.

'We can't be found together,' Harry whispered, standing quickly and crossing to the window. Normally he wouldn't worry for his own reputation in this sort of situation. As a titled and wealthy gentleman he could generally withstand being found in a compromising position with a young lady, even one as notorious as Lady Fortescue. However, following his sister's unfortunate liaison with the dishonourable Captain Mountfield last year and the ensuing scandal, the Edgerton family was not in a position to be embarrassed again. Added to that the look of pure fear in Lady Fortescue's eyes at the thought of giving the gossips of London society something to really get their teeth into, the window escape was looking more appealing every second that passed.

Quickly he unbolted the window, slid it up and motioned for Lady Fortescue to join him. She was at his side in an instant, nodding as he motioned for her to go first. With more grace than should have been possible in this situation Lady Fortescue gathered up her skirts, giving Harry a fleeting glimpse of a slender, stockinged leg, and allowed him to steady her as she stepped up to the windowsill.

Behind them the voices were getting louder still and now Harry had no doubt they were heading for the study. If he could just get Lady Fortescue out of the window he would be able to distract whoever came into the room until she had managed to move out of sight.

She stepped up as the doorknob began to turn. One foot was through the window, balancing on the sill outside as the door began to open. Then Lady Fortescue gave a quiet cry of pain, lost her footing and came careening back into the room. Harry instinctively caught her, spinning round with the impact of her body into his and ending up with her chest pressed against his, one arm looped around her waist and the other resting between her shoulder blades.

At that very instant the door opened fully.

'Merciful Lord,' Mrs Winter, one of the worst gossips in the whole of London, exclaimed loudly.

Quietly Lady Fortescue groaned.

All in all there were four women standing on the other side of the study door. Each and every one looked thrilled to be at the centre of such a scandal.

Slowly, aware his every movement was being observed and mentally recorded for later dissection and discussion, Harry ensured Lady Fortescue had her balance before removing his arms and stepping away.

'Ladies,' he said with a polite bow.

'Lord Edgerton,' Mrs Winter gushed breathlessly, 'and Lady Fortescue.'

Muscling a path through her companions, a well-built lady in her late forties stepped into the room. Harry closed his eyes momentarily, wondering how he'd sinned to be punished this badly.

'Lord Edgerton, this really won't do,' Lady Prenderson, their hostess for this evening, said, her eyes burning with righteous indignation. 'This behaviour is unacceptable—having *relations* with this woman in my husband's study.'

Harry wasn't sure what she objected to the most: the supposed relations between him and Lady Fortescue or the fact that it had occurred in her husband's study.

'I expect this behaviour from certain people,' Lady Prenderson said, giving Lady Fortescue a disdainful look, 'but after the scandal your sister has caused your family I would have thought you would know better.'

Harry had been all ready to apologise, but the mention of his sister made a red curtain descend over his normally cool head. Lady Fortescue must have sensed this change in him and calmly stepped forward.

'Please excuse me, ladies, I have a duty to my cousin.' Her voice was cool and her demeanour poised and collected. Harry supposed she had endured all manner of gossip over the last few years—she must have had practice at dealing with staying calm when faced with further notoriety. He knew she was just as bothered as he by the position they'd been discovered in—her eagerness to climb out the window to avoid exactly this situation was testament to that fact—but the face she showed the world was one of complete indifference.

None of the ladies in the doorway moved, blocking the escape route to the more populated ballroom. With a tremendous effort Harry managed to regain control of his emotions and stepped forward, taking Lady Fortescue's arm. There was only one thing to be done. He took a deep breath, quelled the doubts clamouring for attention in his mind and spoke.

'Ladies, may I present my fiancée,' Harry said with a confident and winning smile. 'Lady Fortescue has just agreed to marry me.'

Shock blossomed on the four faces gawping at them from the study door. Lady Fortescue barely reacted, the only sign she'd heard what he'd just said the subtle stiffening of the muscles Harry could feel where their arms interlinked. She was certainly difficult to shock.

'Surely not, Lord Edgerton,' Mrs Winter said, a hint of disappointment in her voice. Harry remembered she had two unmarried daughters and had to suppress a smile. The work of the meddling matron was never done.

'Now if you would excuse us, I wish to get my new fiancée a glass of champagne to celebrate.'

The crowd of gossips parted silently and Harry led Lady Fortescue through them and down the hallway. Only once they were back in the ballroom did they pause, with Lady Fortescue turning to him with a raised eyebrow.

'Fiancée?' she asked.

'It will save us both from the scandal.' It wasn't exactly true, but it would at least delay the moment of scandal until a point when they were both prepared for it.

'You've just engaged yourself to the most notorious woman in this ballroom. I hardly think you've saved yourself from scandal.'

Harry felt the heat begin to rise in his body. Surely she didn't think this a real engagement. He'd meant for it to be a simple ruse, an engagement that would last a few weeks, perhaps a month until something else noteworthy occurred in society, and then they would quietly go their separate ways. The *ton* would still gossip, but it would not be the most scandalous thing to happen all year.

'Being found together in the Prendersons' study will be all over London by breakfast tomorrow morning. This way we are an unlikely engaged couple, not a disgraced earl and a widow.'

'I thank you for your consideration,' Lady Fortescue said, her grey eyes latching on to Harry's and making him shiver with the intensity, 'but I think it better we dispense with this pretence and ride out the scandal.' Leaning in, she whispered in his ear, 'Trust me, a little gossip isn't the worst thing in the world.'

Chapter Two

'I really wouldn't read that, my dear,' Mr Tenby, Anna's kindly uncle, said, a look of concern in his eyes.

Anna's hand stilled on top of the folded gossip sheets. She'd hoped the news from the Prendersons' ball would not be reported for another couple of days. It was a miracle how quickly they seemed to be able to publish the latest intrigue and style faux pas.

'Words cannot hurt me,' Anna said brightly, picking up the paper and scanning the text, trying to ignore the concerned looks coming across the breakfast table from her uncle and her cousin Beatrice.

'"*Congratulations are due to Lady Fortescue on her engagement to Lord Edgerton at Lord and Lady Prenderson's ball two days ago. Recently out of mourning for her third husband, Lady Fortescue will no doubt be keen to legalise her tie to one of London's most eligible bachelors.*"'

Anna read the offending paragraph out loud, wondering how many other people were doing the same thing at breakfast tables across London.

'What did happen, Anna?' Beatrice asked.

Ever since the Prenderson ball Anna had kept herself

distant from the rest of the household and steadfastly refused any visitors. Even her sweet younger cousin had been kept in the dark.

'A misunderstanding, nothing more.'

'This Edgerton chap has called on you twice,' Mr Tenby said. 'Seems keen to see you.'

'He was merely trying to save an impossible situation.'

'Decent young man by all accounts.'

'Uncle,' Anna said kindly, 'I do not care if he takes in waifs and strays off the streets and gives half his income to the poor, I will never marry again.'

'He's very handsome, in a rugged sort of way,' Beatrice said.

Anna supposed he had been handsome. Sparkling blue eyes contrasting with hair so dark it was almost black, and a toned and muscular physique. She could see why he was dubbed one of London's most eligible bachelors even without the title and the income that went with it.

'He could look like a wild boar for all that it matters,' Anna said.

'And he proposed to you to save you from scandal. He's clearly a gentleman of honour,' Beatrice said, her voice dreamy and distant.

Remembering what it was like to be eighteen and innocent, Anna ignored this last statement entirely, biting back the retort that was on her tongue.

'Anna dear, you know you will always have a home here with me,' her uncle said, 'no matter what happens with your settlement from Lord Fortescue. I enjoy your company and dare say will even more so when my little Beatrice has left for a life with a husband of her own.' Mr Tenby paused, as if considering whether to say more. 'But more than your company, I wish for your happiness. One day you may want to marry again. You're still young, you may want children, a home of your own. Don't rule out anything yet.'

'Of course, Uncle.' Anna smiled at the kindly man who had taken her in after her husband had died. Lord Fortescue had three children from his first marriage. Two brutish sons and a spiteful daughter who had turned Anna out of her home less than thirty minutes after her husband's death. They'd taken everything, left her with nothing but the clothes she was wearing, and even now were contesting the settlements she was due from her late husband's estate. Anna's uncle had travelled halfway across the country when he'd heard of her plight, swept her up into his carriage and brought her back to his home. He'd reminded her that there was kindness in the world and that not everyone was cruel and selfish.

Patting her on the hand, Mr Tenby rose from his seat and made his way towards the door.

'Whatever your feelings for this gentleman, he deserves an audience,' he said softly, 'even if it is just to end this *engagement* between you.'

'Yes, Uncle.'

Anna knew he was right. It had been rude and cowardly to refuse to see Lord Edgerton the past two days. If he came to call on her today, she would see him briefly and clear up any misunderstanding between them.

Harry whistled as he strode up the stairs two at a time. The sun was shining and it was impossible to feel anything but positive on such a day. Today he would insist on an audience with Lady Fortescue and no one would stand in his way.

The door opened before he could raise the polished doorknocker and an elderly butler opened the door.

'Lady Fortescue is in the music room, Lord Edgerton. She will see you directly.'

Perhaps this was going to be easier than he had anticipated.

Looking around him with interest, Harry followed the butler up the sweeping staircase to the first floor. As they climbed Harry could hear an exquisitely played piece of piano music getting louder, as if the pianist was growing in confidence with every note.

'Lord Edgerton,' the butler announced as he showed Harry into a sunny room. The piano music stopped abruptly and Lady Fortescue stood to greet him, her expression as inscrutable as it had been at the Prendersons' ball.

'A pleasure to see you again, Lady Fortescue. I do hope you have not been unwell,' Harry said pointedly, reminding the woman who stood before him he'd tried to visit twice in the last two days. He wondered if she would lie, if she would pretend to have been stricken down with a bad chest or a headache, but instead Lady Fortescue regarded him for a few seconds before speaking.

'I must confess I was hoping to put all this nonsense behind us,' she said quietly.

Harry waited for her to step out from behind the piano and glide towards him before he took her hand and bent over it formally. He felt her flinch ever so slightly at his touch, but her expression did not change.

'Please have a seat.' She motioned to one of two upright chairs positioned a few feet apart.

'The world thinks we are engaged,' Harry said, getting straight to the point. Lady Fortescue's cool grey eyes were disconcerting when she fixed them so intently on his.

'It would seem so.' There was no reproach in her voice, just an air of mild uninterest.

'I suppose that is preferable to the alternative.'

'Which is?'

'The rumours of us being found together in a compromising position.'

Tilting her head to one side, Lady Fortescue appeared to consider this for a moment.

'You're probably correct,' she conceded.

'Forgive me for my bluntness, but you seem wildly unconcerned about the gossip attached to our names,' Harry said.

The situation was feeling rather surreal. Normally if a man and a woman had been found in a compromising position it would be the woman who was eager to save her reputation. Gentlemen, especially titled ones, were forgiven all manner of indiscretions. Gently bred ladies were not. It was perhaps unfair, but it was the way society worked.

Harry watched Lady Fortescue carefully and detected a tiny twitch in the muscles of her forehead. It could mean anything, but he wondered if it was yet another sign that Lady Fortescue was unnaturally good at hiding her emotions.

'Lord Edgerton,' she said with a sigh, 'before you met me what had you heard?'

Harry opened his mouth to answer and then closed it again. He'd heard plenty. The ballrooms and gentlemen's clubs had been rife with rumours and speculation about Lady Fortescue and her three deceased husbands.

'I take it from your silence the rumours were not complimentary…' She paused, smiling to reveal a perfect set of white teeth. 'Ever since my second husband passed away people have talked about me, not to my face, of course, but they have picked and prodded at my life as if it were nothing more than an episode for public entertainment.'

'That cannot be pleasant.'

'It isn't, of course it isn't, but I'm still here. A little gossip isn't the worst thing in the world.' It was the second time she'd made that statement, the second time she'd brushed off the damage unkind words could do, and Harry began to wonder what Lady Fortescue *did* think was the worst thing in the world.

'A scandal can ruin lives,' Harry said resolutely. 'Even end lives,' he added too quietly for Lady Fortescue to hear.

'It depends on the person and the nature of the scandal, I suppose.'

Harry thought of his sister. She'd always been strong, vivacious, until the fateful night when her reputation had been dashed by a scoundrel of a young man and a few malicious onlookers. Before it had happened Harry would have said his sister could withstand anything; now he knew how fragile people could be.

'I am grateful for your concern,' Lady Fortescue said softly, the coolness of her demeanour lifting slightly. 'You want to do the honourable thing and I'm sure any other young woman would be delighted to continue with a sham engagement until the rumours were lessened, if not forgotten.'

'But not you?'

Every word she uttered was considered and carefully chosen, every movement precise. And every moment that passed by Harry found himself becoming more and more intrigued by the notorious Lady Fortescue.

'People already say the worst about me—another rumour is not going to make much difference.'

Harry wasn't so sure. Sometimes even the weakest of gossip could be turned into something hurtful and malicious.

Sitting up even straighter in her seat, Lady Fortescue fixed Harry with an assessing gaze. 'Unless you have a reason to want to avoid the scandal.'

Of course he did. The Edgerton family name had been dragged through the dirt after his sister's disgrace, but Harry was titled and reasonably wealthy and his reputation wouldn't suffer overly much by being caught in a compromising position with Lady Fortescue. Especially if he married a nice, respectable young woman in a few months' time. No, his reason for being here today wasn't for himself or the rest of the Edgertons—in fact, he knew by embroiling himself with such a notorious widow he was opening himself up for more gossip and scandal than if he just stayed away. The real reason for him being here today was a sense of wanting to do the right thing by a young woman who might have a bad reputation, but seemed decent and vulnerable in Harry's assessment. Perhaps he wouldn't have been so insistent a year ago, but seeing his sister go through just such a scandal had awakened him to the hurt a woman could suffer at the hands of an unscrupulous man.

'Not at all,' Harry said. Lady Fortescue did not need to hear the dark, intimate Edgerton family secrets. 'There is simply the matter of our supposed engagement to deal with.'

For the first time today Lady Fortescue smiled, her

eyes sparkling with repressed humour. 'You can throw me over, I really don't mind.'

'Shall I say I caught you in the arms of another man?' Harry couldn't help himself, he wanted to see how far he could push her before she cracked.

There was a beat of silence, then Lady Fortescue's shoulders sagged a little, the perfect posture disappearing and with it some of the formality she exuded.

'I've been rude,' she said, her voice softer, less clipped. 'Inexcusably so. I apologise. I suppose I'm not used to talking to people.'

The door opened before Harry could answer, the elderly butler followed closely by a young maid.

'I thought you might like to offer your guest some tea, my lady,' the butler said.

The maid set down a tray with two teacups, a pot, a jug of milk and a plate of crumbly biscuits before hurriedly leaving the room. The butler hesitated for a moment at the door.

'Perhaps the gentleman will be staying for lunch?' he asked, almost hopefully.

Lady Fortescue laughed, exuding warmth towards the elderly servant, her grey eyes glittering as she turned back to Harry.

'I'm sure you're far too busy.'

He inclined his head. There was always work to be done running his country estate and looking over the accounts, but he could of course have made time for lunch.

The butler left, muttering something about a proper invitation before closing the door behind him.

'Your uncle's butler seems very keen to have guests to wait upon.'

'I expect my cousin, Beatrice, put him up to asking. He is completely devoted to her, probably would jump in front of a horse if she asked him to without a second's thought.'

'Your cousin is playing matchmaker?'

Lady Fortescue grimaced, a reaction that would have normally dented Harry's pride, but he was quickly learning this young widow was strongly opposed to any future romantic link.

'Forgive me for not ordering tea sooner,' she said. 'I am not used to entertaining guests.'

Most wives of titled gentlemen were exemplary hosts, their main role to welcome guests into a well-looked-after home, but perhaps during her mourning period Lady Fortescue had locked herself away out of devotion to her late husband and forgotten the basics of hospitality.

Harry sipped his tea, selected a biscuit and munched on it. All in all it had been a strange morning. He'd expected to come away with an engagement, at least in name, to Lady Fortescue. Instead he'd been more or less dismissed, despite the young widow's softening in the last part of their interview.

Standing, Harry was just about to take his leave when the door opened again and the doddery butler entered.

'A package for you, my lady.'

He'd never seen the blood drain from someone's face as quickly as it did from Lady Fortescue's. Quietly she thanked the butler, who placed the package on the table in front of her before leaving the room.

Her hands were shaking as she stood, an unnaturally sunny smile plastered on her face.

'Thank you for visiting.' Her words came out as a choked whisper, and a hand flew to her mouth as if to claw them back in.

Chapter Three

The world was spinning, or that was how it seemed to Anna. Everything in the room had gone blurry and she felt herself stagger uncoordinatedly a few steps to one side. Before she could get her panic under control strong arms had looped around her waist and were guiding her back to the armchair, pressing her firmly, insistently, into the seat.

'Take deep, slow breaths.' Lord Edgerton's voice was quiet and calm in her ear.

Silently Anna cursed. Two minutes later and Lord Edgerton would have left. Now there would be questions, enquiries about her health, probably even a follow-up visit. At least the rules of politeness meant he would not enquire what was in the package.

'What on earth is in that package?' Lord Edgerton murmured, more to himself than to her. 'That's it, long, deep breaths, you'll feel recovered in a moment.'

Thankfully he didn't seem inclined to call for a servant or her cousin to come and attend her; he seemed perfectly content to deal with this himself. Anna had to admire a man who could deal calmly with a panicking near-stranger—most would just step back and convince themselves it wasn't their problem.

Opening her eyes, she saw the room had come back into focus. In front of her she could see her hands gripping the arms of the chair so firmly her knuckles had turned white, and a few feet further away was the offending package.

'Have some tea,' Lord Edgerton suggested, backing away and sitting down in the other armchair, his demeanour remarkably relaxed.

She declined with a shake of her head. The teacup would only rattle in the saucer and give away quite how discomposed she was, if the attack of panic hadn't done that enough already.

'Tell me it is none of my concern,' Lord Edgerton said, his eyes fixed on hers, 'but what could be so awful about this package on the table?'

'It is none of your concern,' Anna said, trying to inject some haughtiness into her voice, but failing miserably—the squeak that came forth from her mouth was more adolescent girl than woman of the world.

Lord Edgerton actually grinned. 'The gossips say you are unreadable, Lady Fortescue. Unreadable and superior, but I think they've got you all wrong. Right now I can read you as easily as I read the morning papers.' He paused, catching her eye and holding it until Anna was forced to look away. 'You're petrified of whatever is inside that box.'

Slowly she inclined her head; there was no point denying it. He'd witnessed her reaction first-hand.

'What do you think is inside?'

'Truly, I have no idea,' she said honestly. It could be a bloodied rag, a pile of excrement, a particularly graphic and threatening letter. All of these things she'd received in similar packages over the last few weeks. 'But it won't be anything pleasant.'

'There's no markings to say where or who it is from. How can you be so sure it will be something unpleasant?'

Instead of answering Anna stood, steeling herself mentally before raising her hands and starting to open the package. Her fingers were shaking so badly that she fumbled with the string that held the box closed. Quickly Lord Edgerton rose to his feet and placed a cool hand on top of hers, stilling her fingers.

'Allow me,' he said, not waiting for her to reply before unfastening the string and opening the box.

The sharp inhalation of surprise told Anna that he hadn't been prepared for whatever was inside. She stepped forward, but Lord Edgerton moved in front of her, blocking her view. As he raised his hands to her arms she flinched, as she always did whenever anyone touched her, but he gripped her gently but insistently, moving her away from the table.

'What was inside?' Anna asked.

'A dead animal.'

Anna felt the bile rise up in her throat. The vendetta against her was escalating. In a few short weeks it had gone from threatening letters to a dead animal in a box.

'What sort of animal?'

'A cat, I think.'

Anna stiffened, torn between breaking free from Lord Edgerton's grip and seeing for herself, and burying her head in his shoulder and crying for the animal she knew instinctively was in that box.

'A ginger cat? Small?'

Lord Edgerton nodded. 'Was it yours?'

Morosely Anna nodded. Beatrice had bought her the animal soon after Anna had come to live in London. It had been her younger cousin's attempt to brighten Anna's days and in a strange and unexpected way it had worked. At least until a few days ago when the lovely creature had gone missing.

Lord Edgerton turned to her, his face fixed in an expression of determination. 'You need to tell me what is going on here.'

She needed to do nothing of the sort. He was little more than a stranger, albeit a chivalrous one. For a moment she avoided his eyes, trying to work out exactly what she could say to make Lord Edgerton go away and forget what he had seen here. It was a deep instinct, this need to deal with her problems with no help from anyone else. For so long she'd been on her own—even through her marriages she'd never found a true companion, someone to share the difficulties of daily life with.

'I think you should leave,' Anna said quietly, knowing he would protest, but trying all the same.

'Not a chance.'

'This really is none of your concern.'

'Would you rather I called your uncle in here? Or your cousin?'

Silently Anna shook her head.

'I thought not. You haven't told them, have you?' he asked.

'There is no need. I am dealing with it.'

'You've had similar packages before?'

Closing her eyes for a moment, Anna assessed her options. Either she could confide a little in Lord Edgerton, just enough to satisfy his curiosity, or she could insist he leave and risk him informing her uncle of what was happening.

'Can we go for a walk?' she asked, eyeing the package from a distance.

'Of course. What would you like done with the box?'

Anna felt the tears building in her eyes. Although she'd always insisted she wasn't an animal lover, her little cat had brought her happiness in a time of fear and uncertainty.

'Perhaps you would like to bury the cat discreetly?'

Before she could answer he picked up the box, folded the lid over to shield the dead animal from her eyes and tucked it under his arm.

'I will meet you on the front steps.'

Anna watched in amazement as he left the room, crossed the hallway and quickly descended the stairs to the basement, no doubt in search of a servant to help him with whatever it was he had in mind. Although she prized her independence, in this situation it was rather pleasant to have someone else take charge and make the decisions.

Lady Fortescue had just emerged into the hallway when Harry came striding up the stairs from the basement kitchen, taking them two at a time. He'd found a footman and paid him a generous sum to store the package somewhere discreet, warning the man against looking inside. To ensure he would comply, Harry had tied the string in a complicated knot which meant he would know if it had been tampered with. Later he would organise for the box to be buried in the garden and for the gardener to mark the spot with a rose or some other flower of Lady Fortescue's choice.

'Shall we take a walk to the park?' he suggested, offering Lady Fortescue his arm.

She nodded, her face still ashen from the surprise of finding out what was in the parcel.

They left the house and walked in silence for a few

minutes, Harry content to let his companion gather her thoughts before pressing her for answers. He wasn't sure what she'd got herself mixed up in, but his curiosity had been piqued and some deep-seated instinct meant he couldn't abandon a woman in distress even if on the surface she didn't want his help.

'I'm not sure how much you know about me,' Lady Fortescue said quietly as they entered Hyde Park. It was a sunny day, but still chilly for April, and there weren't many people out taking the air at this hour.

'Not all that much,' Harry said, realising it was the truth. He'd heard many rumours, but none of them had included any information of substance.

'I've been married three times,' Lady Fortescue said, looking straight ahead as she spoke. 'My first husband was elderly and infirm, wealthy, of course, with a title. My father arranged the marriage and it was assumed it would not be a long-lasting union. He died seven months after we were married.'

'Lord Humphries,' Harry said. He remembered the announcement now and his mother sympathising with the young debutante who'd been forced into marrying such an elderly man.

'I was in mourning for a year and then I met Captain Trevels. I was a widow of some means and independent enough to make my own decisions, so I married Captain Trevels against my father's wishes.'

This union Harry had been unaware of. No doubt Lady Fortescue's family had wanted to hush up what they saw as an inferior match for their daughter.

'Soon after we married my husband was sent to India for a year. On his return he was dreadfully unwell and died only four weeks after our reunion.'

Two dead husbands in the space of a couple of years,

but despite the society gossip there seemed nothing untoward about the deaths. Elderly men and officers of the army died all too often.

'Unfortunately my second husband had been a little too free with my inheritance and after my mourning period was complete I was dependent again on my father.'

'He chose your third husband?'

'I managed to hold out for two whole months before I agreed to marry Lord Fortescue,' she said with a grimace, 'but even at the very beginning I knew I had no choice. Eventually I would end up as Lady Fortescue.'

For such a private person Lady Fortescue was being remarkably open and honest about her past. Harry wondered if she found it easier talking to him, a relative stranger, than someone who was close to her. If he probed too much, got too close, he was sure it would be easy for her to push him away.

'Lord Fortescue had three children from his first marriage, all grown adults now. They resented our marriage from the very start. My husband was fifty-eight when we married, in good health and very physically active.'

'And then he died,' Harry summarised.

'And then he died. Of course his children tried to blame me. They threw me out of the house, have contested the settlements I am entitled to from the estate and even asked the local magistrate to investigate my husband's death.'

'So they're the ones sending you these horrible packages?'

'I don't know.' The words sounded so pitiful that Harry wondered just how much this young woman was having to deal with all on her own. 'The packages only started arriving when I came out of mourning. I wonder if the Fortescue children would have waited so long.'

'How many have there been?'

'Four packages, and two letters.'

'What was in the other packages?'

Lady Fortescue shuddered, her fingers tightening their grip on his arm involuntarily.

'One was full of excrement, from a horse, I think. One had a bloodied scarf and another an animal's heart.'

'And the content of the letters?'

'Vile words, threats, profanities.'

'But no clue as to the author?'

She shook her head. They walked on in silence for a few minutes, Harry trying to take in everything he'd just been told.

'Have you told anyone?'

She turned to him, her large grey eyes wide, and shook her head. 'Only you.'

Harry felt his pulse quicken as she regarded him with an expression of reluctant hopefulness. Even though their acquaintance was only a brief one already he felt a desire building not to disappoint her. Swallowing, he realised his mouth was dry and his tongue felt heavy behind his lips. Lady Fortescue might not be an exotic beauty, but she possessed a quiet, mesmerising quality that made it difficult to walk away.

'Lord Edgerton, what a delight,' a middle-aged woman called from some distance away and Harry had to search his memory for her name and the circumstances of their acquaintance. 'I'd heard rumours you and Lady Fortescue were engaged, and here you are walking out together. How lovely.'

'Mrs Henderson,' Harry said, taking the woman's proffered hand. 'It has been too long.'

'You must tell me,' Mrs Henderson said, flashing a smile at Lady Fortescue, 'how you managed to catch such a fine man as Lord Edgerton. I have an unmarried daughter and the best offer we've had so far is from the local vicar.'

From many women there would have been at least a hint of envy, but Mrs Henderson was a cheerful, un-judgemental soul who wouldn't begrudge a young couple's happiness.

'I have to confess I have no idea how it happened,' Lady Fortescue said softly.

At least she wasn't denying their engagement to any-one who would listen now. It would work out much better if they could pretend to be promised to one another for a month or two and then quietly break off the en-gagement. Harry was under no illusion that they would be able to avoid a scandal completely, but at least it would be at a moment of their own choosing.

'I will leave you to continue your walk,' Mrs Hen-derson said, 'without the interruptions of a nosy old lady.'

'It is always a pleasure, Mrs Henderson.'

'The entirety of London society will know we have been out walking together by the end of the evening,' Lady Fortescue said with a shake of her head, follow-ing Mrs Henderson's departure with her solemn grey eyes. 'I don't understand why people are so interested in the lives of others.'

'Boredom and human nature,' Harry said with a shrug. Gently he guided Lady Fortescue over to a bench situated just in front of a small pond. 'Let me help you.'

'How? Why?'

'You're not very trusting.' It was said in jest, but he

felt his companion stiffen next to him. 'Let me help you get to the bottom of who is sending you those packages, who is threatening you,' he ploughed on quickly.

'I'm sure you have much better things to be doing with your time.'

'Give me six weeks. If I haven't found out who is behind the threats by then, I will admit defeat.'

Six weeks should be plenty of time to find the culprit. Harry had spent five years in the army and, although he had fought in his share of skirmishes, most of the time he had been deployed to gather information, to blend in with the locals and uncover any plots and plans. Those were skills you never lost once acquired and it had been a while since Harry had been given a challenge like this.

'Why would you?' Lady Fortescue asked, turning those searching grey eyes on Harry and making him feel as though she were staring past his face and into his mind.

'No one should have to live in fear. No one should have to endure what you are enduring every single day.'

There was more to it than that, but Harry couldn't tell Lady Fortescue he'd seen the same desperate expression she'd had on her face when the package had arrived before. That in the weeks after his sister had been humiliated and shamed he'd seen that *emptiness*, that desperation. He had failed Lydia in her time of need and the results had been almost fatal—he would not let another woman suffer alone.

'Let me consider the idea,' she said.

'Shall I call on you tomorrow?'

'I have some business to conduct in the morning, but perhaps you would care to dine with us at lunchtime.'

'Perfect. I will look forward to it.'

Instinctively he raised her hand to his lips, brushing a kiss over the knuckles. Although she concealed it well, Harry sensed her discomfort at even this most innocent of contact. Moving away, he wondered just what had happened to Lady Fortescue to make her so averse to human touch.

Chapter Four

'There's been a problem, ma'am,' Billy Godden said as he rapped on the door and strode into the office, his face grim.

'Tell me, Billy.'

'Reports of a storm off the coast of Portugal. The Tildenhall Shipping Company have lost three ships, the London Shipping Company two and there are rumours many more have gone down.'

Anna closed her eyes for a few seconds, trying to digest this newest disaster that had befallen the company since she had taken over managing it.

'Both the *Lady Magdalene* and the *Norfolk* were scheduled to be sailing along the coast of Portugal.' Anna stood and crossed to the shelving unit on the opposite wall, running her fingers along the handwritten labels until she came to the correct one. Quickly she pulled out a large map, unrolled it and laid it on her desk. 'Where did the storm hit?'

Billy took his time, consulting a small notebook and tracing his fingers over the map before pointing out an area just to the south of the city of Porto.

Trying to keep calm, Anna opened the ledgers that

contained the details of the routes and cargos of the two ships.

'If on schedule, the *Norfolk* should be out of danger—it is due to round the Cabo de Roca tomorrow.'

'And the *Lady Magdalene*?'

Tracing the predicted route with her finger, Anna grimaced.

'There have been no sightings?' she asked. 'No reports of it docking in Lisbon for repairs?' she asked hopefully.

'Nothing, ma'am.'

Resisting the urge to sink to the floor in despair, Anna rolled up the map and then focused on the details in the ledger. Twenty-four sailors were aboard the *Lady Magdalene*—she just hoped they were unharmed.

'Send out messages to anyone who might have information and see if you can persuade one of your men they might like a trip to Portugal to investigate if there are no sightings within the week. I will deal with the clients.'

'Yes, ma'am.'

Once she was alone Anna allowed her body to sag. The loss of a ship was devastating for any shipping company, but many of the larger outfits could withstand one loss here and there. The Trevels Shipping Company was still in its infancy. After the death of Lord Fortescue, the only thing his children had not contested was her ownership of the small shipping company her second husband had owned and run into the ground. When Anna had revived it she'd barely hoped that they would survive a year, but slowly they were emerging from the piles of debts and starting to make a small and hard-won profit. A disaster like this could cripple them.

Straightening up, Anna closed the ledger. She would

not overreact. As yet there was no evidence the *Lady Magdalene* had sunk. The captain was experienced and knew how to handle a ship in a storm, and the ship itself was one of their newer vessels.

With a glance at the clock that hung above the fireplace Anna grimaced. Already she was late for lunch and now she had to compile a list of the clients whose goods were aboard the *Lady Magdalene* and decide when to contact them. Quickly she scribbled a note, explaining the delay to her uncle. Uncle Phillip had never tried to control her movements, never quibbled when she was called out to attend to business or missed the odd meal here or there, but he did worry if she didn't inform him that she would be delayed. The office for the shipping company was situated in the docks, not the most salubrious of areas, and although Anna had become used to most of the more colourful characters, she still ensured she never walked alone outside the office.

'Lady Fortescue, hard at work as usual, I see.' A large man burst through the door without knocking.

Anna forced a smile. Roger Maltravers ran the biggest and most profitable shipping company in London and had his office situated on the other side of the docks, the more prosperous side, but that didn't stop his frequent visits to the offices of the Trevels Shipping Company.

'I've said it a thousand times and I'll say it again, not proper work for a woman, this shipping business. And certainly not one as lovely as you.' As he spoke he wandered around the office, fingering charts and ledgers, peering at the maps on the walls.

Anna clenched her teeth together to try to hide her irritation. It wasn't that she disliked Roger Maltravers, but she didn't particularly like him either. He was too effusive, too sure of himself, and ever since her company had started to have a modicum of success he'd been trying to persuade her to join her company with his.

'Awful storm off Portugal, I hear,' he said casually.

'So I am told,' Anna said, wondering if he didn't notice the coolness in her voice or if he just ignored it.

'Could be devastating if you lost one of your ships.'

'We have insurance.'

'Crafty scoundrels, you'll never see a penny back.' He paused and Anna knew what was coming next. It was the same every week, had been for the past six months. 'You wouldn't have to worry your pretty head about issues like this if you married me. I would look after you.'

Anna stood, smoothing down her skirts.

'A very kind offer, Mr Maltravers, but I am a widow three times over and have resolved not to marry again.'

'Dastardly shame.'

'My mind is made up.'

'You need a man to look after you.'

'I have my uncle.'

'You need a husband.'

Anna felt the irritation bubbling inside, straining for release. She'd had three husbands and not one of them had looked after her, not really. The only person she could truly rely on was herself.

'It doesn't sit well with me the idea of a vulnerable young woman alone in the world. There are bad people out there, people ready to take advantage. I only want to protect you, Lady Fortescue.'

'I have a lot of work to do today, Mr Maltravers, please excuse me.'

She crossed to the door and opened it for him.

'I shall call on you tomorrow,' Mr Maltravers said

as he left reluctantly, calling over his shoulder, 'Think about what I've said.'

Anna resisted the urge to slam the door behind him, instead closing it softly and resting her forehead on the cool wood. She knew it was beyond unusual for a woman to run a business, let alone a shipping company. She was one woman in a world full of men, but there was absolutely no way she would ever give up her freedom and her independence again.

Harry frowned as he strolled through the docks, keeping his wits sharp and his pace brisk. The area wasn't the worst in London, but it wasn't far off. Surely he must have the address wrong, surely Lady Fortescue's uncle hadn't meant to send him here?

He'd arrived for lunch at Mr Tenby's residence at the agreed time, only to find Lady Fortescue hadn't returned home. Her uncle wasn't overly concerned and Harry got the impression this was a regular occurrence.

Rather than dine without his fiancée, Harry had offered to go and find her and escort her home, hence his trip to the docks. When he'd made the offer he had assumed she was out shopping, or perhaps taking tea with a friend, not running a business in one of the most notorious parts of London. Lady Fortescue was becoming more interesting with every snippet of information he picked up about her.

Glancing at the piece of paper with the address, Harry started to ascend a rickety set of wooden stairs, having to pause on the way up to let a large man pass him on his way back to ground level.

Harry knocked on the door and was surprised when it was flung open immediately, with some force.

'Mr Maltravers, I must insist...' Lady Fortescue

trailed off, her eyes widening in surprise. 'Lord Edgerton,' she managed after a few seconds.

'Lady Fortescue.' Harry bowed, trying to conceal a smile. He found he rather liked surprising his so-called fiancée.

'I invited you to lunch,' she said softly, a hand covering her lips. 'And then didn't turn up.'

'A more sensitive man might be offended,' Harry said, following her into the office and looking around him with interest.

'You're not offended?'

'Your uncle tells me it happens all the time. Not forgetting guests, but forgetting meals.'

'I don't often have guests,' Lady Fortescue said quietly.

He'd been in such offices before, when organising shipments or booking passage to the Continent, but usually they were run by weathered old men, men who looked like the sea had chewed them up and spat them out. They were not run by gently bred young ladies, even notorious widows.

'This is your business?' he asked eventually, studying a detailed map of the English Channel.

'My late husband...' Lady Fortescue paused and corrected herself, 'My second late husband, Captain Trevels, owned this business. It came to me on his death and it was one of the few things I was allowed to keep possession of throughout my last marriage.'

'It is an unusual business for a woman,' Harry said bluntly.

Lady Fortescue smiled, not the usual, polite upturning of the corner of her lips, but a proper, full on smile of amusement.

'You're very direct, Lord Edgerton.'

'Perhaps you should call me Harry. We are engaged after all.'

'We're pretending to be engaged,' Lady Fortescue corrected, just in case he forgot. 'Harry,' she said his name quietly as if trying it out on her tongue. He saw the faintest of blushes blossom on her cheeks, gone before he could even be sure it was truly there.

He waited for her to offer her given name. He waited so long he began to wonder if she might insist he call her Lady Fortescue for the rest of their acquaintance.

'My name is Anna.'

'It is a very unusual business for a woman, Anna,' Harry repeated.

She shrugged, that small movement that Harry was beginning to associate with his fiancée, and smiled. 'Most men would say any business is a strange one for a woman.'

'That's very true.' He saw her stiffen a little and leaned in closer. 'But most men are fools,' he said quietly. 'Now, your uncle promised to save us some lunch, if you can spare an hour or two.'

She glanced at the pile of papers on the huge wooden desk and hesitated.

'You'll work more efficiently on a full stomach.'

'A quick lunch,' Anna conceded.

'And you can tell me about the world of shipping.'

Chapter Five

⁓⁓⁓

As the music in the ballroom swelled above the chatter Anna found herself looking around in anticipation. Against her better judgement she had agreed to attend the Carmichael ball this evening, a ball that Lord Edgerton, Harry, would be making an appearance at, too.

She had been doing a lot of things against her better judgement these past few days: agreeing to this sham engagement just to avoid a little scandal, allowing Harry into her life and confiding in him about the malicious parcels she'd been receiving. After a long time spent being a meek and mild wife, Anna didn't usually give in to anyone easily now she had her much wished-for freedom and independence, but Harry seemed to be able to get her to agree to anything with his confident persistence.

'You're thinking about him,' Beatrice said breathlessly, sitting down beside her and taking a large gulp from the glass of lemonade Anna had been holding.

'Who?'

'Who?' Beatrice laughed. 'Your fiancé, who else?'

'Fiancé in name only,' Anna said, lowering her voice. She didn't want her cousin to get carried away in a romantic fantasy.

'For now. Admit you were thinking about him.'

'Shouldn't you find your partner for the next dance?'

'Hah, I knew it. You were daydreaming about him.'

'Beatrice Tenby, don't be so ridiculous. I haven't day-dreamed about anything or anyone in the past five years.'

Handing the glass of lemonade back to her, Beatrice stood.

'I don't think you're half as prim and proper as you make out.' Beatrice flounced off, swishing her skirts and fluttering her eyelashes at any young man who glanced in her direction.

'I do hope not,' a low voice said in her ear.

Anna stood abruptly, using all her self-control not to exclaim out loud. Lord Edgerton—*Harry*, she reminded herself—was standing directly behind her. He took her hand, bowing over it before straightening and giving her a wink.

'It would seem we're the centre of attention,' Harry said quietly.

Nonchalantly Anna glanced to the left and right. Everyone around them was deeply engrossed in conversation. Too deeply engrossed. Behind the uninterested façade they were watching every move Harry and Anna made.

'I trust you are well, Lord Edgerton,' she said loud enough for the gossips to hear.

'Very well, Lady Fortescue. Perhaps you will do me the honour of granting me this dance.'

Anna stiffened. She didn't dance, at least not any more. Her role here was purely that of chaperon to Beatrice. She was expected to sit on the periphery of the ballroom, watch the young women dance and laugh and be merry, and hold the lemonade whenever her cousin retreated to the edges for a rest.

'I'd wager you are a fabulous dancer.'

Once. Once she'd been as carefree and happy as Beatrice. She'd whirled across ballroom after ballroom, content to let her partner of the moment guide her, happy to trust a man she barely knew completely for those few minutes of the dance.

'I don't dance.'

Harry stepped back and regarded her. 'I don't believe you,' he said finally.

'You don't believe me?'

'I don't believe you. You have more grace than a dancer in the ballet.'

He held out his hand, waiting for her to take it. There was no way she could refuse and a part of her felt a spark of excitement at the thought of dancing again.

Slowly she placed her hand in his and stood, allowing Harry to lead her to the dance floor. The last dance was just finishing, the dancers breathless and flushed from the quick steps to a lively tempo. There was a brief pause before the musicians struck up again, this time with the unmistakable first notes of a waltz.

'My lucky night,' Harry murmured.

He gripped her lightly, guiding her to a space on the dance floor and smiling before leading her across the room. As the seconds passed Anna felt herself relaxing, Harry was a good dancer and despite her years spent away from balls and ballrooms Anna felt the steps returning like long-lost friends. As they twirled past the other couples Anna could feel her spirits soaring. There was a freedom in dancing, a wonderful feeling that you might take flight, and she couldn't believe she had gone so long without experiencing it.

They didn't speak while they danced and Anna found herself sneaking the odd glance at her companion. Beatrice was right, he *was* handsome, although maybe not in the conventional sense. Most men of the *ton* followed fashion closely. They wore intricately decorated waistcoats and spent time and money styling their hair as well as their clothes. Harry stood out in the ballroom exactly because he didn't do those things. His hair was cut short and his clothes were no doubt expensive and finely made, but lacked the excessive pomp of the other men in the ballroom. What he did have was presence. He was tall, with broad shoulders and a muscular build, but more than physical size he exuded a confidence that could not be imitated—you were either born with it or not.

As the dance drew to a close Anna found herself disappointed. For a moment she had been transported back to the carefree days when she'd been a debutante. Before the marriages and the husbands, when the only reprimand she would get if she laughed too loud or danced too merrily was a stern word from her father.

'Do you care for a breath of air?' Harry asked as he escorted her from the dance floor. He picked up two glasses of champagne as they passed a table lined with sparkling flutes and offered her one.

'I'm doing all the things I cautioned Beatrice against,' Anna said, still allowing Harry to lead her out on to the terrace.

The raised patio stretched the whole length of the back of the house and was well illuminated with lanterns. Coy young women strolled arm in arm with swaggering young men, while the more daring of couples whispered in darkened corners. Steps led from the raised terrace into the garden, with only the first few feet visible in the moonlight. Every debutante with hopes of a good match would have been warned from straying any further from the ballroom, but inevitably someone would be caught where they shouldn't tonight.

'Did you enjoy our waltz?' Harry asked as he led her to the stone balustrade. They leaned on the smooth stone and gazed out into the garden, their forearms almost touching.

There was no point in denying it. Anna knew her love of dancing had been rekindled and any onlooker would have been able to tell with a single glance how much she enjoyed her first waltz for many years.

'I did, thank you.'

'Your late husband wasn't much of a dancer?' Harry asked.

Anna shook her head, not trusting herself to speak. Early in the marriage they had attended various balls and functions together and Anna had made the mistake of accepting a young man's invitation to dance after Lord Fortescue had made it clear he would not be making an appearance on the dance floor. Her husband had seen the dance as a betrayal and Anna had paid a high price for her few minutes of merriment.

'I thought you didn't like champagne,' Anna said, motioning to the half-empty glass in Harry's hand, latching on to the first thing she'd seen to try to steer the topic of conversation away from her disastrous marriage.

'I thought it best we didn't sneak through the house in search of something more palatable and get caught in a compromising position a second time within two weeks.'

'Probably for the best,' Anna murmured.

'Tell me,' Harry said, turning to her, 'what made you agree to be a chaperon for your cousin?'

'My uncle asked.'

'That was all?'

'I owe him a lot, not that he would ever ask anything I wasn't comfortable with.'

'He took you in after the death of Lord Fortescue?'

'Among other things.'

He'd done so much more than take her in. Anna had been broken, barely surviving when Uncle Phillip came and swept her into his loving home. He'd given her space to heal and provided gentle reminders that not everyone was a monster.

'I think he is the only person to ever love me uncon-ditionally,' Anna said quietly.

'What about your parents?'

She shrugged before she could stop herself. Shrug-ging was a habit she'd always had, but Lord Fortescue had hated the miniscule movement of her shoulder. This past year she still repressed many of her natural reac-tions, but slowly they were creeping back.

'My mother died when I was a young child, I barely remember her. My father…' She paused, wondering how best to describe him. 'I'm sure he *did* care, he just didn't think a gentleman should be affectionate, so most of the time I had no idea what he was thinking.'

'I'm glad you have someone to care for you.' There was a softness to Harry's voice that made her turn and look at him. He was smiling at her, a smile filled with warmth that crinkled the skin around his eyes and sud-denly Anna was aware of just how attractive her com-panion actually was. As her pulse quickened she tried to gain control of herself with a sharp reprimand, but found her body swaying towards Harry before she could stop herself.

Their arms touched, just a sliver of contact, but enough to cause a spark of excitement to jump through

Anna's body. Here in the moonlight, with the beautiful music from the ballroom drifting on the evening breeze, Anna felt the first surge of hopeful anticipation.

Shaking herself, she managed to look away and as soon as she did the spell was broken. Quickly she took a step back, pretending to adjust her skirts to cover her confusion. It was the warm evening's air, and perhaps a touch too much champagne, that had caused her momentary lapse in sanity, nothing more.

Harry was looking at her with an amused expression and she wondered how much he'd been able to read on her face.

'You should be ashamed,' a low voice hissed behind them.

Quickly Anna spun around, stepping back as she recognised the woman striding towards them. Before she had time to react Miss Antonia Fortescue, her spiteful stepdaughter, had stepped much closer than Anna was comfortable with, only stopping when their noses were almost touching.

'Miss Fortescue,' Anna said, her voice devoid of emotion, 'I did not expect to see you here.' It was the politest thing Anna could bring herself to say.

'Look at you, making merry with my father barely in the ground.'

'Your father died over a year ago, Miss Fortescue. My mourning period has finished.'

Anna thought her stepdaughter might reach out and strike her at that comment, but her disdain was limited to a narrowing of the eyes.

'Miss Fortescue?' Harry asked, stepping between the two women.

'Yes?' Miss Fortescue snapped, glancing at Harry before returning her unwavering gaze to Anna.

'I don't think we've had the pleasure of being introduced. I am Lord Edgerton.'

His title, and no doubt his reputation, earned him another glance from Miss Fortescue. Anna prayed he would keep silent about their sham engagement. The last thing she needed was for her late husband's family to find out she'd become engaged again.

'I hope you know what company you keep, Lord Edgerton.'

'Lady Fortescue is the most amenable of companions,' Harry said.

Antonia snorted, an unladylike sound that required her to screw up her nose and turn an already unattractive face into something pinched and malicious.

'Your stepmother was just explaining how she gained an entire family when she married into the Fortescue clan,' Harry said, without a hint of sarcasm in his voice. Anna looked at him appraisingly—he might come across as easy-going and mild-mannered, but her companion was sharp and intelligent along with it.

'She is no stepmother of mine.'

Silence followed. There wasn't really much else to say, but Antonia seemed reluctant to move on.

'I understand you haven't seen much of Lady Fortescue since your father's passing,' Harry said, his voice suitably sombre. 'Perhaps we should remedy that.'

Anna felt her jaw clench as she turned slowly towards Harry. She tried to communicate how much she would like him to be silent with just a dramatic widening of her eyes, but he flashed her a smile and wilfully ignored her, pushing on with his invitation.

'I'm having a little house party, the weekend after next. It's at my country estate, just south of Sevenoaks.

We'd be delighted if you could attend. And your brothers, of course.'

Anna didn't know who was more shocked, her or Antonia, but they both stood with mouths slightly opened, unable to utter a word.

'Fantastic,' Harry said. 'We look forward to seeing you there.'

Anna felt him grip her arm and guide her along the terrace, no doubt planning on escaping before she or Antonia had a chance to collect themselves and protest at the idea of spending more than a few seconds in each other's company.

Harry was feeling rather pleased with himself. The evening was going well, exceedingly well. He'd managed to claim a dance from his initially reluctant fiancée, watch her eyes light up as he whisked her around the ballroom and see some of her legendary composure slip as they stood side by side on the terrace. To top it all, he'd furthered his little investigation into the horrible packages Anna was receiving by inviting his main suspect to a country house party.

Next to him Anna walked with her head held high, but her fingers were digging into his arm through his jacket. He hadn't warned her of his plan, there hadn't been the opportunity, but he was sure once she'd recovered from the shock she would see it was the sensible thing to do: gather all the possible culprits in one place and wait for them to strike.

They'd just reached the end of the terrace when he felt Anna's grip on his arm tighten even more. Before he knew what was happening she'd whisked him around the corner and down a short set of stone steps to the shadowy lawn below. In ten quick paces she'd pressed him into an alcove, hidden from view from the terrace above.

'Lady Fortescue,' he murmured, 'I thought we were going to try our best to behave this evening.'

She was standing close to him, so close he could smell the lavender scent of her hair and before he could stop himself he reached out and tucked a stray, coppery strand behind her ear.

'What do you think you are doing?' Anna asked, her voice barely more than a whisper, but managing to convey the depth of her fury all the same.

'A strand of hair…'

'Up on the terrace, with Miss Fortescue.'

'Being polite.'

'To a woman who might be sending me—' She broke off, her voice faltering at the memory of what was in the last package.

'We're never going to get to the bottom of what's happening if we avoid the people who might be responsible. We need to observe them, confront them, push them into making a mistake.'

'By inviting them to stay under the same roof as us?'

'I'll be there to look out for you.'

Anna closed her eyes and shook her head. 'I barely know you,' she said quietly.

'That's not true.' Although they had only met for the first time a little over a week ago Harry felt as though they'd known each other for much longer.

'You do not get to make decisions about my life,' Anna said, her voice low but firm. 'No one gets to make decisions about my life.'

There was such conviction as she spoke, such determination, that Harry wondered what had happened to drive her to this point. She didn't trust anyone and clung to her independence more than any woman he had ever encountered. It should be annoying, but Harry found himself admiring her more for her strength.

'I'm sorry,' Harry said, knowing when to take a step back and regroup. 'I should have discussed my idea about the house party with you first.'

The apology seemed to disarm her and Harry watched as some of the fury seeped from her body. Without thinking he raised a hand and smoothed the furrow between her eyebrows. She stiffened at his touch, but did not jerk away, instead slowly raising her eyes to meet his own.

For an instant Harry wanted nothing more in the world than to kiss her. He wanted to cover her lips with his own, gather her to his body and kiss her until she forgot whatever it was that was making her frown.

'Perhaps we should discuss it tomorrow,' Anna said, taking a step back.

'Good idea.'

Anna looked around her as if only just realising where they were. A sardonic smile crossed her lips.

'Thankfully the world thinks we are engaged,' she said, 'or this would be an even bigger scandal than us being discovered together at the Prendersons' ball.'

All the same she peered out into the darkness carefully, judging her moment to return to the ballroom. Just as she was about to dash out from the alcove Harry caught her hand.

'Dance with me,' he said.

'Here? Don't be silly.'

'No one can see us.'

'People will be wondering where we are.'

'Let them wonder.'

'This whole engagement is to try to minimise the scandal attached to our names, not increase it.'

'Dance with me.'

He saw her hesitate, torn between returning to the safety of the ballroom and sharing another wonderful waltz. The music from the ballroom was audible down here, muffled by the chatter of people on the terrace, but still good enough to dance to.

For an instant he thought she would and he felt his heart leap in his chest, then she was gone, her dress swishing behind her, her head bent low as she fled back to the safety of the ballroom.

Chapter Six

Distractedly Anna handed her bonnet to Grace, her maid, and patted her hair with both hands to tame any stray strands. She'd been unable to sleep after the ball and early that morning she'd headed to the shipping company offices to try to catch up on paperwork. It had been a gruelling day, with the *Lady Magdalene* still missing and the clients who had their goods aboard the ship getting restless.

'Lady Fortescue would like some tea,' Mr Maltravers said, ushering Grace away with a shake of his hand.

'Grace,' Anna said sharply, 'I have a headache. I think I will lie down.'

Her effusive business rival had insisted on escorting her home after turning up uninvited at the shipping company office earlier in the afternoon. Anna had argued, strongly enough that anyone else would consider her rude, but Mr Maltravers had been unaffected by her protests and escorted her home anyway.

'A cup of tea will cure that,' Mr Maltravers said, taking her by the arm and leading her into the drawing room.

As always Anna stiffened at his touch, visibly shuddering at the feel of his clammy palm on her arm.

'Thank you very much for your escort, Mr Maltravers,' Anna said firmly, 'but I am weary and feel unwell. You will have to forgive me for being a terrible host and not offering you any refreshment before you leave.' Despite her conciliatory words Anna kept her tone and manner as cold as possible. Mr Maltravers was irking her, making her feel uncomfortable in the one place she normally felt safe.

'I could wait.'

'No.' She wasn't above begging him to go, but instead placed a hand on his arm and guided him back to the front door, even opening it herself.

'I shall call on you tomorrow to check you have recovered. I worry about you, Lady Fortescue.'

'Please do not trouble yourself.'

She hadn't once encouraged him, hadn't ever been anything more than polite and most of the time had been downright frosty towards him, but still Mr Maltravers insisted on popping up in every aspect of her life.

Anna shut the door while he was still on the top step, closing her eyes and leaning her head against the wood.

'Shall I bring you a cold compress for your head, my lady?' Grace asked, a mischievous glint in her eyes.

'It is a miracle I do not truly have a headache after spending close to an hour in Mr Maltravers's carriage with him puffing away on that disgusting pipe.'

'Lady Fortescue, you have a guest,' Williams, the elderly butler, announced. He grimaced. 'He is in the garden.'

Uncle Phillip's town house was large and well proportioned, but like many houses in the city it didn't have much of a garden. A small patio with a stretch of grass beyond it, it took less than five minutes to stroll around the whole perimeter.

'The garden?' It was a strange place to put a guest.

'With Mr Tenby and Miss Tenby.' Williams paused and Anna could sense there was more to be said. 'They are playing shuttlecock.'

Of course Harry would come to call today. He came to call most days, but for some reason today seemed more significant than any other. Anna wondered if he'd felt it too, that spark, that flare of attraction as they stood together in the Carmichaels' garden. For a moment she'd wanted to kiss him, wanted to fall into his arms and feel his lips on hers. It was ridiculous, worse than ridiculous, and now Anna could feel the butterflies in her stomach as she walked slowly towards the doors to the garden.

For a few seconds she stood and watched the scene outside. Harry and Beatrice had expressions of furious concentration on their faces as they hit the shuttlecock backwards and forward. Uncle Phillip was seated in the sun, shouting out words of encouragement. It looked like an idyllic family scene.

Harry was in good spirits as usual, his shirtsleeves rolled up to expose strong forearms and his eyes sparkling in the sunshine. He was a good-looking man, there was no denying it, but Anna knew that wasn't the only reason she felt a tightening inside her as she watched him. There was more to him than a desirable exterior. There was a drive in Harry to look after people, to ensure they came to no harm. He quietly got on and made the important decisions without causing too much fuss.

Of course there was a bad side, too. Yesterday on the terrace he'd assumed control, taken over and made decisions that weren't his to make. That was why she had to stop this reaction she had to him before it went any further. Never again would she give up her autonomy, not for anyone.

Pushing open the door, she stepped out into the sunshine.

'Anna,' Harry called as soon as he caught sight of her, 'come join us.'

She hesitated, just for a moment, and then stepped off the patio and on to the grass, picking up a spare racket as she went.

'Our record is twenty,' Beatrice said, her eyes shining. 'Lord Edgerton is rather good.'

Anna regarded her cousin out of the corner of her eye. If she wasn't much mistaken, Beatrice was developing a little affection for Harry.

'I hope you're ready,' Harry said, swinging his racket. 'Whoever misses the shuttlecock first has to do a forfeit.'

'What's the forfeit?' Anna asked.

Beatrice laughed and Harry hit the shuttlecock, powering it towards her. It had been years since Anna had picked up a racket, but she swung it instinctively, hearing the satisfying *ping* as the small shuttlecock bounced off the strings. It looped through the air towards Beatrice who hit it easily. Round and round the shuttlecock flew, faster and faster until Anna had to dive to reach it. The shuttlecock spun off the edge of her racket with a dull *thunk*, losing momentum and heading for the ground. Both Beatrice and Harry jumped forward, angling their rackets towards the small, tumbling object, but, before either of them could reach it, it hit the ground.

'Congratulations,' Harry said. 'You won.'

'What's my prize?'

Harry stepped towards her, his eyes fixed on hers,

took her hand and raised it to his lips. Anna shivered as he brushed the lightest of kisses against her knuckles. For a moment the rest of the world faded into the background and it was just the two of them on this patch of lawn. Then reality came tumbling back as Harry let go of her hand and stepped away.

'An evening of entertainment. How do you ladies feel about the opera?'

Anna felt her heart sink. She hated the opera. All those people watching each other, their eyes fixed on the other spectators rather than the stage. It felt as though you were an exhibit in a museum.

'I love the opera,' Beatrice enthused. Anna had a sneaking suspicion her cousin would profess her love for any activity Harry suggested right now, even something as horrible as bear-baiting. There was a hint of adoration on Beatrice's face every time she looked at Anna's fake fiancé.

'Anna?'

She almost lied, almost found herself professing a love for something that in truth she found disagreeable, but then she paused. After Lord Fortescue had died, after she had recovered from the rawest emotional and physical wounds she'd acquired in that marriage, she'd promised herself she would start to be true to herself. There was no need to do anything to please other people now; she could accept or decline invitations as she desired. No one could cajole or force her to do anything.

'I am not keen on the opera,' she said.

'Anna,' Beatrice said, her voice shocked and admonishing.

Anna shrugged. 'I'm not. I see no reason to lie to Lord Edgerton.'

'Harry,' Harry corrected her. 'And you're right, there is no reason to lie to me.'

'I would be delighted to accompany you to the opera, Lord Edgerton,' Beatrice said.

Harry smiled indulgently, the smile of a big brother to a younger sister. 'As much as I would enjoy that, we must find something that Anna enjoys, too.' He turned to her, eyes narrowing. 'What is it about the opera you dislike? The singing? The impenetrable language? The garish costumes?'

'I find all that quite enjoyable. It is the audience I dislike, the feeling of being on display.'

Lord Fortescue had enjoyed the opera, often journeying to London for a performance. As always he'd required Anna to be exquisitely turned out for the trip, cataloguing any imperfection to punish her for later. Then he would spend most of the performance looking for signs Anna was flirting with other men. Of course it never happened, Anna wasn't foolish—she kept her eyes fixed on either the stage or her husband—but the lack of evidence never deterred Lord Fortescue. It meant the opera had gone from a pleasant excursion to a place of fear and horror.

Harry regarded her, his blue eyes seeming to pierce through her protective layer.

'Let me surprise you,' he said eventually.

'As you wish.'

'Beatrice my dear, help your decrepit father inside,' Anna's uncle called from his spot at the edge of the patio.

Beatrice eyed her father reluctantly before bobbing a curtsy to Harry and gliding off to do as she was bid.

'My cousin seems to adore you after just a few hours,' Anna said as they were left alone.

'She is a young woman of good taste,' Harry said.

'She is foolish and impulsive.'

'Like all girls of eighteen.' It was spoken as if he had personal experience with a foolish young girl.

'You have a sister,' Anna said as she slipped her hand through his arm.

'I do.'

'Is she the same age as Beatrice?'

'She's eighteen.'

'Is she making her debut this year?'

Harry shook his head. Normally so easy to talk to, he was not forthcoming when it came to his family.

'Next year, then?'

'Perhaps.'

'Are you her guardian?'

'In a sense. My mother is still alive, but she leaves most of the decisions surrounding Lydia to me.'

'That must be difficult for you. The minds of young girls are impenetrable.'

Harry smiled stiffly, but didn't answer, then, swiftly changing the subject, he said, 'I thought we should discuss this house party I am arranging.'

'Perhaps we should abandon the idea.'

'No. It is the only way to get all of our suspects in one place.'

'They won't accept an invitation from me.'

'But they will from me.'

'How can you be sure?'

'I'm an earl, people always accept my invitations. Who should we invite? Who might want to cause you harm?'

'*If* we agree to have this party, we should invite my late husband's three children, Miss Antonia Fortescue, the new Lord Fortescue and Mr Ronald Fortescue. Also probably my late husband's brother, Mr Lionel Fortescue.'

'Anyone else?'

'Anyone else dislike me enough to murder my cat?' Anna asked. 'No, I don't think so.'

'I'll draw up a guest list, include some old friends to keep it civil, then we can decide on a date.'

'I haven't decided whether I want to do this yet or not,' Anna said.

'Nonsense, it's the best way. I'll organise everything. All you need to do is turn up.'

'I need more time to think.'

'There's nothing to think about. I have it all in hand. This is for the best.'

Anna stiffened, withdrawing her hand from his arm. 'Do not presume to tell me what is best for me,' she said icily. 'You do not know me.'

'Anna…' Harry started to say, but Anna held up a hand.

'I make my own decisions. I do not need any man to make them for me.'

'I wasn't trying to make any decisions for you.'

'And yet that was the end result. I thank you for calling on me today, Lord Edgerton, but perhaps we should end our acquaintance here.' Before Harry could protest Anna turned and swept away, her heart hammering in her chest. She was inside before he'd moved and safely upstairs before she heard his footsteps in the hallway.

'Anna…' she heard him call, followed by the polite, muted tones from the butler. A minute later the door opened and closed as no doubt Harry was shown out. Anna risked a peek through the curtains at her window, drawing back as Harry stood back from the house and looked up directly at her. She was angry. Angry at the presumptive way he'd tried to make such a major decision for her and angry at herself for allowing him to get so close. Independent and single, that was how she would spend the rest of her life, even if the idea of never seeing Harry again hurt more than it should.

Chapter Seven

'So you're not at risk of being the Black Widow's fourth victim?' Mr James Rifield asked, laying down a card as he spoke.

'Don't call her that. And, no, the engagement is purely a sham, a way to avoid a little scandal.'

'I did hear a whisper you were caught in a rather compromising position, one where neither of you was wearing many clothes.'

Harry grimaced—here was the rumour mill at its very worst. He and Anna had been doing nothing more than conversing, albeit unchaperoned, and now half of London thought they had been caught midway through an evening of passion.

'We were caught alone in a room together, nothing more.'

'And you proposed to save her reputation. Little old-fashioned, isn't it?'

'There is nothing more damaging in this world than malicious gossip.'

Rifield's expression hardened. 'How is Lydia?'

Harry shook his head. 'Just the same.'

'She'll get there, old chap.'

Sometimes Harry wondered if the miraculous improvement he was hoping for would ever happen. It had been over a year since his sister's disgrace, over a year since the scandal had become too much for her. Now she sequestered herself away at Halstead Hall, refusing to come out of her room for days on end. It wasn't the life he wanted for her.

'So what happened?' Rifield asked.

Harry shrugged. It was difficult to know. One minute they had been strolling through the garden, the next Anna had gone very pale and said that she had wanted to end their acquaintance. She'd been angry, although she'd not once raised her voice and her face had remained impassive, but Harry wasn't entirely sure what had upset her.

'Lady Fortescue is very independent. I think she felt I was trying to impose my ideas on her.'

Perhaps he had been a little forceful, ploughing on with the idea of a country house party without stopping to consider her views, but he'd been doing it for her. He hated the idea of her receiving any more unpleasant packages and worried that someone might actually try to do her harm.

'Maybe it's for the best. This engagement had to end at some point and now you don't have to be the one to make the break.'

Harry nodded absently. It didn't feel for the best. He'd promised he would help find whoever was terrorising her and now it looked like he wouldn't even get the chance to look the main suspects in the eye.

'Unless there was more to it than a temporary arrangement of convenience,' Rifield said shrewdly. 'I've never met her myself, but I'm told Lady Fortescue is very attractive.'

'No more so than most of the other young women,'

Harry said. Strictly it was true—she had pleasant features, a slender physique and just the right amount of womanly curves in all the right places. What it was more difficult to explain was how he struggled to look away from her cool grey eyes or how her coppery hair reflected the sunlight on a bright day. There was something enthralling about Anna, something that was difficult to put into words.

'She's not like I expected,' Harry said slowly.

'So there is something more?'

'No. No, I *like* her. I didn't expect that, but she's not exactly a suitable wife for a man who wants to settle down with a quiet and scandal-free wife.'

'In a couple of years people will have forgotten the scandal with Lydia. And then you'll be stuck with a dull wife you care nothing for.'

'You're a romantic at heart, Rifield,' Harry teased and then became serious again. 'I failed her, I failed Lydia. I should have seen how low the whole affair brought her, should have anticipated…' He paused, closing his eyes for a second while trying to block out the awful night he'd found his sister trying to take her own life. 'Anyway, this engagement to Lady Fortescue is temporary. We shall break off our betrothal within a few months and I can go back to looking for an amiable, respectable young woman to be my wife.'

'But what about love, Edgerton? What about passion?'

Harry grunted, flicking open his hand of cards and focusing on the numbers. He didn't believe in love, or at least he didn't believe it was a good idea to base an entire marriage on it.

'Love has no place in a marriage,' he said.

The two men played on in silence for a few minutes.

They'd had this argument many times before, although not of course with the complication of Lady Fortescue. Rifield was a rare man among the titled and wealthy—he believed marriage should be to someone you loved. Harry had no such beliefs. Marriage was about a lot of things—money, titles, land, reputations—but the one thing it wasn't about was love.

'You're nothing but an old sceptic,' Rifield said as he laid down two cards.

'I'd rather a quiet, straightforward companionship with a woman I admire than a marriage filled with destructive passion any day.'

He'd seen what a marriage based on love could be like. His own parents had been madly in love and their union had been anything but content. By the time his father had died, his mother had become a husk of her former self and he wouldn't want to inflict that on anyone. No, he planned on doing his duty by Anna, helping her find whoever was terrorising her and then he would return to his search for a companion he could envisage himself spending a quiet and passionless marriage with.

'Will you try to salvage things with Lady Fortescue?' Rifield asked as he frowned at his cards.

'I must. She needs me, even if she's too stubborn to admit it.'

'So a bouquet of flowers and a trip to the opera?'

Grimacing, Harry shook his head. He knew it would take a lot more than that to win round his reluctant fiancée.

Chapter Eight

'Please, Anna, *everyone* is going to be there. I can't miss out.'

'I thought your father was going to take you.'

'He has one of his headaches, he can't get out of bed.'

'There will be other operas, Beatrice.'

'But what if tonight is the night I'm destined to meet my future husband? If I'm not there, I might be condemned to the life of a spinster.'

Anna fought the urge to roll her eyes. She'd been young and romantically inclined once, too, although possibly not this naïve.

'Who will we be sitting with?' Anna asked reluctantly.

'Thank you, thank you, thank you,' Beatrice gushed, throwing her arms around her cousin. 'Mrs Towertrap and her three daughters.'

Anna wished she could take back her agreement. Mrs Towertrap was pleasant enough, but Anna had met Anastasia, the eldest of the Towertrap daughters before. The young woman had been rude, verging on cruel, and Anna had no desire to renew their acquaintance.

'Will you come home with me now to get ready?' Beatrice asked.

Looking down at the mound of paperwork on her desk, Anna sighed. It would be there tomorrow. The *Lady Magdalene* still hadn't turned up nearly two weeks after the big storm and the losses looked to be catastrophic. Still, there was no point worrying about that now, tomorrow was another day.

'Do you have your carriage?'

'Of course. Father has forbidden me from coming to see you here,' Beatrice said, looking around her in barely concealed excitement, 'but Smith, the coachman, knows I would just find another way to get here if he didn't bring me.'

'You really should listen to your father. The docks are no place for a well-bred young woman.'

'*You* spend all your time here,' Beatrice said.

'That's different.'

'Because you're a widow?'

'Because I know a bit more about the cruel realities of the world.'

Beatrice rolled her eyes. Quickly Anna tidied away the papers she'd been working on and followed her cousin out of the office and down the stairs to the street below.

'What happened between you and Lord Edgerton?' Beatrice asked as the carriage wove its way through the busy docks.

'Nothing.'

'You're refusing to see him because of nothing?'

'I should never have agreed to this sham engagement in the first place,' Anna said. 'I just came to my senses, nothing more.'

'I liked him.'

'He is a very likeable man. That doesn't change the fact that I do not wish to have any man in my life.'

'Not even the perfect man? One who would bring you a lifetime of happiness.'

'No such person exists. Everyone is flawed.'

'You might be lucky with your fourth marriage,' Beatrice said, looking out the window.

'It's not worth the risk,' Anna murmured, too quiet for her cousin to hear her.

Of course she sometimes wondered if she was making the right decision, embracing her widowhood in such a manner. The future stretched out before her, years full of solitude. One day Beatrice would marry and at some time in the distant future her uncle would pass away. She'd have friends, but they would have their own husbands, their own children. Still, a lifetime of loneliness was better than one of misery and that would be what she was risking if she married again. You couldn't truly know a man until you shared a life with him.

'Perhaps I might ask Lord Edgerton to call on me,' Beatrice said, her voice light, her gaze fixed out of the window.

Suppressing a smile, Anna nodded. 'He would be a fine match for you,' she said.

Anna knew her cousin was only trying to bait her, although there had been a hint of infatuation in her eyes the afternoon they had all played shuttlecock together.

The carriage pulled up in front of the opera house and Anna waited for the door to open before stepping down, turning to wait for Beatrice. Theirs was not the only carriage arriving, in front and behind the ladies and gentlemen of the *ton* were eagerly alighting from their coaches and carriages, ready for an evening of people watching and passing judgement.

Linking her arm through Beatrice's, Anna ascended the steps, smiling politely at the gaggle of young women going through the door ahead of them.

'I hear the Duke of Westfield is going to be in attendance tonight,' Beatrice whispered, her face aglow with excitement.

If going on title and wealth alone the Duke of Westfield was considered the most eligible bachelor in society at the present time. Unfortunately he also had a rapidly receding hairline, a pot belly to rival a pig and a voice that could send a listener to sleep in a matter of seconds. Anna had been introduced to him a few years ago and had spent a dull half an hour listening to the intricacies of numismatics, which she had learnt at length meant rare coin collecting. Despite his dull personality he would have his pick of the debutantes when he decided to tear himself away from his coin collection to choose a wife.

As they entered the foyer Beatrice spotted a couple of her friends and rushed over, no doubt ready to discuss the young men in attendance.

'You look ravishing,' a low voice said in her ear.

Anna spun so quickly she almost lost her balance, but Harry placed a steadying hand on her arm.

'Beatrice engineered this,' she said flatly.

'I did enlist her help,' Harry admitted.

'I should go.'

'Please let me apologise.'

Anna hesitated. As usual people were looking at them, but she was still tempted to turn and flee from the opera house. Beatrice was safely ensconced with the three Towertrap girls under the watchful eye of their mother; there was no need for her to stay.

'You know how much I dislike the opera, yet you bring me here to apologise,' Anna said, her voice low.

'I can see that it looks as if I haven't learnt anything, but please give me a chance. Come with me.'

Part of her wanted to. It would be easy to forgive him, easy to return to the pleasant companionship they had shared the last few weeks, but she knew she had to be careful. More than once she'd found herself wondering what it would be like to kiss Harry, how it would feel to have his arms pull her close. Dangerous thoughts, thoughts that could lead somewhere Anna most certainly did not want to go.

'Lord Edgerton,' Anna said with a sigh, 'everything we have done in the past few weeks has been working towards trying to minimise the scandal that surrounds us and now you want me to sneak off and sully my reputation even further?'

'Harry,' he said. 'Last week you called me Harry.'

'Last week was a mistake.'

'Which part?'

'Let's just say everything I have done since meeting you was a mistake.'

'You don't mean that.'

She thought of the glorious waltz they'd shared and the almost magical moment on the terrace afterwards.

'Almost everything,' she conceded. 'Lord Edgerton...'

'Harry.'

'Lord Edgerton,' Anna said firmly, 'you are a kind man with good intentions, but I am perfectly capable of looking after myself.'

'I disagree.'

Anna felt herself stiffen. He was doing it again, speaking in a completely aristocratic, completely *male* way, making statements with such confidence it bordered on arrogance and presuming he knew best.

'You are capable,' Harry said quickly. 'You're the most capable woman I've ever known, but no one, man or woman, should have to deal with the persecution you are suffering alone.'

'Truly, it does not bother me.'

'Don't lie to me, Anna. I was there when you received the last parcel, remember.'

A shiver ran down her spine at the memory, but she managed to suppress it.

Taking her arm, Harry gently led her to one side of the foyer. Multiple sets of eyes followed their every move, no doubt cataloguing their expressions and body language.

'I'm sorry. I was overbearing and controlling. I shouldn't have ploughed on with my plan without consulting you first. It's your life, you deserve to be involved in every decision.'

Anna felt herself softening. It wasn't often anyone had apologised to her and meant it, but, seeing the sincerity in Harry's eyes, she knew he truly did regret how he'd handled the situation.

'Thank you,' she said quietly.

'Forgive me?'

She hesitated for only a second before nodding.

People were starting to move upstairs and find their boxes and Anna knew she would have to rejoin Beatrice for the duration of the performance.

'Stay for the first act and then plead a headache,' Harry said.

'Why?'

'I have a surprise for you.'

Despite her hardest efforts at self-control, Anna felt a spark of anticipation.

'We cannot both leave midway through. It'll look too suspicious.'

'It was a pleasure to see you this evening, Lady Fortescue,' Harry said loudly, bending over her hand as he raised it to his lips. 'Alas, I have a prior engagement, but I did not want to go an entire day without setting eyes on my beautiful fiancée.'

'A bit much,' Anna murmured, trying to suppress a smile. Harry might be too assertive sometimes, but he made her smile more than anyone else ever had. 'Good night, Lord Edgerton,' Anna replied, turning to join her cousin and their companions.

Harry stepped out into the crisp evening air, whistling to himself. It had been easier than he'd envisaged to apologise to Anna. Despite her frosty exterior she was forgiving and Harry had the sense that she hadn't wanted to stay mad at him. Anna might protest that she liked her solitude and privacy, but he suspected underneath that initial private layer there was a lonely young woman just crying to be rescued.

'Not your place,' he murmured to himself. He would help her with the anonymous packages, try to save her from a little scandal, but then they would have to go their separate ways. No matter how much he liked her, she wasn't the right choice of wife for him in the long term. She wouldn't bring the stability and respectability needed to the Edgerton family and he feared after spending a few months in her company he would find it a little difficult to play the role of the distant husband he had planned for himself. There was something enthralling about Anna, something that drew you in.

'Lord Edgerton, isn't it?'

Harry spun around to find himself looking into the face of a vaguely familiar man.

'You have me at a disadvantage, Mr…'

'Mr Maltravers. I'm a close personal friend of Lady Fortescue.'

'That's right, we bumped into each other at the docks.' Harry remembered the brief encounter on the steps up to Anna's shipping office.

'I hear you are engaged to Lady Fortescue.'

'Yes.'

'May I offer my congratulations. Lady Fortescue is a fine woman. I have admired her ever since she took over her husband's company,' Mr Maltravers said.

'Thank you.'

'I have often advised Lady Fortescue she needs a protector. The world is such a dangerous and cruel place.'

Harry murmured in general agreement, wondering how Anna knew Mr Maltravers. He was well dressed, but had an air of desperation about him and kept looking around furtively as if he expected to be thrown out at any moment.

'Please don't take this the wrong way. I have been a close friend to Lady Fortescue for quite some time. She is a vulnerable young woman despite her efforts to seem strong. I trust you will not hurt her.'

Harry frowned. It was an odd thing to say, especially from a man he'd just met.

'Of course not.'

'Good,' Mr Maltravers said, nodding his head once and then again. 'She deserves to be cherished. I'd hoped…' He trailed off. 'Never mind. I must excuse myself, I'm heading to the opera and already I am late.'

'Good evening,' Harry said, inclining his head.

He watched as Mr Maltravers hurried up the steps and through the doors of the opera house, throwing a glance back over his shoulder to where Harry was standing. An odd man, certainly one he couldn't see Anna having much time for.

The first act was not as long as some and Harry found himself waiting with anticipation to see if Anna would emerge early from one of the boxes. There was a chance she would decide not to come, sit through the first interval ensconced safely in the box with her companions, but Harry had seen the spark in her eyes and knew at least a little part of her wanted to see what he had planned.

Just as the crescendo of the first act was being reached Harry slipped back into the foyer of the opera house. It would be difficult to explain his presence if Anna did not emerge and he was instead seen by another member of the *ton*, but it was a risk worth taking. From here in the richly decorated foyer he could hear the impressive vocal talents of Giuditta Felini, the Italian opera singer who was the talk of London at the moment. Just as the audience broke into spontaneous applause a door upstairs opened and Harry saw Anna slip out.

Despite the risk she was taking in coming to meet him she moved slowly, gracefully, gliding down the stairs as if on her way to take tea with a friend. As she reached Harry he had an overwhelming urge to reach out, pull her to him and kiss her, but before he could even smile a greeting other doors began opening and Anna's eyes widened in panic.

'This way,' he whispered, grasping her by the hand and pulling her through a nondescript door, closing off the view of the foyer which would soon be busy with other audience members socialising during the interval.

He'd paid one of the opera-house employees handsomely to leave this particular door unlocked and provide a burning candle to light their way, and the young man hadn't disappointed. Sitting on a ledge at the bottom of a narrow staircase was a flickering candle.

'Where are we going?' Anna asked. She sounded a little nervous and he wondered if she were afraid of the dark.

'Up.' Gently he took her hand again and guided her up the stairs. 'You said the other day that you enjoyed the actual opera performance—it was the rest of the audience that put you off attending the opera.'

'Everyone is looking at everyone else, judging them.'

'Well, I thought you might like to enjoy the rest of this performance without anyone looking at you.' *Except me*, he added to himself.

They climbed in the darkness, flight after flight, until they came to the very top of the staircase. In front of them was a door that Harry pushed open and then they were on a small platform at the very top of the opera house.

'Where are we?' Anna asked.

'This building has so many nooks and crannies I'm not sure what this area was used for originally. Now the staff use it for storage.'

'How do you know about it?'

Harry shrugged. 'I'm observant. More observant than most. I was at the opera one evening when I saw a couple of faces up here. One of the opera girls had smuggled her family in to watch when they couldn't afford tickets. I poked around until I found out how to get up here.'

'So people can see us?' Anna asked, stepping back from the edge quickly.

'If they look up. But they won't be able to see who we are.'

Carefully Anna stepped forward again, leaning on the wooden barrier and looking down on the people below. Many were still in their boxes, talking to their companions, the women fanning themselves in the heat.

'It's not luxurious,' Harry said, pulling up two wooden crates for them to sit on, 'but it is private.'

Gracefully Anna sat down, adjusting her skirts so the material did not snag on the corners of the box.

'And I brought champagne.'

'You don't like champagne.'

'But you do.'

Their eyes met for an instant before Anna hurriedly looked away. Harry busied himself opening the bottle and pouring out two glasses and handing one to Anna. As she took her first sip the audience down below began filing back into their seats, although there was still a substantial amount of chatter as the second act began.

Harry had seen this opera twice before so he sat back and watched Anna's face as her eyes were fixed to the stage. It was the story of Medea, the priestess in ancient Greece who fell in love with Jason and bore his children, murdering them when he abandoned her. It was captivating and emotional, and as Anna relaxed he saw the first flicker of emotion cross her face. Normally she was so poised, so in control, it was wonderful to see her express what she was truly feeling. As the story unfolded he noticed the gleam of tears on Anna's cheeks, but she was too engrossed in the opera to wipe them away.

Gently Harry leaned in, using his thumb to capture the tiny droplets of salty tears, brushing them away. With his hands still cupping her face she turned towards him.

'It's beautiful,' she whispered.

Using every last bit of his self-control Harry nodded and backed away. He'd never felt such desire as he did right now, never wanted to kiss a woman so much, but he knew it would lead down a path he just couldn't follow.

Quickly he stood, needing to put physical distance between him and Anna, allowing her to watch the last few moments of the opera in peace.

'Thank you, Harry,' Anna said as the applause from the audience began. She stood and crossed the small platform towards him, stopping when they were only inches apart. 'That was one of the best evenings of my life.'

He was unable to stop himself from lifting a hand to place on her upper arm, allowing his fingers to trail over her satiny-soft skin. By the flickering light of the candle she looked beautiful and Harry knew if he didn't step away immediately he wouldn't be able to control what happened next. Her cool grey eyes met his and for a moment the noise from the audience below faded into the background.

It was Anna who stepped away, turning quickly and crossing back to the wooden barrier, pretending to be sorting out her skirts so she wouldn't have to look at him.

Harry hadn't expected the sharp pang of disappointment. No real liaison between them could result in anything good, but it seemed his head and his heart wanted two very different things.

'We will wait for everyone else to leave,' Harry said quietly, 'and then I will escort you downstairs. Your cousin will be waiting for you in your uncle's carriage. I thought it best mine was not seen dropping you home at this hour.'

Chapter Nine

'**G**reat news!' Billy Godden shouted as he ran up the stairs and burst into the office. 'The *Lady Magdalene* has docked in Lisbon. She needs extensive repairs, but the cargo is all in good condition.'

Anna felt a great weight being lifted from her and cautiously enquired, 'And the crew?'

'All safe and accounted for.'

'Thank you, Billy,' Anna said. 'That's wonderful news.'

'Should we arrange for another ship to pick up the cargo, ma'am?'

Before answering Anna took out the small notebook she kept with her at all times that outlined the current position of all the ships the Trevels Shipping Company owned. Quickly she scanned the pages, trying to work out a solution.

'The *Elizabeth Rose* is not due to sail for France again for another two weeks. We could send her to Lisbon to take the *Lady Magdalene*'s cargo and arrange a replacement for the run to France.'

'Shall I organise it, ma'am?'

'Please do, Billy.'

As he left Billy paused by the door. 'There's a package out here for you,' he said, picking it up and placing it on the desk.

Anna felt a chill creep over her entire body and quickly sat down in her chair before she collapsed. The package was nondescript from the outside, just a brown box tied up with string. There was no note attached, no card to say who it was from, but Anna knew immediately it was another unwanted present from her tormentor.

She hesitated before pulling at the string. It would be easy to throw it away, discard it without looking inside. That would be one way of taking back control, but she knew she couldn't do it. She *needed* to know what was inside, what part of her life they were attacking now.

For a moment she wondered about sending word to Harry, asking him to come and open the package for her, but as soon as the thought occurred she abandoned it. Harry wouldn't be around for ever. In a month, maybe two at the most, they would go their separate ways and Anna would again be alone. She disliked the idea of having to rely on anyone else, so she wouldn't.

'You're a grown woman,' she murmured to herself, quickly tugging at the string before she could change her mind. The knot unravelled and with a rapid movement Anna tore off the lid of the box and peered inside.

Thankfully there was nothing as gruesome as a dead animal inside. The box was almost empty, with just a folded square of paper at the bottom. Trying to ignore her shaking hands, Anna lifted the paper and began to unfold it.

As she read the writing on the paper she felt the bile rise in her throat and a swell of nausea from her stomach. It was a list of her every movement over the past week, details of where she'd gone, at what times and who she had encountered. It was accurate and detailed and could only have been obtained by someone who was watching her closely.

At the very bottom of the page was a warning written in capitals.

STAY AWAY FROM LORD EDGERTON

'I want to go ahead,' Anna said decisively as Harry walked through the door.

He must have seen her expression as he didn't waste time with a greeting, instead moving to examine the box on the table.

'When was it delivered?' he asked.

'Some time this morning. Did you hear what I said? I want to go ahead.'

'With the house party?'

Anna nodded. 'I need to know who is sending these packages.' She shivered before continuing, 'I need to know who is watching me.'

'Was it just the note in the box, nothing else?'

'The note is bad enough. Someone's been spying on me, following me.'

The thought of an unknown tormentor trailing her as she went about her daily life made Anna feel so sick she had to walk to the window and throw it open, gulping in a lungful of fresh air.

'You haven't noticed anyone?'

Silently she shook her head. There hadn't even been the hint of a shadow or the feeling of eyes on her. She'd been completely oblivious.

'Why the warning to stay away from me?' Harry pondered.

'Perhaps they truly think I murdered my other husbands and want to protect you.'

'These packages aren't about protection, they're about persecution. It doesn't make sense.'

'I don't care,' Anna said, her voice sounding almost hysterical even to her own ears, 'I just want to stop them.'

She leaned her forehead on the grimy glass, closing her eyes for a few seconds while focusing on her breathing. Quiet footsteps told her Harry was approaching behind her, but for once she didn't tense, didn't feel the stiffening of her muscles that occurred whenever anyone got near.

Softly he placed his hands on her shoulders, not trying to move her or spin her to face him, content with just letting her know he was there. As the seconds ticked past Anna felt some of the tension seep from her body until she was composed enough to step away from the window.

'I want this house party,' she said firmly. 'I want to invite all three of Lord Fortescue's horrible children and I want to get to the bottom of who is sending these packages.'

'I'll arrange a date,' Harry said simply.

'You don't mind?' Anna asked. She'd reacted badly when Harry had pushed for this very plan just a few days ago, but it looked as though he wasn't about to bring up her behaviour.

'I will not have you terrorised.'

Quickly Anna stepped away, busying herself at her desk. Harry's desire to protect her was seductive and she had to concentrate hard not to fall under his spell.

'We should invite some other guests, too. I don't

think I could bear being cooped up in a house with just the Fortescue family for a weekend.'

'Do you have any friends you'd like to invite?'

Avoiding Harry's eye, she shook her head. Once she'd had friends, she'd been popular and well liked as a debutante. Even after the death of her second husband she'd had a select group of friends, women she could laugh with and confide in and share the good and bad moments with. Lord Fortescue had put an end to any companionship, systematically isolating her from her limited family and friends until she'd had no one but her cruel husband.

'How about Beatrice?'

'I'd rather she wasn't involved.'

'It might look a little strange if she isn't present.'

'I don't want her getting hurt. If this *person*, this *villain*, catches on to how much I care for Beatrice she might be targeted.'

'Leave the guest list to me,' Harry said with a reassuring smile.

'How will you get the Fortescue children to attend?'

'I'll ask them,' Harry said with a shrug. 'I'm hoping they'll be intrigued enough to accept.'

'Thank you,' Anna said quietly.

'Do I take it our engagement is back on?'

Grimacing, Anna nodded. Right now she would do anything to find out who was sending her these threatening packages, including resurrecting the sham engagement to Harry.

'You look overjoyed at the prospect, Lady Fortescue,' Harry said.

'I'm not sure if we are saving ourselves from scandal or just postponing it.'

'If we wait until some other unfortunate gets caught

in a compromising position, the collective attention of the *ton* will be directed elsewhere and we can quietly go our separate ways.' Harry knew they would still be subjected to gossip and rumour, but perhaps they could lessen the speculation by choosing the right time.

'It may work,' Anna conceded.

'And now I wish to take my fiancée out for an afternoon stroll.'

They took his carriage back to the more salubrious part of London and Harry had the driver stop by the Stanhope Gate while they alighted. Despite the sunny start to the day the sky was now moody and overcast, the clouds like great purple bruises spreading across the sky.

'Afraid of a little rain?' Anna asked as she watched him looking up.

'I wouldn't like for you to catch a chill.'

'Always a gentleman, Lord Edgerton,' Anna murmured.

'Not *always*,' he said, a barely perceptible gleam in his eyes.

Anna had relaxed on the carriage ride through London, the tension slowly seeping from her body and the frown lifting from her face as they got further from the docks. He knew it was the unpleasant packages and her mysterious tormentor preoccupying her mind, but he also wondered if the stress of running the shipping company didn't help.

'I was thinking about your shipping company the other day and I don't think I know a single other woman who is so involved with running a business,' Harry said, keeping his voice light. 'It must be stressful.'

He half-expected a frosty response, but instead got

a wry smile. 'Careful, Harry, or you'll start to sound like the meddling matrons I receive so much *friendly* advice from.'

'Society disapproves.'

'That is an understatement. I do not fit the expected stereotype of a gently bred lady. I prefer world maps and shipping charts to watercolours and dinner parties.'

'What made you decide to run the company yourself, rather than hire a man to do it?'

Anna smiled again and Harry realised this was the most animated he'd seen her. There could be no doubt she loved her unusual work.

'Aside from the fact that the company couldn't afford it?' She linked her arm through Harry's and they began to stroll through the park as she spoke. 'The Trevels Shipping Company had a grand total of three ships when I took over the day-to-day management last year. We were heavily in debt and didn't have a reliable reputation among the traders that mattered.'

'But you could afford to employ someone to manage the company now?'

'Yes,' Anna said slowly, 'but that's never going to happen. It's my blood, sweat and tears that have gone into the company, my hard work that is just starting to pay off. I will not hand it over to someone else to ruin it.'

'I can see it has been an important part of your life,' Harry said, aware he was stepping dangerously close to a line he shouldn't cross, 'although one day you might feel differently. I'm sure you will want to marry again, have children—your focus would shift.'

The main problem would be that most husbands wouldn't want their wives traipsing off to the docks every day to do a job that wasn't even suitable for a woman of a lower class.

'That isn't an issue,' Anna said with a smile on her lips, but fire in her eyes. 'I will never marry again.'

It was said so vehemently that Harry missed a step.

'Of course you'll marry again,' he said before he could stop himself.

'Oh, really, Lord Edgerton, you know my mind better than I, I suppose?'

'I just meant you're young, you're beautiful, you're from a good family.'

'You forget half of society thinks I murdered all three of my husbands. Not many men would want to take on the Black Widow as their wife.'

'No one actually believes that...' He paused and corrected himself after receiving an admonishing stare, 'Well, not many people actually believe that.'

'It is of no concern. *I* do not wish to marry again, so it doesn't matter if anyone would have me or not.'

'Do you not want children?' Harry asked.

Anna's face softened and there was a look of regret in her eyes. 'I always hoped... But it wasn't meant to be. Enough, let's talk of something else. How about you? Have you someone in mind to settle down with?'

Over the past six months he'd attended every ball, accepted every invitation and valiantly tried to find a wife who was respectable and suitable, but also likeable. He wanted a companion, someone he could tolerate sharing breakfast with every day for the next thirty years, someone who would make a good mother to his children. He wouldn't consider anyone he thought there was even a small chance he might fall in love with. Years of witnessing the explosive rows between his parents, seeing the hurt and betrayal in his mother's eyes as his father disappeared with another of his mistresses, was enough to tell him love only set you up for hurt in a marriage. His parents had married for love, his mother had been infatuated with his father throughout their union and she had suffered years of pain and heartache. No amount of passion was worth that.

'No one in particular.'

Smiling, she pulled away slightly and regarded his face for a moment or two. 'Let me guess, you're looking for an accomplished young woman, someone beautiful and poised, someone who was born for the role of countess.'

Harry smiled, too, playing along. This was a new side he was seeing of Anna. He felt as though slowly he was breaking through the façade, knocking down the wall she'd constructed to keep everyone out brick by brick. For the first time she was teasing him and she'd actually opened up a little about her hopes for the future, although he'd clearly got the message that the subject of her past was still strictly out of bounds.

'Only women from the purest aristocratic stock may be considered,' Harry joked.

'So you *do* have someone in mind?'

'No.'

'But you do want to marry?'

'Of course,' he answered before thinking, but then considered the question. He'd always been expected to marry, to carry on the Edgerton family name and ensure the status and wealth built up over the last few centuries didn't dissipate and leave the immediate family. It was his role in life, just as much a responsibility as running the large estate in Kent and looking after his mother and sister now his father had passed away.

'It's strange, isn't it—we're brought up being told we must marry well, make a good match in life, that sometimes we don't consider what we really want.' Anna looked off into the distance as she spoke, her expression inscrutable.

'What is it you want?' Harry asked.

'Peace. But we were talking about you. You don't give much away about yourself, Harry. You're a hard man to get to know.'

'Nonsense. Everyone tells me I'm amiable enough.'

'Oh, you're amiable, more than amiable, but in the weeks that we've known each other you haven't told me much about yourself.'

'That can't be true.'

'You're very good at getting others to talk, Harry, so much so that they forget you haven't said much about your life.'

'What do you want to know?'

'I can ask you anything?'

'You can ask...' He trailed off, grinning. 'I might not answer.'

They strolled arm in arm for a few minutes in silence. Every time Harry tried to speak Anna stopped him, admonishing him for interrupting her train of thought. It was a beautiful day in the park, despite the menacing clouds overhead. The trees that lined the pathways were beginning to fill out with their new leaves and dotted along the grass verge were the earliest blooms of spring flowers. Harry realised he felt content and more at peace than he had in a long time.

'What's your dream, Harry?' Anna asked eventually.

'My dream?'

'What do you want most in the world?'

He considered for a few moments. In most people's eyes he was blessed. He owned a large country estate which provided a decent income, had had a distinguished career in the army before he'd left after his father's death and could afford to spend most of his time as he pleased.

'Happiness for my family. For my sister and mother. A good marriage to a decent man for my sister, for her to settle down and have a family.'

'That is a very selfless dream,' Anna said quietly.

Perhaps it seemed that way to someone else, but Harry knew if his sister were happy he would be able to shed the guilt that followed him everywhere. If she could move on with her life, return to society and find herself a husband, then he might be able to forgive himself for failing her so badly.

'Is she not happy now?' she asked.

Harry shrugged, hoping he could deflect Anna's interest on to a different subject. Apart from Rifield, who'd been his closest friend since their days in the army together, no one knew the full extent of Lydia's despair following the scandal she'd suffered last year.

'She's eighteen,' he said slowly. 'It is difficult to know what an eighteen-year-old girl is thinking at the best of times.'

That much at least was true. This past year Harry had tried to get closer to his sister, tried to break down some of the barriers Lydia had constructed to shield her from the outside world, but in truth he hadn't made much progress. When he was at home in Kent he insisted she dine with the rest of the family, that she go out on rides with him and spent time strolling through the grounds with their mother. Lydia complied, but although she was physically present, it was still obvious her mind was elsewhere.

'So you say your sister won't have her debut this year?' Anna asked.

The Season in London was just winding down, with

most of the *ton* spending the warmer months outside the city on their country estates. The best time to re-introduce Lydia to society would be at the start of the next Season in the autumn, but Harry doubted she would be ready for that.

'No. She had attended a few functions when she was seventeen,' he said, trying to keep his voice light, 'but nothing this past year.'

Out of the corner of his eye he saw Anna frown in confusion. Normally once a young woman had made her debut she attended as many balls and soirées as possible. To find a suitable husband you had to be out there actively looking and being seen.

For a few moments they walked on in silence, skirting round the edge of a small pond, nodding in greeting to the few couples they passed. It was quiet in the park; one of the first fine days of spring had caught people unawares and as yet they had not ventured out from their sitting rooms and gentleman's clubs. If the good weather continued Hyde Park would be crowded in a few days. Harry was grateful they didn't have to stop every few paces to talk to some acquaintance or other, but he did wish there would be a distraction before Anna could ask any more difficult questions about his sister.

'Will she be there at the house party?'

'Yes,' Harry said slowly. She'd be there, but he probably wouldn't be able to cajole her into socialising.

'And your mother?'

'She doesn't mix much since my father's death.'

It wasn't the whole truth, but Anna didn't need to know the intimate details of his mother's anxiety. She'd always been of a nervous disposition, but these past few years her circle of comfort had shrunk and shrunk until she wasn't happy anywhere but home and only then when there were no strangers about. She'd spent her entire life tormented by the love she'd felt for her husband, but now he was dead she was overcome by grief and foreboding.

'It sounds like you have a lot of responsibilities,' Anna said softly as she guided him to a bench situated under a towering oak tree.

They sat side by side, Anna's hand resting in the crook of his elbow, looking out over the park. Despite the almost depressing talk about his family Harry felt a peculiar sense of contentment sitting here with Anna. Once her icy demeanour had cracked she was warm and interesting, and she was sensitive enough to know when not to push him further with her questions.

'Tell me about your time in the army,' Anna said.

He shifted slightly, wondering how to start. The years he'd spent in the army were some of the best of his life. He'd enjoyed the sense of purpose, the camaraderie, the knowledge that the junior officers and soldiers relied on him for guidance and advice. Of course there were bad parts, too—battles where he had lost friends, skirmishes he hadn't seen the point of.

'For most of my service I was posted to the Cape,' Harry said. 'It was hot, it was volatile and it was beautiful.'

'It's unusual for a first son to go into the army,' Anna said quietly.

It had been more than unusual—it had been a subject of much argument and debate with his father. Of course his family hadn't wanted him to join the army, but after the cloistered life of university Harry had felt lost, directionless. His father was still strong and capable of running the family estates so Harry had felt surplus to requirements. His solution had been to join the army.

'My mother sobbed for an entire week when I informed her of my plans,' Harry said grimly. 'But I was young and I'd already made my decision.'

'So they sent you to Africa.'

'Not immediately. When I joined the army the conflict with Napoleon was just in its infancy. I was deployed to various places, but much of the fighting was done at sea. It wasn't until I went to the Cape that I saw much in the way of action.'

It had never been his role to be at the forefront of a battle. His talents at negotiating, his ear for languages and his ability to blend in with different groups of people meant he was often used for the intelligence-gathering side of things before a conflict or negotiating a resolution afterwards.

Just before he could regale her with any tales of swashbuckling heroism a movement on the other side of the pond caught his eye. It was another couple, the man dressed in a garishly coloured jacket and the young woman giggling coquettishly. Normally he wouldn't be in the slightest bit interested in the romantic liaisons of anyone else, but there was something about the way the man walked that made every muscle in his body tense and gave him the sensation of ice in his veins.

'Harry?' Anna said, turning towards him and placing her free hand on his upper arm.

Everything faded into the background, everything except the man approaching ceased to exist and Harry felt his body move without instruction. As if wading through treacle he stood and walked towards the couple, his hands bunching into fists by his side. The man hadn't seen him yet, he was too engrossed in the words he was whispering to his companion, too enamoured with the sound of his own voice to notice Harry approaching.

'Mountfield,' Harry growled.

At first Captain Mountfield didn't seem to recognise him and this made Harry even more irate. The scoundrel had ruined his sister, nearly been the cause of her death, and he didn't even recognise Harry.

'Lord Edgerton.' The name finally passed Captain Mountfield's lips after a few seconds.

The seconds ticked past as the two men stared at one another, the tension mounting until the lady on Captain Mountfield's arm gave a nervous titter.

'You haven't introduced me, darling,' she said.

Harry didn't even look at her, finding it impossible to tear his eyes away from the only man in the world that he had ever hated.

'Miss Francesca Pont,' Captain Mountfield said quietly, his eyes never leaving Harry's.

'A pleasure to make your acquaintance, Lord Edgerton,' Miss Pont twittered.

All the hurt and distress his sister had suffered over the past year flitted before his eyes and Harry felt his fists tense. After five years in the army he abhorred violence, but right now it wasn't his rational brain in control of his body.

'Hit me and you'll regret it,' Mountfield hissed.

After Lydia and Mountfield had been found in a compromising position and the captain had refused to do the honourable thing and marry Lydia, Harry had challenged him to a duel. Captain Mountfield had refused, laughing in Harry's face. He'd said he would tell the world all the dirty little details of his affair with Lydia if Harry didn't leave him alone. Of course Harry had backed down, but part of him still really wanted to face this scoundrel with a gun or a sword in his hand.

'I'll remind all of society exactly how your sister disgraced herself last year.'

'Be careful of the company you keep, Miss Pont,' Harry said, stepping back and letting the couple past.

His whole body was shaking as he watched them walk away. As they disappeared into the distance he let out a muted growl and turned to look for some inanimate object to take out his pent-up rage on. Instead he found Anna standing behind him. Gently she took his hand in hers and squeezed his fingers.

'I know a little about hatred,' she said softly, 'so I know how hard that must have been to let him walk away. Whatever he did, however you want to punish him, your love for your sister prevailed over that.'

Harry studied Anna's face, letting his eyes roam over her pale skin, the curve of her perfectly pink lips and into her cool, grey eyes. As he focused on her he felt some of the rage start to seep away and his muscles begin to relax.

'I don't believe in fate,' Anna said as she linked her arm through his and began to lead him back the way they had come. 'I don't believe that bad people get punished for their deeds, but perhaps one day whatever it is that he holds over your sister will not matter any longer and then you will be able to expose him for the scoundrel that he is.'

Chapter Ten

The carriage sped down the country lanes, winding this way and that over the rutted road, making it impossible for Anna to stay in one place on the narrow cushion, let alone focus on the book in her hand. Across from her sat her maid Grace, somehow managing to doze despite the jolting of the carriage. She felt a cautious optimism about this weekend. She dared not believe this might be the day they exposed her tormentor, but underneath careful layers of realism she was a little hopeful. It would be wonderful not to be always looking over her shoulder, not worrying about who might be watching her and following her. For months she had felt a sick anticipation every time the butler entered with a letter or a package.

Settling back on to the seat, one hand gripping the small ledge below the window, Anna turned her focus to the scenery outside. If her calculations were correct she should be arriving at Halstead Hall very shortly. Harry had gone on ahead a few days earlier to get everything prepared for the weekend and for propriety's sake she was arriving along with the other invited guests.

All in all they had agreed on a guest list of twelve.

It included the three Fortescue children, as well as the wives of the new Lord Fortescue and Mr Ronald Fortescue. Mr Lionel Fortescue, Anna's brother-in-law, had sent his apologies, but was spending a few months in Scotland. They'd ruled him out as a likely suspect as it would be difficult for him to orchestrate the sending of the packages from so far away and by all accounts he'd been in Scotland for over two months already.

Harry had invited a couple of old friends, single young men who were there to keep the peace and also to entice Miss Antonia Fortescue to attend. She was in search of a husband and Anna suspected the only reason she'd agreed to come to the gathering was the prospect of wealthy, titled gentlemen in a confined area.

To finish off the guest list there was also Harry's sister Lydia and the local vicar and his wife from the village of Halstead. All in all a strange party, but Anna knew the purpose of the event wasn't to enjoy herself or make friends, it was purely to find out who was tormenting her.

Nevertheless she felt a surge of excitement as the carriage swerved into a wide driveway and Halstead Hall came into view.

It was a beautiful old house, set in magnificent rolling Kentish countryside. As they rattled up the long drive Anna could see a group of deer in the distance, the tiny fawns frolicking alongside their mothers. The house itself looked old but well maintained, perhaps originally Elizabethan, but with extra wings added over the centuries as was common in many of the country estates.

At each end of the property was a tower, complete with crenellations, and over the heavy front door was a coat of arms. Looking at Halstead Hall, she was in no doubt it was the home of one of the oldest families in England.

The carriage came to a stop and a footman was at the door immediately, offering her his hand to help her down. As her feet hit the floor the footman stepped back and Anna saw Harry emerge from the house, a delicate-looking young woman on his arm.

'Lady Fortescue,' he greeted, taking her hand and brushing a kiss against her knuckles. 'Welcome to our home.' His eyes twinkled in the sunlight and Anna knew he was enjoying himself already. In the short time she'd known Harry it had become clear he was an intelligent man, made for more than the dull life of the wealthy gentleman. She didn't know much about his time in the army, but whenever he mentioned that part of his life he grew animated and his eyes lit up with enthusiasm. She supposed helping her find out who was sending her the unwelcome packages took him back to his army days a little.

'This is my sister, Lady Lydia Pershore. Lydia, this is Lady Fortescue.'

Anna stepped forward and dipped into a curtsy in front of the young woman, as was the correct formal greeting. Lydia looked a little overwhelmed, so as she rose Anna gave her a conspiratorial smile.

'You must call me Anna,' she said.

'I am Lydia.'

'I have been wanting to meet you ever since your brother first spoke of you,' Anna said, gently linking her arm through Lydia's. She'd heard the gossip, pieced together a little of what had happened to Harry's sister a year ago after she'd witnessed the confrontation between Harry and Captain Mountfield in Hyde Park. According to Beatrice, the scandal had been monumental, although her cousin seemed to think many things were worthy of that title. No one had seen or heard from the disgraced Lydia since she was found with very few clothes on in the arms of an army officer. As often seemed to be the case, Beatrice couldn't even remember the army officer's name, it was the daughter of an earl the society gossip had focused on.

Whatever had happened Anna didn't want to know any more. She knew better than most how malicious gossip could hurt. No matter what rules of propriety Lydia had broken, Anna had no doubt she had been punished more than enough in the months since.

'Am I the first to arrive?' Anna asked.

'I was meant to invite other people?' Harry asked, barely able to keep the smile from his lips.

'It would probably make for a more pleasant weekend without the Fortescues,' Anna admitted.

Harry led them inside, and Anna tried not to look around with open-eyed amazement at the beautiful entrance hall. Her family had been wealthy, as had two out of three of her husbands, but never had she been anywhere with such plush furnishings.

'We should have time for a quick tour,' Harry said as they passed through the hall into a sitting room illuminated with the afternoon sunlight.

'Won't the other guests be arriving soon?' Anna asked.

'I might have told them an hour later,' Harry said, not a hint of embarrassment for his deception evident in his voice. 'I wanted to show you Halstead Hall first, without the Fortescues trying to push you down the stairs or poison your teacup.'

'Harry,' Lydia admonished with a gasp.

He shrugged. 'The awful thing, dear sister, is that it could happen.' He turned to Anna. 'Come with me.'

Taking her by the hand, he pulled her quickly into room after room after room, explaining what they all were in a couple of words before moving on. He reminded Anna of an excited young boy, eager to show his new friend his home.

'The music room,' he declared as they entered a large room with a grand piano at one end. 'Perhaps you'll play for me one day.'

Letting go of Harry's arm, Anna walked the length of the room and stood behind the piano, running her fingers across the shiny veneer on the lid before gently caressing the keys. As a young girl she'd spent hours playing the piano, loving the emotion that could be expressed in a single piece of music. No other instrument had the versatility of the piano, allowing soft, gentle notes to be followed by the loud, marching tunes.

'Perhaps,' she said, pressing a couple of the keys, hearing the perfectly tuned notes and wondering if she would ever feel that same love for music as she once had.

After a few moments they moved on, the tour taking her through the dining room and out on to the terrace before returning to the house.

'Let me show you to your room,' Harry said, leading her up the sweeping staircase to the first floor.

He unlocked the door to a large room filled with natural light. In the centre was a four-poster bed, flanked by two comfortable-looking armchairs. A dressing table and a wardrobe made up the rest of the furniture, but it was the view that commanded the most attention. Two large windows, both with window seats, looked out over the parkland. Rolling green hills dotted with oak trees stretched as far as the eye could see.

'This bedroom has one of the finest views in the

house,' Harry said softly. He was standing right behind her, so close she could feel his breath on her neck. Ordinarily she would feel unsettled by having anyone so close to her, but not with Harry. She'd realised over the last few weeks that she felt safe with him, a peculiar sensation for someone who was used to living in fear, always wondering where the next unprovoked attack would come from.

'Thank you,' she said, turning to face him. He didn't step away, instead moved a fraction closer, his hand reaching out to find hers. Anna looked up into his eyes, felt her heart pounding in her chest and couldn't deny any longer the physical pull she felt whenever Harry was near.

For a long few seconds he studied her face, his free hand reaching up to brush her hair back from her forehead. Her skin tingled as his fingertips made contact and she shivered with anticipation as he traced a route past her temple and around her ear.

Never before had she wanted to be kissed as much as she did right now and as Harry stepped away she had to choke back a cry of frustration.

'Let me show you my favourite part of the house,' Harry said, taking her hand and pulling her from the bedroom, striding so quickly along the corridor Anna almost had to run to keep up. They passed door after door, room after room, so many that after a minute Anna had lost count. 'This way,' he said, leading her through a tiny, inconspicuous door at the end of the corridor, then up a tight spiral staircase. As they climbed the temperature dropped a few degrees and Anna got a sense of what Halstead Hall would have been like a few hundred years ago soon after it was first built. The walls were smooth stone and at regular intervals there were iron brackets on the walls, no doubt for a lighted torch to guide the way in the dark.

They emerged at the top of one of the towers Anna had noticed when she'd first alighted from her carriage. Although the day was still and calm, up here there was a little breeze, enough to rustle her skirts and whip the loose strands of hair across her face.

Carefully they picked their way over the uneven flagstones to the edge, where Harry leaned easily on the low stone wall. Anna wasn't nearly so confident in the old stone's stability, instead choosing to stand a pace back from the parapet.

'It's beautiful,' Anna said, shielding her eyes from the sun as she looked out over the rolling countryside.

'You can see for miles. I used to come up here when I was a boy and spend hours daydreaming.'

'It's very peaceful.'

'That's why I wanted to show you.' He handed her a heavy iron key. 'I know this weekend might be difficult for you, so many people who dislike you under one roof. If it ever gets too much, then I wanted you to have somewhere private, somewhere safe to come.'

Anna felt the weight of the key in her hand, swallowing the lump that was forming in her throat.

'Thank you,' she said softly.

'There are only two keys—you have one and I the other. If you come up here and lock the door behind you, then only I will be able to follow you.' He paused, continuing slowly, 'If you do come up here, could I ask that you lock the door after you come back down. It doesn't do to have the tower easily accessible to everyone.'

'Of course.'

For a few minutes they stood side by side, looking out over the countryside. Anna had the sense Harry wanted to say something more, but he couldn't find the words.

'I know this weekend will be hard for you,' he said eventually, 'but do you think I could ask a favour of you?'

'Anything.'

'You shouldn't agree before you know what I'm asking,' Harry said with a mischievous glint in his eyes. 'I could be requesting you join us for dinner in just your undergarments or run naked through the halls at dawn.'

She fixed him with an admonishing stare.

'Of course I wouldn't do that to my lovely fiancée...'

'Pretend fiancée,' Anna corrected him.

'Would you help my sister a little?' he asked, his expression turning serious again.

'Help in what way?'

'You're so good at being in society, socialising with people, even when you know they're saying horrible things about you. I don't know if you just don't care what other people think, or if you're very good at putting on a show of not caring, but it's hard not to admire you for it.'

Harry's words came out quickly. He was anxious, Anna realised. For the first time since they'd met he was actually nervous.

'Lydia gets very upset by people, by the unkind things people say...' he sighed '...even the unkind things she imagines people might be thinking.'

'That's no bad thing,' Anna said quietly.

'You don't. Do you?'

She shrugged. Of course being called a murderer, a black widow and a harlot hurt, but long ago she'd realised they were only words and they could only do her damage if she let them. She supposed in a perverse way she had Lord Fortescue to thank for making her so strong, so resilient. He'd called her names and accused her of all sorts of untrue things every single day of their marriage—after a while she'd learnt to block out most of what he said.

'I've had a lot of practice at ignoring them,' Anna said. 'It's hardened me, made me cynical and untrusting. You don't want that for your sister.'

'She's so unhappy,' Harry said quietly. 'I just want her to be happy.'

Anna reached out and placed her hand over his.

'I will do anything to help you,' she said, stepping closer. 'Whatever you think is for the best.'

Harry was doing so much for her, going above what anyone could ever expect of him to help her find out who was tormenting her, the very least she could do was try to help his sister find her confidence in socialising again.

Chapter Eleven

Standing outside, Harry forced a smile to his face as Miss Fortescue stepped down from her carriage. Despite the almost permanent sneer he could tell she was impressed by Halstead Hall. To him it was just home, but he knew it was one of the grandest residences in the country.

'Miss Fortescue, welcome to Halstead Hall.'

She inclined her head, shot a look of disgust at Anna and allowed the butler to show her inside.

'Please take your time to settle into your room. We shall meet for drinks before dinner, at seven in the drawing room.'

'She looked happy to be here,' Anna said as she watched her stepdaughter and a flustered young maid disappear into the house. 'Remind me how you persuaded me this would be a good idea?'

Harry suppressed a grin. Throughout the arrival of the guests Anna had stood by his side, elegant and poised, but distant. He was reminded of the first time he'd met her at the Prendersons' ball. It had taken a lot of work for him to slowly break down the barriers she'd erected around herself, but slowly he felt like he was getting through. Seeing her formal behaviour crack when there was no one else around warmed him, probably more than it should.

'Just think, three days and hopefully we will know which of the Fortescue children is sending you those packages,' Harry said, giving her arm a quick, reassuring squeeze. He had also noticed that she'd stopped flinching whenever he touched her now. Early on in their acquaintance she'd jumped every time he brushed against her, as if expecting something awful to occur because of the contact. Now she didn't pull away at the slightest touch and seemed comfortable walking arm in arm with him.

'How are we going to work out which of them is guilty?' Anna asked, narrowing her eyes as another carriage appeared on the horizon.

'It's simple. We observe them, provoke them to anger and watch to see how they react, who threatens you, who seems to want to cause you the most harm.'

'It seems a little unsubstantial,' Anna said. 'The Fortescues aren't dim-witted, they will be on their guard while they are here.'

'Then we confront them,' Harry said with a shrug. 'One by one, ideally in the company of the other guests, and we watch their reaction to that. I've dealt with enough scoundrels in my time to know if one is lying.'

Anna nodded slowly, but Harry could see she wasn't quite convinced.

The next carriage was pulling up to the house and this time Harry didn't have to force a smile on to his face. He recognised the coat of arms painted on its side and sure enough, before the carriage had come to a complete halt, Rifield was jumping down. Anna had initially been concerned at the idea of involving his friend in their attempt to uncover the perpetrator behind her persecution, but Harry had reminded her that Rifield would be perfectly placed to see what people were saying when neither Harry nor Anna was present. He had been glad when Anna had agreed.

Harry watched with curiosity as his old friend turned and took the hand of first an older woman, then a younger one and helped them alight.

'Rifield,' he greeted warmly, clasping his old friend's hand.

'Foxton sends his apologies,' Rifield said as he gripped Harry's hand firmly. 'Been struck down with a bad chest and couldn't make the journey.'

Sir Thomas Foxton was another of Harry's old friends and meant to be making up the numbers this weekend as well as providing a little moral support. Although roughly the same age as Harry and Rifield, their friend suffered with repeated chest infections no doctor seemed to be able to cure, hence Harry wasn't overly surprised by the cancellation.

'I have brought Mrs Wright and her charming daughter, Miss Caroline Wright, with me,' Rifield said. 'Didn't think you'd mind.'

Harry turned to the two women. He recognised them both, thought he had probably danced with Miss Caroline Wright at a ball the past Season.

'Mrs Wright is a friend of my mother's,' Rifield explained, 'and Miss Caroline Wright made her debut this year.'

'A pleasure to meet you. You are very welcome at Halstead Hall,' Harry said, greeting first the mother and then the daughter. 'May I introduce Lady Fortescue.'

Anna stepped forward and greeted the newcomers

formally, smiling at the young Miss Wright who recoiled away before she could stop herself.

'Harrison, please ask the maids to make up two more rooms and escort Mrs Wright and Miss Caroline upstairs. We will meet for drinks at seven in the drawing room,' Harry addressed his efficient butler.

Once the two women had disappeared inside Rifield turned to Anna.

'Lady Fortescue, I have heard so much about you,' he said.

'Hasn't everyone?' Anna sighed. 'Lord Edgerton tells me I'm quite notorious.'

Rifield threw his head back and let out a hearty chortle.

'I'm intrigued to find out who our villain is this weekend,' Harry's friend said. 'It'd all be rather exciting if it wasn't so ghastly.'

'You wouldn't be so keen on this weekend if you knew our guests of honour well.'

'The Fortescues? They do have a bit of a reputation. I've met the new Lord Fortescue and his younger brother, but never had the pleasure of Miss Fortescue.'

'She's husband hunting,' Anna said, a wicked gleam in her eyes, 'and you're just the sort of man she's looking for.'

'Now I see why Edgerton was so keen to get me here.'

'There's no denying it, you're bait, old friend,' Harry said, clapping Rifield on the back.

'I am completely at your service, madam,' Rifield said with a theatrical bow.

'And now I must go and change for dinner,' Anna said, bidding the two men farewell.

They watched her go, both standing in silence as she glided gracefully up the stairs and out of sight.

'I see why you're infatuated,' Rifield said quietly. 'There's something rather enchanting about the notorious Lady Fortescue.'

'I'm not infatuated,' Harry protested.

'Good. Then you won't be mad I decided to invite Miss Caroline Wright to this little party.'

'You're interested in her?' Harry asked. In all the years he'd known Rifield he hadn't known him to favour any young woman, despite his romantic views on life.

'Good Lord, no. She's pleasant enough, I'm sure— my mother certainly approves of her, and you know how difficult she is to impress. No, I brought Miss Wright here for you to get to know.'

'Why on earth would you do that?' Harry asked.

'She's exactly what you told me you're looking for— respectable, reliable, amiable. Perhaps a little dull, but she's generally well liked. And I can't see you being burdened by falling in love with her.'

Harry exhaled loudly.

'Don't be like that. She's just what you say you want.'

'You're worse than a meddling mother,' Harry said. This wasn't the first time Rifield had introduced him to some young debutante. Normally on paper they looked perfectly pleasant, but in the flesh there was something missing, some quirk that irked Harry more than it should. 'And bringing her here for this weekend, what were you thinking?'

Rifield shrugged. 'If she's the one for you, then why waste time?'

'Has it escaped your memory that I'm currently engaged to Lady Fortescue.'

'Pretending to be engaged,' Rifield corrected him.

'I can hardly court Miss Wright while the world thinks I am promised to Anna.'

'Don't worry, I explained the situation to Miss Wright, she's understanding.'

'You did what?' Harry forced himself to lower his voice. 'What did you tell her?'

'Just that you had proposed to Lady Fortescue to save her from a scandalous situation, not of your own making, of course. And that once the scandal had blown over you would both be going your separate ways.'

'Rifield, I know you have the best of intentions...'

'Always, old chap. Just want to see you happy and settled.'

'But I do wish you hadn't invited Miss Wright. This weekend is going to be difficult enough without having to pretend to be interested in a dull debutante.'

'Not pretend, Edgerton. Miss Wright could be the woman who becomes your wife.'

The idea sent an unwelcome shiver down Harry's spine. He knew he was meant to be looking for someone respectable and amiable, but the idea of actually having to choose a wife made him shudder every time he thought about it.

'Just give her a chance, Pershore,' Rifield said, calling his old friend by his family name just as he had in the army before Harry had inherited the title. 'You might find you like her. I'll keep an eye on Lady Fortescue while you woo Miss Wright, although by all accounts Lady Fortescue doesn't need anyone to defend her.'

'I wouldn't be so sure,' Harry murmured. Anna was fantastic at projecting a strong façade to the world, but underneath she was just as vulnerable as any other young woman. As she had been widowed three times it was easy to forget she was still young, still only a few years older than Lydia.

'Just think, in three days' time you could have found out who is sending Lady Fortescue those ghastly packages and secured yourself a wife.'

Anna hesitated before knocking, her hand hovering a few inches from the wood. She'd asked one of the many housemaids which room was Lydia's and the young girl had directed her to a quieter wing of the sprawling house. Now she was here she wasn't sure what she was going to say, but she'd promised Harry she would try, so she steeled herself and knocked.

'Come in,' a soft voice said.

The room was beautifully decorated, the walls covered in wallpaper of an oriental design and the curtains and bedsheets matched. Lydia was sitting on the window seat, gazing out over the countryside, only turning to face Anna after a few moments. She was still wearing the dress she had been earlier that day, despite there being less than an hour until dinner.

'We didn't get a chance to talk earlier,' Anna said, stepping into the room and closing the door behind her.

The woman in front of her looked a little like Harry, she had the same dark hair and piercing blue eyes, but her features were much softer, her frame more petite. Although she wasn't as thin as some young debutantes, she looked a little frail and her skin had the translucent quality that hinted at an indoor lifestyle.

'Harry's told me about you,' Lydia said quietly. 'He admires you very much.'

'He is almost alone in that regard.'

Lydia cocked her head to one side, regarding Anna for a moment before motioning to a chair. Anna sat, aware that she felt a little nervous. It was important to her that she didn't fail Harry in this, not because he would blame her, but because he had done so much for her and asked for so little in return.

'I am not a popular woman in society.'

'He didn't tell me that,' Lydia said.

Anna shrugged. 'You'll probably pick up on some of the dislike these next few days.'

Immediately Lydia looked away. 'I'm not sure I'm going to come down tonight. I feel a little unwell.'

'I understand,' Anna said. 'For a long time I wished I could just hide away for ever.'

'I'm not hiding.' Lydia paused. 'Did he tell you what happened? Did he tell you what everyone thinks of me?'

Anna shook her head. 'I can guess enough, though. Thousands of women go through the same thing. Some scandal, some disgrace, the man gets off lightly, boys will be boys after all. The woman is ripped apart by the gossips.'

'Is that what happened to you?'

Laughing, Anna shook her head. 'No, society thinks I murdered my husbands.'

Lydia's eyes widened and for the first time Anna saw a hint of a smile on the young girl's face.

'Ridiculous, isn't it? But I had three husbands in the space of six years, and my stepchildren from my last marriage really did not like me. A rumour was started and I was the perfect target.'

'You must think me overdramatic,' Lydia said quietly. 'You're dealing with all of this and I—' She broke off, her voice wavering.

'Not at all.' Anna stood and crossed the room, sitting down next to Lydia. 'I spent months hiding away in my uncle's house. For a while I thought I would never attend another ball or accept another invitation ever again.'

'What changed?'

'I was given the right motivation to start socialising again. My uncle asked me to chaperon my young cousin and it was something that I wanted to do.'

Lydia nodded, her gaze wandering until it focused on a spot somewhere in the distance.

'No matter what your brother says, what anyone says, it is perfectly fine for you never to socialise again, if that is what makes you happy,' Anna said, trying to find the right words to make Lydia see she was in control of her own life. 'But if it doesn't, if you want to go to balls and socialise and dance until the early hours, then a little malicious gossip is not a good enough reason to hide yourself away.' She paused, allowing the young woman time to digest her words. 'It's your life, Lydia. Only you know your hopes and dreams, and only you can change your future.'

'I don't know if I can bear it,' Lydia said quietly. 'Walking into a room and knowing everyone is talking about me.'

'Then walk in next to me. I will guarantee you people will be too busy wondering who I am going to marry and murder next to think about the scandal between you and your young man.'

Slowly Lydia nodded and Anna felt like shouting for joy. There was still a sadness about Harry's sister, something deep-seated and almost melancholy, but she could see her words had penetrated through to Lydia's mind and hopefully the young woman would at least consider them before deciding what to do.

'Shall I help you dress?' Anna asked.

'Would you?'

'Of course. I often help my cousin, Beatrice, get ready before a ball.'

Together they selected a demure white dress with a bright blue sash and carefully Anna helped Lydia into it. Aware of the minutes ticking by, she styled the young woman's hair simply but elegantly, sweeping most of her locks back and securing them at the back of her head, leaving some wisps to frame her face.

'Ready?' she asked as Lydia inspected herself in the mirror.

There was a moment's hesitation before Harry's sister nodded, then arm in arm they left the room.

Chapter Twelve

⬥⬥⬥

The conversation was flowing in the drawing room and Harry took a step back to watch the assembled guests. The Fortescues were huddled together in one corner, heads lowered as if discussing something important. Another group, much more friendly in demeanour, stood in the centre of the room as Rifield entertained them with tall tales from his time at university a decade ago.

The only people missing were Anna and his sister. Every few seconds he found himself glancing at the door, wondering who would come through. He barely dared to hope Lydia might decide to join them, but perhaps the safety of a small group in a familiar environment might entice her.

'You seem distracted, Lord Edgerton,' Miss Wright said as she slipped away from the main group and came to his side.

'Not at all.' He flashed a sunny smile, at the same time finding his gaze wandering again to the door. Even if Lydia didn't show, then Anna should be here by now.

'Mr Rifield told me a little of your situation,' she said, touching him lightly on the arm to bring his attention back to her. 'I think it is wonderfully selfless what you are doing for Lady Fortescue.'

Harry blinked, unsure how to answer.

'I know the engagement is not real,' Miss Wright whispered, leaning in so only he could hear her words. 'There aren't many gentlemen who would risk their own reputations for a stranger.'

'It seemed the right thing to do,' Harry murmured.

'You're too generous, I'm sure, Lord Edgerton. Mr Rifield said that Lady Fortescue was about to be embarrassed and you stepped in and proposed to save her from scandal. Is that what happened?'

'More or less,' Harry said vaguely.

'I admire your discretion,' Miss Wright said, in a tone that hinted that she wished she could know more.

'How did you find your first Season, Miss Wright?' Harry asked, trying to move the conversation on to safer ground.

'Tolerable. I enjoy the balls and the socialising, but now the Season is over I am keen to focus on my charity work.'

'What do you do?'

'My mother and I are patrons of an orphanage in Bath.'

Rifield was right, Miss Wright was just the sort of young woman he should be considering for a wife. She was well liked in society, from a good family and even did charity work. Why then did he find the idea of spending more than a few hours in her company completely unappealing?

Harry opened his mouth to compliment Miss Wright for taking on such a cause, but before the words left his tongue he was distracted by a movement at the door. As he turned his head he saw Anna stepping into the room, dressed in a simple pale green dress made of fine silk, cinched in at the waist with a white ribbon. As always she looked poised and elegant, with no hint of the nervousness Harry knew she must be feeling deep inside. Her expression remained serious as her gaze swept over everyone in the room until her eyes met his. It could have been his imagination, but he was sure he detected just the flicker of a smile, a crinkling of her eyes, as she spotted him, and then as if nothing had happened she moved on. Harry watched as she stepped to one side, glancing behind her. To his amazement Lydia followed her into the room, looking nervously at Anna for reassurance. Anna took his sister by the arm and whispered something in her ear. He couldn't believe his eyes when Lydia actually smiled and for the first time in over a year he felt a little surge of hope.

'May I introduce my sister, Lady Lydia Pershore,' Harry said as Anna and Lydia came to join them.

Miss Wright greeted the two women, smiling kindly at Lydia, although Harry noticed she barely spared a glance for Anna.

'You look lovely, Lydia,' Harry said, taking his sister's hand and kissing her gently on the cheek. He always felt as though she were a delicate porcelain doll, about to crack at any moment, and as such he knew he treated her with too much caution.

'Anna helped me to dress.'

For a moment he felt like picking Anna up and twirling her round, and proclaiming himself as her eternal servant. He wasn't sure how she had convinced his sister to come downstairs, to put on a ballgown and do up her hair, but he would be grateful for ever that she had.

'What a fine gown you are wearing tonight, Miss Wright,' Anna said.

For the first time Harry looked at what Miss Wright

was wearing, taking in the pale pink dress, rich with embroidered patterns over the bodice area.

'Thank you, Lady Fortescue. Do you like it, Lord Edgerton?'

Harry murmured an inane compliment, picking up on the tension between Anna and Miss Wright. He supposed in order to entice Miss Wright to the house party Rifield had made Harry out to be completely blameless and chivalrous in the situation he found himself in with Anna. As such, Miss Wright probably didn't have too good an opinion of Anna, even before you took into consideration her reputation among the *ton*.

He was thankful when his butler announced dinner was ready to be served and his guests all started to make their way through to the dining room.

Without thinking he stepped forward to take Anna's arm, but before his fingers touched her skin she gave a subtle shake of her head, glancing towards Lydia as she did so.

'Allow me to escort you to dinner, Miss Wright,' Rifield said, coming up to their little group and taking the young woman's arm and whisking her away before she could protest.

'Lydia, can I escort you in?' Harry asked.

His sister smiled again, placing her hand daintily in the crook of his arm. Together they walked side by side into the dining room. Harry glanced back at Anna, the last one left in the drawing room. She had no one to escort her in to dinner, she would have to walk alone into a hostile environment, and not for the first time Harry wondered how she managed to stay so composed.

Small steps, Anna told herself, *one foot after another.* It was tempting to run away, to flee upstairs to her bedroom, lock the door behind her and shut out the world, but she knew that wasn't the way to solve anything.

Without having to think Anna went through the routine of putting on her invisible armour. Head held high, shoulders rolled back, chin tilted, facial features set into an impenetrable, neutral position. Every day of her marriage to Lord Fortescue she'd done exactly the same thing, from waking up in the morning until she went to bed at night.

Gliding into the dining room, she saw that everyone else had taken their places; there was just one seat empty, between the new Lord Fortescue and his brother Mr Ronald Fortescue, two of her adoring stepchildren.

Anna sat, inclining her head in greeting to the men on either side, before turning to face the woman seated directly opposite. She was relieved it wasn't Miss Fortescue—being completely surrounded by Fortescues would have been too much to bear.

'Antonia tells me you're still running that grubby little shipping company,' Lord Fortescue said part way through the first course.

The eldest of the Fortescue children, the new Lord Fortescue resembled a bull in both looks and temperament. Easy to anger, slow to think, his round face and short neck seemed always to be flushed an unsightly shade of red. He looked much like his father, so much so that Anna had to remind herself it wasn't her late husband sitting next to her when she caught a glimpse of him out of the corner of her eye.

'Indeed,' she said.

'I suppose it's better than whoring.' Lord Fortescue laughed heartily at his own joke, thumping the table with a beefy fist and making the soup jump off Anna's spoon.

'I wouldn't know,' Anna said quietly when he'd finished laughing. 'I have only experience of running the company, not working in any other occupation.'

'I don't know,' Mr Ronald Fortescue said from her other side, leaning in closer so only the three of them could hear what he was saying. 'Surely only a woman of experience, *a professional*, could lure three husbands into marriage in such a short time.'

Ronald Fortescue was the youngest of the three children, but also the sharpest. He was cruel, vindictive and Anna suspected he had inherited many of his father's worst traits.

'Don't forget victim number four,' Lord Fortescue said through a mouthful of soup. He waved his spoon in Harry's direction.

'How is your wife, Mr Fortescue?' Anna asked, turning to her left. The new Lady Fortescue, wife to the eldest Fortescue son, was sitting further up the table, but Mr Ronald Fortescue's wife was not present. Anna suspected she had once again gained an injury she could not easily hide.

'Mrs Fortescue suffers from her nerves,' he said, adding under his breath, 'Stupid woman.'

'I suffered from my nerves a lot when married to your father,' Anna said quietly, her voice hard. 'But isn't it peculiar I haven't suffered at all since his sad passing?'

Lord Fortescue pushed his chair out noisily from the table and stood up, his face turning an even deeper shade of red.

'Ladies and gentlemen,' Harry called from the top of the table, interjecting before Lord Fortescue could say anything he might regret. 'It may be a little unorthodox, but can I propose a little game while we eat.'

Anna felt Lord Fortescue's eyes boring into her as he reluctantly took his seat. She flashed a glance at Harry, who gave her a quick, reassuring smile. He might have put her in this situation, insisted that she be thrown in straight away to sit between the two Fortescue brothers, but he was there keeping an eye on things, ready to step in if things got too heated.

'Some of us know each other very well, but others are not so well acquainted. Seeing as we are a small party, I suggest a little game to allow us to get to know one another better.' He paused as a footman took away his empty bowl of soup. 'In turn we must each tell the table three things about ourselves, things that not many people would know. Two of those things will be true, the other a lie. As a group, we have to work out which is the lie.'

A murmur went along the table as the assembled guests discussed the unorthodox idea with their neighbours.

'Let me start,' Harry said, standing up. 'I was once attacked by a lion in Africa,' he said. 'My favourite drink is champagne. I can speak four languages fluently.'

Anna felt the shift of focus from her to Harry and allowed herself a small sigh of relief. After living with her last husband she could maintain a composed façade for days on end, but she was a little out of practice and she disliked the scrutiny of the Fortescue children.

'No one can speak four languages, that must be a lie,' Mr Ronald Fortescue said.

'Wait,' Mrs Wright called. 'If that was the lie, then it would mean he's been mauled by a lion in Africa.'

'Vicious beasts, no one survives a lion attack,' Lord Fortescue said. 'I witnessed a man get torn to pieces by a lion as if he were no more than a rag doll during my time in Africa.'

'Lord Edgerton did serve in the army, if my memory is correct,' the local vicar said. 'And I think he was posted to Africa.'

Anna glanced at Harry and saw him give her a conspiratorial wink. She'd been dubious about this whole weekend, worried about gathering together all the people who hated her most in the world, but Harry had promised he wouldn't let anything untoward happen and for the first time in a long time she was realising she could trust someone to do what they said they would.

'Lord Edgerton did serve champagne in the drawing room,' Miss Wright said. 'And I'm sure I saw him take a glass.'

'It's got to be the lion. That's the lie,' Lord Fortescue insisted. 'Rifield, you must know.'

'I am abstaining from comment. I've known Edgerton for far too long for him to have any secrets from me,' Rifield said.

'And you?' Lord Fortescue asked, not deigning to say Anna's name. 'Do you know anything about your new fiancé?'

'Lord Fortescue, I *know* which statement is a lie. I won't ruin the game by giving you the answer.'

'Shall we agree on the lion?' the vicar asked.

A murmur of agreement went around the table.

'That's your final answer?' Harry asked.

'Yes, we're right, aren't we?' Lord Fortescue said.

'Lady Fortescue, would you like to reveal the correct answer?' Harry asked.

All heads turned in Anna's direction.

'Lord Edgerton can speak four languages,' Anna

said. 'And he must have been attacked by a lion, as he strongly dislikes champagne.'

'Surely not,' the vicar's wife said, her eyes widening in disbelief.

'You must tell us how you survived a lion attack,' Miss Wright said, her face a picture of concern.

Anna wasn't sure exactly why Miss Wright had been invited to the house party. She was a last-minute addition, someone Harry had not even been aware of until she'd arrived with Rifield. At first Anna had assumed she was some romantic conquest of Harry's friend, but the pair didn't seem overly interested in one another. Now she was beginning to wonder if Miss Wright had her sights set on Harry and, if so, how he felt about the matter.

Sitting back in her chair, Anna inspected the young Miss Wright. She was plain but not unattractive, her hair was pulled back sharply from her face and her demeanour was earnest and upstanding. All in all she was the complete opposite of Anna and would make a respectable wife for a man worried about his family's, and more especially his sister's, reputation.

'That is a tale for another time,' Harry said. 'Who's next? Miss Fortescue?'

As Antonia stood Anna realised she was still looking at Miss Wright. She was surprised to find it was jealousy she felt at the idea of Harry turning his attention to another young woman. Not that she saw a future between her and Harry, she knew she could never give up her independence again, couldn't bear to take her chances in another marriage, but she did care for him.

Don't be selfish, she told herself silently. She couldn't ever marry Harry, so she should be happy for him to find someone to settle down with. Although she doubted

Miss Wright was the right woman for him. Harry needed someone who challenged him, someone who made him laugh and shared his interests, not someone who stood meekly by his side, agreeing to everything he said, no matter how respectable she was.

'I'm not entirely sure...' Miss Fortescue said.

'Just any three facts,' Harry said, flashing Anna's stepdaughter his most charming smile. 'I'm sure whatever you choose will be fascinating.'

'My brothers will have to keep quiet,' Miss Fortescue said. 'I can play three instruments, I once broke my ankle when thrown from a horse and I correspond with friends on three different continents.'

On either side of Anna the two Fortescue brothers looked completely bemused.

'What fascinating facts,' Rifield said in encouragement. 'And you are adept at lying for such a respectable young lady.'

Harry had instructed Rifield to charm Miss Fortescue, in the hope of getting her to open up about her hatred of Anna.

'Three instruments seems rather a lot,' Mrs Wright mused. 'My daughter is talented on the piano and has a beautiful voice, but I wonder if anyone could play *three* instruments.'

'I believe Miss Fortescue could well correspond with friends on three continents. People travel at the drop of a hat nowadays and it is common to have friends in Africa as well as India,' the vicar said.

'Lady Fortescue?' Harry asked. 'Do you have any idea?'

Anna inclined her head gracefully at her stepdaughter. 'I do not wish to spoil the game. I'm afraid I am certain of the answer.'

'What do you know?' Miss Fortescue hissed, causing the whole table to fall silent.

'I was married to your father for a year, part of the family in every way.'

When she had first arrived in the Fortescue household Anna had tried her very best to fit in. Both Lord Fortescue's sons lived elsewhere, but Miss Fortescue was unmarried and as such still resided in the family home. Anna had tried to befriend her, tried to forge an alliance with the unhappy young woman. As the weeks passed she'd realised Antonia was almost as spiteful as her father, so the attempts to assimilate had stopped, but she'd still lived under the same roof as the young woman for a year.

'You play the piano, the violin and the cello to a very high standard,' Anna said, no hint of emotion in her voice. 'You have a friend in India—Miss Fiona Dotwell, if I'm not mistaken—and a friend in Egypt, as well as many correspondents in this country.' Miss Fortescue opened her mouth to speak, but Anna carried on. 'And you were thrown from a horse when you were ten years old, but you broke your wrist and not your ankle.'

The silence stretched out as Anna finished speaking, none of the assembled guests wanting to come between the two women.

'Is Lady Fortescue correct?' Harry asked quietly after thirty seconds had passed.

'She is correct,' Miss Fortescue confirmed.

'I did try to be your friend,' Anna said quietly, angling her head to Antonia so the other guests wouldn't be able to hear.

'You seduced my father, betrayed him and may well have killed him. You were never a friend of mine.' Miss Fortescue's voice was not so quiet, projecting the accusations down the table. As the silence stretched out two spots of colour appeared on her cheeks and with a jerky, rushed movement she stood, dropping her napkin and pushing her chair back with a loud scrape. 'Please excuse me, I have a terrible headache all of a sudden.'

Miss Fortescue left the room, throwing Anna a look of hate on her way out. As the other guests tried to fill the ensuing silence with embarrassed chatter, the Fortescue brothers both turned to Anna.

'You're a disgrace,' Lord Fortescue muttered in her direction.

Mr Ronald Fortescue was looking at her with more curiosity than contempt. 'Why are we here, Lady Fortescue?' he asked quietly.

'Would you believe me if I said to mend the family rift?'

Mr Ronald Fortescue laughed, a spiteful, ugly chortle. 'I don't believe a word that comes out of your mouth, dear Mother.'

'Then perhaps it would be better if I said no more.'

Chapter Thirteen

It was another unseasonably warm evening for so early in the spring so Harry had instructed the servants to throw open the doors to the terrace from the drawing room. After dinner the women had filed through, leaving the men in the dining room, discussing whatever it was they discussed when the women left.

Anna surveyed the room. Mrs Wright and Miss Wright were perched on two straight-backed chairs, talking to the vicar's wife. Lydia stood awkwardly to one side, as if unsure if she should join in the conversation. She'd remained quiet throughout dinner, barely saying a word, but she had eaten a little, sipped on some wine and answered any questions directed only at her.

'Tell me,' Anna said, approaching Lydia and taking her arm, 'what do you think of our guests?'

A small smile flickered across Lydia's lips, only present for a second, but welcome all the same. 'They're a little odd,' Lydia whispered. 'Individually I'm sure they're all perfectly pleasant.'

Anna grimaced—she wouldn't call Miss Fortescue or her brothers perfectly pleasant in any situation.

'But it is a strange group to be gathered together.'

'Did your brother tell you why he arranged this house party?' Anna asked.

Lydia shook her head. 'A little, but not much.'

Harry probably thought he was protecting his sister, shielding her from the unpleasantness in the world, whereas in truth he was likely just isolating her more from the real world.

'The three guests, Lord Fortescue, Mr Ronald Fortescue and Miss Antonia Fortescue, are my stepchildren,' Anna explained, drawing Lydia to one side. 'They all completely despise me—they have done since the moment I married their father and it has only got worse since his death.'

Lydia looked at her with wide eyes and Anna wondered if she was doing the right thing. Part of her thought it would be good for Lydia to be involved with the wider world again, to have something to think about other than her own unhappiness, but she also realised she was probably telling Lydia this against Harry's wishes.

Quietly she explained about the packages and the letters, about her suspicions that it was one of the Fortescue children behind the campaign of hatred. As they talked she saw Lydia slowly become more animated, more interested.

'Do you think they'll do something while you're here?' Lydia asked after Anna had finished her story.

'That is what we hope. Then we can catch them at it and put a stop to the packages once and for all. Will you keep your eyes open for anything suspicious?'

'Of course.'

'Lady Fortescue.' A voice behind Anna made both her and Lydia jump. 'Please forgive me for the interruption.' It was Miss Wright, smiling sweetly. 'I was hoping you might like to join me for a stroll along the terrace. It is such a lovely evening.'

Anna allowed the other woman to take her arm and lead her out to the terrace, checking over her shoulder that Lydia was not too uncomfortable at being left alone.

'What a beautiful evening,' Miss Wright said as they walked away from the dining room.

'Indeed.' Something about this young woman made Anna raise her guard, but she smiled politely and waited for her to say whatever it was she wanted to say.

'I understand the nature of your agreement with Lord Edgerton,' Miss Wright said quietly.

'Oh?'

'No one could say he is not chivalrous, coming to your aid to save you from scandal, but I fear such a kind and generous man might be taken advantage of in that sort of situation,' Miss Wright said smoothly.

'Taken advantage of?' Anna asked mildly, feigning confusion.

'We all know this engagement between you is nothing more than a ruse, something that Lord Edgerton plans to break when the time is right,' Miss Wright said. 'But I fear an unscrupulous woman might pressure such a kind-hearted man into a more lasting agreement.'

'For a woman who only met Lord Edgerton and myself today you seem to have a lot of insight into our situation,' Anna said, keeping her voice impassive.

'You have a reputation, Lady Fortescue, and not a good one. Any connection with you is not good for Lord Edgerton, or his sister. And everyone knows *she* can't afford to have any more scandal attached to her name.'

'I was under the impression Lord Edgerton was a grown man and not a child,' Anna said, 'and as such is perfectly capable of making his own decisions.'

'Even the noblest of men can be led astray by a pretty face and a devious mind.'

'Tell me, Miss Wright, do you have intentions on my fiancé?' Anna couldn't help herself. 'Stealing another woman's betrothed is hardly decent behaviour for a respectable woman.'

'Mr Rifield has made it clear that Lord Edgerton wants a respectable wife who is well liked and well thought of by the rest of society. You are neither respectable, well liked or well thought of. I suggest you gracefully step out of the way and let Lord Edgerton get on with his life without the burden of you.'

'Thank you for your advice,' Anna said, inclining her head politely to Miss Wright. 'You certainly have given me much to think about.'

It would be so easy to go on the attack, but Anna had realised long ago that nothing was ever gained by making a dispute public. Quickly, before her anger could get the better of her, she spun on her heel and glided away, ensuring all traces of anger and passion had been cleared from her face before she stepped back into the drawing room.

Holding a flickering candle, Harry climbed up the winding staircase, feeling his head clear as he breathed in the fresh air. Quietly he stepped on to the parapet, smiling to himself as he saw Anna looking out into the darkness. He'd thought she might be up here. After a challenging dinner no doubt she needed time to process everything that had happened before retiring to bed.

As he stood watching her it became clear she hadn't heard him approaching. She didn't turn round or speak to him, instead lifting her face to the moonlight.

'Anna,' he said, coming up behind her and touching her lightly on the shoulders.

She stiffened and let out a gasp of surprise, but quickly recovered, turning to him with a half-smile.

'You did very well tonight,' he said softly.

'Did I? I couldn't tell.'

'Lord Fortescue's children are absolutely awful. You were wonderfully detached from their spitefulness,' Harry said. He'd watched her throughout dinner, admired the way she hadn't risen to any of the cruel comments the new Lord Fortescue or his brother had made. He'd known she was skilled in hiding her emotions, but until tonight he had never seen anyone deal with such outright disdain with so much dignity.

'Remind me why this is a good idea,' Anna said, turning away and resuming her perusal of the night sky.

'One weekend of discomfort will be worth it if we can put an end to the persecution you've been suffering.'

'Perhaps you're right,' she said, a hint of sadness in her voice.

Carefully Harry reached up and adjusted the shawl around her shoulders, covering the exposed skin against the chill of the night. His fingers lingered, feeling the heat of her body even through the thick wool of the shawl.

'Why are you doing this for me, Harry?' Anna asked, turning to face him.

'I told you before, no one should have to suffer what you're going through.'

'That's too noble,' she said with a little laugh.

'We might not really be engaged,' Harry said, stepping closer so their bodies were almost touching, 'but over the last few weeks I've come to care for you, Anna.'

Her eyes met his and he felt as though she were searching his entire soul, the deepest recesses of his being.

'I do not like to think of you alone, suffering,' he said.

He wanted to kiss her then, even though he knew it would only complicate things. Before his rational mind could make him step away Anna had swayed towards him, one hand reaching up to touch his face. With her fingers on his cheek, her eyes looking into his, Harry knew a kiss was inevitable and with a low groan he gave in and covered her mouth with his own.

She tasted sweet and her lips were warm, just as Harry had imagined them to be. As he kissed her a torrent of desire crashed through him and he looped an arm around her waist, pulling her closer to him. Even in the midst of passion Harry knew this was wrong, but nothing in the world could have stopped him.

Anna's fingers trailed down his cheek, tracing their way along his neck and coming to rest on his chest. The skin where she'd touched him felt as though it were on fire and his entire body was on edge, as if each and every nerve was waiting to discharge.

With a soft sigh she pulled away.

'I'm sorry, Harry,' she said. 'I shouldn't have done that.'

He half-expected her to flee, that was what most women of his acquaintance would have done after a situation such as this, but instead she embraced him, wrapping her arms around him and burying her head in his shoulder.

'You're a kind man, Harry Edgerton,' she said, her voice muffled by his clothes. 'And I am a foolish woman.'

Gently he lifted her head so she was once more looking into his eyes. For a moment he forgot all the reasons why they couldn't be together, forgot his resolve to find a wife he could never fall in love with and Anna's vehement objection to the idea of ever marrying again.

'Can we forget this ever happened?' she asked. 'I value what we have too much for this to ruin things.'

'Of course,' Harry said, knowing he was lying. He wouldn't ever be able to forget how her lips felt on his, the taste of her mouth in his own, the way her body fitted against his as if they were made for one another.

She smiled at him then, a smile that could melt the heart of any man, then turned and slipped down the staircase back to the main house. Harry stayed where he was for a few minutes, looking out at the stars and wondering when his life became so complicated.

Chapter Fourteen

As the first light of dawn filtered through the thick curtains Anna rose from her bed, slipped into a dress she could fasten without the help of a maid and quietly left her room. She'd always risen early, always enjoyed the peace of a new day before the household started to wake, but today she felt heavy and tired.

She'd barely slept, too many conflicting thoughts racing through her mind, whipping her up into a state of confusion and anxiety and chasing away even the possibility of sleep. Every time she tried to settle Harry's face would flash before her eyes and the memory of his lips on hers, his fingers on her skin, pushed out anything else clamouring for attention in her mind.

Of course the kiss had been a mistake. Anna wasn't sure what had come over her. There had been something almost magical about the moment up at the top of the tower, something irresistible about Harry.

He was unlike any man she had ever known, although she supposed a list of five wasn't very many to compare to. Apart from her three husbands and her father—a man who had frowned upon displays of affection or sentimentality—the only man she'd ever been relatively close to was her beloved uncle. Despite living for a few years as a widow in between her marriages she'd kept herself quite private, never been in a position to start an illicit affair, never indulged in an inappropriate friendship with a gentleman, until now of course. Nevertheless, she knew Harry was different to other men. He was kind and generous, perhaps too generous. He took the problems of others and made them his own, often shouldering the burden when he shouldn't have to. There was no arguing he was a good man.

After Lord Fortescue's death Anna had vowed never to marry again, never to give a man that ultimate power over her. While married she'd suffered daily at her late husband's hands. He was a cruel man and a crueller husband, and she had the scars to prove it. Even after knowing Harry for just a few short weeks she knew he would never beat her, never raise his hand in anger, but all the same she needed to keep her distance.

It would be all too easy to fall for Harry, to find herself seduced by his charm and his kindness, and once again to lose her autonomy, to become a wife rather than a woman of independence.

'Keep your distance,' she murmured to herself as she glided down the stairs, turning back on herself in the grand hallway to slip through the door to the kitchens below where she thought she might find a door a little easier to open than the heavy oak that guarded the grand entrance.

Outside the air was damp and in the distance Anna could see wispy tendrils of mist floating low over the hills. With the sun just starting to peek over the horizon it looked more like a fairy-tale land than England and Anna found it difficult not to smile. Despite the reason she was here, despite all she'd suffered over the years, she couldn't help but appreciate this moment. Right here, right now she felt happy and it was a long-forgotten emotion.

As she stepped on to the immaculately kept lawn that swept the entire length of the back of the house she could feel the dampness seeping through her shoes and knew it wouldn't be long until the hem of her dress was sodden with water, but even this was not enough to make her turn back.

In the distance she could see two deer, a mother and her baby, trotting through the parkland, and closer, just twenty feet away, a group of rabbits were hopping about in the early morning air.

Anna walked for a few minutes with no certain destination in mind, just content to be out in the fresh air. As she headed away from the house the outline of a summer house became visible, the white boards reflecting the sun. Without too much thought she headed for the small structure, but as she drew near she heard a faint sobbing.

Pausing, Anna wondered whether to push on or retrace her steps before anyone saw her. She didn't like to leave whoever it was inside the summer house in distress, but she also knew all too well how sometimes a witness to sorrow was the last thing that person might need.

Quietly she stepped up to the open door and looked inside. For a moment she thought it was Lydia sitting on the bench—the woman had the same dark hair, the same delicate, almost fragile physique. As she looked up Anna realised this woman was older, but most certainly related.

'I'm sorry to intrude,' Anna said. 'I heard you crying, but I understand if you wish to be left alone.'

'Come sit,' the woman said, brushing the tears away from her eyes. 'You must think me very foolish sitting here crying all by myself.'

'Not at all.' Anna meant what she said. She didn't know what troubles this woman faced and sometimes a few quietly shed tears in private were all the outlet a woman was allowed.

'You must be Lady Fortescue,' she said with a soft smile. 'Lydia told me all about you last night.'

'Lady Edgerton?' Anna ventured, guessing this must be the countess, Harry's mother.

Anna had thought it a little strange the countess had not been present to greet the guests as they'd arrived, or been part of the gathering the evening before, but Harry had hinted that his mother suffered deeply from her nerves.

The older woman frowned, looking past Anna and her eyes glazing over slightly.

'You must be careful, my dear—an ill wind follows you here.'

Anna glanced over her shoulder, shivering slightly, knowing it was from the damp morning air but wondering what Harry's mother was looking at.

'Would you like me to take you back to the house, Lady Edgerton?' Anna asked.

Harry's mother sighed and Anna saw her hands were trembling in her lap. Cautiously, moving slowly so as not to alarm the older woman, she reached out and placed one of her hands over the top of Lady Edgerton's fingers. Momentarily Lady Edgerton stiffened, but then seemed to relax a little.

'There has been much heartbreak here.'

'I know, Lady Edgerton,' Anna said placatingly.

'My poor Lydia. She's so sensitive, so delicate.'

Looking at the countess, Anna knew Lydia had inherited more than just her looks from her mother. Harry had hinted that his mother was prone to fits of melancholy and was plagued by her nerves, and now Anna could see just what a toll this had taken on her.

Suddenly the older countess's eyes swung back to Anna's, focusing intently on her.

'He's very taken with you.'

'I'm not sure...'

Lady Edgerton shook her head vehemently. 'He is very taken with you. Nothing good can come out of it.' She wrung her hands together, squeezing and pinching at the skin until Anna felt like reaching out and pulling them apart. 'First Lydia and now him, how am I to bear it?'

'Bear what, Lady Edgerton?'

'Losing them. My lovely children. First my husband and now them.'

Anna wanted to point out that she hadn't lost either of her children, Harry and Lydia were still resident at Halstead Hall, still very much alive, but didn't want to add to the older woman's distress.

'It nearly killed me when poor Lydia—' She broke off, letting out a sob. 'My poor heart, it won't stand any more pain.'

'Please don't suffer on my account, Lady Edgerton.'

'They say you're engaged to my son,' Lady Edgerton said, turning and fixing Anna with a hard look.

'Your son is helping me through a difficult time.'

'He must marry a nice girl. A respectable girl. He needs to settle down and produce an heir with someone from a good family.' Lady Edgerton's voice was becoming higher in pitch and more hysterical with every syllable. Anna wished she knew how to calm Harry's mother, but was aware a few poorly chosen words could have the opposite effect.

'I'm sure he will, Lady Edgerton.'

'How can he, when…?'

'Mother.' Harry's voice was quiet but firm and both women turned in surprise to look at him.

The silence stretched out, Anna feeling as though she couldn't be the one to break it, but feeling decidedly uncomfortable being in the middle of the tension between mother and son.

'Let me escort you back to the house,' Harry said kindly after a long minute of silence. 'You'll catch a chill in this damp air if you stay out any longer.'

'Yes, dear,' Lady Edgerton said.

Gently Harry took his mother's arm, flashed an apologetic smile over his shoulder at Anna and led the older woman back over the damp grass towards the house.

'You must think my entire family mad,' Harry said, ten minutes later as he met Anna on the lawn in front of the summer house.

'Not at all.'

'Sometimes I do,' he murmured, running his free hand through his hair, resting it at the nape of his neck before letting it fall to his side.

'All families have their challenges,' Anna said.

'What a wonderfully uncontroversial way to put it.'

Harry offered Anna his arm and they walked side by side away from the house across the wet lawn. He was a naturally early riser, normally one of the first awake in the household, but this morning he'd opened his curtains to see Anna strolling through the gardens just as the sun was rising above the horizon. When he'd gone out to meet her he hadn't expected to find his mother sat in the summer house in just her flimsy nightclothes.

'My mother hasn't been the same since my father passed away,' Harry said quietly, feeling as if he needed to tell Anna his family weren't completely crazy.

'There's no need to explain anything, Harry.'

'She was always nervous, but nothing like this. Now it seems she's governed by worry and superstition.'

'Were she and your father close?'

He grimaced, remembering the blazing arguments, the screaming matches that he would watch from the top of the stairs, his parents oblivious to his presence.

'They loved each other,' he said slowly. 'Completely adored each other, especially at the beginning.'

There had been good times, Harry remembered, the walks they would all take together though the fields, his parents arm in arm and smiling up at each other. But as the years went on the good times had diminished and instead their lives had been full of arguments and rows.

'They loved each other *too* much. It wasn't healthy to have so much passion in a marriage. They were always destined to hurt one another.'

'Surely love in a marriage is a good thing,' Anna said softly.

Harry shook his head vehemently. 'Mutual respect and companionship, that's what a good marriage is built on, not love. My parents loved each other so much it was destructive, especially for my mother. As time went on, after an argument my father would goad her, flaunt his latest mistress in front of her. He knew it would destroy her, but he still did it. And this was to the woman he loved.'

'That doesn't sound like love…' Anna murmured.

'But they did love each other, madly at first. It turned bad and ruined them both.'

'And your mother's still mourning him?'

'Ever since he passed away she's shut herself off from the rest of the world, and it was worse after Lydia…' He trailed off.

'It sounds like you've had a lot to deal with these last few years.'

'No more than any other head of the family,' he said. 'They don't tell you what a difficult job having responsibility for the ones you love actually is.'

'Does your mother have a companion?' Anna asked.

He shook his head. 'She and Lydia used to be inseparable, but I think Mother became a little too overbearing even for my sister.'

'Are you happy, Harry?' Anna asked quietly, the question causing him to pause and look at her.

'Happy?'

'Yes, happy.'

'I suppose so. At least I will be when Lydia finds a husband and is settled.'

'You're a very kind man,' Anna said, looking up at him, her cool grey eyes piercing into his core, 'but you must remember to please yourself as well as others.'

'What do you mean?'

'Correct me if I'm wrong, but society tells me you are looking for a wife.'

He shrugged—it wasn't a great secret.

'But instead of looking to find someone you actually care about, someone who you can see would make you happy, you're looking for a woman who is respectable and dull.'

'As I said, I don't believe in love matches. For centuries people have been marrying for much more sensible reasons than love.'

'Are you looking to save the Edgerton family name, to marry a woman so respectable she could champion Lydia back into society?'

Harry sighed—the thought had crossed his mind on more than one occasion. 'A respectable wife certainly wouldn't hurt the reputation of this family, but that is not the main criteria I am basing my search on.'

'What is?'

'I'm looking for an amiable young woman who would make a good mother to my children, a respectable countess, someone I like, but don't feel anything more for.'

'What about love, Harry? What about happiness?'

'I think my marriage will be much happier if love doesn't complicate it.'

'What happened to your parents doesn't have to happen to you,' Anna said.

'Were you happy?' he asked, slightly more abruptly than he meant to. 'In your second marriage, the man you married for love?'

'No,' Anna said without hesitation. 'But I see now it was an infatuation with a dashing young man, not true love.' He watched as Anna hesitated and he realised she was wondering whether to give up a little more about her own past.

'I've had three marriages, Harry, none of them particularly happy, but one was the worst year of my life. I wouldn't want anyone to suffer through a marriage like that.'

Harry watched her intently. From the little things she'd said, from the reactions she had whenever anyone touched her, he'd worked out her last marriage had been difficult, but now he was wondering if it had been more than that.

'Marriage is for life,' Anna said, stopping and turning to him, 'and I wouldn't like to think of you being stuck with someone who didn't make you as happy as you could be for the rest of your life.'

Rifield had said the same thing many times, had cautioned Harry about choosing his wife based on purely her reputation and her amiability, but they didn't understand, neither of them did.

'I thank you for your concern,' Harry said quietly, 'but our situations are very different.'

Anna sighed, turning to smile at him brightly after a few seconds. 'It is none of my concern, I know that,' she said, patting him on the arm like an elderly aunt. 'You have been so kind to me, I do not like to think of you as unhappy, but I will keep my views to myself.'

There was an awkwardness between them for a few minutes and Harry was reminded of the evening they had first met in Lord Prenderson's study. Anna had been stiff and formal then, but as the weeks had passed by she had revealed more of her true self, little by little.

'Let us return to the house,' Anna said, her expression inscrutable. 'Your guests will be rising for breakfast shortly and it is probably wise we are not seen out in the gardens together with no chaperon.'

The walk back to the house only took a couple of minutes and as Harry left Anna in the entrance hall he found himself mulling over her words. His views on marriage weren't that unusual. Most of the unions between titled ladies and gentlemen were arranged for far less sensible reasons than he was proposing. Most people of his acquaintance married for money, a title or links to an influential family. He was merely looking for a wife he could rub along well with for thirty years, someone who could never hurt him because he wouldn't be head over heels in love with them. He'd seen the destruction a marriage built on love could cause—he wasn't about to impose that on his own life or his future children.

Chapter Fifteen

'**P**all-mall,' Harry had announced to the guests who had made it down for breakfast. 'It's the perfect day for it.'

Now about half of the party had traipsed out to the gardens where Harry was enthusiastically hammering the hoop into the grass and setting out the course. To one side, just off the patio, Harry had set the heavy wooden mallets and the hefty ball, and as she watched the rest of the guests emerge from the house Anna walked over and picked up one of the mallets, testing its weight in her hand.

'I hope you're not planning to use that as a deadly weapon,' Rifield said quietly in her ear, smiling as he did so.

From most people it would have been an unkind reference to the rumours of how her husbands had died, but Anna could detect no malice in Harry's friend.

'Who wants to go first?' Harry asked.

There were six of them in total: Harry and Anna, Rifield, Mrs and Miss Wright, and Lydia. The Fortescues had all taken breakfast in their rooms and were yet to emerge to join the other guests. The vicar and his wife had returned home the evening before, but would be joining them for dinner again tonight.

'I'm not sure it is entirely appropriate for a young lady...' Mrs Wright said, eyeing up the ball and mallets.

'Perhaps you gentlemen could show us how the game is played,' Miss Wright suggested.

Anna took a seat on the patio alongside the three other women and watched as Harry and Rifield hefted the mallets and took some preparatory swings.

'The aim of the game is to hit the ball along the course and through the hoop at the end in the least number of hits,' he explained.

'I've never seen pall-mall being played in a garden before,' Miss Wright remarked.

Harry went first, hitting the ball a good distance with his first swing before lining up and aiming for the hoop further down the garden. The ladies all let out a cheer as the ball shot through the hoop on the fourth hit.

'Your turn, Rifield,' Harry said.

Rifield stepped up to the starting point and tapped the ball, sending it hurtling across the grass. It took him five hits to get the ball to pass through the hoop and by the time it sailed under the metal bar the spectators were all laughing at his antics.

'Who is next?' Harry asked.

'If you would be so kind as to show me how to hit the ball,' Miss Wright said, standing up and ignoring the warning glance from her mother.

Miss Wright took the mallet from Harry and positioned herself as he directed. Reaching around her waist, Harry showed her how to hold the heavy wooden mallet, how to line up the hit with the hoop at the other end of the garden and the desired force to hit the ball with. Although their bodies did not touch at any point

Anna felt a sharp stab of jealousy and had to remind herself that Harry was not really her fiancé to covet.

Miss Wright hit the ball along the garden with delicate little taps, succeeding in pushing it through the hoop after eight hits.

'Lady Fortescue?' Harry asked as he and Miss Wright headed back to the patio.

Anna stood, allowing Harry to lead her to the start point.

'Have you played before?' he asked.

'No.'

'Would you permit me to assist you?'

She nodded, allowing Harry to adjust her grip on the mallet, show her how to position her body and finally loop his arms around her waist much as he had done with Miss Wright. Their bodies didn't once touch, but every second she was aware of his presence just inches away. As she hit the ball for the first time, sending it spinning across the garden, she felt his breath on her neck and had to force herself to concentrate on the game before her.

'Good hit,' Harry called, a trace of admiration in his voice.

Anna squared her stance, looked backwards and forward between the hoop and the ball a few times and then swung the mallet again. The ball bounced, flying along the course and Anna felt a swell of pleasure. She liked to do things well.

'Four hits,' Harry called from further up the garden. 'If I'd have known you were this good I'd have tried harder.'

Anna handed the mallet over to Lydia and watched as the young woman tapped the ball gently down the garden. Harry was with her every step, every hit.

'He's so good with his sister,' she heard Miss Wright murmur to Mrs Wright.

'Many men wouldn't have the patience to molly-coddle a young woman of such tepid character,' Mrs Wright whispered.

'It is certainly a point in his favour.'

As if Harry needed any more points in his favour. He was an earl, from one of the oldest families in England. He owned a large estate and beautiful property, and probably many more houses dotted around the country. He'd served his country while in the army and now was devoted to serving his family.

'You'd have to get the sister married off quickly, though,' Mrs Wright murmured. 'No sense in having to share Lord Edgerton's attention.'

'I'm sure there would be no shortage of candidates once a suitably large dowry was suggested,' Miss Wright said, looking thoughtfully at Lydia. 'And it would do the poor girl good to make a life of her own.'

'Ah, Miss Fortescue,' Harry called as Lydia hit the ball through the hoop at the end of the course. 'You're just in time to play pall-mall.'

Anna turned to see her stepdaughter walking stiffly on to the terrace. There was still no sign of her brothers and Anna wondered if they had decided to pack for London.

'I do not play games,' Miss Fortescue said.

'Nonsense, everyone plays games.' Harry motioned towards Rifield, who summoned his most charming smile. 'Rifield will show you how it's done.'

Stepping back off the course, Harry wandered back to Anna's side, picking up a glass of water from the table on his way.

Quietly they watched Miss Fortescue stiffly allow

Rifield to demonstrate how to play pall-mall, wondering whether she would hit him with the mallet if he got too close.

'I think she's developing a soft spot for Rifield,' Harry murmured, quietly enough so only Anna could hear him.

'I don't wish to be uncharitable, but I don't think Miss Fortescue is capable of affection.'

'Under that unwelcoming demeanour there might be a romantic side struggling to get out.'

Anna had lived under the same roof as Miss Fortescue for a year. She very much doubted there was a hidden romantic under the spitefulness, but she had been wrong about people before.

The sun peeked out from behind a cloud as the rest of the guests got into the spirit of the game and for a few minutes at least it felt like they were at a normal, amiable house party with friends rather than people who detested her.

To everyone's surprise Mrs Wright, who had to be coaxed from her seat on the patio, won the game of pall-mall, managing to knock the ball through the hoop in just three hits. She reddened at the congratulations and hurriedly returned to her seat before she could be pressed into repeating the performance.

'Time for archery,' Harry declared.

'Are you mad?' Anna hissed at him as he took her arm and led her to a different part of the garden. Up ahead three well-worn targets had been set up and closer to the house a selection of bows and arrows lay on the ground.

'Can't have my guests getting bored,' Harry said.

'Someone is threatening me and you provide the deadly weapons to help them make good on their threats.'

'No one will harm a hair on your head while you are under my protection,' Harry said so confidently it left Anna speechless.

As the footmen carried the seats from the patio, arranging them a little distance away from the targets, the guests chattered and eyed up the assorted bows on the ground.

By the time the ladies were seated Lord Fortescue and Mr Ronald Fortescue had joined the group and each were eagerly inspecting the bows, picking them up to feel the weight and testing the tautness of the string.

'Brings back memories of the good times, eh, Lady Fortescue?' Mr Ronald Fortescue said.

Anna fixed him with an icy stare, but decided not to answer.

'Perhaps we should play Fortescue rules,' Lord Fortescue murmured to his brother. 'Might get rid of our little problem with the settlements.'

'Fortescue rules?' Harry asked Anna, quietly so he wouldn't embarrass her.

The two Fortescue men laughed at their private joke and Anna felt an unfamiliar rage building inside her. Of course she could control it—during the terrible months of her last marriage she'd felt everything from terror to rage to sorrow, but she'd become expert at hiding every emotion, of constructing a wall to hold back her feelings. Now there was no need, no reason to remain calm and detached. No one to hurt her, no one to make her regret her actions.

'Lord Fortescue has suggested we play Fortescue rules,' Anna said, her voice ringing clear and loud, silencing the rest of the guests.

The look of surprise on her two stepsons' faces was enough to encourage her to go on.

'My husband, the late Lord Fortescue, always had an archery target set up on the lawn, with a bow and arrows handy.'

'That's quite enough, Lady Fortescue,' Mr Ronald Fortescue hissed.

'No, no, Mr Fortescue, you suggested Fortescue rules, I'm just explaining them to our companions.'

'I really don't think…' Lord Fortescue bumbled, his face turning an even deeper shade of red than normal.

'My dear husband, the late Lord Fortescue, was very particular in how he liked the members of his household to behave,' Anna said, seeing the horrified fascination in the faces of the assembled guests. It wasn't the done thing to discuss the intimate details of a marriage, especially when a peer of the realm was involved, but everyone was hanging on Anna's every word. 'If I had committed a transgression he felt was very severe, he liked to punish me in novel and *amusing* ways.' Amusing to him, certainly not to her.

'That is quite enough, Lady Fortescue,' the new Lord Fortescue said, grabbing Anna by the arm roughly.

Immediately Harry had intervened, taking Lord Fortescue's wrist and squeezing until he let go, muttering in pain.

'He would make me stand in front of a target, just like this,' Anna said, walking slowly up to the middle target. She stood with her back to the board and spread out her arms. Everyone was watching her, no one able to tear their eyes away. 'And then he would ask me if I was afraid.'

The first time he'd done it Anna had thought it a joke. She'd laughed merrily at her new husband until he fired an arrow that thunked into the target so close to her shoulder it tore the fabric of her dress.

'I think he wanted me to be afraid,' Anna said, looking directly at the three Fortescue children, each in turn. Not one of them would meet her eye.

'You deserved everything you got,' Miss Fortescue said after a few seconds, her voice no more than a low whisper, but Anna heard every word all the same.

'For what? For laughing too merrily at the dining table? For playing the piano too loudly in the middle of the day? For receiving a letter from a schoolfriend?' All transgressions she had been punished for.

'You were an unfaithful harlot…' Miss Fortescue said, echoing her father's words, even her father's tone.

'It's just not true. You know it and he knew it.'

'Shut up,' Miss Fortescue whispered. 'Stop slandering a dead man's name when he can't defend himself.'

'We both know what your father did to me…'

'Shut up, shut up, shut up.' Miss Fortescue's voice raised from a whisper to a croaky shout.

Anna should have seen the flash of desperation in Miss Fortescue's eyes, should have stopped there, but she felt liberated, finally free of the hold her late husband held over her even after his death. If she wanted to she could tell the whole world what a cruel violent man Lord Fortescue had been.

'He—' She didn't get to say any more. Time seemed to move slowly as she saw Miss Fortescue lift the bow that was in her grip, pull back the string and loose the arrow. Anna was frozen, unable to move, the arrow heading straight for her when Harry's solid body careened into hers, knocking her to the ground.

Silence stretched out, no one moved for what felt like an eternity. Finally Harry shifted, moving the weight of his body on to his arms and pushing himself up.

'Are you hurt?' he asked, cupping her face with his hands.

She considered for a moment. She felt a little winded from where he'd landed on top of her, but she wasn't hurt. Slowly she shook her head.

With everyone's eyes on her, Anna stood, turning to inspect the arrow in the target, still quivering from the impact, embedded right where her head would have been if Harry hadn't pushed her to the ground.

Miss Fortescue let out a sob, covered her mouth with her hand and fled swiftly in the direction of the house.

'I shall see to my sister,' Mr Ronald Fortescue said quickly, beating a hasty retreat, closely followed by his brother.

Anna felt her pulse begin to slow as she looked away from the target and up into Harry's reassuring eyes.

'What an action-packed morning,' Rifield said, his eyes still wide with shock.

'I will escort Lady Fortescue to her room,' Harry said, taking Anna's arm.

'Good idea.' Rifield leaned in. 'Don't worry, I'll look after your guests. Take all the time you need.'

As Harry led her gently across the lawn they heard Rifield gathering up the rest of the bewildered guests and suggesting a nice sedate stroll about the gardens.

Chapter Sixteen

'I'll kill him,' Harry growled, pacing backwards and forward across Anna's bedroom floor. He shouldn't be in here, certainly not alone with the woman he was pretending to be engaged to, and most certainly not with the door firmly closed and locked.

'If you mean my late husband, he's dead already,' Anna said, calmly, with that little shrug of the shoulders he was coming to like so much.

'He used to stand you in front of the target and shoot arrows at you? That's disgusting, it's barbaric.'

'Only in the first few months of our marriage,' Anna said quietly.

Somehow he didn't think Lord Fortescue had stopped due to a reformation of character.

'Did he harm you? Is that why he stopped?'

Harry stopped pacing in front of Anna and held her gently by both upper arms, looking her over head to toe as if for arrow wounds.

'No, whatever else Lord Fortescue was, he was a good shot, could hit where he wanted to on a target with an arrow from thirty feet.'

'So why did he stop?' Harry asked quietly, wondering if he really wanted to know.

'He liked to see the fear in my eyes, to know he had absolute control not just over my body but also my mind, my emotions.'

'You can't mean to say you stopped being afraid.'

Anna looked down at the ground for a few seconds before answering, 'I stopped caring. I stopped caring whether the arrow hit me or not.'

He couldn't find the words to respond for a few seconds. It was unconceivable, a husband putting his wife in such danger, all for a little amusement, to see the fear in her eyes. What kind of man…what kind of *monster*… could do such a thing?

'Did he do other things to you?' Harry asked, his voice no more than a whisper. He had to know, but at the same time dreaded her answer.

'Harry,' Anna said, raising a hand and trailing her fingers down his face, 'you don't need to know.'

No wonder she'd been so adamant she would never marry again.

'Tell me,' he said, raising a hand so it covered hers, looking deep into her unwavering grey eyes.

'We should…' Anna started to say.

'There's no rush. Rifield will keep the rest of the guests busy. Tell me.'

With a sigh Anna turned away. He thought she would refuse again, tell him to get out of her rooms, perhaps even start packing to return to London, but instead he saw her fiddling with the fastenings of her dress.

'Help me,' she said, looking over her shoulder.

'What…?'

'You wanted to know, so help me.'

Motioning to the fastenings at the back of her dress,

those normally a maid would help her with, Anna began to pull at the pale green cotton. In a daze Harry stepped forward, his fingers fumbling as he reached out for the first of the fastenings. He couldn't deny he'd thought about undressing Anna, couldn't deny he'd imagined this moment a thousand different ways. He'd desired her from the moment their bodies had careened into one another in Lord Prenderson's study, but never had he thought he would be undressing her in the middle of the morning in his family home.

After a few seconds he'd loosened the dress just enough for Anna to slip it down. The rustling of material revealed a thin white cotton chemise, which went from the top of her back to well below the knee, covering her body and preserving her dignity, but Harry felt as though he were looking at her naked. As he watched she tugged at the ties at the front of the chemise.

'Anna?' he asked, trying to be a gentleman, trying to give her the opportunity to stop.

'You wanted to know, you wanted to see.'

'Stop,' he said, hearing the lack of emotion in her voice. The last thing he wanted was for her to do anything against her will. 'Stop, Anna.'

She shook her head, pushed the chemise from her shoulders and pulled down. Harry heard himself take a sharp intake of breath as the skin of her back was exposed. Her skin was milky white, just the colour of the cream off the top of the finest milk. He'd touched her hand, her arm, her cheek enough times to know the skin would be soft and velvety to the touch.

Latticed across her back were a half-dozen pale scars. Long and thin and straight, there could be no mistake they'd been made by a rod. Without thinking Harry raised his fingers and gently touched one of the scars. It was well healed and one day far into the future probably would disappear, but to make such a scar would have required a deep wound and a cane wielded with a monstrous force.

'He beat you,' Harry said quietly.

'Among other things.'

He had so many questions, so many things he wanted to ask, but hearing the emptiness in her voice Harry gripped the edge of her chemise and tugged it back up over her shoulders.

He gently tightened the fastenings of her gown and once she was dressed again Anna turned to face him.

'Why?' he asked.

'I don't think you'd understand, Harry,' Anna said with a small, brave smile.

'Try me.'

'He was cruel. He was evil. He revelled in holding power over me, by seeing the naked fear in my eyes, by finding new ways to torment me.'

'He did this to you for a whole year?'

Harry felt sick to his stomach, roll after roll of nausea working its way through his body. Who could do such a thing to such a woman? Who could do such a thing to anyone?

'It was worse at the beginning. I learnt to submit.'

'Submit?' He echoed the word with horror.

Anna shrugged. 'I conducted myself in the manner he wished me to, after a few months of beatings. I sat straight, didn't fidget. I didn't look at anyone else when we socialised, didn't speak to anyone else except on his express command. I did everything he told me to. Everything.' There was disgust in her voice, as if she thought she should have been stronger, should have stood up to her late husband more.

'That made him stop?'

Anna laughed, but it was humourless. 'No. Of course not. He always found an excuse, always found a reason.'

'How did you survive?' Harry's words were hushed, awed, and he saw Anna close her eyes for a moment before answering.

'I don't know,' she said, as the tears started to glisten in her eyes.

In two steps she was in his arms, her head buried deep in his shoulder, her body racked with sobs. Harry wrapped both arms around her, pulled her close and stroked her hair. Murmuring soothing sounds, he held her minute after minute, wondering if this was the first time Anna had allowed herself to crack a little, to cry about the terrible things she'd suffered during her year of marriage.

As Anna cried Harry felt a rage like no other building inside him. Here was a kind and gentle woman who had been terrorised throughout her marriage, persecuted by the man who was meant to protect her.

'Did they know?' Harry asked, as Anna pulled away for a second, wiping the tears from her cheeks.

'Who?'

'His children. Those cretins I have invited into my home.'

When Anna didn't meet his eye Harry had his answer.

'Promise me you won't do anything, Harry,' Anna said, regaining some of her usual poise.

'I can't do that. They knew what their father was doing to you, yet they did nothing?'

'What could they have done? I was his wife, his property.'

'Not his property,' Harry protested. 'You're a per-

son, a woman, not a piece of furniture he can smash
up on a whim.'

'The law is very clear, Harry. Once a woman marries everything she has, including her person, belongs
to her husband.'

'Not to abuse and injure.'

'He can do whatever he likes. Lord Fortescue used to
discuss with his cronies the best size and thickness of
rod to keep a woman in line. Apparently it is frowned
upon to use a rod thicker than a man's thumb.'

Unable to resist a quick peek at his own thumb,
Harry felt the blood surge to his head.

'He beat you with a rod as thick as a thumb?'

'I'm not sure he stuck to that rule exactly. I think the
rods he used were often thicker.'

'Did he…?' Harry closed his eyes, knowing he had
no right to ask the question, but somehow needing to
know the answer. 'Did he rape you?'

'It would have been well within the law,' Anna said,
'but no, he didn't. He was unable to…' She trailed off,
staring at a point on the wall. 'Sometimes I wondered
if it would have been better if he wasn't unmanned, if
his rage for me would have been less.' She shook her
head as if trying to get rid of an unpleasant thought.

'How did you bear it?' Harry asked, knowing that
many women would have been completely destroyed.

'I didn't have a choice. He was my husband, until
one of us died.'

'I don't know how you survived,' he said quietly,
'but I'm glad you did.'

Anna rested her head on Harry's shoulder. For a
whole year, ever since Lord Fortescue's death, she'd
clung on to the secret of the abuse she'd suffered, not

wanting to taint anyone else with it, not trusting any-one with her secrets. Today, as she'd stood in Har-ry's garden, listening to her stepsons chuckling at the memory of just one of the many terrible ways their father had sought to demean and terrorise her, she'd felt something snap inside her. She didn't have to be afraid any more. Her husband was dead and his chil-dren couldn't touch her. Whoever was sending her the packages and threatening letters didn't know who they were up against. She'd survived a year of physical and psychological torture, she could survive a few nasty surprises in the post.

When Harry had escorted her back to her room she hadn't meant to tell him quite so much and certainly had never planned on dropping her dress and chemise to expose her back and the scars that told a little of the beatings she'd received. There was something about him that made her want to open up, to share her secrets and share her past, to let him into all the dark corners of her soul that she didn't even dare to peep into.

'I suppose the Fortescues will leave now,' Anna said quietly, 'before we can work out which of them is send-ing the packages.'

Immediately Harry sprang to his feet and strode to the door.

'Please don't do anything,' Anna said, her voice calm but authoritative.

'I won't stand by while those brutes walk away, thinking there is no shame in laughing at how their fa-ther abused you.'

'Please, Harry. I ask you not to do anything.'

He hesitated and she felt a weight lift from her as he crossed the room and cupped her face in his hands.

'Stay here,' he instructed.

Of course she followed him, having to run through the corridors to keep up with his long, purposeful strides.

He flung open the door to Mr Ronald Fortescue's room, catching him shouting at his valet who wasn't packing quickly enough for his master's liking.

'What is the meaning—?' Mr Ronald Fortescue asked, his question cut off as Harry barrelled into him.

There was a short tussle, but it was obvious from the outset Anna's stepson hadn't a chance against Harry's superior size and strength, and especially not when he was bursting with fury.

'Did you know?' Harry asked, his voice low but dangerous.

'Know what?' Mr Fortescue tried to sound defiant, but there was a tremor in his voice.

'Did you know what your father was doing to her?'

'I... I...'

Harry flung him away, disgusted, and Mr Fortescue staggered back.

'Why are you sending Lady Fortescue the letters and packages?' Harry asked.

A look of genuine confusion passed across Mr Fortescue's face.

'What?' he asked.

'Not him,' Harry growled and walked from the room, catching Anna's hand and pulling her behind him.

Next on his list was the new Lord Fortescue, Anna's oldest stepson.

'What the devil—?' Lord Fortescue started to bluster as Harry burst into his room.

'I'll be quick,' Harry said. 'I want you out of my house as much as you want to leave. Why are you sending Lady Fortescue packages?'

'Packages?'

Even Anna could see Lord Fortescue was not lying. He had no idea what Harry was talking about. That was two off the list, leaving only Miss Fortescue.

'Come on,' Harry said, pulling Anna behind him again, marching her along to her stepdaughter's room.

This time Harry knocked and waited for the door to open a crack instead of bursting in. Even in his anger he couldn't bring himself to act ungentlemanly towards a female guest in his house.

Miss Fortescue's face was pale and drawn and Anna realised with a jolt of surprise that she had been crying. Red-rimmed eyes and the red tip of her nose gave it away, as did the three handkerchiefs discarded on the bed.

'What will you do to me?' Miss Fortescue asked, managing to stand up straight and look Harry in the eye as she spoke.

'Do to you? Nothing.'

'I thought you might summon the magistrate.'

'Antonia,' Anna said, stepping forward, 'I'm sure what happened in the garden was an accident.'

Shifty eyes hinted that it perhaps wasn't entirely accidental, but Anna chose to ignore it.

'At least I'm sure you never meant to hurt me. Sometimes when we hear something we don't like we react in a way we can't control.'

Miss Fortescue nodded as if in agreement, still unable to meet Anna's eye.

'I won't summon the magistrate—in fact, I will let you leave here with no further consequences to your actions, if you answer a couple of questions truthfully,' Harry said, his voice stern. 'If you refuse to answer or lie to me then I will need to reconsider what I do about the incident in the garden.'

Smoothing down her skirts, Miss Fortescue motioned for him to continue.

'I understand you dislike Lady Fortescue and have done since she first married your father.'

'Yes,' Miss Fortescue answered, her voice quiet but clear.

'Why?' Anna asked the question before Harry could continue, realising she had many theories on the reasons her stepchildren hated her so much, but no definite answers.

For a few seconds she didn't think Miss Fortescue would answer, but then a petulant mumble came from her mouth, a cascade of reasons why she'd disliked her father's new wife from the moment they'd met.

'My mother had been dead less than six months when you seduced my father. You're six months younger than me, it's disgusting, and we all know you only married my father for his title and his money.'

Most of what Miss Fortescue said was true. Anna had married Lord Fortescue when he should still have been in mourning for his first wife, but it hadn't been her choice. What Miss Fortescue didn't know, and Anna was certainly not going to tell her stepdaughter now, was that her father and Anna's father had met to discuss a possible marriage before the first Lady Fortescue had passed away, when she was lying sick in her deathbed.

'We women are not often lucky enough to choose our own fates,' Anna said quietly. 'I did not ask to marry your father, did not even know who he was before the arrangement was made.'

Miss Fortescue looked away rather than acknowledge the truth in Anna's words.

'What do you think you will gain by sending me those horrible packages?' Anna asked softly.

'What packages?'

Just like her brothers there was no hint of guilt on Miss Fortescue's face, just a look of mild confusion.

'Never mind,' Anna said. 'I wish you a safe journey, Antonia.'

Chapter Seventeen

Anna pulled her shawl tighter around her shoulders and shivered. It was a beautiful sunny day, but still early in spring and the sunshine couldn't make up for the crisp bite of the April air.

After ensuring the Fortescues had all been escorted from his property Harry had gone to check on the rest of his guests, promising Anna he would slip away as soon as possible and come meet her here in the formal gardens. His voice had brokered no argument when he'd insisted they needed to talk further, and Anna found she couldn't be angry with his authoritarian tone as she agreed they should discuss the events of the morning.

Watching two blackbirds tapping at the grass with their beaks, Anna sank back on to the stone bench, allowing her body to relax. When she had been married to Lord Fortescue she had got into the practice of always sitting straight, never slouching, even when she was alone, just in case her husband surprised her and found her in a position he did not approve of. It was a hard habit to break, but slowly Anna was finding she could will her body to relax if she reminded herself no one would ever again reprimand her for sitting comfortably.

With her eyes closed she turned her face up to the sun, enjoying the warm rays as it peeked out from behind a cloud. It had been a strange morning, one of high tensions and dramatic revelations, and she felt physically tired from all the excitement. When she'd stepped in front of the target, meaning to shame her two stepsons into realising how their father had treated her was not acceptable, and most certainly not a topic to find merriment from, she could never have envisaged how the morning would turn out. She hadn't planned on sharing a little of the abuse she'd been subjected to with Harry, certainly hadn't ever imagined she would have dropped her dress quite shamelessly to let him see the scars on her back. It had been an impulsive action and at the time had seemed the best way to show him the physical damage her late husband had inflicted. And physical scars were a lot easier to explain than mental ones.

'Sorry,' Harry said, striding along the gravel path towards her, 'that took longer than anticipated.'

'Are the rest of your guests mollified?'

'Thankfully we're only a small group, otherwise someone would be bound to talk.'

It was true, seeing as the local vicar and his wife were only joining them at dinner and the Fortescues had now all left, the remaining guests at this little house party included only Mrs Wright and her daughter, Rifield and, of course, Lydia.

'Will they stay?' Anna asked.

'I think so. Unless you'd prefer me to cut our house party short.'

There were pros and cons to staying and leaving. The main point of the party had been to find out which of the Fortescues had been sending Anna the packages. Now it looked as if they were going to have to look elsewhere for the culprit. However, Anna didn't feel overly inclined to head back to London just yet. Harry's estate was peaceful, even more so now the Fortescues had all left, and she secretly relished the idea of spending another couple of days here enjoying his company.

'Did you believe them?' Harry asked as he offered Anna his arm and they began to walk through the formal gardens. 'You know them better than I do.'

She considered for a few moments. It would have been easy for any of them to lie, easy for them to anticipate the question and feign confusion, but she hadn't seen any deception in any of her stepchildren's expressions. None of them had known about the packages or the threatening letters.

'I believed them,' Anna said. It was horrible to say it out loud for it meant admitting she had another enemy, one she knew nothing about.

'I believed them, too,' Harry said thoughtfully. 'Complete waste of time, this house party. I'm sorry, Anna.'

'There's no need to be sorry.'

'It was unnecessary. We could have just confronted the three of them in London without having to put you through the torment of staying under the same roof as them.'

They fell silent as Harry led her around the freshly dug-over borders, which no doubt in summer would hold a dazzling array of brightly coloured flowers.

'We will have to regroup,' Harry said, sounding every inch the military officer. 'Make a list of everyone who might hold a grudge against you. Any servants you have dismissed, business rivals, clients who feel your shipping company has done them wrong. We will go through the list systematically, questioning everyone until we find the culprit. Never fear, we will get to the bottom of this matter.'

Anna had to suppress a smile. 'I just want to forget about it for a couple of days,' she said. 'Forget about the packages and the letters and the unknown person who hates me so much they feel moved to be so cruel.'

'There's no time like the present. Why don't you draw up a list and we can discuss it after dinner tonight?'

'Harry, did you listen to a word I just said?'

'I just think we should keep up the momentum on this.'

'And I said no,' she said firmly.

'But we could use this time…'

'I said no, Harry,' Anna repeated. 'I want to have a couple of days where I feel normal, where I'm not always thinking about what the next package might contain, what the next letter might threaten.'

'If you're sure.'

'I'm sure. When we return to London we can go back to searching for whoever is tormenting me. For the next couple of days I wish to at least pretend I'm a carefree young woman.'

They fell silent, continuing their stroll through the gardens, each lost in thought.

'Anna, what you told me earlier,' Harry said eventually as they made their way on to a tree-lined boulevard, 'I can't stop thinking about it.'

At least he was honest. Most people would skirt around the subject, dropping hints that they wanted to know more, but never asking directly.

'What would you like to know?' she asked.

'Did your other husbands…?'

She shook her head. 'My first husband was much older than me, benignly uninterested in our marriage, but never unkind. Captain Trevels I barely saw after our marriage vows until he returned home when he was so unwell he couldn't sit up in bed without my help.'

'Just the thought of Fortescue hurting you…' Harry trailed off, shaking his head as if the image was too much.

'I think violence and abuse in marriage is much more common than we all care to admit,' Anna said quietly. 'I survived, Harry, that's all that matters now.'

'But the awful things people say about you and after all you've endured.'

Anna shrugged. 'I told you once before a little gossip isn't the worst thing in the world,' she said. 'I don't care what people say about me. They cannot hurt me like my late husband hurt me. He is dead and I am free, and no amount of horrible gossip will ever change that.'

'I can see why you never want to marry again,' Harry said softly.

She doubted he truly understood. Of course she never wanted to put herself in a position where a husband could physically hurt her again, where it became legal for a man to beat her, as long as the rod wasn't *too* thick. What she doubted he realised, what she doubted anyone could realise unless they had been in a similar situation, was her complete reluctance to ever give anyone power over her life again. Now she lived by her terms, did as she wished, talked to whom she wished, ran her business and accepted or declined invitations as she desired. No, nothing was worth giving up that control.

Chapter Eighteen

Harry was glad to see Anna at breakfast the next morning. She'd understandably been reluctant to re-join the other guests for the afternoon stroll into the village and for dinner yesterday, and had sent her apologies. This morning she looked bright and fresh, her head held high as she took her place at the breakfast table. No one mentioned the events of the day before and, if they had, no doubt Anna would shut down any enquiries politely but firmly.

'What shall we do with the morning?' Harry asked, smiling at his assembled guests as they finished breakfast. In truth, he wanted nothing more than to whisk Anna off to a remote corner of his estate and show her not all men were cruel, but he knew that was never going to happen. With great effort he focused on Miss Wright, who was looking at him with her encouraging dark eyes. Rifield was right, he should be thinking of finding himself a nice, amiable bride and here was one served up without any effort, but he just couldn't find any enthusiasm at the idea of getting to know her.

'How about a scavenger hunt?' Rifield suggested.

Harry could always rely on his friend to fill a long silence with a suggestion.

'How would that work, Mr Rifield?' Miss Wright asked.

'We draw names out of a hat for our partners and then in pairs we set off around the estate and have to find three items of interest. The couple with what is judged to be the most interesting item by everyone else wins.'

'What a lovely suggestion,' Mrs Wright said, her eyes already gleaming. No doubt she was hoping her daughter would be paired with either of the eligible young gentlemen.

Harry went to fetch some paper from his study and wrote the six names down on pieces of paper, folding them in half before placing them in Miss Wright's proffered bonnet.

'Miss Wright, would you like to pick the first two names?'

She dipped her slender hand into the bonnet and took out two pieces of paper.

'Mother and Mr Rifield,' she said, her tongue darting out over her lips as she spoke.

Rifield moved soundlessly over to Mrs Wright, as always uncomplaining in doing his bit to help Harry out.

'Lydia, would you like to pick the next two names?' Harry asked.

His sister had barely said a word all day, but he supposed it was something to be celebrated that she was still socialising rather than retreating off to her room.

With her cheeks flushing Lydia stepped up, dipped her hand into the bonnet and took two names.

'Miss Wright and myself,' she said, glancing nervously at her chosen partner.

Harry felt like shooting his fist up into the air. That left him and Anna, just the person he wanted to spend the morning with, and now good fortune or fate had thrown them together.

'I am quite happy to swap with one of you young ladies,' Mrs Wright said. 'It wouldn't feel right me enjoying the company of such a lovely young gentleman when he could be with someone closer to his own age.'

It was an obvious attempt to pair her daughter off with Rifield, but Miss Wright shook her head and took Lydia's arm.

'Not at all, Mother, I'm very much looking forward to spending the morning with Lydia.'

'What are the rules?' Harry asked, eager to be off.

'Two hours to find three interesting items from around the estate. Nothing from inside the house.'

'Shall we start?' Harry asked, offering Anna his arm.

She looked up at him with warmth in her eyes and Harry knew immediately where he wanted to take her for the morning. They might not find many interesting items, but right now winning the game was the last thing on his mind.

'This way,' Harry murmured quietly in Anna's ear, guiding her away from the other couples.

'Where are we going?' Anna asked.

'Somewhere private. Somewhere I guarantee you will love.'

'That is a bold statement, Lord Edgerton,' Anna said, a small smile lighting up her face.

After finding out what she had endured through the year of her marriage Harry wanted nothing more than to put a smile on her face. That was what this morning was about. Tomorrow he would think about his future, tomorrow he would work on getting to know the

respectable and slightly bland Miss Wright, but today
he would dedicate to making Anna smile.

They walked briskly, fast enough to stop the chill in
the air from bothering them, Anna peeking out from
underneath her bonnet every few seconds to glance up
at his face. Out here in the countryside, without anyone
else watching them, it was hard to believe she was the
same Lady Fortescue the gossips whispered about, the
same Lady Fortescue who had a reputation for being
icy and unapproachable. Here she was just a vulnerable young woman, a young woman who made his pulse
race every time he looked at her.

'Where did you grow up?' Harry asked, as they came
to the top of the hill and began their descent into a shallow valley.

'My family home was in Hampshire,' Anna said, 'but
we spent most of our time in London. My father didn't
much care for country life.'

'And you?'

She looked up at him, tilting her head back so he
could see the soft line of her jaw and the delicate skin
of her neck.

'I love the countryside,' she said. 'I think I'd be
happy if I never had to set foot into London again.'

'Then I think you'll like where I'm taking you.'

Harry had been treading this very path for nearly
thirty years, often escaping on his own during his childhood to come and explore the dense forest in the valley.
It only covered a small area, but the trees were close
together, their leaves tangled and dense overhead, and
the paths covered in moss. It felt like a little enchanted
forest in the middle of Kent.

They left the long grass on the hillside and stepped

into the wooded area, and immediately next to him Anna gasped. Harry suppressed a smile.

'It's beautiful,' she said.

Along the edges of the overgrown path were hundreds upon hundreds of bluebells, their violet flowers hanging low, a carpet of colour against the green. The flowers stretched out into the distance, crowded between trees, huddled into clearings and growing even where the light barely penetrated.

Anna rested her hand lightly on his arm, allowing him to guide her through the dense forest along the barely visible path. Once, when he was young, Harry's father had ordered the forest to be tidied, the trees chopped back, the paths cleared, but Harry and his sister had begged him not to spoil the magical place. Their father had relented and now Harry loved to stroll in the dappled sunshine whenever he came home.

'How is your mother?' Anna asked as they walked.

'Let's not talk of our families for once.'

'What do you wish to talk about?'

He knew this was the wrong time to start a flirtation. Anna had made it very clear she wasn't looking for a romantic relationship and who could blame her after all she had suffered in her last marriage, yet sometimes he thought he saw a flicker of attraction in her eyes.

'How about us?' he said, gripping her firmly as she stumbled on the uneven path and taking the opportunity to pull her a little closer to him.

'Us?' She turned to him with amusement in her eyes. 'Which *us* would you like to talk about? The *us* who are pretending to be engaged? Or the *us* who are foolishly trying to play at tracking down this mysterious person who's sending me horrible packages?'

'How about the *us* who's walking arm in arm through

a beautiful wood on a sunny spring afternoon.' She was exactly the sort of woman he *couldn't* marry, someone he knew he might very well fall in love with if he spent too much time with her, but still he couldn't stop himself from imagining a future they couldn't have.

'That *us* is nothing more than a fantasy,' Anna murmured.

So he had been right, she did feel the spark between them.

'Sometimes it is fun to indulge in fantasy,' Harry said, bending down to whisper in Anna's ear.

'As long as everyone is clear that is all this is,' Anna said, turning her grey eyes to look at him, searching his face for reassurance.

'I know nothing can happen between us, Anna,' Harry said, his lips almost tickling her ears. 'You're hardly the mild wife I'm looking for and you have plenty of reasons never to want to marry again, but don't you want to forget that for one afternoon?'

When she didn't say anything, Harry felt his heart soar. For just one afternoon they could be irresponsible, they could pretend they were unencumbered young lovers.

'If we were courting,' Anna said, 'what would you say to me?' Her voice was light, her manner so different to how she'd been just hours earlier. He wondered how many people got to see this side of Anna and doubted it numbered more than one or two in the past few years.

'Most men would tell you how the sunlight glints off your coppery hair and your lips curve into the most wonderful smile. They would sing odes to your grace and compare you to a rose on the most magnificent summer's day. They would profess to be blinded by your beauty and overcome by your sweet nature.'

'But not you?'

'Not me. The things I admire about you are a little less superficial, although I do have to admit every time I look in your eyes I forget every thought in my head...' He paused, seeing Anna unsuccessfully try to suppress a smile under her bonnet. He loved how her lips quivered ever so slightly as she fought her urge to grin. 'I love the determined look you get on your face whenever you talk about your company. I love how to the world you can seem dignified and aloof, but then I see a tiny smile, a tiny flicker of amusement in your eyes and I know what you're really thinking. I love your courage and determination to hold your head up high no matter what and I even love how you think you have to deal with everything alone.'

'That's quite a list of things you love,' Anna said quietly, her face completely unreadable.

For a moment Harry felt a panic seize him as if someone had him by the throat and was slowly squeezing. Of course he didn't *love* Anna. He loved lots of things about her, but that wasn't the same as love. He admired her, it was hard not to. And he *liked* her, there wasn't a single other person in the entire world he enjoyed being with as much as Anna, no one else even came close. But love was another matter. Love was... Well, love was...

He took a deep breath. This was why he could never let this relationship go any further. It would be so easy to fall in love with Anna, so easy to share an intense and passionate relationship, and that was exactly what Harry didn't want for himself. A nice, bland wife, someone he could share a calm and placid marriage with.

'If I was courting you, I'd need to declare myself

early,' Harry said glibly. 'You would have a number of suitors, of course.'

Anna smiled at this. 'All lining up to become the fourth victim of the Black Widow?'

Harry bent down, plucking a handful of wild bluebells and arranging them into a messy bouquet.

'For my lady,' he said with a theatrical bow, pulling back the flowers as Anna reached out to take them. 'In exchange for a kiss.'

'That is quite a steep price for a bouquet of flowers.'

'That depends…' Harry said.

'On what?'

'On how much you want to kiss me.'

For a long few seconds Anna just looked at him, that inscrutable expression on her face.

'No consequences?' she asked. 'After we return to the house we go back to how we were?'

He couldn't believe she was asking the question. It meant she was actually considering kissing him.

'No consequences,' he said. 'We never even mention it again.'

'They are particularly beautiful bluebells.'

'Surely worth a single kiss.'

'Perhaps.'

Gripping her hand, Harry pulled her gently from the path and into the woods, stepping a path that he'd known since he was a boy, yet was all but invisible to the naked eye. Carefully he picked his way across gnarled tree roots and through ferns as tall as his shoulder until they came to a clearing. It had been years since he'd last set foot here, but barely anything had changed. There was still the huge trunk of an oak tree lying on the ground where it had fallen many years ago in a storm, still the dense silence of the forest, interrupted only by small creatures rustling through the undergrowth, still the same earthy scent and the same dappled sunshine.

'No one will stumble across us here,' Harry said, watching as Anna perched on the edge of the felled tree and then taking his place beside her.

'This is rather a convenient spot,' Anna said, looking at him with a small frown. 'Did you plan on bringing me here all along?'

Not consciously, although he did wonder if somewhere deep down he'd known what he wanted to happen and had engineered everything to make it as he'd pictured.

'No plans,' he said, 'but perhaps some unacknowledged desire pushing me subconsciously towards this place.'

Slowly he reached up and gripped one end of the ribbon that secured Anna's bonnet under her chin. A gentle tug was all it took to untie it and carefully he lifted the bonnet off her head.

'Do you think anyone would notice if I pulled down your hair?' Harry asked. For weeks he'd been wanting to see Anna shake her coppery locks loose, to see her hair cascade over her shoulders and down her back, but even he knew that was too much to ask. Only a husband or a lover ever got to see their woman's hair unfastened and loose. No respectable young lady would ever take down her hair in public.

He felt his pulse quicken as Anna raised her hands to her hair, slowly pulling out the pins. One after another, each allowing another few strands to uncurl and tumble over her shoulders.

'Maybe I *should* write an ode to your hair,' Harry

murmured, lifting his fingers and running them through her loose curls.

His fingers lingered as they brushed against her neck, picking out all the spots he wished he could kiss. There was a hollow just behind her earlobe that begged for his lips, but Harry knew he had to tread carefully. If he didn't control himself he might find himself ravishing Anna in the middle of the clearing and that would ruin all their plans.

Tentatively Anna reached up and touched Harry's shoulders, gripping them gently and pulling him closer to her.

'What was the price for my flowers?' she asked.

'Two kisses.'

'Two kisses? That seems rather steep. Surely I did not agree to that.'

'I'm sure you did, my lady.'

Their bodies were close now, thighs side by side, separated only by the thick layers of her skirts, swaying closer together with every passing second.

Slowly, taking his time, Harry leaned in, the desire in him building to an excruciating high as he watched her close her eyes and tilt her chin, inviting him to kiss her. His lips met hers, gently at first, revelling in the sweet taste of her mouth, the softness of her lips, the warmth of her skin. He stiffened as her tongue flicked out to meet his and felt his entire body clench and tighten as she clutched at his shoulders and pulled him closer.

His hands were moving now, caressing her neck, her shoulders, her back. He wanted to touch her everywhere, run his fingers over every exposed bit of skin. He felt her breasts brush against his chest and wanted more than anything to push down her dress to expose the milky skin beneath and to trail kisses over the most private parts of her body.

'Harry,' Anna whispered, inflaming his desire even more as he heard his name on her lips.

He wouldn't have ever pulled away. If it were up to him they would still be locked together as the sun set on the horizon and the day turned to night, but Anna must have had more self-control as she eventually sat back, her eyes a little glazed and her mouth beautifully pink.

'That was unfair, Harry,' she said after a minute.

'Unfair?'

She nodded. He understood. They might have laughed and joked about never mentioning their little intimacy again, but it would be impossible to forget that kiss. It *was* unfair. Right now he couldn't remember a single reason why he and Anna couldn't be together. He liked her. He desired her. He wanted to get lost in her kisses all day long. There was a small voice in the back of his mind shouting about duty, but Harry found it very easy to silence as he glanced again at his fake fiancée.

He never thought Anna would kiss him again, despite upping the price of the flowers to two kisses, but as he turned back to her he wondered if he was in heaven as her fingers snaked around his neck, tickling the skin before she leaned in closer.

There was nothing gentle or delicate about this kiss. Harry found it impossible to hold back. All the pent-up desire that had been building over the past couple of weeks erupted and he found himself gripping Anna hard, kissing her as if they would never get the chance again. She returned his passion, running her hands over his body and kissing him deeply.

He couldn't help himself, he needed more. With dextrous fingers he traced the edge of her dress, where fabric met the skin of her chest. Anna stiffened for a second and then melted into him, pressing his hand deeper under the fabric. Inch by inch he exposed the silky-smooth skin of her breasts, pushing at her dress and chemise, knowing he had to see her, had to taste her.

'Harry,' Anna whispered, a plea for more that inflamed him like nothing else could.

With an almost imperceptible ripping of fabric Harry managed to push her dress down, taking a moment to watch how the soft cotton pooled at her waist, wishing it would just fall over her hips and leave her completely naked.

'I need to kiss you,' he said, his voice gruff with pent-up desire.

She nodded, her eyes wide, and before she could say anything his lips were on her skin again. He trailed kisses from her collarbone to the groove between her breasts, finally pausing before capturing one dusky-pink nipple in his mouth. Anna sighed, a sound that went straight to his very core, and out of the corner of his eye he saw her head drop back, her eyes glazed with desire.

After a few seconds of teasing and kissing he moved his lips to her other breast, eliciting the same deep sigh, and he wondered if it was the most perfect sound in the world.

It would have been so easy to lay her down, to strip her entirely naked right here deep in the forest and worship her body until the sun went down, but reluctantly Harry pulled back. He wanted her badly, but this wasn't the right way. Despite being a widow and not a shy virgin Anna was still vulnerable and he wouldn't be the man to take advantage of her, not like this. Even if he had to suppress a groan as he looked at her wonderfully dishevelled appearance.

Wordlessly Anna moved away a few inches, as if she didn't trust herself to remain quite so close. He felt bereft without her body pressing against his, but contented himself with watching her straighten her dress and pin her hair up. In the dappled sunlight she looked like some Greek goddess, some deity sent to bewitch and bedazzle him.

'I'm sorry. I couldn't help myself,' Harry said eventually.

'Don't apologise,' Anna said softly. 'It was wonderful.'

Harry knew then how close he was becoming, how close he was to falling in love. He needed to distance himself, to step away from Anna and her sweet, strong nature and her beguiling looks, but right now that seemed impossible to do.

'We need to find something to take back from our scavenger hunt,' Anna said, standing and brushing small pieces of moss from her skirts.

'A bluebell,' Harry said, plucking one of the hundreds that surrounded the small clearing and tucking it carefully in the pocket of his jacket so the head of the flower poked out the top.

'Weren't we meant to bring back three things?'

'Let's pretend we forgot that part.'

He'd promised her they wouldn't discuss the kiss, the intimacy, promised her things would go back to normal, but he wondered if her heart was still hammering in her chest. He couldn't imagine never thinking about those few minutes in the clearing again—right now it seemed like it would be at the forefront of his mind for eternity.

'We should return,' Anna said, placing her hand in

the crook of Harry's elbow. 'Otherwise we will be late and the others might get suspicious.'

'Perhaps we could linger just a few minutes more,' Harry suggested hopefully. It really was beautiful under the trees and out here he didn't have to share Anna with anyone else.

'The whole purpose of this pretend engagement is to save us both from further scandal and gossip,' Anna said, trying to look haughty, but instead just looking delightfully dishevelled. 'And all we've done these past few weeks is jump from one scandalous situation to the next.'

She was right: first their little trip into the darkness of the Carmichaels' garden, then the unchaperoned private platform to watch the opera from, then the kiss at the top of the tower and now this wonderful interlude in the forest. They hadn't really been behaving as they should, but Harry found he couldn't regret it.

'We're among friends here,' he said. 'Who is going to care if we return a little late?'

'Perhaps the upstanding Miss Wright and her mother,' Anna said, casting a sideways look at Harry.

He shook his head, but couldn't find the words to refute Anna's statement. He didn't really know Miss Wright or her mother well. They might be the sort of people who loved to be witness to a scandal so they could tell all their friends.

'She's pursuing you,' Anna said, just the tiniest hint of emotion in her voice.

Now wasn't the time to talk about this. Not five minutes ago he'd been kissing Anna, completely lost in her, willing to give away his fortune for just a few more minutes alone with her. He couldn't think of any other woman right now, even if there was no way of him and Anna having a future.

'Do you mind?' he asked.

Anna sighed, not answering for a few seconds, before shaking her head. 'I don't mind you having admirers, Harry. As much as I like you I know we aren't really engaged and one day soon we will go our separate ways. But I do want you to be happy and I'm afraid you'd be marrying Miss Wright for all the wrong reasons if you did court her.'

She'd said the same to him before, only a couple of days ago.

'People get married for all sorts of reasons,' Harry said. 'Money, titles, allegiances. Love doesn't often come into it. Why would my reasons be any different?'

'You deserve happiness, Harry,' she said, stopping abruptly and turning to face him. 'And an unhappy marriage is not a good start to a happy life.'

'That's exactly why I want to marry some respectable young woman that I can see myself tolerating for the rest of our married lives. Much better to have contentment than passion.'

'Toleration is no substitute for love,' he heard her murmur, but she shook her head and dropped the subject.

They continued walking in silence, emerging from the woods and back into the long grass before finding the path that led back up the hill to the house. As they began the descent to the house they saw Miss Wright and Lydia walking arm in arm back from wherever their scavenger hunt had taken them.

Next to him he saw Anna surreptitiously smooth down her creased skirts and pat at her hair so no one would suspect anything untoward had happened between them. The tear in the fabric of her dress she'd cleverly concealed by holding it together with a hairpin and arranging a few loose strands of hair over the new seam.

'Lord Edgerton,' Miss Wright called as the two pairs neared each other. 'Lydia has been telling me of her love for music.'

He glanced at his sister and was surprised to see a hint of excitement in her eyes.

'My mother is hosting a small piano recital next week at our London house and I have invited Lydia along. Of course you'd be welcome to accompany her.'

No invitation was forthcoming for Anna, but he pushed this to the back of his mind.

'Would you like to go, Lydia?' he asked, hardly daring to hope.

With a small nod his sister indicated she would and Harry felt like falling to his knees and praising every saint that had ever lived. A piano recital was hardly a bustling ball, but it was a start. It was a social event that his sister had agreed to go to and without him having to cajole her a single bit.

This morning was turning out to be a great success. With a spring in his step he turned towards Halstead Hall, trying to stop the triumph from showing on his face.

Chapter Nineteen

'Play for me,' Harry murmured in Anna's ear, sending shivers down her spine. They were in the drawing room, awaiting the other guests to gather before dinner, and Anna had gravitated towards the piano without realising it.

'I haven't played for anyone in years,' she said, trailing her fingers along the keys.

'I heard you, a few weeks ago when I came to visit you for the first time at your uncle's house. You were good.'

'I play for myself, when no one else is around, but I don't think I've had an audience in the last five years.'

'Indulge me,' Harry said.

'I think I've indulged you enough today,' Anna muttered, flushing as she remembered their intimacy in the clearing. She hadn't been able to look at Harry for the rest of the day without feeling the heat rise in her cheeks and the blood pound in her ears. Never had she felt the kind of attraction she did for Harry. Of course she'd found men attractive before, but with Harry it went deeper. Her body craved him, but it wasn't just a primal desire, there was so much more.

'Please.'

With that one word she melted. Before her marriages she hadn't realised how attractive good manners were.

Carefully she sat on the piano stool, arranging her skirts around her.

'Do you need any music?'

She shook her head. Dozens of pieces were seared into her brain from years of practice. It might have been a few years since she last played them, but once learnt a piano piece wasn't something easily forgotten.

Stretching out her fingers, she began to play, choosing something which started slowly, building in tempo and difficulty as she gained confidence. After a few minutes she felt all her worries lifting from her shoulders, all the uncertainties, all the dilemmas just fading away. Right now the only thing that mattered was the music.

As she finished the piece and drifted back to earth she became aware of Harry again, standing far too close for propriety, especially as the other guests were expected in the drawing room at any moment. He laid a hand on her shoulder, his fingers trailing against the bare skin of her neck, the contact sending tiny jolts through her body.

She dared not turn to face him, knowing he would have *that* look in his eyes, the one she found impossible to resist. He would suggest a kiss and before she knew what was happening they would be in each other's arms when the rest of the guests arrived for pre-dinner drinks.

'Tell me why you don't play much any more,' Harry said, his voice quiet.

'Lord Fortescue didn't like it,' Anna replied simply.

'I like it.'

She turned to face him then, wondering when this strong, kind man had crept into her heart where he certainly did not belong. No man did.

'I like it, too,' she said.

Perhaps, a little voice in her head said. *Perhaps he is your chance at happiness.*

She did feel happy when she was with him, more happy than she had been in years.

The door to the room opened and Miss Wright entered with Lydia, the two women arm in arm.

'What marvellous music,' Miss Wright said, smiling sweetly at Anna. 'We couldn't wait to see who was playing.'

'Lady Fortescue is very talented,' Harry murmured, stepping away slowly as if trying not to draw attention to how close he'd been standing.

'Perhaps you could play for us after dinner,' Miss Wright suggested.

Anna inclined her head, knowing it would seem petty if she said no. Hopefully she could just play one piece and then someone else would take over. Both Miss Wright and Lydia would be proficient at playing the piano—all young women of good birth were, although not many enjoyed it as much as she did.

Within a few minutes their party was complete with Rifield escorting Mrs Wright into the room. They were just about to move into the dining room when the door opened again and Lady Edgerton entered the room, her hair hastily pulled back and her dress crumpled, but nevertheless dressed for dinner.

'Mother,' Harry said, frowning. 'I didn't expect you to join us.'

He moved quickly to his mother's side, bending his

head and talking quietly, trying to stop everyone from overhearing.

'I should be here,' Lady Edgerton said, wringing her hands.

'There really is no need. If you would be more comfortable in your rooms…'

'No. I can't hide away on such an important night. I must be here. I can't fail you.'

Harry flashed his sister a concerned glance, but Lydia just shrugged and he had no choice but to escort their mother in to dinner.

'Thank you for a lively weekend,' Rifield said, lifting his glass once everyone was seated. 'It has been most memorable.'

Anna's eyes darted to Harry's. She certainly would never forget the moment they'd shared in the clearing and the rest of the weekend wasn't easily forgotten either.

'I wanted to say something,' Miss Wright said, ignoring the plate of food in front of her and fixing Anna with a steady stare. 'Many things have happened this weekend that I am sure the rest of society does not need to know about and I wanted to assure you, Lady Fortescue, that they will not hear any details from me or my mother.'

Mrs Wright nodded her head in agreement.

'Thank you,' Anna said quietly.

'Well said,' Rifield agreed. 'There is no need for any details from this weekend to be discussed by anyone who wasn't here.'

All eyes were on her as Anna took a sip of wine to wet her throat. 'Thank you all for your kindness. I feel I must apologise for the drama that unfolded over the weekend and embroiling you all in that. It was never my wish for things to happen as they did.'

Harry gave her a reassuring smile and Anna felt the corners of her mouth quiver as she tried to maintain her serious façade.

'Please, don't apologise,' Miss Wright said. 'I don't know anything about the difficulties you faced in your last marriage, Lady Fortescue, or the disputes you have with your stepchildren now, but I do understand they must be substantial if Lord Edgerton is willing to put his own reputation on the line to try to resolve some of these issues. Especially as your engagement is not a true one.'

Stony silence followed for a few seconds. Most people around the table knew Anna and Harry had agreed to pretend to be engaged while the gossip died down, but no one was meant to say it out loud.

Harry cleared his throat, but before he could speak there was a clatter of cutlery as his mother dropped her fork.

'Not true?' Harry's mother asked. 'What does she mean, Harry?'

'I'm sorry,' Miss Wright said quickly. 'I just assumed everyone knew.'

Anna scrutinised the young woman. She looked mortified by letting slip something she shouldn't, but there was no way to be sure if the mistake was genuine or not.

'Mother,' Harry said, his voice steady with no hint of the trepidation he must be feeling at trying to explain the situation to his mother.

'None of your clever words, Harry, tell me truthfully—are you engaged to this woman or not?'

'It's not that simple.'

'I don't see what about the question is difficult to answer. Are you engaged?'

Anna felt her heart hammering in her chest. She

knew the answer, she'd always been the one going around reminding everyone that their engagement was only for convenience, a ruse only to be maintained until society had found someone else to gossip about. Nevertheless she found herself holding her breath.

'No, Mother.'

Deflating, Anna bowed her head so no one would see the disappointment in her eyes. His answer was never going to be anything but *no*. All the same, some part of her had wanted him to proclaim his affection for her, confess that although their arrangement had started off as a way to avoid a little bit of scandal it had ended with him falling in love. After this morning in the clearing she knew he desired her, just as she did him, but part of her was hoping for something more than that, something deeper.

'No?'

'I found myself in an embarrassing situation,' Anna said. 'Lord Edgerton was chivalrous enough to step in and offered to pretend to be engaged until the scandal was forgotten about.'

'Harry, is this true?' Lady Edgerton asked, a tremor in her voice.

He inclined his head.

'What on earth were you thinking? What about your reputation? This family's reputation?'

'You raised me to think of others,' Harry said quietly. 'Lady Fortescue was in need and I was in a position to help.'

'But this will ruin you. No decent woman will associate with you now.' Her voice was becoming shriller and shriller and Anna could see Harry glancing uncomfortably at the rest of the guests. 'This was your idea, wasn't it? A way to trap my son into marriage.'

Anna shook her head. She didn't want to tell everyone that Harry had insisted on their fake engagement, that he wouldn't take no for an answer.

'It was my idea, Mother,' Harry said abruptly. 'Lady Fortescue is a friend, she needed my help and I was more than happy to give it to her.'

'You're ruined, we're all ruined. There will be just as much scandal when you break off the engagement.'

The countess was probably right, Anna reflected. They wouldn't avoid all gossip by pretending to be engaged and then ending their relationship, but at least it gave them some power over when and how they made the announcement.

'You're ruined,' Harry's mother repeated.

'No, I'm not. I am an earl and a wealthy one at that. I come from one of the oldest families in England and I will have absolutely no problem in securing a respectable wife.' Harry spoke firmly but quietly, his tone brooking no argument, and Anna was glad to see his mother looked a little mollified, although her hands were still shaking as she picked up her fork again.

'It's not good,' she mumbled to herself as she began eating. 'It's not good.'

Harry flashed Anna an apologetic glance, but she shook her head, a minute movement that she hoped portrayed that she wasn't upset by the revelation.

Of course it was a lie. Inside Anna was crying, although she wasn't quite sure why. She'd been the one pushing Harry away on every occasion, the one who had insisted over and over again that she did not ever want to marry. And she didn't. It was just…

She couldn't finish the thought, there were too many things that made her like Harry. Time and time again he'd swooped to her rescue, calmly dealing with whatever new problems arose. He was kind, but more than that he truly wanted to help people in meaningful ways. And then there were his kisses. Anna knew she would never be kissed like that again. Every time she looked at him she felt her pulse quicken and her skin flush. Just the memory of their kiss earlier in the day made her feel giddy with excitement.

'I am so sorry,' Miss Wright was murmuring to Harry. 'I just assumed everyone knew. We're such an intimate group after all.'

'Please don't apologise. Everyone but my mother was aware of the situation, and it was my fault for not enlightening her sooner.'

Anna saw the fingers that brushed against Harry's arm and forced her gaze down to her plate. It didn't matter, she told herself. She found Harry attractive, she enjoyed his company, but they were never going to end up together. That meant she had no right feeling jealous when Harry didn't brush away Miss Wright's hand or when he leaned his head in closer to hear what she was saying.

Anna tried to excuse herself after dinner, but was pressed into playing a couple of pieces on the piano before she could persuade Miss Wright to take over. Despite her objections the young debutante looked thrilled to be able to show off her own musical talents, Anna thought, acknowledging her thoughts as uncharitable.

Rather than returning to her bedroom, she slipped out on to the patio, meaning to take a stroll around the gardens to clear her head before bed.

'It's a beautiful night,' a voice came out of the darkness, making Anna jump and let out a small cry. 'Sorry to startle you.'

It was Lydia, who must have also slipped away between the dining room and the drawing room, sitting on a low stone bench and looking up at the stars.

Anna walked the length of the patio and perched on the bench beside Lydia, feeling the cold of the stone even through the layers of undergarments and skirts.

'I'm sorry about Mother,' Lydia said quietly.

'There's nothing to apologise for.'

'You must think us an odd family.'

'Every family is a little odd in their own special way,' Anna said, reflecting on the peculiar foibles of her own family.

Lydia gave a short, sharp laugh. 'I suppose that's true.'

'I understand you are going to be accompanying Harry to London next week,' Anna said, trying to keep her tone light. If she understood correctly this was the first time Lydia had agreed to go out into society since the scandal with Captain Mountfield last year, so quite a monumental event.

Lydia shrugged, looking down at her shoes that were peeking out from under her dress. 'Miss Wright invited me to a piano recital. I thought it might be a pleasant way to spend an evening.'

Cautiously Anna searched for the right words. Just one ill-timed comment could be enough to push this nervous young woman back into her self-protective shell. 'It'll be a small, select group, I'm sure.'

Sighing, Lydia looked up at Anna. 'I suppose you think me very foolish,' the younger woman said.

'Why do you say that?'

'Hiding away here when you've been so brave to face the people who call you names and whisper about you.'

'I think everyone deals with it in a different way,' Anna said. 'Neither is right or wrong.'

They were silent for a few minutes, both looking out into the dark garden and the starry sky beyond. The night was clear, probably the reason there was a noticeable chill in the air, but Anna felt no compulsion to get up and go inside, not yet. She had an instinct Lydia hadn't quite finished with what she was trying to say, despite her silence.

'The first night you were here, when you came and helped me dress for dinner, you said something to me,' Lydia said after a few minutes. 'You told me it was my life, that my decisions were my own and that if it made me happy I could stay away from society for ever.'

Anna remembered saying the words and nodded.

'I've thought a lot about what you've said over the last few days and I realised you were right. I'm not happy shut away here, of course I'm not, but the only person keeping me here is *me*.' Lydia bit her lip and Anna was reminded how young Harry's sister was. At just eighteen she'd coped with so much already; no one this young should be having to make such monumental decisions. 'It's just that I've locked myself away for so long, I don't know...' She trailed off, shaking her head as if she couldn't find the words.

'You feel like by trying to return to a normal life you're acknowledging how you've been living these past months was the wrong course and that doesn't feel right?' Anna ventured. She'd felt the same thing.

Lydia nodded, her eyes wide. 'I don't think I could have even thought about going to a piano recital or even socialising with Harry's guests here a few months ago, maybe not even a few weeks ago.'

'That's perfectly natural,' Anna said, giving Lydia a quick squeeze on the arm. 'Time heals most wounds, even to our most fragile characteristics like our self-confidence. In a year's time you'll feel completely different to how you do now. In five years' time this part of your life will be a distant memory and when you're fifty and surrounded by children and grandchildren it will just be a short episode of a rich and varied life.'

Lydia gently placed her hand in Anna's and looked up at her. 'Thank you,' she said quietly. 'I can see why Harry cares for you so much.'

Anna felt a lump beginning to form in her throat. She knew Harry cared for her, it was obvious in everything he did, every way he tried to help her—the problem was she was starting to care for him rather deeply, too.

'Your brother is very kind,' Anna said carefully, trying to keep any hint of emotion from her voice.

'He tries to help everyone,' Lydia said. 'He's been like it ever since we were young. But he really does care for you.'

'I value his friendship.'

'There's nothing more between you?' she asked, her tone hopeful.

'Your brother is looking for a quiet, scandal-free society wife,' Anna said, 'and I am certainly not that.'

'But if he weren't? If he were able to follow his heart and choose the wife he wanted?'

'He doesn't believe in following his heart,' Anna said quietly. 'He thinks love has no place in a marriage.'

'Foolish man,' Lydia said with a shake of her head. 'Our parents…' She trailed off. 'Has Harry told you about our parents?'

'A little.'

'They were very much in love and they made one another miserable. I think it was worse for Harry, they'd mellowed a little by the time I was aware of what was going on, but they still sometimes had huge rows.'

'That's why Harry would never marry anyone he cared for. It seems so obtuse, thinking history would repeat itself.'

'And he is nothing like our father. Father might have loved Mother fiercely at the beginning of their marriage, but he was selfish and thought only of himself. A man who truly loves a woman wouldn't parade a string of mistresses in front of her eyes, he wouldn't say things purely to cause hurt.'

'Harry would never do that,' Anna agreed.

'Foolish man,' Lydia said again. 'I suppose he thinks he needs to protect me as well, marry someone with a good reputation, someone who might ease my passage back into society.' She shook her head. 'I just want him to be happy.'

They sat in silence for a few moments, both contemplating the reasons Harry was set on orchestrating his own unhappiness.

'What if he realised he was wrong?' Lydia asked. 'What if he realised he wanted to marry you, someone he *did* care for?'

Anna couldn't meet Lydia's hopeful eyes. Of course she'd considered this very scenario, imagined Harry being free of responsibility, free of the fear that he might care too much for his wife, and asking her to marry him. Part of her would say yes without any hesitation, the part that acknowledged she was well on her way to falling in love with him. Then the sensible part of her stepped forward and made her remember her vow never to marry again, not because she was against breaking a vow, but because of the reasons behind the vow. She would never give a man that power over her again, not even a man as kind and generous as Harry.

'I don't think I'll ever marry again,' Anna said eventually.

'He'll end up with someone like Miss Wright. I know that's the kind of wife he thinks best for him, someone pleasant and dull and respectable. And although my brother can make the best of most situations, a wife who does not challenge and stimulate him, who he does not care for, would make even him miserable,' Lydia said.

'I thought you liked Miss Wright.'

Lydia pulled a face that reminded her so much of her cousin Beatrice, Anna wanted to wrap her arms around the young woman.

'She's perfectly *nice* to my face, but I'm not convinced she doesn't talk about me behind my back.'

So Lydia was much more astute than Anna had given her credit for.

'Even if she doesn't, she wouldn't make Harry happy and that's what is important. He doesn't look at her like he looks at you.'

Smoothing down the satin material of her dress to keep her hands busy, Anna inclined her head, not trusting herself to speak.

'Of course I appreciate what he's trying to do for me, but sometimes I wish he'd be a little less selfless.'

'Perhaps you should tell him that,' Anna suggested.

Lydia sighed, but nodded all the same. 'He still looks at me as if I'm going to shatter at any moment.'

'It must be hard seeing someone that you love suffer,' Anna said.

'I know. And I know every time he looks at me he sees me up on the rooftop, thinking about doing something very stupid, but I just want him to get past that, to see I'm not the same person any more.'

Anna tried to keep her eyes from widening at the revelation Lydia had just made. She'd known Harry's sister had been brought very low indeed by the scandal following her liaison with Captain Mountfield, but she'd never imagined the young woman had tried to take her own life. But Lydia hadn't revealed the depths of her desperation in a bid for attention, so Anna wouldn't make a fuss of it.

Keeping the shock from her face, Anna said kindly, 'He will. Give him time. Let him see you socialising a little, let him see you enjoying yourself and smiling and slowly he'll realise how you've grown and moved on.'

'But it might be too late by then. He might have already married someone who will make him miserable.'

Anna didn't have an answer for that. Knowing Harry, he probably would have. It was going to take a long time for Lydia to find her confidence, to start socialising and for Harry to see that she was slowly getting better.

'Talk to him then,' Anna urged. 'Tell him all this. Explain how you're feeling, how you've grown. Perhaps that will be enough.' Perhaps it would be enough to show him he didn't need to marry a respectable woman for his sister's sake, but it wouldn't do much to shift his deep-seated belief that marrying someone he actually cared about would only end in disaster.

They sat in silence for a few more minutes, both lost in thought as they gazed up at the clear night sky.

Chapter Twenty

The rain was hammering on the stairs as Anna dashed
out of the carriage and up to the Shipping Company office. Even though she was only out in the open for at
most twenty seconds she was dripping wet by the time
she swung the door shut behind her. Rainwater dripped
from her hair, down the front of her dress and even off
the tip of her nose. The hem of her dress was discol-
oured and muddy and already she could feel the wet material beginning to stick to her skin. The weather was a
far cry from the beautiful days of Harry's house party,
but Anna couldn't find it in herself to be miserable.

In the three days that had passed since she had returned home she'd felt light and high-spirited, so much
so that both her cousin and uncle had commented on
numerous occasions. Beatrice had pushed her again
and again to talk about what had occurred during her
trip to Kent, but Anna had wanted to keep the memories to herself, as if in sharing them they might escape
and diminish.

Now, even shivering in her damp clothes, she found
she couldn't keep the smile from her face. Nothing had
been resolved, they still didn't know who was send-

ing her the horrible packages, but the memory of the time she'd spent with Harry was in the forefront of her mind.

'Dreadful weather,' Mr Maltravers bellowed as he came bursting through the door without knocking. Normally Anna would stiffen at his presence, but today she even managed to smile at her business rival.

'Good morning, Mr Maltravers,' Anna said, wiping the wet tendrils of hair from her face.

'What are these rumours I hear about you being engaged to some blue blood?' he asked abruptly, without any of the normal pleasantries.

'Lord Edgerton. He's a good friend.'

'But are you engaged? I saw the chap a couple of weeks ago and he didn't deny your connection, but I'd hoped you'd have seen sense by now.'

Mr Maltravers had proposed to her formally three times, but managed to bring up informal proposals in almost every conversation they had. Anna wasn't sure if he wanted her or her Shipping Company more, but he was determined to pursue her despite the multiple rejections.

'Yes, we are engaged,' Anna said. Perhaps this would finally discourage him from proposing yet again.

'Man like him won't have any business sense,' he said, shaking his head. 'The company will be run into the ground within six months.'

'What makes you think he will take over?' Anna asked.

Mr Maltravers barked a harsh laugh. 'Of course he will. No man would let his wife run a shipping company. It's unheard of.'

'We live in modern times, Mr Maltravers.'

'If you care about the company you should marry

me. I'd whip it into shape in no time and you have to admit we rub along pretty well.'

Anna couldn't stand the man and had made it quite clear that they didn't *rub along* well at all, but he was just so persistent.

'I thank you for your proposal, Mr Maltravers, but you see I am engaged to Lord Edgerton,' Anna said, wondering what she would do once they broke their sham engagement and Mr Maltravers proposed again.

He moved towards her, dripping rainwater all over the wooden floorboards, and took her fingers in his large hand.

'I've admired you for a long time, Lady Fortescue. Your beauty and grace do not belong in this office, and I will make it my goal to be the one to free you from this work. I will not give up hope that one day you will be my wife. I hate to see a woman alone and vulnerable. There are too many terrible people in this world ready to take advantage, ready to hurt a woman who doesn't have a strong man to protect her.'

Anna was saved from answering as the door flew open and Harry came bounding in, grimacing as he wiped the water from his face.

'Am I interrupting?' he asked, his eyes flickering from Maltravers to Anna, resting on their linked hands, but his smile never slipping.

'Ah, the fiancé,' Mr Maltravers said, summoning a small bow of his head and a polite smile for Harry. 'You are a very lucky man, Lord Edgerton.'

'I am thankful every minute of every day.'

'I shall leave you,' Mr Maltravers said. 'Consider what I said, Lady Fortescue. You know where I am.'

They waited until Mr Maltravers's footsteps had

faded into the distance, covered by the hammering sound of the rain on the roof before moving.

'Should I be concerned?' Harry asked, shrugging his soaking overcoat from his shoulders and draping it over the coat stand.

'Mr Maltravers has been suggesting marriage almost every week for the last six months. I haven't been tempted so far.'

'He's a man of good taste.'

Anna shrugged. 'I'm not sure if it's me or the company he wants more.'

'Trust me,' Harry said, moving closer and lifting her hand to his lips, 'it's you.'

Anna's heart was pounding in her chest as he lingered with his lips on her skin and she imagined those very same lips tracing a path up her arm and across her body.

'What are we doing, Harry?' she whispered. 'We both know this can't lead anywhere.'

Slowly he dropped her hand and stepped away, his eyes never leaving hers.

'You are a very difficult woman to resist,' he murmured.

Anna couldn't hold his gaze, moving away and shuffling papers on her desk, not even noticing when the water droplets from her hair smudged some of the ink on her important documents.

'I was hoping to steal you away from your work for a couple of hours.'

Ever since she'd met Harry she had been spending a little less time at the Shipping Company office and a little more time socialising. In truth, she didn't mind. The company was beginning to do well so didn't need such close supervision and Anna knew it was healthy to have a more balanced lifestyle. All the same she hesitated.

'Just two hours,' Harry said, 'and then I'll deliver you back here myself and offer my services as your personal scribe, accountant and odd-jobs boy for the afternoon.'

It was hard to resist him.

'Two hours?'

'Two hours, no longer on my honour.'

Harry ran first, dashing to his waiting carriage and flinging the door open, waiting for Anna to make her way down the stairs before helping her up. Once she was seated he bounded inside, giving a shout for the coachman to set off, sparing a thought for the poor man sitting in the pouring rain.

He swept his hair back from his face, brushing the droplets of water from the tips and realising he was fighting a losing battle; his entire body was wet, a few more drips weren't going to make much difference.

Across from him Anna was tentatively touching her own hair as if wondering if any kind of style could be salvaged from the sodden tendrils.

'Where are we going?' Anna asked, settling against the backrest while rearranging her skirts.

'I have a surprise for you. Did you know we've been *engaged* for an entire month now?'

'You're proposing that we celebrate the one-month anniversary of our fake engagement?'

'We may not get to two months,' Harry reminded her softly.

She turned her head to look out the window then, studying the empty streets with an air of nonchalance and not for the first time Harry wished he could tell what she was thinking. Every day they spent together she warmed to him more, so much so that Harry was certain that she *liked* him, even cared for him, but he just couldn't tell if there was anything more to it than that.

On his part he knew he was falling for her. Ever since their kiss in the clearing at Halstead Hall he'd fallen asleep dreaming of her body pressed beside his and woken up tight with desire. And more than the physical attraction was his need to see her every day, to just be with her. He found himself making up excuse after excuse to call on Anna at home or at her company's office. It would only take one little slip and he would be professing his undying love for a woman he could never marry.

'Will you be attending the piano recital this evening?' Harry asked, steering the conversation to neutral ground.

Anna sighed. 'I'm not sure I'd be very welcome. I think Miss Wright only invited me because your sister insisted.'

'What does it matter why you were invited?'

'I think Miss Wright would prefer to have your attention to herself,' Anna said quietly.

'And I would prefer it if you were there.'

This earned him a little smile before she turned back to the window and continued her perusal of the empty streets.

'Harry, where on earth are we going?' Anna asked after a few minutes.

Instead of heading towards the more illustrious part of town their coach was weaving its way through the back alleys of Southwark, an area no sensible aristocratic lady would ever venture and gentlemen only went to have their vices satisfied.

'Nearly there,' he said cheerfully, poking his head out of the window for a second.

Two minutes later the carriage stopped and Harry instructed Anna to wait while he jumped down and rushed towards a nondescript door. After a hurried conversation with the occupant he ran back to the carriage and motioned for Anna to get down.

'If you're trying to sell me into service in a brothel, I won't be pleased,' Anna grumbled, but underneath it he could tell she was intrigued.

They ran inside where a young woman waited to show them into a tiny kitchen with a welcome fire.

'Anna, meet Miss Polly Proctor, daughter of the very talented cook in my London house.'

'Pleased to meet you, your ladyship.' Polly bobbed a curtsy, looking completely overwhelmed to have two titled visitors in her home.

'Lovely to meet you, Polly,' Anna said kindly.

'Would you like a cup of something warm, your ladyship? And please take a seat by the fire.'

Anna took the proffered seat, thanking Polly for the warm cup she pressed into her hands a few minutes later.

'What beautiful girls,' Anna said, motioning to the two toddlers who were gripping on to Polly's skirt and following their mother around the kitchen closely.

'My twins. Gilly and Kate.'

'They're lovely. A credit to you.'

As the two women talked about children Harry sat back and listened contentedly. If there was any topic of conversation that could unite women from all different backgrounds it was the subject of children. Soon Polly had relaxed enough to giggle and chat freely and one of the two girls was sitting happily on Anna's lap.

'Shall I bring them in now, sir?' Polly asked as Anna finished her drink.

'Yes, please.'

'What are we doing here?' Anna whispered as Polly left the room.

'Just wait.'

A minute later Polly came back in, carrying a large wicker basket which she set down in front of the fire. Harry watched as Anna craned her neck to see what was inside.

'I saw how much your cat meant to you,' he said quietly, 'and thought now might be the right time to consider another little companion.'

Anna sank to her knees in front of the basket and peeked inside. Harry saw her face light up at the sight of the kittens, all sleepy and curled up next to their mother, and wanted to capture how she looked right at that moment, the radiance and happiness that emanated from her.

'I need to find homes for them,' Polly said. 'My sister will take two and my next-door neighbour will have one, but the other two don't have anyone to take them. Sir said you might be interested…' She paused, looking hopefully down at Anna.

'I'd love them,' Anna said, stroking the soft fur and murmuring at the tiny kittens.

'You'll take both?' Polly's face lit up. 'Truly?'

'Truly. I wouldn't want to leave one homeless. Which two?'

'Your pick, your ladyship.'

Harry wasn't surprised when she picked out the two smallest, handling them with as much care as if they were her own babies. Both had a distinctive tortoiseshell pattern on their backs, but one had white feet and the other a white tip of tail.

After bidding Polly farewell they ran back to the

carriage and climbed up, Anna sheltering her two new kittens from the rain as best she could with her cloak.

'That was a very sweet thing to do, Harry,' Anna said as she settled back into her seat, stroking the two sleeping animals in her lap. 'I don't think anyone has ever been as thoughtful.'

She reached across the gap between them and grasped his fingers in her own, her eyes filled with happiness.

Chapter Twenty-One

'They've been engaged a month and there's still no sign of a wedding date.'

'He's probably realised who he's tied himself to and can't bring himself to go through with the marriage.'

'The Edgertons are a good family, and he's an earl. Of course there was that unfortunate *business* with his sister last year, but it's hardly his fault. He could do so much better than Lady Fortescue.'

'It's a disgrace, such an eligible bachelor being snapped up by a woman who's already got through three husbands.'

Anna suppressed a smile as she listened to the two middle-aged women seated in front of her gossip with no idea she was sitting behind them. She knew both the women vaguely, had been introduced on a couple of occasions, but she had no qualms about embarrassing them for their unkind words.

'I heard she's already lining up husband number five for after she's got rid of Lord Edgerton,' Anna said, leaning forward and inserting herself into the conversation.

Both women spun in their seats, realised it was Anna

who had spoken to them and turned varying shades of crimson. They gave her disgust-filled looks and moved away quickly, muttering behind their fans as they found new seats.

'Making friends?' Harry observed as he slipped into the seat next to her.

'Just fuelling the gossip about us.'

He raised an eyebrow. 'Trying to prolong the scandal and therefore our engagement, Lady Fortescue? If I didn't know better I'd say you were falling for me.'

'Well, according to the gossips you could do *so* much better than me.'

Harry pretended to preen, then bent down to whisper in her ear, 'Ah, but they don't know what a good kisser you are.'

Anna considered this for a moment. 'I think that's probably a good thing.'

'Perhaps.' Harry's eyes flickered to her lips and Anna felt an all-too-familiar shiver run down the length of her spine. All he had to do was look at her in a particular way and she was ready to disgrace herself in front of a room full of witnesses.

'Where's your sister?' Anna asked, trying to distract herself.

'She went to talk to Miss Wright.'

'I'm glad she came.'

'Me, too.'

'Lord Edgerton,' Beatrice, Anna's cousin, said as she flopped down into a seat beside Anna. 'It's lovely to see you, although I'm still miffed I didn't get an invitation to your little party.'

'Blame your cousin,' Harry said, settling back in his seat.

'I do. Anna said your sister was coming tonight.'

At that moment Lydia joined them, greeting Anna and slipping into her seat as Harry introduced Beatrice.

'Come sit with me,' Beatrice said. 'I'd love to hear all the juicy details of what occurred at your brother's house party and Anna is not very forthcoming.'

Anna watched for any sign of discomfort from Lydia, but she seemed happy enough to link arms with Beatrice and allow Anna's cousin to start gossiping.

She caught the flash of hope in Harry's eyes as he realised Lydia was slotting right in during a social situation and gave him a reassuring pat on the forearm.

'Beatrice will be kind,' Anna whispered. Her cousin might be confident and outspoken, but she was sweet underneath it all. Just the sort of friend Lydia needed.

At the front of the room Mrs Wright clapped her hands, smiling at her assembled guests. All in all there were about twenty-five people in the room, mainly women, but with a smattering of men.

A tall man with a neat little moustache took his place at the piano and began to play. He was talented, hugely so, and within minutes he had the entire room enthralled. As Anna listened she felt the music washing over her and taking her back to simpler times.

Her fingers sought out Harry's and they sat side by side with their fingertips just touching, hidden from the view of everyone else by their position between the chairs. She dared not turn her head sideways, knowing one glimpse of Harry's smile, one twinkle of his eye, and she would do something they would both come to regret.

Too soon the first piece was over and Harry stood, breaking the contact before anyone could see them. Quickly he moved away, ducking out on to the terrace. Anna was just about to follow him when Mrs Wright came and sat down beside her and launched into a long history of how she'd come to discover the talented musician playing for them today. As she spoke Anna kept glancing at the door to the terrace, expecting Harry to reappear. She was completely trapped, unable to go to him, and it felt like torture.

Harry took a long, deep breath of the cold evening air and steadied himself. They'd only been holding hands, not even that, just the gentlest touching of the fingertips, yet here he was about to burst with desire like some green boy.

The door opened and he spun, smiling, expecting to see Anna, knowing that he wouldn't be able to keep his hands from her, but not caring.

'Miss Wright,' he said, trying to keep the disappointment from his voice.

'Thank you for coming this evening, Lord Edgerton,' Miss Wright said, crossing the terrace to him.

'My sister was most eager,' he said.

'I found myself missing your company after we spent the weekend together.'

He wanted to move away, but knew he had to tread carefully.

'I am glad you enjoyed yourself, even with the unpleasantness of the second day.'

'I think you handled that unpleasantness very well, Lord Edgerton. I admire you very much.'

'And I you, Miss Wright.' It was perhaps the wrong thing to say and he realised it as he noticed the flare of triumph in her eyes, but he was just trying to be polite.

'I have been talking to my select group of friends,' Miss Wright said, changing the direction of the conversation so abruptly Harry wasn't sure what was going on. 'I thought it might be prudent if we welcome your sister into our group. We are regarded in society as respectable debutantes, we all involve ourselves heavily in charity work and ensure no hint of scandal touches our names.'

Harry wasn't sure if she were proposing a friendship for his sister or that Lydia would be the charity work Miss Wright's friends engaged in.

'That is very generous,' he said, trying to dampen the feeling of discomfort building.

'I am sure with our support she could re-enter society and find herself a respectable husband. Perhaps not a duke or an earl or a marquess, but most certainly a baron or a second son.'

It was exactly what he'd wanted for his sister, so why did it feel so underhand, so sneaky?

'Of course she would have to engage in charity work and behave in an exemplary fashion, but with a little time I think her little indiscretion could be glossed over.'

'Mmm,' was all Harry could bring himself to say. He wanted Lydia to be accepted back into society, even wanted her to find a good husband and settle down with a family of her own, but this just didn't feel like the right way to go about it.

'It would be my pleasure to help her in this way,' Miss Wright said, stepping closer, but still maintaining an appropriate gap between them. She certainly was a stickler for the rules of propriety.

'That is very kind, Miss Wright,' Harry murmured.

'There was one other little matter I thought I might mention,' she said quietly. 'Your engagement to Lady Fortescue.'

The fake engagement that Harry just couldn't seem to bring himself to end.

'Although I can see Lady Fortescue has some wonderful qualities, she does have a certain reputation. I wondered if you appreciated how much your association with her damages your reputation and, by extension, your sister's.'

'Lady Fortescue is a friend,' Harry said softly but firmly. 'I would not abandon a friend in their hour of need.'

'But surely you have done enough, Lord Edgerton. And if Lady Fortescue considers you a friend, then she will not hesitate to distance herself from you at such an important time. A respectable marriage for you could make all the difference to your sister's chances.'

It was exactly what Harry had been telling himself for the past few months, but as he looked at Miss Wright and imagined a future with her in it he found himself shuddering and not in a good way.

'Thank you for your concern, Miss Wright,' he said, trying to keep his voice light. 'I shall certainly consider what you have said.'

As a well-brought-up young woman she didn't press the matter any further. There was no way for a respectable debutante to declare her desire for a man to start courting her, especially not outright. Many indicated interest with a flutter of the eyelashes or fleeting glances, but Miss Wright could do no more than curtsy and take her leave.

Harry was still outside five minutes later when most of the guests had trickled back into the large drawing room for the second part of the recital. He was gazing out over the darkened gardens, his eyes wandering over the immaculately kept grass and the neatly dug borders as a fine drizzle began to fall. He knew he should be grateful to Miss Wright—her offer to take Lydia under her wing was exactly what he had hoped for. With Miss Wright's influence and reputation Lydia's past indiscretion would eventually be forgotten, at least enough for her to find a husband.

If he were truly being selfless and working towards helping his sister recover from the scandal, he'd marry Miss Wright without a second's thought and bring some respectability back to the Edgerton family, but he just couldn't do it. It was ridiculous, Miss Wright was exactly the sort of woman he'd always been determined he'd marry one day: amiable, level-headed and someone he absolutely would never fall in love with. He should be dropping to his knees and begging the young woman to marry him, but he couldn't, not now he'd met Anna.

Running a hand through his hair, he inhaled deeply. He was falling in love and no matter how hard he tried there was no way of stopping it. A sensible man would distance himself, would take himself away from the woman he couldn't stop thinking about, but Harry was in too deep already. The situation was everything he'd always vowed to avoid—a woman he loved, someone he could actually hurt and who could hurt him. Not that he could imagine Anna doing anything to harm him deliberately…

'The performance will be starting again in a minute,' his sister said as she stepped outside. Despite her words she seemed in no rush to return to the audience and gently closed the door behind her.

'Are you enjoying it?' Harry asked, taking her arm as she approached and leading her for a slow stroll along the terrace.

'The pianist is very talented,' Lydia said, 'but it feels a little strange to be out in society after so long.'

'You don't regret coming?'

He found himself holding his breath as he waited for her to answer.

'No. Anna and her cousin, Beatrice, have been very kind and Miss Wright has introduced me to quite a few people. No one has said anything unkind.'

'Good. I wouldn't want you to be unhappy.'

Lydia smiled at him, the impish smile he remembered so well from her childhood, one he hadn't seen much this past year.

'No one would dare with you scowling at them.'

'I don't scowl.'

'You're scowling now.'

Harry didn't have an answer for that, instead deepening his scowl to make his sister giggle.

'I don't want you to be unhappy either, Harry,' Lydia said once she'd regained her composure.

'I'm not unhappy.'

'Not now, but you could be. I know what you're planning and I think it would make you miserable.'

'What do you think I'm planning?'

'Marrying someone you don't love, someone like Miss Wright.'

'I thought you liked Miss Wright?'

'She's pleasant enough, at least to my face. And she's probably pleasant enough behind my back. But pleasant doesn't make a good choice for a wife.'

'I think I'd like a pleasant wife.'

'Not if that was all there was, Harry,' Lydia said, her large blue eyes staring up at him with more wisdom than an eighteen-year-old should have. 'You deserve someone who adores you, who challenges you, who you think about every moment of every day.'

Anna, his mind screamed, that was who he thought about every moment of every day.

'We've seen what happens when people marry for love,' Harry said softly.

'That wasn't love, Harry,' Lydia said in a voice much older than her years. 'Two people who love each other don't go out of their way to hurt one another. Father was cruel and Mother provoked him again and again. I don't know what their relationship was built on, but that wasn't love.'

Harry frowned, but before he could speak Lydia continued.

'Love is caring for another person more than yourself. It's doing anything and everything to protect them and never knowingly causing them harm. Love is beautiful, Harry, and what our parents had wasn't beautiful.'

'You're eighteen, Lydia…' Harry began.

'I don't pretend ever to have been in love, but I watch people. I can see when two people truly care for one another—they're the happy ones. Not those who marry for money or titles or some other silly reason.' She reached out and squeezed his hand. 'Don't let our parents' disastrous marriage ruin your life. You're not like Father, Harry, you're a better man. I know you would never hurt someone you loved, you wouldn't intentionally hurt anyone.'

'Who would you have me marry?'

She levelled a completely grown-up stare at him that made him wonder where the little girl who loved pony rides had disappeared to.

'Someone who makes you smile when you see her, someone who makes you whistle as you come down for breakfast, someone that has you acting like a carefree young man and not someone with the weight of the world on his shoulders.' She patted his arm as if he were a little boy.

'But if I take a well-respected wife, someone who could help you back into society…'

Lydia grimaced. 'Then you will be unhappy and I will be unhappy because you are unhappy.'

Standing on tiptoes, she reached up and gave him a kiss on the cheek before turning and slipping back into the drawing room. Harry knew he should follow her, but lingered for a few minutes longer, too deep in thought to hear the piano music start again.

Chapter Twenty-Two

'Rebecca Tointon has had four proposals this month,' Beatrice said as she flopped on to Anna's bed, creasing up the delicate silk of her gown in one swift movement.

'Rebecca Tointon is the richest debutante London's ever seen,' Anna said, smiling at her cousin in the mirror. 'And it's not like you haven't had any.'

'Two, that's barely anything. And both were entirely unacceptable. Sir Witlow is barely out of the schoolroom and Mr Gainsborough has a daughter older than me.'

'You've only been out in society a few months,' Anna said soothingly. 'I'm sure an earl or a marquess will fall head over heels in love with you soon.'

'You can joke, but you're engaged to the most eligible bachelor in London. And he's an earl.'

'Pretending to be engaged,' Anna corrected.

Beatrice levelled her with a hard stare. 'No one believes that any more. You two are besotted with each other.'

'I am not besotted,' Anna said, feeling the heat rise in her cheeks as she came out with the lie. 'And Lord Edgerton is just being chivalrous and trying to save me from a little gossip.'

'If that was true he'd have broken the engagement this week when Lady Arrington got caught in a rather compromising position with Lord Wilbraham. Apparently her husband is thinking of *divorcing* her.'

Anna had half-expected Harry to suggest they quietly end their engagement once society was preoccupied with the rather scandalous discovery of Lady Arrington half-naked in the arms of a man who was most certainly not her husband, but he hadn't. He hadn't even hinted that it might be a good opportunity.

'Lord Edgerton has made it very clear he wants to marry a well-respected young woman, not an old widow who everyone gossips about.'

'That's what he thinks he should want, but not what he really wants,' Beatrice said with all the self-assurance of a confident eighteen-year-old. 'He wants you.'

Anna remembered their kisses, the stolen caresses, the looks that turned his eyes dark with desire.

'And you want him,' Beatrice said, holding her hand up to stop Anna from interrupting. 'I know you've vowed never to marry again, you've told me a thousand times, but that doesn't stop you from being besotted with Lord Edgerton. It's rather sweet and tragic, of course.'

A knock on the door halted the rebuke Anna had been forming as Beatrice skipped across the room to answer.

'Lord Edgerton, we were just talking about you,' Beatrice said with a dazzling smile.

In the mirror Anna watched as he raised a questioning eyebrow, but Beatrice just shook her head.

'I suppose I must have something to busy myself with before the rest of the guests arrive.'

Anna saw her cousin give Lord Edgerton a rather salacious wink that she suspected Beatrice had picked up from somewhere and someone entirely inappropriate and felt a prickle of guilt. It was truly scandalous that Harry be in her bedroom with her and Anna felt once again that she wasn't the most conscientious chaperon for the young girl.

As she tried to secure a dainty gold chain with a tear-drop ruby on the end around her neck she saw Harry check over his shoulder and then close the door completely, turning the key until the lock clicked. She felt a shiver of anticipation as he slowly turned back to face her.

'Allow me,' he said, coming up behind her and taking the two ends of the gold chain in his hands. His fingers brushed against her neck as he secured the clasp and then lingered for just a second longer than was necessary. 'I thought we should discuss how to move forward with finding who has been sending you those horrible packages.'

'I haven't received any more,' Anna said, feeling a little disappointed he didn't want privacy for any other purpose. 'Perhaps it was one of the Fortescues and now they've been scared off.'

'Perhaps, but it is unlikely. We both saw their reactions when we mentioned the packages—they didn't have any idea what we were talking about.'

'I don't know who else would want to harm me.'

'No spurned lovers? No spiteful wives who have a reason to hate you? No business rivals who would prefer you cowed and afraid?'

Anna shook her head. She truly couldn't think of anyone.

'No gossips you've publicly humiliated? No men you've turned down?'

'I really can't think of anyone,' Anna said. 'I have not ever had a lover to be spurned and the only man to propose to me in the last year is Mr Maltravers, and he's harmless.'

'Ah, yes, the man who's proposed to you nearly every week for the past six months.'

'But he wouldn't be sending me the packages, it wouldn't make sense.'

Harry looked thoughtful for a moment, then shrugged. 'Let's add him to our list. I'm told unrequited love is a large burden to bear. Anyone else?'

'I will think the matter over tonight,' Anna said with a small shake of her head, 'but I can't think of anyone else at present.'

'We should go downstairs,' Harry said, but didn't move from his position standing behind her.

'The other guests will be arriving soon.'

Anna's uncle, Mr Tenby, was hosting a small dinner party for a select group of friends as he did most months. He'd insisted Anna invite Harry, but most of the other guests would be middle-aged men and their wives, all friendly enough but not overly interesting.

'Perhaps they wouldn't notice if we were a couple of minutes late,' Harry murmured, dropping a hand lightly on Anna's shoulder. Her dress was low-cut with a wide neck, exposing her collarbones and the tips of her shoulders, and now Harry's fingers were tracing a path along the bare skin.

'Harry, we shouldn't,' Anna said, regretting the words as soon as they left her mouth.

'I know.'

He didn't stop, but in the mirror Anna saw he

closed his eyes for a moment as if trying to reason with himself.

'What are we doing here, Harry?' she asked quietly.

'We're just two people, pretending to be engaged and finding it damn difficult to keep our hands to ourselves,' Harry said bluntly.

'We should break off our engagement.'

'We will. Just not yet. Give me a few more days.'

'What for, Harry?'

'To enjoy you.'

She turned and stood, facing him so they were chest to chest, body to body. Anna was not small in stature for a woman, but she had to tilt her head back to see Harry's face she was so close.

'Lydia thinks I should marry you,' Harry said, trailing his fingers from her temple down to the tip of her chin. 'She thinks you make me happy.'

'Doesn't she know I wouldn't have you?'

Harry shrugged, leaning in closer. 'She thinks I'd be able to persuade you.'

Right now Anna was feeling as if she would be very easy to persuade.

'It got me thinking, my conversation with Lydia, about what life is all about.'

Anna was finding it hard to concentrate with Harry standing so close. She could feel the heat from his body, the tickle of his breath on her neck and the completely distracting fingers on her skin.

'I started wondering if maybe I'd been approaching things all wrong.'

Managing a non-committal squeak, Anna looked up, knowing it was the wrong thing to do even as she did it.

'I've been too preoccupied with worrying about

not repeating my parents' mistakes that I have nearly made an even graver one myself. I thought marrying a woman I cared deeply for would make me unhappy, but really *not* marrying for love would be a much greater source of misery.' He dropped his fingers to her neck, his touch feather-light and oh, so seductive. 'And here you are, a woman I care deeply for, and we're already engaged...'

'Pretending to be engaged,' Anna corrected, half in a trance-like state. The correction made Harry smile.

'Do you know what would make me extremely happy right now, Lady Fortescue?'

Anna shook her head, hoping with every fibre in her body that it would involve a meeting of their lips.

'Kissing you right here.' He dipped his head and brushed his lips against the patch of skin that sat in the hollow just above her collarbone. 'And here...' His lips moved across her neck, pausing at the angle of her jaw before he groaned softly and covered her mouth with his.

Anna felt time stop. She wasn't aware of anything but Harry's lips on hers, his tongue, his hands, his body. Already her head was spinning and her heart pounding.

Never had she been kissed like this before. None of her husbands had ever made her feel even a fraction of what Harry did whenever his lips met hers.

'What would make you happy, Anna?' Harry asked, pulling away just enough to whisper the question.

She couldn't form any words, couldn't think of anything but Harry's firm body and their slow movements towards her large, inviting bed.

'Tell me,' he murmured, 'what would make you happy?'

She couldn't bring herself to utter the words, couldn't bring herself to admit out loud that she wanted him to lay her down on the bed and make love to her. Despite all the rumours and all the gossip she *was* a respectable widow. She'd only ever shared a bed with her husbands, never even entertained the idea of a lover.

'How about if I kissed you here?' he suggested, moving his lips down to the base of her neck.

Anna heard the sigh leave her mouth before she was even aware of it. Harry grinned and edged her a step closer to the bed.

'Or how about if I kissed you here.' His lips trailed ever lower, dancing across the skin of her chest, pushing against the material of her dress.

Feeling the edge of the bed behind her Anna sank down, looking up at Harry towering over her. Despite his physical advantage in size and strength she felt completely safe with him. Even after thinking she would never trust a man again, it was impossible not to trust Harry.

Holding out her hand, she waited until he'd taken it and pulled him to sit beside her. As soon as he was back on her level his lips found hers again, kissing her so deeply, so passionately, that Anna felt her head begin to spin. Her hands were on his body, her palms caressing his torso through the layers of his eveningwear, and suddenly Anna realised that she had to feel more of him, to touch his bare skin, to run her fingers over the firm muscles of his back.

Pulling away slightly, she took his cravat and untied it in one swift movement, then moved on to his jacket, pulling it from his shoulders.

'My turn,' Harry said, lifting Anna to her feet and quickly spinning her so he could unfasten her dress. His fingers worked quickly and, before she could compose herself, Anna's dress was pooling around her ankles.

Harry whispered, 'What are you doing to me?' He motioned to the white stockings she wore under her dress. Anna glanced down. She'd put them on to keep out the chill of the cool evening, not as a seduction technique.

While he was distracted Anna quickly untucked his shirt, pulling it off and pausing to lay her hands on his chest. His skin was soft, but the muscles underneath firm and solid, and Anna knew that before the evening was over she would feel her own body pressed against those very muscles.

'Lie down,' Harry said and as Anna fell back on to the bed he gripped the top of one stocking and slowly started to pull the material down her leg. His fingers grazed her skin, sending wonderful sensations all through her body, and soon Anna was offering up the other leg quite shamelessly for him to divest of her stocking.

Soon she was clad only in her chemise, the thin white cotton barely any protection from Harry's burning gaze.

'Do you want me to stop?' Harry asked as he gripped the hem of her chemise. The strained expression on his face hinted at how hard he would find it if she said yes, but Anna knew he wouldn't continue without her agreeing completely. There was no way of hiding from the fact that she wanted this as much as him.

'Don't stop,' she whispered.

It was enough. Within seconds he'd whipped her last piece of clothing off over her head and was regarding her naked body. Anna didn't feel ashamed or self-conscious—this was Harry, he could put even the most timid mouse at ease.

While Harry began to caress her body, Anna reached up and unfastened his trousers, gripping the waistband and pushing them down as far as she could reach.

'I've been dreaming of this for a long time,' he said as he dipped his head and caught one of her nipples between his teeth. 'You've bewitched me, enchanted me, and now I can't stop thinking about you.'

Anna was too overwhelmed by the wonderful sensations coming from where his mouth met her skin to answer coherently.

'I fall asleep every night wondering how you would taste, how you would feel. Imagining touching you here...' he grazed his fingers across her abdomen '...and here...' he moved lower with his feather-light touch '...and here.'

Anna gasped as his fingers sent little jolts of pleasure through her body as he caressed her. Never had she been touched like this, never had she been made to moan in pleasure involuntarily.

'I've even imagined kissing you,' he said, causing Anna to pause. Surely he was kissing her already? As he pushed himself down the bed Anna's eyes widened and she struggled up on to her elbows, only to fall back with a soft whimper as his lips brushed against her most sensitive spot.

'Harry,' she moaned as he kissed and caressed her, her hand bunching the sheets beneath her, holding on tight to try to anchor herself to the bed. Every second that passed made her feel like she would float away on a cloud of pleasure, until something burst deep inside her, consuming every inch of her body.

As she opened her eyes and looked up she saw Harry moving up towards her, looking like some Greek god with bronzed skin and hardened muscles. She gripped his arms, pulling him towards her, and gently he slipped inside her.

He kissed her as their bodies came together and they moved as if one, rising and falling on the soft bed until Anna felt the pleasure building and building before the wonderful release. As she clung tight to Harry's back he stiffened and then collapsed on top of her.

Anna felt herself come drifting back down to earth as Harry raised himself on his arms and looked down at her. She couldn't help but smile, a dreamy, faraway smile. In a few minutes they would have to return to reality and discuss the future, but right now she just wanted to revel in the warm sensation of feeling completely and utterly cherished.

Harry stretched out beside Anna, pulling her body closer in to his and resting his hand on her hip. He knew they should move, knew a rather respectable dinner party was just about to start directly below them, but he couldn't find it in himself to spoil this moment.

He'd known what would happen the moment he'd locked the door behind him on entering Anna's room. If he was honest with himself, he'd known what would happen long before that. Ever since his realisation that he could not marry Miss Wright, or anyone like her, and Lydia's frank words trying to make him see he wasn't anything like their father, that he *could* marry for love and be happy, he'd known it was only a matter of time before he and Anna fell into each other's arms.

'Marry me,' Harry murmured, saying the words into the soft skin of Anna's neck.

'We're already...' she started to say.

'I mean for real. Marry me. Be my wife.'

Anna turned to face him, her eyes searching his. For once the cool greyness that normally hid all her emotions was alive with hope and worry and disbelief.

'I...' Before she could answer there was a quick rap on the door, followed by a low hiss that sounded like muffled words through the thick wood.

Anna sprung up from the bed and began to struggle back into her dress. There was another knock, this one louder and more insistent.

'Anna, open up. Now.'

With a quick glance at Harry, Anna rushed over to the door and opened it a crack. Beatrice hurriedly pushed inside, closing the door behind her. Anna's cousin's eyes widened as she took in the scene. Harry had just had time to pull the bedcovers over himself, but there was no hiding what had just occurred in this bedroom.

'Father sent me to fetch you. All the guests have arrived.'

Harry looked at Anna's completely dishevelled hair, her delightfully pink cheeks and her crumpled dress she'd only managed to get halfway on.

'Tell your father Anna has a headache, a bad one. She won't be able to attend the dinner party.'

Beatrice nodded, glancing at Harry out of the corner of her eye, but not able to bring herself to look at him directly.

'And you?'

'Does your father know I arrived?'

Beatrice shrugged.

'Only one of the footmen saw me come up. I don't think anyone else knows I'm here.'

Harry wrapped the sheet around his lower body,

not wanting to embarrass Anna's cousin any further. Quickly he crossed to Anna's small writing desk and took a sheet of paper, penning a quick note of apology.

'Give this to the tall footman, the one with white-blond hair. Ask him to deliver it to your father as if it were just dropped off.' Harry handed her the note of apology along with a couple of shiny coins to ensure the footman's silence.

'And what will you do?' Beatrice asked, then shook her head, holding up her hands. 'Forget I asked, I don't want to know.'

With a backwards glance at her cousin, Beatrice left the room and Anna hurriedly locked the door behind her.

'We'll never get away with it,' she whispered.

Harry shrugged. It didn't much matter either way. If they were found together in Anna's bedroom they would just have to marry sooner and that would suit him just fine. Now he'd made up his mind to follow his heart and not his head he was rather eager to make everything legal.

'Everyone will know and then they'll really have something to gossip about.'

'Hush,' Harry said, crossing the room and taking her in his arms. 'What does it matter?'

Anna looked up at him as though he'd grown a second head.

'Of course it matters. Your reputation will be ruined completely and by association your sister will be subject to further rumour and scandal.'

'What is it you always say?' Harry asked. 'There are worse things than a little gossip.'

This at least got a smile from her. A little upturning of the corners of her mouth, but a smile all the same.

'Marry me, Anna,' Harry said again, 'and it won't matter.'

'You don't want to marry me.'

He kissed her, a slow, gentle kiss full of passion and promise, then pulled away and cupped her face in his hands.

'I've been trying to tell myself I don't want to marry you for six weeks,' he said, dropping a kiss on the end of her nose. 'I can't pretend any more.'

He waited, watching the emotions flit across her normally inscrutable face. It was unsurprising that she was hesitating, after her last disastrous marriage she had every right to be cautious, but Harry knew she cared for him and surely that was more important than her worries.

'It's not that I don't care for you, Harry,' Anna said, biting her lip. 'I care for you rather a lot.'

'I love you,' Harry blurted out, unsure where the words had come from, but realising they were true all the same. He did love Anna and he would make damn sure they spent their lives together.

Anna glided towards him, her eyes locked on his. 'I think I might love you, too, Harry,' she said, but there was a hint of sadness in her voice. Harry chose to ignore it and pushed forward.

'Then that's settled. We'll marry as soon as possible.'

Anna shook her head. 'I'm not sure…'

'I love you, you love me. What else is there to consider?'

'I need to think about this. I need some time.'

Harry sank to his knees in front of her and took both hands in his own. 'I promise to cherish you, to protect you, to allow you to flourish.'

'I need time, Harry.'

It wasn't an outright 'no' and with a little work Harry was sure he could turn it into a 'yes'. She was just cautious and rightly so after the abuse she'd had to endure from her last husband. All he had to do was show her he was different, show her how their lives could be together.

With a gentle squeeze of her hand he backed away.

'I can give you time, Anna. I don't want to rush you. Just know that I love you and I want us to be together.'

'You said you wanted to marry someone you would never fall in love with.'

'I was a fool, too preoccupied trying to avoid the harm my parents caused each other, too blind to see what they shared couldn't have been love. I could never hurt you like my father hurt my mother, could never set out to make you cry or make you want to hide in shame. I want to cherish you, protect you, show you how much I love you every single day,' Harry said.

'And your mother? She will not approve.'

'My mother is consumed by her nerves, I'm not sure she'd approve of anything. But I will break the news to her gently and she will come around.'

Anna fell silent, all her protestations answered for a little while.

'Just consider my proposal, Anna. That's all I ask. Think of the life we could have together. Think of the happiness.'

'I might not be able to have children,' Anna said quietly, glancing up at Harry for a second as she spoke. 'Three husbands and not one pregnancy does not bode well.'

He took her hand in his own and kissed her knuckles. 'Then we don't have children.'

'You'd make a wonderful father.'

'And you would make a wonderful mother, but sometimes these things are just not meant to be.'

'I will consider it,' Anna said, a little frown on her face. Harry knew the war that was waging inside her, knew enough about her character and her past to piece together the internal argument that was raging in her head. Part of her wanted to throw caution to the wind and say yes to becoming his wife. She loved him, he loved her, and the carefree romantic was telling her that things would be different this time. The other part of her was much more cautious. She'd been hurt, irreparably so, and didn't want to ever put herself in a position where anyone had power over her again. He just hoped the positive side won.

'I shall call on you tomorrow,' he said.

'I might need more time than that.'

'Then I shall call on you the next day as well.'

'Harry…'

He held his hands up. 'I'm not pressuring you, take all the time you need. We can be engaged for another six months if we so desire. I just don't want to go too long without seeing you.'

'I've got the accounts to go over tomorrow. Perhaps you could call on me at the Shipping Company Office and we could go for a stroll in the late afternoon.'

'I'm looking forward to it already,' Harry said, pulling her in closer and kissing her deeply.

Humming to himself as he slipped out the back door, Harry skirted around the side of the house, quietly opened and shut the gate behind him, and was back on the street without anyone seeing him. All in all it had been a successful evening. He had never planned to seduce Anna, although he had been fantasising about tumbling into bed with her for weeks. And he had never planned on proposing, at least not right then.

Ever since his talk with his sister when he'd realised she was right, he knew he could never hurt Anna the way his father had hurt his mother. He'd been consumed with the idea that he and Anna could have a future. A future where they strolled through his country estate arm in arm, spent long, lazy mornings in bed together, and sat side by side while she worked on her shipping company accounts and he those for running the estate.

For so long he'd been focusing on the wrong things, thinking a dull, amiable wife would stop him from spending the rest of his life miserable, when the exact opposite was the truth.

So here he was, just a man in love with a woman, trying to persuade her to marry him. Harry knew he had a huge grin on his face, he probably looked like a lunatic escaped from an asylum, but he couldn't stop smiling. Anna would come round, if he didn't press her too much, and she'd realise by herself how they were meant to be together.

He was just crossing the street when a movement in a carriage fifty feet away caught his eye. Pausing for just a second, Harry glanced at it, trying not to let on he'd noticed. Sure enough there was a shadow inside, someone shifting behind the curtain, trying not to be seen.

Nonchalantly he continued walking, his natural path taking him past the carriage. As he drew closer he could see the curtains were drawn tightly together and there were no identifying markings on the exterior, no family crests or coats of arms, just plain black paintwork.

He debated whether to fling open the door and expose whoever was sitting inside, but his impeccable manners and good upbringing prevailed. This coach might have nothing to do with Anna or the mysterious packages she'd been receiving. It might simply be two lovers out for a secret assignation who'd chosen this street to stop in at random. Harry rounded the corner, ducked behind the wrought-iron fence so he was hidden by the thick bushes and looked back. The carriage hadn't moved. The coachman was sitting holding on to the reins with a drooped head and Harry wondered if he was dozing. Perhaps he would be able to sneak back and...

Before he could finish the thought he saw the coachman jerk awake and gather the reins tighter. Whoever was inside the carriage was evidently ready to leave. Looking about him, he searched for another carriage, something he could follow in at a discreet distance. There was nothing. Anna's uncle lived in a respectable residential street where many people would have carriages of their own. No need for a hired conveyance to be touting for business.

Cursing, Harry sprang into action. They knew whoever was tormenting Anna was watching her closely. The last package had just contained a list of dates and times and locations where she'd been. This could be his best chance at finding out once and for all who was behind the packages.

He ran at a full sprint down the pavement, throwing himself at the carriage door just as the coachman urged the horses forward. Clinging on to the handle, Harry pulled, opening the door as the carriage started moving. He was balancing on the footplate of a rapidly accelerating carriage and he knew a fall could cause him to have at least a few broken bones. Gritting his teeth, he pushed the door open a little further and threw himself inside.

As he landed on his face inside the carriage he felt the driver pull on the reins to slow the horses, shouting in surprise at his new passenger.

'Mr Maltravers,' Harry said, greeting Anna's business rival. 'What a surprise to see you here.'

'What is the meaning of this…this…intrusion?' Mr Maltravers spluttered, his face rapidly turning crimson.

'I could ask you the same thing.'

'Stop talking in riddles, man, and tell me why you've thrown yourself into my carriage.'

Harry picked himself up from the floor and took a seat across from Mr Maltravers.

'Tell me, why were you outside Lady Fortescue's house, watching?'

'I don't know what you're talking about.'

'Your carriage was stopped outside Lady Fortescue's house.'

'Indeed it was. There's no crime in it.'

'No…' Harry shook his head '…but it is a crime to send threatening messages, to kill a cat and send it to their owner.'

'What are you going on about?' Mr Maltravers bellowed. 'You're making no sense.'

Harry watched carefully and saw a flicker of fear in the portly man's eyes. He knew exactly what Harry was talking about.

'Why were you here, then?'

'Not that it's any of your concern, but I had in mind to pay Lady Fortescue a little visit this evening, then I remembered her uncle was hosting a dinner party so thought it better not to intrude.'

'So why did you not instruct your coachman to leave straight away? You were watching the house.'

'I was doing nothing of the sort. Get out. Take your vile accusations and leave my carriage.'

Harry had seen enough. Mr Maltravers wasn't going to admit he had been the one terrorising Anna, much less explain why he'd done so. Nothing more would be gleaned tonight.

'I must insist you have no further contact with my fiancée,' Harry said. 'Do not visit her on business, do not run into her on the street by accident, do not ever come by her house. Is that clear?'

Mr Maltravers bristled, but did not protest.

'I shall inform Lady Fortescue of this in the morning,' Harry said.

'No, you won't.'

Harry had just turned to get down from the carriage when Mr Maltravers grabbed him by the jacket.

'I saw you go into her room, saw the shadows behind the curtains,' he hissed. 'I don't think you or Lady Fortescue would like the world to know what happened between you tonight.'

Harry shrugged, pulling himself free of Mr Maltravers's grip. 'I don't much care what you tell the world. Soon Lady Fortescue and I will be married and if the gossips want to talk about us, then so be it. There are worse things in the world than a little gossip.'

Quickly he jumped down from the coach, turning to address the coachman.

'Get this scoundrel out of my sight.'

As the coach raced off around the corner Harry glanced back at Anna's window. Now she could go about her life in peace, not always wondering where the next threat was coming from. Tomorrow he'd tell her about Mr Maltravers and, once he'd informed her, he would talk to a magistrate he knew well and see what could be done to keep Mr Maltravers from ever bothering Anna again.

Chapter Twenty-Three

'I'm not sure I believe it,' Anna said. 'I've never liked the man, but I didn't think he was capable of this.'

She sank back into her chair behind the desk and absentmindedly stroked the small kitten in her lap. She'd brought both kittens into the office today as they were already causing chaos around the house, scratching furniture and ripping fabrics. They were sweet little things, just wanting to frolic and play all the time, but they didn't realise yet that the whole world wasn't theirs to paw and scratch.

'I found him sitting in a carriage outside your uncle's house.'

Anna nodded. 'Why would he do it?' she asked. 'I thought he liked me—the man proposed to me often enough.'

'I suspect he wanted to make you feel vulnerable, so you would think you needed a husband to look after you and run to him for comfort.'

Anna shuddered. It was a cruel thing to do.

'I never even suspected him.' Mr Maltravers had suggested she needed protection on a number of occasions, but she'd never thought he was terrorising her to scare her into marriage.

Harry shrugged. 'Sometimes we need to be more wary of the people who act in secret than the people who are unpleasant to our faces.'

'He actually thought it would make me marry him?' Anna asked, incredulous. Mr Maltravers was the last man she would ever consider marrying.

'He didn't admit as much, but I suspect that was the reason. He had no other motive I can see. And he did propose to you rather a lot.'

Anna nodded. 'And I suppose the packages started when I came out of mourning, the point when I *could* start considering marriage again.'

'It's not just me that finds you irresistible,' Harry said, moving closer and taking Anna's hand.

'He killed my cat, he watched me and recorded all my movements.'

'Men can do terrible things when they're thwarted.'

'I was never sure if he wanted to marry me for *me* or for the business.'

'I think we can assume it was you he was obsessed with. I've never known a man to go to such lengths for anything other than an infatuation.'

Anna shuddered, thinking of all the times she'd been alone with the man, all the carriage rides home, the conversations in her office.

'I don't think he would have ever harmed you,' Harry said.

'You warned him to stay away?'

'Of course.'

'I'm glad the matter's resolved,' Anna said with a sigh, taking Harry's hand. 'Thank you. I don't think I truly believed this would ever be over.'

'It's over,' Harry said, pulling her closer to him and

kissing her lightly on the forehead. 'I won't let anyone harm you, I won't let anyone threaten you.'

'I just want to forget this all ever happened.'

'And you can, my love. I'll sort things out with the magistrate.'

Anna stiffened and pulled away. She didn't want to involve a magistrate, she just wanted to forget Mr Maltravers even existed, forget about the horrible packages and the feelings of unrest and fear at the thought of being watched.

'No magistrate,' Anna said. 'I don't want to report this.'

'We must, Anna. He's tormented you for months, he can't be allowed to get away with it.'

'No, Harry, no magistrate. I don't want anyone else knowing about this. I don't want to have to relive everything that's happened.'

'You won't have to. I'll talk to the magistrate, make sure everything is kept discreet.'

'I said no, Harry,' Anna stood back and folded her arms.

'What if he does it again? What if he thinks he can get away with it and torments another woman?'

'I don't want to report it,' Anna said firmly.

Harry hesitated and then moved forward, engulfing her in his arms. At their feet the two kittens jumped and rolled, vying for her attention, and with a laugh Harry bent down and scooped them up.

'I can see you two are going to be trouble,' he said, giving both tiny balls of fur a stern look before giving in and stroking them until they purred. 'Do you mind if I take your mama out for a little excursion?'

Anna tidied up the papers on her desk, putting the large accounts book into a drawer and locking it afterwards. Then she gathered her cloak and slipped it on, glancing out the grimy window at the grey sky.

'Don't worry, I have the carriage waiting,' Harry said, following her gaze. 'And it means these two beauties can come along with us.'

The streets were busy as they weaved their way towards Ludgate Hill. Women selling flowers competed with men pushing wheelbarrows and children hurrying along behind governesses, and there was a crush of carriages travelling in all directions.

'What did you name them?' Harry asked as he stroked the kitten that had decided to settle in the crook of his arm, oblivious to the hairs that were already falling on his jacket.

'He's Apollo and this little lady is Artemis.'

'Twin gods. Very apt. I think they'll like Halstead Hall. Lots of curtains for them to get their claws into.'

'They're going to stay with you?' Anna asked, her expression serene.

'I'm sure you'll want to bring them with you when we take up residence.'

'Harry...'

'I'm not rushing you.'

Anna had to suppress a smile. It was hard to resist his easy charm and even harder to remain annoyed at him when he flashed that rather dazzling look. She still felt as though she were in a dream. Ever since their intimacies the night before Anna kept wondering if things were real. She shouldn't want to fall into Harry's arms, agree to everything he was proposing and allow him to sweep her off into the sunset, but she did. Part of her wondered why she was still resisting. She didn't really think Harry was like any of her other husbands.

He would never be cruel, never hurt her. Sometimes he liked to make decisions for her, but surely she could work on that. She just wanted to be sure she would be able to maintain her independence if she agreed to this marriage. And that she was almost sure of. Almost.

'We're here,' Harry said, jumping down from the carriage and holding out his hand to Anna. Before she could protest he had handed the two kittens up to the coachman, instructing him to guard them with his life.

Anna allowed Harry to lead her to a shop a few doors down, noting the elegant displays in the window and the fancy lettering above the door. Augustus Grey Jeweller's, it read, and as they pushed opened the door a small man with a clipped moustache and small spectacles halfway down the bridge of his nose rushed forward to greet them.

'Lord Edgerton, what an honour. Please come in and look around. Is there anything in particular I can help you with today?' The words came out in a rush, so much so that Anna had to pause for a moment to separate the sentences.

'I wish to buy an engagement gift for my fiancée,' Harry said.

'May I offer my congratulations to you both,' the jeweller said, giving a funny little bow and flushing with pleasure. 'Please have a look around and if anything catches your eye I will get it out for closer inspection.'

'We're not *really* engaged yet,' Anna whispered to Harry as they began to stroll around the shop.

'I'm hopeful,' Harry said.

Anna tried giving him her sternest glare, but in truth she wasn't in the slightest put out. It was another generous act in a string of generous acts that showed the sort of person Harry was. She'd be a fool to turn down his proposal.

'What would you like?' he asked. 'Perhaps a necklace, or a ring to mark our engagement.'

Anna paused by a beautiful necklace. A string of iridescent pearls of the highest quality, shimmering under the glass. She didn't have much jewellery, only the pieces she'd saved from her adolescence and year as a debutante. Her first husband had gifted her a few pieces, but her second husband had promptly sold them to raise funds before his posting to India. Lord Fortescue had never bought her any jewellery of her own, instead making her wear items that had belonged to his late wife and were certainly never Anna's to keep.

'I can imagine you in pearls,' Harry murmured in her ear. 'Just in pearls.'

Refusing to be embarrassed, Anna moved on, her eyes flitting across the beautiful pieces set out to entice and enthral.

'I don't need anything, Harry,' she said.

'I know, but I would like to get you something all the same. Sometimes it's nice to be spoiled, to have someone buy you a gift.'

Anna stepped up to a case containing multiple beautiful rings, bands of gold and silver all set with different stones. There were some with huge diamonds and rubies, rings that would be noticed and commented on, and one particularly beautiful ring with a perfectly cut emerald, but Anna's eyes focused on something much less ostentatious, much more simple.

'Could I have a look at this one?' she asked.

It had a simple gold band with a green jade stone, unostentatious and beautiful.

The jeweller obligingly took it from the case and offered it to Anna for closer inspection.

'Allow me,' Harry said, taking the ring from her and slipping it on to her finger. It fit perfectly and looked as if it had been made to sit on her hand.

Anna regarded it, trying to suppress the tears that were threatening to form in her eyes. Why couldn't she have met Harry before her father had arranged her first marriage with Lord Humphries? Why couldn't she turn back time and be an eager debutante again, ready to fall in love without all the complications the last six years had added to her life?

'We'll take this one,' Harry said and Anna didn't even bristle at him assuming control of the situation and making the decision for her.

Chapter Twenty-Four

Resisting the urge to twiddle with the ring on her finger, Anna suppressed a smile as she glanced impatiently at the clock. Harry was due to visit and today was the day she was going to accept his proposal. First she was going to gently bring up the subject of her independence and her continuing to run her business, but if that went well she would agree to be his wife.

A bubble of excitement welled up inside her, threatening to burst and make her giggle or clap her hands with joy, but with some difficulty Anna managed to suppress the urge to show how giddy this was making her feel.

She was sitting with her legs underneath her, curled up in the drawing room with her two beautiful kittens frolicking at her feet. Another glance at the clock revealed only a minute had passed since she'd last checked and with a groan of impatience she got to her feet, sidestepping to avoid Apollo and Artemis, and crossed to the piano. Music would make the time pass more quickly.

With an ease that showed her talent at the piano Anna began to play, not bothering to flip through the sheets of music, but instead choosing a piece that was imprinted into her mind. As she played she felt a peculiar sense of contentment. Today she was going to leave her past behind and start to plan her future with the man she loved. Of course she still had a few misgivings, concerns that were only natural for a widow who'd survived three disastrous marriages, but that was not going to stop her from admitting she loved Harry and realising it would only be herself she was hurting if she chose to live her life separate from him.

She kept telling herself that if she went into this marriage making it clear to Harry she would never give up her business, that she would not sit at home organising the domestic matters like most wives, then surely they would have a chance at happiness.

There was a murmur of voices in the entrance hall, inaudible under the piano music, but Anna knew within a few seconds her future husband would be shown into the room. She had butterflies in her stomach as the door opened and couldn't resist the smile that took over her face when Harry walked in.

Just as she was about to stand and fling herself into Harry's arms another man entered the room behind him. Without missing a note Anna continued playing the piano as she assessed the newcomer. He was in his mid-forties, his expression serious, but as Harry leaned in and said something he gave a jovial little laugh.

Anna came to the end of the piece and stood, stepping out from behind the piano and gliding towards Harry, her movements slow and controlled and her expression neutral.

'Lady Fortescue, may I introduce Sir Gregory Hicks.'

Anna inclined her head in greeting before meeting his steely gaze with one of her own.

'Sir Gregory is a magistrate, he's discreet and I trust his judgement.'

'A magistrate,' Anna murmured. 'How interesting.' Pulling Harry to one side, she gave Sir Gregory a polite little smile before turning her back on him so her words were not overheard. 'What is he doing here?'

'Lord Edgerton told me of your little problem,' Sir Gregory interrupted, stepping forward and inserting himself in between her and Harry. 'He thought I may be able to advise you.'

'My little problem?' Anna asked, hardly believing what she was hearing.

'With an overzealous suitor. Malicious letters and packages, following your movements, all in all a very unpleasant episode.'

'Please excuse us for a few minutes, Sir Gregory, I just need to discuss something with Lord Edgerton. Would you care for some tea while you wait?' Anna was so irate she had nearly forgotten to offer the man some refreshments and was glad when he shook his head. It would mean he could be got rid of quicker.

She half-dragged Harry from the drawing room, not trusting herself to speak until they were safely ensconced in her uncle's study, with two doors firmly closed between them and Sir Gregory.

'Explain yourself,' Anna said, her tone clipped and harsh even to her own ears. She was finding it hard not to raise her voice.

'I thought it would be wise to consult a magistrate about how best to proceed with this Maltravers situation.' Harry placed his hand lightly on her shoulder and Anna had the urge to shake it off—instead she focused on maintaining her composure.

'Why?' she asked.

'Why? Because he killed your cat. Because he had been following you and watching you for months. Because he's been threatening you and who knows what he'll do now he's been found out. I want to keep you safe.'

'I asked you not to do anything,' Anna said, shaking his hand off her shoulder and moving away. Her hands were trembling and she felt her breathing becoming quicker and more laboured.

'I know, Anna, but…'

'But what? My opinions don't matter? Is that it?'

'Of course they matter,' Harry said, his voice soothing.

'Clearly they don't. You heard what I said, but just decided to do the opposite anyway.'

'I want to protect you. It's in your best interests.'

Anna let out a short, almost hysterical laugh as she tried to gain control of herself and failed miserably. 'I never asked you to protect me, Harry. I never asked you to do anything except let the matter drop.'

'I wasn't going to just let him get away with all the upset he's caused you.'

'What right have you to make that decision?' Anna asked, her voice rising in volume, but she was helpless to stop it.

'I love you, Anna, I care for you. That gives me the right.'

She shook her head, feeling the anger bubble up and almost close off her throat. Her next words were tight and a little muffled. 'You're just like the rest of them.'

'The rest of who?'

'Men. Thinking you know what's right for me. Making decisions for me.'

'You were just going to let him get away with it. Who knows, he might even have carried on.'

'And that was my decision to make, Harry. It's my life and if I choose to shave off all my hair and disguise myself as a man to join the army, then it is none of your concern. If I choose to give all my money away to the orphans of London, again it is none of your concern. And if I choose to put this matter with Mr Maltravers behind me rather than be tied up in lengthy legal arguments, then it is none of your concern.'

Harry grasped her upper arms and waited until she looked at him.

'I love you, Anna. That means everything you do is my concern.'

As he held her eyes Anna felt herself soften slightly. Perhaps it had all been in her best interests...

Then as suddenly as the thought had entered her mind she felt her resolve stiffen and her jaw clench. His motivations didn't matter. He was still trying to rule her life, to make her decisions for her, and he saw nothing wrong in his actions. Now it might just be an argument over whether to consult a magistrate about Mr Maltravers's persecution, but it would lead to other things. Before she knew it she would be married to a man who didn't see he was taking away her autonomy.

Trying to suppress the tears in her eyes and the sob that threatened to burst from her throat, she pulled the ring from her finger. It had only been there for two days, but already she'd got used to the weight and the feel of it. Her hand felt naked without it, but she couldn't keep it.

'Take it,' she whispered, not trusting her voice to speak any louder.

'No,' Harry said, shaking his head.

'Take it. I was a fool to think this could ever work.'

'Anna, don't.' His voice was firm and authoritative. 'I love you. You love me. This is just a misunderstanding.'

'I can't have a man tell me what to do again. I can't have someone controlling me.'

'I wouldn't try to control you.'

'You already are.'

He took her hand, raising the fingers to his lips. 'I'll send Sir Gregory away. We can talk about it and, if you truly don't want to do anything more, I will never mention Mr Maltravers again.'

With tears running down her cheeks, Anna pulled away. It shouldn't be this hard, doing the right thing. She'd known all along marrying again would only lead to pain, but right now it felt as though her heart was ripping in two.

'I can't marry you, Harry,' she said, wishing it weren't true. 'I can't give up my freedom.'

'Damn it, Anna, I'm not trying to lock you in a room for the next forty years. I want to love you, cherish you, give you the life of happiness you deserve. I'm not going to take away your freedom. I'm not going to try to make your decisions for you.'

But you already are. Anna couldn't bring herself to say the words, instead she reached up and let her fingers trail down Harry's cheek, knowing this would be the last time she saw him. Desperately she tried to imprint every detail of his face into her memory, knowing she would never feel like this about another man.

'Goodbye, Harry,' she said, turning and sweeping from the room. It took a gargantuan effort not to turn and look back, but she knew if she hesitated for even a second she'd run back to his arms and forget all her misgivings.

Chapter Twenty-Five

'Again,' Harry barked, taking up his starting stance and brandishing his sword.

'Take it easy, old chap,' Rifield said, wiping sweat from his brow. Despite his protestations Harry's friend turned and steadied himself, raising his sword and indicating he was ready to begin.

Metal clashed against metal as they began the drill, one of hundreds they'd perfected during their time in the army together. Harry had met Rifield on his very first day after signing away his freedom when they'd been partnered together for training. They'd quickly come to appreciate one another's skill and agility and soon after become good friends.

'I take it she turned you down?' Rifield asked during the next break.

Harry grunted, stalking back to his starting position. It had been three days since he had last seen Anna, three days since she'd told him *goodbye*. In that time he'd tried on numerous occasions to see her, but every time he'd failed. Once he'd even attempted to climb up the outside of the house to her first-floor bedroom, only to find she'd anticipated the move and decamped elsewhere. He'd waited outside her office at the docks for a whole day, but only saw weathered old men going in and out. She'd completely cut him off.

'You knew she was going to be a hard one to convince. What's stopping you now?'

Harry thought of the raw pain in her eyes as she'd told him they couldn't be together. He knew she loved him, that was the worst part. He loved her and she loved him, but she was too scared to let them be happy together. It was entirely understandable after the ordeal she'd endured with her last husband. He'd thought he was breaking down that fear, then he'd gone and brought Sir Gregory into the picture.

When he'd first approached the magistrate he had done it with the best of intentions. There was a deep-seated worry that wouldn't be dismissed inside Harry that Maltravers would continue to watch Anna and perhaps when they were least expecting it he would strike. Harry wasn't sure what he thought Maltravers might do, but he had proved himself to be a malicious and cruel man, and the risk to Anna was significant. So he'd ploughed on despite knowing full well Anna would not like it.

He had underestimated how much value she put on her freedom to make decisions. Many times she'd told him that she didn't want a husband to order her around, to take charge of her business, but he hadn't listened, not properly. He'd thought the main reason she didn't want to marry again was because she was afraid to enter a relationship where she might be mistreated. Of course he would never hurt her, never raise a hand to her, and he thought Anna knew that. Now he was realising that she was more afraid of losing her independence than worrying he might strike her.

'She's refusing to see me,' Harry said, swinging his sword in a practised arc.

'So you're just going to give up?'

Panting hard as he defended himself when Rifield took a few attacking steps, Harry shook his head. No, he wasn't going to just give up.

'No,' Harry said, striking his friend's sword so hard the metal vibrated long after they'd disengaged.

'I need a drink.' Rifield placed his sword in its sheath and laid it on the grass, then disappeared inside the house to find a maid.

Harry allowed his body to slump on to the bench. They were in the garden of Rifield's London town house. It was a tiny patch of grass, barely big enough for their drills, but army life had taught them both to be adaptable and now they were used to fighting in such a confined area.

Rifield was right, of course; he wasn't going to just give up because Anna was refusing to see him.

'This takes me back,' Rifield said as he returned, trailed by a maid carrying two tall glasses of water. 'Practising swordplay while solving the problems of the world.'

Silently Harry gulped down his glass of water.

'Do you remember Blaauwberg?' Rifield asked quietly.

Harry nodded. It had been an unfair fight. Two British infantry brigades against a handful of Batavian troops and some local militia, fought on the side of the Blaauwberg mountain. The British army had taken Cape Town the next day, with surprisingly few casualties.

The Batavian General who had led the defence had retreated inland and Harry had been included in the party to negotiate his surrender. The first round of negotiations had failed, but then they'd tried a different method. Instead of drilling in the facts of the British superiority in numbers of troops, the hopelessness of the situation for the Batavians, Harry had suggested starting the next round of negotiations with a list of the concessions the British were willing to make. Highlighting the good instead of the bad.

As he sat there, remembering the hot lowlands and cool mountains of the Cape an idea began to form in Harry's mind. Rifield was right, he needed to show Anna just how much he was willing to sacrifice to have her in his life.

'You're a very astute man,' Harry murmured, clapping his friend on the back.

'Anything to stop you battering my sword arm. I don't think I can take any more drills with you in such a dark mood.'

Quickly Harry stood, handed over the sword he'd been using and strode towards the door.

'Next time I see you I'll be engaged,' he called over his shoulder. 'Properly engaged.'

Sacrifices, that was what he needed to highlight. Show Anna exactly what he was prepared to do for her, how he would protect her, even against himself.

Leaning back in the comfortable leather chair Harry declined the offer of a drink from the solicitor's assistant with a shake of his head.

'This is most irregular, Lord Edgerton,' Mr Crosby said. He was a tall man with a hawk-like nose and small eyes, giving his face a predatory appearance.

'I am aware how unusual my request is,' Harry said,

smiling at the man in front of him, 'but all I want to know is can you do it?'

'Well of course, it is just a matter of the right paper-work signed in front of witnesses, but I must caution you against this. Have you sought advice from anyone?'

'I do not need advice, Mr Crosby. My mind is quite made up.'

'And what do your family think of your proposal?'

Harry gave the solicitor a hard stare. 'I hardly think that is any of your concern. Now will you do as I ask or shall I take my business elsewhere?'

'As you wish, Lord Edgerton. The papers will be ready to sign in three days.'

Harry stood, holding out his hand for Mr Crosby to shake, then left the office with a spring in his steps and a whistle on his lips.

Anna sat stroking Apollo while Artemis frolicked around her feet. Morosely she stared out the window, half-hoping Harry would appear around the corner with a grin on his face and hard perseverance in his eyes. She'd done the right thing, sending him away, but that didn't mean it hadn't hurt. Even now, six days later she had a deep ache in her chest and a longing that seemed to come from her very soul.

'You're moping,' Beatrice announced as she twirled into the room.

Anna gave her cousin a weak smile but couldn't summon the energy to argue. She *was* moping.

'We've got a ball to go to this evening,' she said, running her critical gaze over Anna's red-rimmed eyes and flushed cheeks.

'I'm not going,' Anna said.

'Yes, you are.'

'Your father has sent a note to Mrs Towertrap, letting her know I am unwell and asking if she will be so kind as to chaperon you tonight.' The Towertrap girls were good friends with Beatrice and their mother had chaperoned her on numerous other occasions.

'I know. I sent one half an hour later saying I no longer needed a chaperon as you were feeling much improved.'

Anna blinked in surprise. 'Why?'

'Otherwise you'll sit around here moping for ever.'

'Is this one of Harry's schemes?' Anna asked. 'Has he told you to ensure I go to the ball so he can ambush me there?'

'No. Although I think you are being an utter fool, I wouldn't force you to see Lord Edgerton. Not when you're hurting so much.'

'Then why do you want me to go so badly tonight?'

Beatrice sighed a sigh of a much more mature woman. 'You're miserable, you're dwelling on whatever it is that's happened with Lord Edgerton, and sitting here by yourself is just making everything worse. Come to the ball with me. You might not have fun, but at least there will be something to distract you.'

Opening her mouth to refuse once and for all, Anna paused. She didn't want to go out. In truth, right now she didn't feel like she'd ever want to venture out of the safety of her uncle's house ever again, but there was a matter she needed to see to. In the eyes of the world she and Harry were still engaged. It would make the whole matter neater, more final, if she openly broke off the engagement.

It would have to be her to do it. Harry still thought he would be able to persuade her she'd made a mistake so he wasn't going to go around announcing to the world that they'd decided to go separate ways. No, she had to be the one to end things and the sooner she did it the easier it would be to move on.

Tears welled up in her eyes at the thought of never dancing with Harry again, never taking a stroll through the park or never hearing him bound up the rickety stairs to her little office at the docks.

'What time are we leaving?' Anna asked, summoning a little smile for Beatrice.

'Eight.'

Anna nodded, trying to keep her expression unreadable as her cousin scrutinised her. Tonight she would attend the ball and she would ensure the whole of society knew her and Harry's engagement was broken. Of course she would have to do it in such a way that cast Harry in the role of the injured party. He still had a chance at a happy future, a respectable wife. She had turned down the only man who could ever make her truly happy, so what did a little more malicious gossip about her matter.

Chapter Twenty-Six

Steeling herself for the unpleasant task ahead, Anna smiled warmly at the middle-aged gentleman in front of her. His name was Mr Warner and he had propositioned Anna on a few occasions in the past, mainly after she was widowed for a second time before she became Lady Fortescue. He was good-looking, well connected and likely the most arrogant man Anna had ever met. Their encounters in the past had consisted of Mr Warner paying her a few tepid compliments, talking about himself for a good long while, then suggesting they retire somewhere a little more private.

Anna hadn't seen the man for a couple of years, but he was perfect for what she had to do this evening.

'Of course I reminded the man of the penalty for trespassing and then had a quiet word with the magistrate.'

'What else could you do?' Anna murmured, laying a feather-light touch on Mr Warner's arm.

'Exactly. These riff-raff need to be reminded of the social order and their need to respect their betters.'

Anna suppressed the urge to tell Mr Warner exactly what she thought of his view on society and instead gave him an encouraging look, then dropping her eyes and biting her lip.

'Perhaps you would like a breath of fresh air,' Mr Warner suggested.

'It is rather warm…'

She allowed him to lead her out on to the terrace, shuddering as he placed a hand in the small of her back to guide her. For a moment she wondered if she could abandon her plan and just announce to the assembled guests that she and Lord Edgerton had called off the engagement. The idea of allowing Mr Warner's hands to roam over her body, his lips to meet hers, disgusted her, but she knew it was the only way to cause enough scandal and make Harry out as the victim. Then he would be free to marry someone respectable, someone who could give him the trust there should be between a husband and wife.

They strolled outside and Anna felt the chill of the evening air on her skin. It was a typical spring evening, overcast and threatening rain, but it did mean they had relative privacy on the terrace. Just as long as someone appropriate came out and caught them mid-kiss.

'I understood you were engaged to Lord Edgerton,' Mr Warner said as they paused at the edge of the terrace.

'A passing fancy, nothing more. We have decided to break the engagement,' Anna said, the words almost catching in her throat.

'Sensible decision. There was some big scandal with the family last year, something to do with Edgerton's sister…' he paused and brought her hand up to his lips '…and I am most pleased you are free to do as you wish. With whoever you wish.'

Anna watched as he glanced over his shoulder to ensure no one was observing them and then pulled her around the corner away from the lines of sight of the ballroom. Now if anyone exited through the doors on to the terrace they would have to step right up to the stone wall to catch a glimpse of her and Mr Warner.

'Perhaps we can come to some sort of arrangement,' Mr Warner said as he looped one arm around her waist and pulled her closer to him.

Anna worked hard to keep her expression impassive, not wanting to let him catch a glimpse of how repulsive she was finding the whole situation.

'Take your hands off my fiancée,' a low voice growled from somewhere in the shadows.

Guiltily Mr Warner and Anna jumped apart, both looking round for the source of the voice.

'Harry,' Anna whispered. He was standing behind her, half-hidden in the darkness, his hands bunched into fists.

'I thought…she said…' Mr Warner stuttered, his normally arrogant posturing replaced by meekness in the face of Harry's hostility. 'She said you were no longer engaged,' he managed eventually.

'Lady Fortescue is mistaken. We are still engaged. So I suggest you leave me and my fiancée in peace.'

Mr Warner glanced at Anna and then shrugged, as if it were too much bother to protest.

'Harry, it's not what it looks like,' Anna said, feeling the tears welling up in her eyes. The whole point of this little escapade was to be discovered, but she hadn't wanted Harry to be there when it happened.

He stepped towards her, emerging from the shadows like a predator stalking his prey. Anna felt an instant thrum of desire and knew that this reaction to him would never fade. That was why she'd been so keen to make him hate her. She couldn't bear to see him at social events and if he hated her then he might keep away.

Now she could see that her plan had been flawed. She didn't want him to hate her, couldn't bear the thought of him thinking she could be so fickle in her feelings.

'It looks like you were trying to seduce Mr Warner to create a scandal and publicly end our engagement, leaving me as the victim and free to marry some nice, respectable, dull young woman.'

Anna opened her mouth to protest, but realised he was pretty much right in every detail.

'I never thought she had to be dull,' she mumbled eventually.

'Praise be!' Harry exclaimed. 'For the woman I'm going to marry is anything but dull.'

She felt all her resolve slipping away as he reached out and took her hand.

'Harry…'

'Come here,' he said, his voice soft but authoritative. Anna felt her body sway towards him and before she could stop herself her lips were meeting his. He kissed her deeply, passionately, and for a long moment Anna forgot all the reasons they couldn't be together and lost herself in his embrace.

'Well, I never! The disgrace!' A voice came from behind them.

Slowly they broke apart, turning to see Mrs Winter, the middle-aged woman who had discovered them together all those weeks ago at the Prendersons' ball, glaring at them indignantly.

'Go away, Mrs Winter. I'm having a private moment with the woman I'm going to marry,' Harry said, turning away and taking Anna back into his arms. Anna had to suppress a giggle as she heard Mrs Winter huff in indignation. 'Where were we?' he murmured, and kissed her again.

'Harry…' Anna said as he pulled away after a few minutes.

'Hush. I know you're worried about marrying again and giving up your independence, your freedom to make all your own decisions.'

'I know you wouldn't treat me badly, Harry, it's not that.'

'I know, my love. I understand how few choices you were allowed to make in your last marriage and how hard you have fought to become independent now.'

'I can't give that up,' Anna said, her voice quavering.

'Do you trust me?'

Without any hesitation Anna nodded her head.

'Then I have something to show you.'

He took her by the hand and led her back along the terrace and into the ballroom. All eyes turned to them as they entered and Mrs Winter was talking loudly with her group of indignant friends.

They didn't stop to talk to anyone, just marched straight through the ballroom and out the front door.

'I'm meant to be chaperoning Beatrice,' Anna said, hesitating as Harry helped her up into his carriage.

He laughed. 'You must be the worst chaperon in London.'

He wasn't wrong. The number of times she'd left early or abandoned Beatrice in the middle of a ball and it wasn't as though she was setting a good example to her younger cousin either.

'I'll let you into a little secret,' Harry said. 'Your cousin helped me to get you here this evening. She knew you'd be leaving early and has made arrangements to stay under the watchful eye of Mrs Towertrap for the duration of the ball.'

'The sly little—' Anna started, cut off by Harry's

deep laugh. 'She assured me she wasn't scheming with you to get me to go to the ball.'

'She lied. She's very good at lying, I think.'

The carriage started moving, weaving slowly in and out of the rows of other waiting coaches, picking up speed a little as it got away from the house.

'I'm sorry about how I tried to end everything,' Anna said after a few minutes of silence, 'but nothing has changed, Harry. We still don't have a future together.'

'Give me ten minutes. Let me show you how much I care for you. And how much I respect you.'

Anna nodded. It was the least she could do after her antics of the evening, but she knew whatever it was Harry wanted to show her, whatever grand gesture he had made, it wouldn't be enough. Nothing could be.

They travelled in silence the rest of the journey to Harry's town house, sitting side by side, Anna's small hand engulfed by Harry's larger one. As they slowed to a halt he jumped down, helping her from the carriage before pulling her up the steps. Anna could see how eager he was to get inside.

'This way.' Once inside the house he led her to his study, a large, airy room filled with books and with a desk at one end. He led her to the desk and motioned for her to take a seat.

Lamps were burning, giving the room a warm glow, and several candles were dotted around in various nooks, meaning the documents on Harry's desk were well illuminated.

'I went to see my solicitor,' Harry said without any preamble. 'I explained our little impasse when it comes to the subject of marriage, and discussed how to get around it.'

'With your solicitor?'

Harry grimaced. 'He wasn't the most supportive, but he drew up the documents I asked him to nonetheless. Everything I show you tonight is legal and binding once we obtain your signature in the presence of a witness. I have already signed both documents.'

'Harry, what are you talking about?'

'This first document states that when we marry I will have no claim over the Trevels Shipping Company. I cannot make any decisions pertaining to it, withdraw any money from it or borrow against it. It will remain completely yours.'

Anna's eyes flitted over the legal document. It was written in complicated legal terms, but in her year running the shipping company she had become used to decoding difficult papers. Laid out on the three sheets of paper was the agreement that the Shipping Company and any profits from it were to remain solely Anna's property and Harry would never have any rights over them.

She glanced at Harry, trying to swallow over the lump that was forming in her throat. It was a lovely gesture, probably the most thoughtful and sincere thing anyone had ever done.

'Wait,' Harry said, 'there's more.'

He took a second set of papers from the pile and laid them in front of her.

'This document will be kept with a solicitor of your choice. You do not have to tell me where or who. It is a document that agrees to a divorce between us at any point in the future. It states you do not need to give a reason for the divorce, you do not need to prove adultery or anything similar. It gives you equal rights to any children we have during our married life together.'

Anna was frowning. She couldn't quite believe everything Harry was saying. Surely such a thing wasn't possible.

'It safeguards you entirely, Anna. It means we can marry without you worrying about becoming unhappy in the future. If I ever raised a hand to you, if I ever belittled and abused you, you could get out of the marriage without any difficulty.'

'Is it legal?' Anna asked.

'It is.'

She shook her head, her eyes flitting over the words. 'Why? Why would you do this?'

'I want to marry you, Anna. I want to love and protect you, and most of all I want to make you happy. This was the only way I could think of to make you see I will not take away your independence. We will be equal partners in everything, and if in a year you find you are unhappy, then I wouldn't want you to remain tied to me for ever. I would never deny you a divorce if you asked for it, but this document just gives you that extra reassurance that you will never suffer by being married to me.'

'It's not possible.'

'My solicitor advises me that it is. Highly irregular, but possible.'

She ran her hands over the two sets of documents, trying to process what had just occurred. In one swoop Harry had removed all the obstacles to them being together.

'If we married,' Anna said slowly, trying to ignore the giant smile on Harry's face, 'I would be free to carry on running the business? Free to make my own decisions?'

'I hope you'll run it, because I'm not allowed to.'

Anna stood abruptly and flung herself into Harry's arms.

'Yes, yes, yes,' she said, her voice muffled by the fabric of his jacket.

'I love you,' he said, dropping a kiss on the top of her head. 'And I promise every day I will strive to make you feel safe and loved.'

Reaching into his jacket pocket, he withdrew the ring she'd given back only a few days earlier and slipped it on to her finger.

'Is this really possible?' Anna asked, pulling away slightly to look up into Harry's face.

'It's not just possible. We're going to be married and within the month if I have my way.'

Nestling her head back into his chest, Anna glanced at the documents on the desk, wondering if she should just tear them up. A man who was willing to do so much for her wasn't going to try to stifle her independence. He loved her and she believed he would support her to do whatever was important to her.

She felt his fingers on her chin, tilting her face up for a kiss. Suddenly all thoughts of legal documents were wiped from her mind as she kissed the man she loved, the man who was going to become her fourth, and final, husband.

Epilogue

Hitching up the beautiful gold silks of her gown, Anna ignored the shouts from her cousin and ran down the length of the docks. Today was her wedding day and, despite her protestations that she didn't need a grand affair, Harry had insisted they celebrate their union in appropriate splendour.

The ceremony was to take place in less than an hour in the drawing room of her uncle's house. Harry had insisted on obtaining a special licence so they could enjoy their wedding in private, with just a few select guests attending.

Scanning the horizon, her eyes flitting over the ships sailing to and from London, she knew she should listen to Beatrice and return home. There was no excuse to be late to her own wedding.

'Thinking of hopping on a ship and sailing for Australia?' a low voice said into her ear, making her jump.

She spun around, allowing the surprise to register on her face as she looked into Harry's eyes.

'What are you doing here?' she asked.

'I could ask you the same. You should be spending your last minutes as an unmarried woman preparing for married life and instead I find you down at the docks, mixing with rowdy sailors.'

'Hardly rowdy,' Anna said, looking around. It wasn't yet ten o'clock and most of the sailors currently ashore hadn't slept off the excesses of the night before.

'Hardly respectable.'

'If you'd wanted respectable, you should have married Miss Wright.'

Harry dropped a kiss on her lips as he pulled her towards him. 'Perhaps I'll admit I like chasing you, never knowing where you're going to end up next.'

Anna turned back to the docks and motioned to the ship that had just appeared in the distance. 'The *Lady Magdalene*,' she said, a smile crossing her face. 'The ship I told you about, the one we nearly lost in the storm off the coast of Portugal.'

They watched as the sailors busied themselves on deck, shouting orders and scuttling about as the ship came in to dock.

'All the crew survived?' Harry asked.

Anna nodded her head. Since taking over the running of the Trevels Shipping Company they'd only had three fatalities among the crews of the various ships, much better than almost every other shipping company Anna knew, but still not as good as she wished their safety record to be. Still, she was making improvements all the time, and with the extra money she now had available from the settlements she'd been due from the late Lord Fortescue's will the company was going from strength to strength.

Marrying an earl did have its advantages, Anna had to admit. Harry had taken a few key people aside and murmured in their ears about the difficulties Anna was facing with the Fortescue children denying her the settlements that were due. Suddenly Anna's stepchildren had capitulated and the money was paid almost immediately.

'Let's go,' Anna said, taking Harry's arm.

'You don't want to stay and greet the captain?'

Anna shook her head, motioning to the middle-aged woman a hundred feet away.

'The captain will be more interested in seeing his wife. Perhaps we could come back after the ceremony, before we leave for our honeymoon.'

'Whatever you wish, my dear.'

They walked arm in arm back towards Beatrice, who was tapping her foot impatiently as she waited next to the carriage that had brought her and Anna to the docks. A few feet further away was Harry's own carriage.

'She's impossible,' Beatrice declared, addressing herself directly to Harry. 'Who runs off to the docks on their wedding day?'

'I wanted to see the *Lady Magdalene* returned safely.'

Beatrice shook her head in disbelief. 'And now I suppose you two are going to ride back into town together.' She held up her hand before either of them could say anything. 'No, I don't want to know any more. I'll stop the carriage around the corner so you can at least *appear* to arrive separately.'

Anna silently kissed her cousin on the cheek, watching as the younger woman hopped up into the carriage and instructed the driver to leave.

'Shall we get to our wedding, Lady Edgerton?' Harry asked, helping Anna up into his carriage.

'You're not having doubts?'

'No doubts at all. You?'

'Oh, lots,' she said breezily, 'but none that are going to stop me from marrying you.'

'I'm glad to hear it. Otherwise I might just have to kidnap you and whisk you away in the biggest scandal London society had seen in a decade.'

'I'll come quietly,' Anna said, leaning in to Harry and feeling the warmth spread through her as he placed his arm around her shoulder.

The carriage weaved its way through the docks, dodging the seamen and traders as they unloaded the cargo ships and whisked the goods away to the local warehouses. Anna looked back at the spot reserved for the *Lady Magdalene*, watching with contentment as the large ship docked and the sailors threw the ropes to the waiting men, ready to secure the storm-battered ship for unloading.

As they lurched forward, swerving to avoid a stray dog that dashed in front of the horses, Anna felt a swell of nausea in her stomach and had to close her eyes for just a minute. Placing one hand on her lower abdomen, she took a deep breath, steadying herself before opening her eyes again. It was another little sign, another little ray of hope. The nausea had been coming for four weeks now, never bad enough to make her vomit, but an almost constant disequilibrium that made her wonder if she might just be growing a little life inside her.

It was possible. She and Harry hadn't exactly had a chaste engagement. There had been that time before her uncle's dinner party when she and Harry had first been intimate. And then the time they'd been a little overcome with passion in the carriage…twice. And of course the time she had visited Harry's town house with the expectation of taking Lydia shopping, but had been cornered by her husband-to-be and they'd spent a wonderful afternoon in his rather masculine bedroom.

So a pregnancy was possible, it was just not something Anna had ever dared to hope for. Three marriages and no hint of a child, she'd assumed she was the one who was barren. Admittedly Lord Humphries had been quite elderly and Mr Trevels was barely in the country during their marriage. And Lord Fortescue hadn't been able to consummate their union, but still she'd assumed she had been the one unable to conceive.

She glanced at Harry. Soon she would tell him, but not yet. She barely dared to hope it might be true, so she didn't want to speak the words out loud. Instead she closed her eyes and leaned back into the strong arms of her husband-to-be.

Harry was whistling softly, stroking her arm and dropping the occasional kiss on her head. It would only be half an hour until they were home and the small number of guests would be gathered to watch them say their vows. The start of a new life.

'What happened to Mr Maltravers?' Anna asked quietly. Their carriage was just passing his office as she asked the question, keeping her demeanour calm and non-accusatory.

'I heard he decided to work on expanding his business on the Continent,' Harry said mildly.

'Did he have any help making that decision?'

'Will you still marry me if I say yes?'

Anna regarded him for a few seconds, searching his honest, open face and realising there wasn't much he could say to stop her from wanting to marry him.

'Yes.'

'I challenged Mr Maltravers to a duel,' Harry confessed.

Straightening, Anna turned to her fiancée and shook her head in disbelief.

'I challenged him to a duel. He refused. I told him

I would seek justice for his crimes, that he'd better remain vigilant at all times.'

'He believed you?' Anna asked, trying to suppress the smile forming on her face.

'He believed me.'

She supposed if you didn't know Harry well he *might* be able to convince someone he was a violent man. And an earl was a powerful enemy to make.

'I suggested he take a long trip to Europe and while he was there forget he ever knew you.'

'Thank you,' Anna said quietly. Despite her reluctance to involve a magistrate in the matter she had dwelled on what might happen in the future with Mr Maltravers. The idea of bumping into him in the docks or hearing his heavy footfalls ascending the staircase to her office had preyed on her mind, and now Harry had quietly and efficiently resolved everything. It was rather refreshing to have a husband who actually cared about her.

'I hear there are bookmakers in London taking bets as to how long before you dispose of me, now you're Lady Edgerton,' Harry murmured into Anna's ear, dodging the hand that swatted at him.

'How long do you think you've got?' Anna asked.

'I believe I can keep you interested for at least a few months.'

Anna regarded him seriously, looking over every inch of him with her businesswoman's eye.

'Perhaps a month or two, and then you'll have to go,' she said, her serious façade cracking as Harry nodded in agreement. 'Or perhaps I'll keep you for eternity.'

'Four husbands is quite enough,' Harry agreed. 'Any more would be greedy.'

'I wouldn't want to be greedy.'

'That's settled then, you'll remain Lady Edgerton for ever.'

They were sitting at the dining table, having a late wedding breakfast with their assembled guests. The ceremony had been a private affair, with only four guests, who were all sitting around the table talking amiably. Harry's mother hadn't been persuaded to leave the safety of Halstead Hall for the wedding, but Harry had his sister and Rifield as his guests. Rifield was deep in discussion with Anna's uncle, leaving the two young girls, Lydia and Beatrice, free to discuss whatever young women of eighteen talked about.

Harry ran a critical eye over his sister. She looked happy today, at least as happy as he'd seen her in a long time. She'd been with Anna to purchase a new dress and had allowed the maids to style her hair in the latest fashion. She didn't smile as much as Anna's cousin, or laugh in the same carefree way, but slowly he was starting to see flashes of the old Lydia returning. She was engaging a little more with the world now, seemed to spend less time inside her own head and more time experiencing what was going on around her. Slowly, Harry could see progress.

'She'll find her way back,' Anna said softly, nodding towards Lydia.

A few months ago Harry would have overanalysed a comment like that, wondering if it was possible, wondering if he was doing everything he could, but now he just nodded. He believed she *would* find her way back. It might take longer than he liked and she probably wouldn't be the same person as she had been two years ago, but that wasn't the end of the world either. Together they would make it through and one day he would be able to look back on these past couple of years and realise what a small part of their lives they had been.

'I would like to propose a toast,' Rifield said, standing and raising his glass. 'To the happy couple, Lord and Lady Edgerton.'

Everyone around the table stood and raised their glasses and Harry felt a moment of complete happiness. He had just married the woman he loved and was surrounded by people who cared about them both. What more could a man ask for?

'No killing this one off until we've had a rematch,' Rifield said to Anna. 'The last time we went through our sword drills he made me look like a beefy drunkard and that's not how I want to remember our friendship.'

'Slander my wife one more time, Rifield, and I'll make you look worse than a beefy drunkard,' Harry said with a grin.

'Forgive me, Lady Edgerton. I was wrong,' Rifield said with a little bow. 'Dispose of him as soon as you see fit, perhaps even before you leave for your honeymoon.'

Harry felt Anna's hand take his own, her fingers lacing in between his.

'The *ton* will have to find someone else to gossip about,' Anna said serenely. 'From now on I'm going to be the perfect embodiment of respectability.'

Unable to resist, Harry leaned down and whispered in his new wife's ear, 'We'd better hope our baby isn't born *too* early then, otherwise the gossips will be talking again.'

The hand that flew to her lower abdomen confirmed what Harry had suspected for the past week. Anna was carrying his child. The bouts of nausea, the subtle changes in her body, the lack of her monthly courses, all had made Harry suspect, but now he knew. Soon there would be another addition to their family.

'I'm not sure,' Anna said quietly.

'I am.'

'I don't know if I can…'

'You can. You were just waiting for the right time. The right husband.'

'And that's you?' There was a twinkle of humour in her eyes.

'That's me.'

* * * * *

A RING FOR THE PREGNANT DEBUTANTE

For Luke and Jack. You keep me smiling.

Chapter One

Rosa lifted her head from the pillow as the door opened and looked at the unappetising bowl of stew before turning her gaze to her odious cousin. He watched her as she dismissed first the dinner and then him, a cold contempt behind his eyes.

'You should be grateful for the scraps I bring you,' Antonio Di Mercurio sneered as he flung the bowl of brown slop on to the rickety wooden table. 'Whores don't deserve to eat with the rest of the family.'

'Would it hurt you to be civil?' Rosa replied in her broken Italian. She tried to remain aloof, but could already feel the anger threatening to take over. Her cousin had been needling her for the past four weeks, trying to provoke some kind of reaction, and Rosa knew it wouldn't be long before he succeeded. There were only so many insults she could turn the other cheek to before retaliating.

'Civil? Maybe you should work on being less civil. Might save the family from further shame in the future.' Antonio laughed heartily at his joke, made the protective sign against the evil eye with his hands and turned to leave.

Rosa picked up the bowl Antonio had just set down and flung it at her malicious cousin, but he was already out of the room and the dinner splatted against the closed door. Letting out a growl of annoyance, Rosa flopped back on the bed and tried to relax. She knew she shouldn't let Antonio upset her so much, but it was difficult being in a foreign country with people she didn't know. The Di Mercurios might be her family on her mother's side, but they didn't act warm or loving. In the four weeks she'd been staying in the villa in Italy not one of them had said a single kind word towards her.

Rosa suddenly sat up straight and looked at the door. In Antonio's haste to avoid her flying dinner he might have forgotten to lock it. She didn't remember hearing the click or the grating of the metal key in the ancient lock. Hardly daring to hope, Rosa stood and crossed the room. She gripped the handle, wondering whether it was a trick, an unkind ruse planned by her cousin to give her the hope of freedom.

Knowing she couldn't give up on even the slightest chance of escaping her imprisonment, Rosa pushed down on the handle and nearly cried out with happiness as the door opened. Quickly she glanced out into the corridor and saw it was deserted; the Di Mercurio family had no need to station a guard outside her door when they kept it locked all day and night.

Rosa carefully closed the door and rested her head against the rough wood. This was her one and only chance to escape. For twenty-three hours a day she was locked in this small chamber, only let out for one hour's exercise around the grounds daily. When outside her room she was always watched closely by one of her numerous uncles or cousins, all intent on keeping her hidden from the world so she wouldn't bring shame to their family. So now really was her only chance and she wouldn't let the nerves that were bubbling away inside her spoil it.

Grabbing her travelling cloak, Rosa collected together the few items she felt she couldn't leave behind and made a neat bundle. Just before leaving the room she pushed her hand under her mattress and removed the small purse of money she'd managed to keep hidden throughout her journey to Italy and subsequent imprisonment in the villa. Then, without a backwards glance at the room that had been her prison cell for the past month, Rosa darted out into the courtyard.

The garden was shrouded in an inky blackness and it took Rosa's eyes a few minutes to adjust. Luckily she knew this part of the grounds from her daily exercise excursions from her room and as she felt her way along the villa wall an escape route began to form in her mind.

'Don't be like that, Maria.' Antonio's voice carried through the night.

Rosa stiffened, her heart pounding in her chest so loudly she thought the whole world must be able to hear.

'I never promised this would be anything more than a few nights of fun. You're only a maid after all.'

Rosa couldn't hear the words of Maria's reply, but she understood the gist of her feelings from the tone. No doubt Antonio had implied he would give the servant much more than a quick fumble. Normally Rosa would have stormed over and confronted her cousin, but tonight she had to be selfish. She couldn't bear to be locked up for another five months, but more importantly she wouldn't let the Di Mercurios snatch her baby away and send it to live with some other family. Going forward, Rosa would have to be selfish, it wasn't just her own future she was fighting for now.

Creeping softly through the night, Rosa moved further away from the villa, making sure she kept the perimeter wall to her right. She was heading for a huge lemon tree at the southernmost corner of the grounds. There she was confident she could make it over the wall and to freedom, and even the most vigilant of her family wouldn't be able to see her climbing the tree that far from the house.

With the lemon tree looming above her Rosa checked she hadn't been followed before testing out the branches. There was no movement from the villa, even Antonio and his disappointed maid had fallen quiet and Rosa concluded they must have returned inside.

Rosa had been climbing trees since she was a little girl, but concern for the baby inside her made her pause and evaluate for a moment longer. Knowing she had no choice, she hiked up her skirt and began to climb. Within two minutes she was sitting on the stone wall, regarding the drop on the other side. It was further down than on the villa side of the wall, due to a sloping of the land, maybe six or seven feet. There was a rough path running alongside the wall with nothing to cushion her drop. She could probably jump without doing herself too big an injury, but the tiny life inside her was another matter. Maybe if she lowered herself slowly whilst holding on to the top of the wall she would be safe.

She was still contemplating her options as she heard movement coming along the path. Footsteps and a low whistling became gradually louder as Rosa pressed herself into the stone and wondered what to do. At this height whoever was approaching might not see her, but if they happened to look up for any reason her escape attempt would be ruined.

The whistling got louder and Rosa knew there was nothing for it but to climb back over the wall until the man had passed. It went against every instinct to return to the grounds of her prison, but she kept telling herself it was only temporary. In a few minutes she would be back on top of the wall and on her way to freedom.

As she swung her legs over she felt herself toppling slightly. With the extra weight she was now carrying around her middle her equilibrium was off just slightly and as she windmilled her arms to try to regain her balance Rosa knew it wasn't going to be enough. With a scream she fell backwards, wrapping her arms protectively around her belly and praying for a miracle.

Thomas felt his breath knocked from his lungs as something careened into him from above. One moment he'd been walking along lost in thought and the next he was flattened, unable to move.

'Oooh…' a soft voice moaned on top of him.

Thomas reached up and his hand met soft fabric. If he wasn't much mistaken there was a woman lying on top of him, but he had no idea where she had come from.

'Excuse me,' he said in Italian eventually when the woman made no attempt to move. He almost laughed at the stiff formality of the words—even after three years of living abroad you still couldn't remove his innate good manners.

There was some wriggling, then fingers digging into his ribcage as she manoeuvred herself upright. Thomas watched in a daze as the young woman ran her hands over her body as if checking for bumps and bruises, caressing her abdomen through the material of her dress.

'Are you hurt?' she asked eventually, once Thomas could see she was satisfied she had not injured herself in any obvious way. She spoke in Italian, but there was an accent that made him wonder if she was not native to this part of the world.

Testing out his theory, Thomas replied in English, 'Just a little winded.'

'You're English.'

He could hear the note of fear in her voice and noticed how she begun to lean away from him as if he were about to do her harm.

'Yes,' he replied tersely. 'Would you mind letting me up?'

'Oh,' the young woman said, mortification in her voice as she looked down and realised she was still straddling him. Quickly she stood, but as she transferred her weight to her left foot she cried out in pain. From his position on the ground Thomas saw her stumble and then come lurching back towards him. This time it was her elbow that caught him in the stomach and a slender knee in the groin area. For a moment Thomas felt the whole world blur with pain before he was back on the dusty country road with a woman on top of him.

'I'm sorry,' the young woman mumbled, too focused on her own pain to realise the extent of the damage she had inflicted on him.

Thomas just grunted, lying still until the ache had subsided, before gripping the young woman around the waist and firmly setting her on the road beside him.

Before deciding what to do next, he regarded the

woman in front of him for a few moments. She was dusty and dishevelled, and at the moment her face was screwed up with pain, but if Thomas wasn't much mistaken this was no common thief or intruder trying to escape the Di Mercurio property. She was too well dressed, her bearing and her speech too polished.

'Why did you jump off the wall?' Thomas asked.

Immediately he saw the young woman bristle.

'I didn't jump. I fell.'

'Let me rephrase the question. Why were you climbing over the wall in the first place?'

'That is none of your concern,' she said primly.

Thomas watched her for a few seconds and then shrugged nonchalantly. He wasn't about to browbeat the information from her, but she would tell him.

'Would you like me to escort you back to the Di Mercurio villa, or fetch someone to come and get you?' he asked lightly.

He actually saw the pallor bloom on her face as the blood drained away.

'Please do not concern yourself,' she said. 'I'll just get on my way and you can continue with your evening.'

'You will need my help…' he motioned to her left ankle '… I'd wager you won't get far on your own.'

'Truly, please do not let me detain you further,' she said with exaggerated politeness. Thomas could see he was beginning to irk her, but found himself unable to stop with his goading. He was enjoying this interaction more than he had any for months now.

He looked on with interest as she tottered to her feet, grimaced and bit down forcibly on her lower lip, presumably to stop her crying out in pain as she tried to put weight on her left foot. Thomas's concern turned to amusement as she began hopping down the road and he had to stop himself from laughing out loud.

'I don't think anyone has ever gone to such lengths to avoid my company before,' he mused loudly as he pushed himself upright and began to stroll along beside her.

She didn't even spare him a look, just hopped resolutely onwards.

'I hope you didn't need to be somewhere in a hurry. You're rather slow at hopping.' This did earn him a glance, but no conversation.

Suddenly she stopped, changed direction and hopped unsteadily to the side of the road. Thomas watched with interest as she hefted a heavy fallen branch from the ground and tested it as a makeshift crutch. It didn't look that helpful.

'So let me guess,' he said as she staggered onwards. 'You're a disgraced maid and you stole the family silver.'

'Don't be ridiculous.'

Two more steps, then she rested, looking back over her shoulder and appearing disappointed with how little progress they'd made.

'You're being forced to marry one of the unpleasant Di Mercurio boys and you're fleeing on the eve of the wedding.'

'That would be a very good reason to run,' the young woman muttered under her breath.

'I've got it,' Thomas exclaimed. 'They were going to offer you up as a ritual sacrifice to the devil.'

'Why are you following me?' she demanded.

'I thought you might need some assistance.'

She stared at him with wide eyes and motioned to the nearly useless crutch. 'You're not providing any assistance so will you just leave me alone.'

'I *could* provide you with assistance,' Thomas said with a charming smile, 'If you ask nicely. And tell me what you were doing climbing over the wall.'

She had a stubborn streak running through her, Thomas mused as she limped a few more paces with her head held high before relenting.

'I was being held prisoner. Now, please will you help me?'

'Well, that wasn't the most gracious of pleas, but a gentleman can overlook these things.' Thomas scooped her up into his arms, hiding a grin at her squeal of surprise and the initial stiffness of her body. 'Where to, my lady?'

No reply was forthcoming and Thomas could see the thoughts tumbling through her head. For some reason she had felt she was being held prisoner by the well-to-do Di Mercurios and had manufactured her escape, but he would wager his entire inheritance that she hadn't really planned beyond getting over the wall.

'Maybe to the residence of the local magistrate so you could report your imprisonment?' Thomas suggested, suppressing a smile as she tensed. 'Or we could go straight to the *governatore*, the man in charge, seeing as they are such an influential family in the region.'

Still no reply from the woman in his arms.

'What's your name?' he asked.

'Miss Rosa Rothwell.'

'Well, Rosa,' he said, enjoying her scowl of indignation at his use of the overfamiliar form of address, 'it is decision time. What's the plan?'

'I would be grateful if you would take me to a local *pensione*,' she said decisively.

'I don't like to criticise a well-thought-out plan, but

won't the village guest house be the first place the Di Mercurios look for their runaway?'

'I will ask the owner to be discreet.'

'It will all come down to who has the bigger purse, you or the wealthiest landowners around the lake.'

Rosa fell quiet again and Thomas adjusted his grip on the pensive young woman in his arms.

'Are you sure you can't sort this feud out with the Di Mercurios?' Thomas asked softly, the levity gone from his voice. 'It would be the easiest way.'

'No.' The force behind that one short word told Thomas all he needed to know about Rosa's predicament. She was in trouble, real trouble, and it wasn't going to be sorted with an apology and a friendly handshake. He couldn't imagine the Di Mercurios had actually kept Rosa locked up, they were a respected and important family, but he was well aware he didn't know the details. 'I need to get away from here,' Rosa said quietly. 'I need to get back to England.'

Thomas quickened his pace along the dusty road and felt Rosa squirm in his arms.

'Where are we going?' she asked.

'I'm renting a villa about a mile from here,' Thomas said. 'You will stay tonight and arrangements can be made in the morning.'

'I'm not sure that is an appropriate—'

'You don't really have a choice,' Thomas interrupted her. 'It's this or the Di Mercurios finding you within the hour.'

'I am a young woman of a good family,' Rosa said stiffly.

'Trust me, there is nothing further from my mind than ravishing you. You'll be perfectly safe.'

Not that she wasn't pretty enough, in a wholesome, innocent sort of way, but Thomas had not been tempted in a long time and he wasn't going to let this dishevelled young woman be the reason he stepped off his predestined path.

Chapter Two

Thomas set her down gently on a wooden chair positioned on the terrace to the rear of his rented villa. Rosa was momentarily mesmerised by the view over the lake to the mountains beyond, the inky blackness of the water giving way to the solid outlines of the snowy peaks silhouetted against the starry sky. Although she'd been in Italy for a month she hadn't seen past the walls of the Di Mercurio villa since her arrival.

'Beautiful, isn't it?' Thomas commented as he caught her looking at the view.

She regarded her host for a few moments, trying to decide what she thought of him. He was confident and arrogant, a man used to getting his own way. She had bristled earlier when he'd made the decisions about her immediate future without really consulting her, but she'd bitten her tongue because…well, because she didn't have anywhere else to go.

'Who are you?' Rosa asked as she took in the expensive furniture and no doubt expensive view.

'Hunter. Lord Thomas Hunter. It is a pleasure to make

your acquaintance, Miss Rosa Rothwell.' Her name sounded seductive on his tongue.

'Do you live alone here?' Rosa asked.

'Don't worry,' Thomas said, flashing her a lazy grin, 'I meant what I said, your virtue is safe.'

Rosa instinctively laid a hand on top of her lower abdomen, stroking the fabric of her dress and thinking of the growing life that was to be her ruin. She'd lost her virtue long ago, but that didn't mean she couldn't hold some moral values. Staying in a house alone with a single, rather attractive gentleman was certainly on the list of *Things a Young Lady Must Never Do* that her mother had often recited to her when she was younger. Nevertheless, here she was, without any other option and ready to put her fate and her already sullied virtue into the hands of Lord Thomas Hunter. Her mother would be appalled.

Lord Hunter disappeared for a few minutes before re-emerging from the villa holding a bottle of wine and two glasses. Rosa watched as he pulled out the cork and filled both glasses, before pushing one towards her.

'So, tell me, whatever have you done to make the Di Mercurios lock you away?' He held up a hand as he took a mouthful of wine. 'No, no, no. Let me guess. It's more fun that way.'

'It's a private matter,' Rosa said, watching as Hunter leaned back in his chair and swung both feet on to the table.

'Did you steal something?'

Rosa refused to be drawn in and focused instead on her wine glass.

'Something more scandalous, then,' Hunter mused.

'Did you insult one of the old women, the ones that look like mean English Bulldogs?'

'Those *old women* are my grandmother and great-aunt.'

'Oh, I am sorry. Well, maybe you won't be quite so wrinkly when you're older. All is not lost.' He paused, then pushed on, 'So they're family, are they? The plot thickens.'

Rosa took a sip of wine and felt the warmth spreading out from the throat and through her body. It was warming and delicious and already a little intoxicating.

'I was sent here in disgrace,' she said eventually.

'Your family sent you all the way to Italy? You must have done something pretty unsavoury for that amount of distance to be required.'

She supposed getting pregnant before marriage was pretty disgraceful, her mother at least had enough to say on the matter. Rosa was *a disgusting harlot, an ungrateful wretch* and *as bad as a common streetwalker.* The strange thing was, despite having been brought up with her mother's strict set of moral values, Rosa didn't feel disgusting or unsavoury, and she couldn't summon anything but warmth for the small life blossoming inside her.

Uninvited tears sprung to her eyes at the thought of the venom in her mother's voice as she'd told her she never wanted to see Rosa, or her child, ever again. They'd always had a difficult relationship, but the finality of her mother's goodbye had hurt Rosa more than she would have imagined.

What had hurt even more had been the look of shock on her father's face when Rosa had admitted her pregnancy. She and her father had always shared a close and loving relationship. It was her father, not her mother, who had played with her as a child, who often would call her into his study so they could spend hours discussing books. So when he'd been unable to rally on hearing the news that his only daughter was expecting a child out of wedlock Rosa had felt her heart rip in two.

Dipping her head, Rosa quickly blinked away the tears. She would not cry in front of a stranger, not about something that could not be changed.

'I suppose it was unsavoury,' she said, smiling sadly.

'The Di Mercurios were meant to look after you?' Hunter asked and Rosa was glad of his change of direction.

Rosa shrugged. She didn't know what their instructions had been, but as soon as she had arrived it had been made clear she was not a welcomed guest.

'They locked me in my room for a month.'

'And fed you gruel, no doubt.'

She looked at him sharply, wondering if he was mocking her, but saw the joviality that had filled his eyes earlier had gone.

'Well, sometimes they treated me to stew and a stale piece of bread.'

'How generous. No wonder you wanted to escape.'

Rosa looked past her host, out over the dark water and to the night beyond and knew she would have put up with the cruelty if it hadn't been for the threat of losing her child. On one of her daily walks around the grounds a maid had sidled up to her and whispered, 'Don't worry, *signorina*, the family they have chosen are kind and loving. Your little one will be well looked after.'

The girl had risked a beating for just talking to her and the words had meant to be reassuring, but Rosa had felt her heart fill with dread and known there and then she needed to escape. No one would take her child from her. She would fight with every ounce of strength and determination in her body and nothing would keep them apart.

'So what is the plan, Rosa Rothwell?' Hunter asked.

'I will seek passage to England.'

'Back to the family that sent you here?'

Rosa grimaced. She had no doubt her mother would pack her straight back to Italy the moment she turned up on the doorstep.

'I have a good friend who will take me in, I just need to get to her.'

Rosa was aware of Hunter's eyes scrutinising her. He did it brazenly, as if he didn't even consider it would make her uncomfortable, or he wasn't concerned if he did. Roaming eyes taking in her every movement, her every expression, making her feel exposed and as if he knew all of her secrets.

'Time for bed,' Hunter said abruptly, standing and draining the dregs of wine from his glass.

Rosa was just about to say she would stay on the terrace a while longer when Hunter's strong arms whisked her up from her seat and carried her over the threshold into the villa.

'What are you doing?' Rosa asked indignantly.

'Taking you to bed.'

'Put me down.'

He ignored her, manoeuvring round the furniture in a plushly decorated living room before kicking open the door to a bedroom. Quickly he strode into the room and deposited her on the rather inviting four-poster bed.

'I might not want to go to sleep,' Rosa said.

Hunter shrugged. 'You're here now.'

Rosa clenched her jaw to stop the flow of uncomplimentary phrases that were trying to escape.

'Only because...' Rosa began, then stared in surprise as Hunter left the room, closing the door behind him. It was difficult to have an argument with a man who refused to listen half the time.

Rosa nearly struggled to her feet, thinking she would hop back out on to the terrace just to show she couldn't be ordered around and sent to bed like a child, but her body was already sinking into the soft mattress and freshly laundered sheets. Tomorrow she would stand up to Lord Hunter, tomorrow she would thank him for his assistance but firmly insist she go her own way from now on. Tonight she was going to enjoy the comforts of Lord Hunter's guest room and rather welcoming bed.

Chapter Three

Thomas tossed and turned, throwing the light sheet from his bed with a growl of frustration. It was nearly dawn yet he hadn't slept for more than a couple of hours and now he felt groggy and unsettled.

Reaching out to the small table beside his bed he picked up the well-read letter, the real reason for his disturbed night. Every time he read the now-familiar words his conscience collided with his more selfish needs and he came away uncertain as to what course of action to take. And if there was one thing Thomas didn't like it was uncertainty. With a sigh he sat up in bed and started to read again, wondering if he was just punishing himself or hoping for divine inspiration, a new point of view, knowing the words and the pleas would still be the same as all the other times he'd read it.

My darling son,
I hope you are well and are finding what you need
to soothe your soul on your travels. It has been
three years and eight months since I last set eyes
on you—one thousand three hundred and forty-

five days since you left. You must know I don't blame you for leaving—I actively encouraged you to go—but I miss you every minute of every day that you are gone.

I am keeping as well as can be expected. My friends ask when I will come out of mourning... when I will start to move on. They don't understand what it is like to lose a husband and a son. I don't think anyone does, apart from you.

Ever since you left I have tried to be patient, tried to allow you to grieve and come to terms with the uncertain future in your own way. You know I have never pressured you to return, never pushed your responsibilities or the estate's need for a master. I truly hoped you would find peace on your travels, revel in new experiences and return to me with a renewed passion for life, but three years and eight months is a long time to wait and now I want my son home.

I'm lonely, Thomas. I'm surrounded by friends, by extended family, by servants I have known for half my life, but without you it all seems empty. So I have decided to be selfish. I know you have lost a father and a brother, and I know you've needed to come to terms with a possibly cruel and difficult future, but now I ask that you think of me.

Come home to me. Fill the house with laughter once again. Allow yourself to think about the future, to hope. A wife and child might be too much to ask, I know that, but please consider returning home and taking up your birthright.

I live in hope that I might embrace you in my arms one day soon.
Your loving mother

He wanted to put the letter out of his mind, to forget the hurt and loneliness that must have triggered his mother to write in this way after allowing him to fulfil his own wanderlust for nearly four years without a word of protest. She had been the one who'd encouraged him to leave in the first place, who'd urged him to travel and experience a bit of the world so he would have no regrets about his own life. Thomas knew soon he would have to return to England, return to the memories and the half-empty family home. He was not cold-hearted enough to refuse a direct plea from his mother.

A swim, that was what he needed, a bracing and refreshing start to the new day. Maybe then he could find it in himself to start planning the long journey back home. Thomas jumped out of bed, grabbed a towel and tucked it loosely around his waist. He padded barefoot through the villa, resolutely not looking at the closed door to the guest room, and out on to the terrace. Even though the sun's rays were just beginning to filter over the horizon Thomas could already feel the heat in the air. It would be another scorching day, the type that sometimes made him long for the cool breezes and cloudy skies of England.

It only took him thirty seconds to reach the lake, two more to stretch and brace himself for the icy shock of the water and then he dropped his towel to the ground and dived in. The blackness consumed him immediately and as Thomas glided deeper he could barely make out the shape of his hands a few inches in front of his face. The water skimmed over his skin, washing away the remnants of the restless night and invigorating him for a new day. Forty seconds in and his lungs began burning, but still he glided deeper. Fifty seconds and he felt the tremor in his muscles from lack of air. Sixty seconds and little grey spots began to appear before his eyes. One more pull of his arms, and then another, the ultimate test of his mind's control over his body. Only when his head began to spin did Thomas relent and kick powerfully to the surface, breaking free of the water and taking in huge gulps of air.

He floated on his back for a while, allowing his body to recover and his breathing to return to normal. As the sun started to rise over the hills and reflect off the water's surface Thomas began to swim. He took long, leisurely strokes, propelling himself through the water at a moderate speed and focusing on the horizon.

This was his favourite time of day, whilst he was powering through the water he could plan and reflect without any distractions. It was just him, the early morning air and the silent lake.

He swam for about fifteen minutes before turning back, the villa now the size of a model house on the banks of the lake. It was still peaceful, but there were signs of life stirring around the edge of the lake. A farmer's cart trundled along the dusty track, kicking up a plume of dirt. A young boy chased an eager dog down to the water's edge and further away to his left the sleepy village was beginning to show signs of activity.

As Thomas reached the edge of the lake he paused, turning to look out over the murky blue water before pulling himself up the old wooden ladder on to the shore.

It was getting light when Rosa awoke and for a few moments she allowed herself to lie in bed and watch the soft light of dawn streaming in through the windows. She wasn't a natural early riser—at home she would

often indulge in breakfast in bed late in the morning—
but these last couple of months she had found herself
waking early with an entrenched sensation of nausea
that could only be cured by a cold glass of water and
something to eat.

Rosa knew she was lucky, many women at her stage
of pregnancy spent their days vomiting and confined to
their beds. A little early morning nausea was not something that stopped her from getting on with her day at
least.

Rising slowly, Rosa straightened her dress, aware of
the creases from where she'd slept fully clothed, and
patted the loose strands of hair into place. She took a
moment to examine her ankle, which had swollen over-
night and had a purple hue to the stretched skin. Even
placing it lightly on the floor made her wince in pain,
but she gritted her teeth and managed to hobble to the
door, leaning heavily on furniture as she went.

Outside her bedroom the villa was quiet and Rosa
sensed she was alone. Of course Lord Hunter would be
an early riser, he was just the type to be cheery at an
ungodly time in the morning. Rosa was just about to
admit defeat and flop into a chair when she spotted an
ornate walking cane leaning up against the wall next to
her bedroom door. Hunter must have put it there after
he'd bid her goodnight, ready for her to use this morning.

Grasping the carved knob, Rosa tested the cane out,
finding she could walk a little better with the extra balance it gave her, although the pain was still there. She
would have to remember to thank Lord Hunter for his
kindness.

Not wanting to rummage through his cupboards, but
desperate for something to eat, Rosa ventured outside

on to the terrace. She recalled from the night before the large orange tree overhanging the seating area and her empty stomach growled at the thought of a juicy orange to start the day.

Rosa had to stretch to reach even the lowest branch, but her efforts were rewarded when she began to peel a ripe and fragrant orange and popped the first segment into her mouth. Chewing slowly, she savoured the sweet juice, licking the remnants off her fingers before biting into a second segment. She had to stop herself from wolfing the whole orange down in a few seconds as she peeled the remainder of the skin from the flesh it was so delicious, but somehow she managed to resist the urge. With the first orange gone Rosa stretched up and plucked a second from the branches of the orange tree, grasped hold of her cane again and limped to the edge of the terrace.

As she looked out over the lake, admiring how the sun reflected off the smooth surface making the water look blessed by the gods, her eyes came to rest on the small figure propelling himself towards the villa. He was swimming quickly, but in a way that looked as though it required hardly any effort on his part. As he got closer Rosa realised it was her host, Lord Hunter. She almost laughed—she'd known he would be a morning person, he probably swam a mile first thing every morning whilst she would normally be languishing in bed.

Rosa watched as he approached the shore, mesmerised by the rhythmic movement of his arms and the effortless way he glided through the water. She'd felt the hard muscles of his arms and chest when he'd picked her up yesterday and wondered if this was how he stayed quite so toned.

With a final pull of his arms Hunter reached the small wooden jetty that jutted out from the grounds of the property. Rosa could see his shoulders bobbing up and down as he gripped the ladder and began to pull himself out.

Time slowed and Rosa found she couldn't look away. Inch by inch Hunter's body rose from the water, his chest, his abdomen, the water pouring off him and leaving his skin shimmering. Rosa felt the heat begin to rise from her core as her eyes locked on to Hunter's naked form. Only when he pulled himself fully out of the water did Rosa realise he wasn't wearing anything at all, but still she couldn't look away. He stood, indifferent to his nakedness, seemingly unconcerned that anyone might see him, and brushed the water from his skin before picking up a towel and wrapping it around his waist.

Only then did he glance up to the terrace. Rosa knew the moment he saw her, the moment he realised she must have been watching him the entire time. For a fraction of a second his whole body went still, like a wolf catching sight of its prey, then he raised a hand and waved cheerily at her.

She wished she could just disappear, that an earthquake would open up the ground underneath her and she could fall inside. He would think that she had been watching him. Well, she *had* been watching him, but not purposefully. She wasn't to know he swam naked, but now she looked like a shameless voyeur.

'Good morning,' Hunter said with a smile as he approached the terrace.

'Good morning,' Rosa managed to mumble, trying to look anywhere but the expanse of exposed skin at her eye level. He was tanned, wonderfully so, his skin a deep bronze hinting to the length of time he'd spent in warm climes.

'Did you sleep well?'

How could he ask such a mundane and ordinary question when he was standing there half-naked in front of her?

Forcing herself to look up and meet his eye, Rosa smiled.

'Very well, thank you.'

Her cheeks were burning so much it felt as though she'd just stepped out of a blacksmith's forge and her heart was beating so loudly she was sure it could be heard for miles, but if Hunter refused to be embarrassed by his lack of clothing then she would not let her discomfort show.

'Isn't the view beautiful first thing in the morning?'

Unbidden, her eyes flicked down to where the towel was tucked around his waist and Rosa heard him utter a low chuckle.

'I find the early morning light to be the most flattering,' Rosa said, watching as Hunter's grin widened.

'Everything looks even better from the middle of the lake,' he said, moving a step closer, 'You should join me next time. A swim can really get the blood pumping at this time of day.'

Rosa was sure he knew exactly what he was doing, no young woman from a good family would feel comfortable standing here talking about the weather and the view with a man she'd just seen emerge naked from the lake, but Hunter was pushing her, seeing how much it would take to make her flee in embarrassment or swoon. Well, she'd never swooned in her life and a little bit of naked flesh wasn't about to make her run. Even if it was particularly smooth and sculpted flesh.

'I can think of better ways to exert myself so early in the morning,' she said with a sweet smile. Without glancing at his face Rosa limped back over to the orange tree and plucked another of the round fruit from the branches. Carefully she began to peel it, worked a segment free and only when she was about to pop it between her lips did she look up and meet Hunter's eye. 'Can't you?'

It was, oh, so satisfying to see him lost for words, his eyes glued on the orange segment as it passed her lips. Allowing herself a small, triumphant smile, Rosa turned and headed back to the villa, her walk of victory only slightly spoiled by the clicking of the cane on the tiles.

Chapter Four

❦

'Last night you were telling me about the disgrace that had your family disowning you,' Thomas said as he helped Rosa up into the curricle.

'No,' Rosa said pointedly, 'I wasn't.'

'Well, we've got an hour's ride to the village of Malcesine, and it will be a terribly dull journey if you sit in silence the whole way.'

Thomas had suggested a day trip to the next sizeable village around the lake when Rosa had talked about seeking a passage back to England. The Di Mercurios would no doubt be searching for their runaway prisoner and there was no point in making it easy for them. In Malcesine they would find the date and time of the next coach leaving for one of the port cities where Rosa would be able to buy a fare home.

'You could tell me what you're doing hiding away in Italy,' Rosa suggested with that sweet smile she used when she was determined to get her own way.

'What if we play a game?'

'I'm listening.'

'We each get three questions. The other has to answer truthfully and fully.'

'I get to go first?' Rosa asked.

'Ask away.'

She sat in silence for a while, watching the countryside passing by and pressing her lips together as she thought. Thomas glanced at her every now and again. Ever since he'd caught her looking at him as he emerged from the lake he'd felt a spark of excitement, a slowly building intrigue at the woman hiding beneath the composed façade. He felt he needed to be close to her, to touch her, to find out what was really going on behind those calm, cool eyes. It wasn't often Thomas met a woman he could fully engage with intellectually. So many of the debutantes his mother had introduced him to before he'd fled England had seemed to want to appear less intelligent than they actually were, wittering on about the weather or the latest fashion. Admittedly he didn't know Rosa well, but there was something more to her—something bold, something that refused to back down.

'Why do you live in Italy?' Rosa asked eventually.

'I like it here.'

She shook her head and actually wagged an admonishing finger at him like some disapproving elderly aunt. 'You're breaking the rules,' she said. 'You said we had to answer truthfully and fully. Why do you live in Italy?'

Thomas broke out into a grin. 'You caught me. I will try to be more honest,' he said, trying out a contrite expression and finding it didn't sit well on his face.

The intensity of her gaze was a little unnerving as she waited for him to speak.

'The past four years I have travelled as far east as India, as far south as Turkey, stopping at various places for a few weeks, maybe a couple of months. I've been here beside the lake for six months, the longest I've stayed anywhere. I suppose I feel at peace here, waking up to such beauty every day is humbling. It makes you admit how insignificant your problems are.'

Although he had never set out to be quite so honest Thomas realised it was the truth. He could have settled anywhere, but he'd chosen Lake Garda to make his home at least for a while.

'Why do you feel the need to move around so much?'

'Is that question number two?'

Rosa nodded.

'When I first left England I didn't know what I wanted to see, I just knew there was a whole world out there waiting for me to discover it. I marvelled at the ancient temples in Greece, climbed an active volcano in Italy, was stalked by a tiger in the jungles of India and spent three glorious weeks floating adrift in a rickety old boat in the Black Sea.' He paused to see if Rosa looked as though she believed him. It was partly the truth, but it did not explain his need to run from his fate, a strange compulsion to keep moving, as if staying in one place too long might let the disease he was so afraid of catch up with him. 'Once I started discovering new places I was like a laudanum addict, I needed to see more, experience more. It was like an illness—if I didn't keep moving on I would become restless and anxious.'

'So why have you stopped now?'

Thomas pulled on the reins to slow the horses as they rounded a tight bend and considered Rosa's question. In truth he wasn't quite sure. The answer he'd given earlier, talking about the humbling beauty of Lake Garda, was true, but he'd visited many beautiful places in the past few years. He wasn't sure what had made him slow, what had made him start thinking of home, yearning for the green fields and grey skies and all the places he had known as a child.

He thought of the letter from his mother, asking him to return, and knew that even without her plea it wouldn't have been that long before he boarded a ship and sailed for England. Something was pulling him home, but he wasn't sure what.

'I suppose everyone needs a rest now and again.'

'You're being flippant again,' Rosa challenged him.

'Sorry. I suppose I don't know. For a while I grew tired of new places, not knowing anyone, never being sure of where I would rest my head from one day to the next.'

'So will you stay here, in Italy?'

Thomas smiled and shook his head. 'That's question number four, Miss Rothwell. You've had your turn, now it's mine.'

Rosa stiffened as if actually nervous about what he would ask, but nodded for him to continue.

'How many months pregnant are you?' He hadn't meant to be quite so blunt and as the shock and hurt flashed across her eyes he cursed his clumsy handling of the question.

'What makes you think I'm pregnant?'

'Look how you're sitting,' Thomas said softly.

Rosa glanced down and grimaced as she realised one hand rested protectively against her lower abdomen.

'I suppose it's natural, a mother's instinct,' Thomas said. 'You've had a hand on your abdomen throughout most of the morning, and every so often you will look down fondly when you think I'm not paying attention.'

She nodded, mutely. They continued in silence for nearly ten minutes before Rosa spoke again.

'Four months, nearly to the day.'

Thomas did a few quick sums in his head, and realised things didn't quite add up.

'And that was why you were sent away in disgrace? You must have known pretty early on that you were pregnant.'

It wasn't a subject Thomas was well schooled in, but he did have a vague idea that most women weren't sure until they were about three or four months along in their pregnancy.

'I knew as soon as I missed my courses, by that time I was only about a month gone. I spoke to the father a week later, confessed to my mother the same evening and the next day I was packed off to Italy.'

That explained the timings a little more.

'What if you were wrong?'

Rosa shrugged. 'I suppose my mother thought it easier to recall me if it turned out I wasn't pregnant than to explain an ever-growing bump.'

Thomas detected a note of bitterness alongside the sadness and wondered if the relationship between mother and daughter was a little strained.

'It took five weeks by boat, a couple more overland, and then the Di Mercurios kept me locked away for a month. That makes four months.' She said it in a matter-of-fact voice that belied the pain on her face.

'What about the father?' Thomas asked, wondering if that was who she was running home to.

Rosa gave a bitter, short bark of a laugh and shook her head instead of answering.

'What do you plan to do, Rosa?' he asked, aware that this game of theirs had become very serious very quickly.

'Stop the horses,' Rosa said sharply.

Thomas glanced at her in puzzlement.

'Stop. The. Horses.'

He pulled on the reins, slowing the horses down to a gentle walk before coming to a complete stop. As soon as the curricle had stopped moving Rosa slid down, grabbed her cane and began to limp away. Thomas frowned, wondering exactly what it was about his question that had caused so much offence.

'Rosa,' he called, jumping down after her and jogging to catch up.

'Leave me alone.'

Thomas realised she was crying and slowed as he approached her.

'I'm sorry. I never meant to upset you.'

She shook her head, turning her back to him.

He stood undecided for a moment, unsure whether to step back and give her space or take her into his arms and comfort her.

'Shh…' he whispered as he wrapped her in his arms and gently pulled her head to rest on his shoulder.

He felt the sobs rack her body, her shoulders heaving as the tears ran down her cheeks and soaked through his shirt.

'I'm sorry,' she said quietly.

Thomas didn't reply, instead tightening his hold on her, running a hand over her raven-black hair and murmuring soothing noises.

'Come back to the curricle,' he said as her sobs died down.

'I don't know—' she started to say, but Thomas interrupted her with a shake of his head.

'I'm not a man who is used to having his requests refused,' he said in an overly serious tone and felt supremely satisfied when Rosa broke into a smile. It was small and uncertain, but a smile all the same.

Giving her his arm to lean upon, Thomas led her back, placed his arms around her waist and lifted her easily back into the seat.

'No running off whilst I climb up.'

'I'm sorry,' Rosa said as he took his place beside her. 'I never cry.'

'Half a day in my company and already you're breaking habits of a lifetime.'

'It's just so frustrating, so completely unfair. Every person who has found out about my predicament has expected me to give my child up. To be thankful for the suggestion that a nice family could raise my baby and no one will ever know.'

The thought had crossed his mind, and although that hadn't been the question he'd asked, it had been the answer he'd been expecting.

'So what are you going to do?'

Rosa took a deep breath, raised her chin and straightened her back. 'I will raise my child myself.'

It was an admirable idea, but not an easy one to fulfil.

As soon as the words had passed her lips Rosa deflated again, her chin dropping closer to her chest and her eyes focused on the ground beneath them as if searching for answers there.

Thomas thought of all the arguments against her plans, thought of all the struggles she would face raising a child alone. It wasn't so much her practical ability to care for and love a child he doubted, or the fact that she would be raising it without a father—many women raised large families after they were widowed. No, the struggle for Rosa would be how she would be shunned and hounded from society. Right now she might not think she cared about other ladies gossiping and pointing, snubbing her in the street and not inviting her to any of the social events of the year, but Thomas knew too well how lonely solitude could be. It would be a miserable existence.

'I know,' Rosa said softly. 'You don't have to tell me how difficult it will be. I will be an outcast, even my child might be an outcast, but I believe that love can make up for all of that. And I will love this baby much more than any family paid to take him or her.'

He nodded mutely. Who was he to disagree with her, his choices hadn't exactly been well thought out or well reasoned these past few years. After his father's and brother's deaths he'd more or less fled the country. He'd been halfway to France before he'd even stopped and thought about his decisions. If Rosa wanted to return to England to find a way to raise her child, then he had no business judging her.

Rosa wondered if he was judging her and then realised she didn't much care. It was true, she had thought of all the drawbacks to raising her child herself, but every single negative point was outweighed by the overwhelming love she already felt for the small life inside her.

'Do you think you'll ever go back?' Rosa asked, trying to change the focus of their conversation back to Lord Hunter.

'To England?' For a few moments he looked off into

the distance as if he were deep in thought. 'I have a mother,' he said eventually.

Rosa laughed, she couldn't help herself. 'We all have mothers.'

Hunter sighed. 'Mine is particularly loving and understanding.'

'How awful for you,' Rosa murmured, thinking of her own mother's parting words to her. They had not been kind.

'She's lonely, rattling round in our big old house, and she's asked me to go home.'

'Will you?'

'She hasn't asked a single thing of me since...' He paused for a moment. 'Since I left England.'

'You might find you enjoy being back home, surrounded by the people who know and love you.'

Hunter grimaced, as if the idea was completely unpalatable. Rosa wondered if there was something else that made him reluctant to go home. All his talk of restlessness, of wanting to see the world and discover new places, was all very well, but she was astute enough to know it was a pile of lies. Hunter might feel all of that, but it wasn't the reason he was so unsettled, so reluctant to return home, Rosa could see it in his eyes. Something much bigger was keeping him away.

She was just settling back on to the seat of the curricle, making herself comfortable for the rest of the journey ahead when a movement to the side of the road caught her eye. She leaned forward, peering into the undergrowth to see whether it was some sort of animal or a person loitering where they shouldn't be.

'*Alt!*' a man shouted in Italian as he jumped from the bushes in front of the curricle. *Halt.*

Hunter didn't have many options. It was either rein in the horses or trample the tattily dressed young man.

Rosa felt her heart begin to pound in her chest and she had to keep her hands in her lap to keep them from trembling. She didn't recognise the man standing in front of the restless horses, but he must be there for her. In her month-long imprisonment in the Di Mercurios' villa she hadn't laid eyes on this man, but she had learnt that the Di Mercurio family was vast and the number of young men she could call cousin reached well into double figures. This must surely be some relation come to take her back.

Just as Rosa was about to grab hold of the reins and urge the horses forward she saw the pistol in the man's hand and paused for a second. Not because of the gun, not really. Of course the man could aim and fire and hit one of them, but hitting a moving target was difficult and she reckoned they had a good chance of getting away without injury to either of them. Rosa paused because of the strip of fabric covering the lower half of the man's face, as if he didn't want to be recognised.

'Don't move or I will shoot the lady,' another voice came from behind the curricle.

Rosa spun round and saw three more men similarly attired.

She glanced at Hunter, saw the expressions of irritation and disbelief flit over his face before it settled back to a stony, unreadable façade.

'Sorry, gentlemen, I don't speak Italian,' Hunter said, in an exaggerated, loud voice. 'English.'

Rosa frowned. She knew he spoke Italian, or at least

she thought he did. She opened her mouth to translate for him and got a sharp dig in the ribs from his elbow. Quickly she closed her mouth again and moved a little closer to Hunter. She wasn't going to succeed in escaping from the Di Mercurios only to be killed by bandits on a dusty Italian road.

'Denaro!' the chief bandit shouted, then slowly, working his mouth around the unfamiliar word, 'Money!'

The three bandits from behind the curricle edged closer.

'I'm afraid I don't carry much with me,' Hunter said a little too flippantly for Rosa's liking. They were being threatened by four men with pistols and swords and here he was pretending not to understand them and refusing to hand anything over.

'Money,' the chief bandit demanded again.

A squat, swarthy man with the complexion similar to that of a toad jabbed Rosa lightly with the tip of his sword and leered at her, giving her a perfect view of his three remaining teeth, all black and rotten in his lower jaw.

Rosa fought the nausea that rose up from her stomach, desperately trying to suppress the gag that threatened to escape from her throat. Although she reasoned vomiting over a bandit might not be a bad way to get him to leave you alone.

'Money,' the toad man repeated, his accent thick and his eyes roaming over Rosa's body.

She felt Hunter shift in his seat beside her and wondered if he was reaching for his coin purse. Thinking of the small amount of money she'd been able to keep safe throughout the journey to Italy and her subsequent imprisonment, Rosa felt her fear melting away and a white-hot fury consuming her instead. They had no right to steal her money, no right to ruin her plans for the future.

Leaning forward, Rosa made to stand and give these bandits a piece of her mind when she felt a restraining hand on her arm.

'Sit down,' Hunter said calmly, as if he were talking about the weather at a garden party. 'Or you'll get us both killed.'

'At least I'm trying to do something,' Rosa hissed.

'Something reckless and stupid.'

'They will not get my money.'

'Is that small purse of yours worth your life?'

Rosa hesitated. He didn't understand. That small purse *was* her life. Without it she wouldn't have a way to fund her passage back to England. She wouldn't even have a way to feed herself. She'd be forced back to the Di Mercurios, forced to throw herself on their mercy. No doubt she would be locked away for another five months and once she'd given birth they would take her child away from her.

Rosa was saved from having to answer by the toad man grabbing her by the waist and squeezing in a lascivious manner. With a squeal of outrage, she thumped him on the head and was just steadying herself to throw another punch when there was a flurry of movement beside her.

Hunter leapt from his seat, barrelled into one of the bandits, sending him crashing into the second man. Whilst the two criminals struggled to disengage from one another Hunter softly grabbed both their flailing pistols and fired a shot towards the chief bandit, making him dive back into the bushes.

Rosa watched in disbelief as Hunter sprinted after the

man, leaping through the air as he reached the under-growth and throwing a punch that sounded as though it hit its mark. There was a distinct crunch of bone and a yelp of pain, followed by a few moments' silence. Eventually Hunter hauled himself up out of the undergrowth with a casual grin.

The two men he'd disarmed moments ago glanced at one another, then rushed towards him and Rosa heard herself gasp as Hunter sank to the floor and kicked out with a foot just as they reached him. Both men tripped, sprawling to the ground with shouts of pain. Quickly he aimed both pistols and fired a shot from each towards the bandits' heads.

Rosa squeezed her eyes shut, not wanting to see the explosion of blood and brains from the two bandits, but as she pressed her lids together she heard a low whimpering. Cautiously she peeked and saw a spasm of movement from the ground. For a moment she wondered if Hunter had missed from such a short range, but then realised he'd aimed a few inches above the men's heads.

'Run,' Hunter ordered. 'Now.'

Rosa watched as the two bandits wobbled to their feet and ran, not sparing a backwards glance for their compatriot left behind.

As Hunter turned slowly Rosa could feel her pulse beating in her throat, a warm, rhythmic reminder of how alive she felt right now. He strolled nonchalantly back towards the curricle, as if he was out for an evening walk and hadn't just single-handedly bested three armed bandits. In the mid-morning sun his blue eyes sparkled and Rosa had the sense he was enjoying himself.

Beside her the toad man hesitated, looking over his shoulder as if checking for possible escape routes.

'Run,' Hunter repeated, his voice low and dangerous.

For a moment Rosa thought the toad man would obey, but she saw the flash of defiance in his eyes just a second before he looped his arm around her waist and pulled her body tightly against his. She felt the cool metal of the pistol against her neck and knew this scared man holding her captive was very dangerous. He had been abandoned by his comrades and could see no way out. One false move and he would probably fire out of fear.

'There's no need for that,' Hunter said, keeping his tone soothing. 'Let the lady go and you have nothing to fear from me.'

Everyone present knew Lord Hunter was lying. He'd taken three men out without even breaking a sweat in the mid-morning sun, Rosa couldn't see a situation that worked out well for the toad man.

She felt the tremor of the bandit's hands, sensed his uncertainty as he shifted from one foot to the other.

'What's your name?' Hunter asked in flawless Italian.

'Er-Er-Ernesto,' the bandit stuttered.

'Well, Ernesto, why don't we make a deal? You let go of my friend here and I will let you walk away.'

'Walk away?' Ernesto asked in surprise.

'That's right. You haven't hurt either of us, haven't taken anything. I see no reason you can't just walk away from this.'

'I'm not stupid,' Ernesto said with a sneer. 'You'll kill me as soon as my back is turned.'

'Like I killed your comrades?'

Ernesto the toad man hesitated.

'Just start backing away. If you see me raise my pistol before you get out of range then shoot me, but I give you my word I will not harm you unless you make me.'

Rosa studied Lord Hunter's calm demeanour and reassuring expression. It was hard not to trust him, she realised.

'The money?' Ernesto asked, but Rosa could tell his heart wasn't in it.

'No, Ernesto. We leave here with our money. You leave with your life.'

Ten seconds passed, then twenty. Rosa could hear a soft mumbling as Ernesto reasoned his options out to himself. After what seemed like an eternity his grip on her loosened.

'Keep your pistols low,' Ernesto said. 'Or I'll shoot.'

Slowly he began backing away down the road, his eyes fixed on Thomas. Thomas stood still, his arms relaxed by his side, watching the bandit calmly. Rosa couldn't quite believe his heart wasn't pounding or his hands slick with sweat, but he looked completely composed.

As Ernesto got to the bend in the road he stopped for a moment before turning and running. They could hear his heavy footsteps for at least thirty seconds after he'd disappeared.

Rosa felt her body begin to shake and immediately Lord Hunter was by her side.

'Sit,' he commanded. 'Take deep breaths. You were very brave.'

As she attempted to limp back to the curricle Hunter gripped her gently and scooped her into his arms. The contact between their two bodies was a welcome comfort for Rosa and she held on tightly to his shoulders. As she felt his firm body pressed against hers Rosa glanced up and caught him looking down at her. He could feel it, too, she was sure of it. That need for physical touch, that desire for intimacy. She told herself it was just the shock, the stressful situation they'd been through to-gether, but as he held her a little tighter Rosa wondered if that was all it was.

She half-expected her body to tense, to remember the last time a man had held her so closely, encircled her with his arms, but instead she felt her breathing become more steady and her racing heart slow as she was reassured by Lord Hunter's touch.

'You let him go,' she said as he placed her gently on the seat of the curricle.

'I gave my word.'

'You let all of them go.'

Hunter shrugged, but Rosa could see there had been a reason behind his decision. Most men would have inflicted maximum pain on bandits who threatened them and Lord Hunter had disarmed and bested them all without much effort. Rosa wouldn't have blamed him if there were four dead bodies strewn on the road right now.

'They would have killed us.'

Hunter chuckled. 'Bloodthirsty wench, aren't you?'

Rosa managed to smile.

'I don't think they would have killed us,' Thomas said simply. 'They were desperate, driven to do something terrible.'

'How do you know they were desperate?'

'Did you see the way they were dressed? How gaunt they were? These weren't successful criminals. And none of them knew how to fight.'

Rosa fell silent, contemplating what Hunter had just said.

'Circumstances can drive decent human beings to do almost anything,' Hunter said, looking off into the distance. 'And I suppose hunger is a real motivator.'

'Surely there have got to be better ways to make money than stealing, though?'

Hunter shrugged. 'Of course. But if you've been turned away from work, unable to provide food for your family, who knows what you might do.'

He moved away from her and began checking over the horses, murmuring soft words to soothe the skittish animals.

As she sat and watched him Rosa felt a new respect blossoming for the man who had saved her twice now. He might be a little arrogant and unapologetic at times, but there was something more to Lord Hunter. Rosa knew most men would have either panicked at being surrounded by bandits or become so furious they showed no compassion or mercy. It was rather refreshing to see a man think with his heart and not his fists.

'Where did you learn to fight like that?' she asked.

'Here and there.'

'In India?'

'Amongst other places.'

She wondered why he was so reticent talking about where he learned to defend himself so effortlessly.

'Ready?' he asked as he vaulted back up beside her.

Rosa nodded. Although they had come out unscathed she felt more than a little shaken by the encounter and was keen to be on their way.

Lord Hunter urged the horses forward and soon they were gliding through the country lanes. As Rosa felt her anxiety levels begin to drop she began to relax into the man beside her. It felt good to have even the slight physical contact of thigh against thigh after her months of isolation.

As her thoughts started to run away from her, tentative hopes spiralling out of control, Rosa forced herself to pull away. She'd lost her virtue and her future to one man, she would not lose anything else to another.

Chapter Five

'Tell me about the father,' Hunter said as he leaned back in his chair.

They were sitting on a terrace in the bustling village of Malcesine, sipping a rather delicious concoction of juices from tall glasses.

Rosa started in surprise at the bluntness of his question and coughed as the juice tickled her throat.

'The father?' she asked. She knew exactly what he was talking about, but she couldn't believe he'd asked the question so directly.

Hunter gestured to her abdomen and Rosa quickly laid a protective hand on the growing bump beneath her dress.

'The father of your baby. Who is he?'

'No one you would know.'

'An unsuitable suitor? A dastardly married man? A dashing young footman?'

'Shall we set about our enquiries?' Rosa asked.

'Sit back, relax. You've had a stressful morning. We can ask about a passage to England in an hour, nothing will change between then and now.'

'Except my desire to murder you,' Rosa muttered under her breath.

'What was that?'

She smiled sweetly and took another sip of her juice. It really was delicious. She could taste orange and a hint of lemon, but there was something else there, too.

Rosa tried to ignore Hunter's intense gaze as she drummed her fingers on the table, shifted in her chair and traced the condensation as it ran down the edge of the glass. He didn't ask the question again, just sat watching her, as if he knew she would crack and tell him eventually.

'What beautiful trees,' Rosa said, gesturing to a cluster of short trees near the water's edge.

Still Hunter said nothing, but that lazy smile she had begun to know well danced across his lips. She wondered how she could find a man so irritating, but still so attractive. It was his eyes, she pondered, you couldn't stay annoyed at a man whose eyes sparkled and glimmered with amusement all day long.

Again she shifted, trying to focus on watching the locals strolling arm in arm along the waterfront. It was unnerving, having someone watch you for such a length of time, and Rosa felt her composure slowly beginning to slip.

'Do you come here often?' she asked, trying to force a response out of Hunter.

'No.'

'You should. It truly is a beautiful spot.'

Silence again.

'Have you always been this annoying?' she asked with a sigh.

'My mother tells me I'm persistent.' Hunter gave a small shrug.

'That's a nice way of putting it.'

'Tell me about the father.'

'Why do you want to know?'

Hunter shrugged again. 'I'm interested. And it'll take your mind off our encounter today.'

That was true, Rosa hadn't thought of the bandits for a whole five minutes.

'He's our neighbour, a boy I grew up with.'

'Boy?'

Rosa grimaced. 'Man. He must be twenty-seven or twenty-eight by now, I suppose.'

'Old enough to behave better.'

'You don't know how he behaved.'

'You're here in exile in Italy rather than happily married in some country house in England.'

It was the truth, but that didn't mean it didn't hurt. For a long time Rosa had imagined a life with David. A home of their own filled with beautiful children, the life she had been brought up to expect.

'So what happened?'

Rosa shook her head. She really did not want to talk about this. Even uttering David's name had the bile rising up in her throat and knots of tension forming across her shoulders.

'How about you?' she asked, desperate to change the subject. 'Any great loves in your life.'

Hunter smiled and shook his head, 'I've never found that special someone.'

'But you've looked?'

'Some people aren't destined to settle down.'

It was an odd statement, one that made Rosa pause and study the man in front of her for a moment.

'But you're titled, you have an estate. Isn't there a need for an heir?'

He shrugged. 'The estate will pass to some distant relative when I die.'

Although it was said casually she could see the pain in his eyes at the idea. Whatever he might say, this was an uncomfortable subject for Hunter.

'You wouldn't rather it went to your son, your own flesh and blood?'

'That is never going to happen so there is no point in mourning what never could be.'

'Why—?' Rosa started, but a small hand tugging at her sleeve cut her off.

'Please, miss, spare some money. I haven't eaten for three days.' A small girl stood looking up at her with large brown eyes in a skinny face.

Rosa hesitated and then reached for her coin purse. She might not have much money, and what she did have she needed for the passage home and her new life, but it was hard to ignore the real pleading in the young girl's eyes.

'Rosa, no,' Hunter shouted, trying to grab her hand, but it was too late. As soon as the coin purse was out in the open an older boy swooped in and grabbed it from her palm. At high speed both he and the girl ran in different directions, weaving through the crowd.

'No,' Rosa whispered, her heart plummeting as she realised her whole future had just been ripped away from her.

Hunter was on his feet immediately, darting after the boy, but Rosa could see straight away he would never be able to catch him. Hunter might be fast, but the boy knew the streets and was small enough to slip between the crowds.

Gripping the edge of the table, Rosa felt her breathing become shallower and could hear a harsh rasping coming from her throat. Without any money she was doomed. She had the choice of life on the streets in a foreign country or crawling back to the Di Mercurios.

'I can't go back,' she whispered. 'I won't go back.'

She looked down at the dress she was wearing, that would fetch her a small sum, but her modest jewellery had been taken from her by her grandmother when she had arrived at the villa. She owned nothing else in the world except the clothes she was wearing.

'I'm sorry,' Hunter said, returning to the table, his face flushed from exertion. 'I lost him in the crowd.'

Rosa shook her head, unable to get any words out. She'd been so pleased when they had escaped the bandits with her purse intact, she'd never thought it might be at risk here in this idyllic village.

'Was that all the money you had?' he asked. Gone was his normal jovial tone, replaced by concern and compassion.

'Everything.'

Hunter raked a hand through his short hair, causing tufts to stick up at the front.

'I can't go back to them,' Rosa whispered again to herself.

Anything would be better than that. Maybe she could find work somewhere, save up the money for a passage home. As soon as the idea entered her mind she dismissed it. If there was no work for able-bodied young men then no one was going to employ a pregnant woman.

'Rosa, look at me,' Hunter said, taking her hand in his own.

As his fingers gripped hers Rosa felt some of her panic begin to subside. It was as if Hunter was tethering her to reality, stopping her from plummeting into a deep despair.

'We will figure something out. All is not lost.'

'That was all my money. Everything I own.'

Gently he stroked the back of her hand with his thumb. Rosa looked up and met his eyes and realised that whatever he said she trusted him. It was ridiculous, she'd only known the man a day, but if he said all was not lost then maybe it would work out.

'Come,' he said, pulling her to her feet. 'I need to think.'

She allowed him to tuck her hand into the crook of his elbow, lay down a few coins for their drinks and lead her away from the riverside tavern. She leaned heavily on his arm, tapping the cane against the cobblestones for a little extra support, but out here in the heat of the day her ankle ached.

'I'm ruined,' Rosa murmured as they weaved their way through the crowds. Not ruined in the sense of a loss of virtue, that had happened many months ago, but all the way through her ordeal she'd had some hope, a plan to make things better.

Hunter didn't say anything, just continued down towards the water's edge.

'Look out there,' he said as they reached the promenade that ran along the edge of the lake.

Rosa looked, following the direction his extended finger was pointing in. The sun glinted off the water and in the distance the hills surrounding the lake were shielded in a thin heat haze.

'What am I looking at?'

Hunter didn't answer, he was looking down at his hand in horror. Rosa followed his gaze, but as soon as he noticed she was looking, too, it was as if a mask came down over his face and his hand promptly dropped to his side.

'What's wrong?' Rosa asked.

'Stay there,' he ordered her, not giving her a chance to answer before striding off along the promenade.

He had to get away. Away from the crowds, away from Rosa's concerned enquiries and away from the stifling heat that threatened to consume him. Forcing himself to walk and not run, Thomas headed away from the village.

'Lord Hunter,' he heard Rosa call in the distance, but her voice barely registered in his mind.

I will not look.

Resolutely he kept his eyes fixed on a tree in the distance, willing himself not to look down.

His resolve cracked within thirty seconds. The first glance was fleeting and brief, but when he saw his hands weren't moving rhythmically and of their own accord he managed to gain control of himself a little and take a second look.

Sinking down on to the stone wall that ran along the lakefront, Thomas held his hands out in front of him. As he had pointed out over the lake there had been a definite tremor, an uncontrolled shaking of his hand. It had been small, probably unnoticeable to anyone but him, but he could not pretend it hadn't been there.

Now his hands were steady and unmoving as he studied them. Thomas exhaled, trying to calm his racing heart and dampen the nausea that rose from his stomach. For a few moments he had thought it was the beginning of the end, that the disease that had claimed his father and his brother was starting to develop in him.

It always began this way—a minor tremor, an uncontrolled movement. Followed by memory loss, personality change and the ever-worsening rhythmic jerky movements and a loss of co-ordination. His older brother Michael had developed his first symptoms when he was just twenty and died at twenty-eight. Thomas's age now. Their father had been a little more fortunate, surviving into his forties. It was a well-kept secret, the Hunter family curse, but generation after generation showed signs of affliction.

Maybe I'll be one of the lucky ones.

It was what Thomas prayed for every day, that he would be one of the few the disease skipped. Not every member of the Hunter family was affected, but there was no way to know if you would succumb until the day you died.

Thomas rested his head in his hands and closed his eyes. Every morning he inspected his body for any unnatural movements, any clue that he might be developing the thing he feared the most. For a moment there he had been convinced that was it for him, that his time on earth was up. One thing Thomas was sure of was that he wouldn't let this disease rob him of his dignity and his hope. If he was ever sure his turn had come, then he would find a more dignified way to depart this world, even if it was considered a mortal sin to commit suicide.

'Lord Hunter,' Rosa said as she approached him slowly, warily.

She'd followed him. Of course she had.

'What's wrong?'

He took a second, flashed a charming smile and stood. 'Nothing, nothing at all.'

'Then why did you run off?'

'I have a proposition for you,' he said, knowing it was the only way to get Rosa to drop the subject. 'Let me escort you home.'

He had to smile at Rosa's shocked expression: the gaping mouth, wide eyes and rapid blinking of her eyelids. Over the years he had become a master of concealing his fears of the illness that might one day claim him and distraction was a great technique.

'Home?'

'Back to England. To whatever friend you hope will take you in.'

'Why would you do that?'

Thomas shrugged. He'd made the suggestion impulsively, but the more he thought about it the more he warmed to the idea.

'I need to return home. I owe that much to my mother. It wouldn't be gentlemanly to abandon you in your hour of need, so why not combine the two objectives?'

'It's too much, I could never ask that of you.'

'What other options do you have?'

Rosa fell silent. She was in no position to turn down the offer of assistance in whatever form.

'You are sure you're happy to return to England? I wouldn't want you to return solely on my account.'

Thomas thought about it before answering and found he was. It would be pleasant to stroll around his estate and reminisce with his mother. He knew he would not stay there indefinitely, but a few weeks, maybe a month, and then he could pick a new destination for his travels. Thomas found the idea of revisiting the home he had once been so happy in rather appealing and knew if he wanted to return for a short period he should do so soon. Who knew if he would get another opportunity?

'Quite sure.'

Rosa shook her head in disbelief, then threw her arms around him.

'Thank you,' she whispered.

He had never heard two words uttered so sincerely or with such relief.

'I will find a way to reimburse you any expenses accrued once we get back to England.'

Thomas waved a dismissive hand—the cost of a passage on a ship and a few weeks in various guest houses was the least of his worries. It wasn't as though he would be able to take his money with him when he died.

'Thank you, Lord Hunter,' Rosa replied. Thomas could see she was struggling to hold back the tears.

'Call me Thomas. We're going to be spending much time together.'

'Thomas,' she repeated, smiling up at him.

'And I shall call you Rosa.'

'You do already.'

He grinned, took her hand and kissed her just below the knuckles. It felt good to have a purpose after all this time.

'This afternoon we shall return to the villa. There are a few things I will need to tie up before we depart. I will arrange for us to leave early next week.'

He would terminate his lease on the villa. As much as

he loved the comfortable dwelling and beautiful views, he realised it was time for him to move on. The momentary fear that he might be entering his last few months of healthy life had jolted him into action. There was more of the world to see, more to experience. He would travel home with Rosa, visit his mother for a few weeks and then spin the large globe that sat in his father's study. *His* study. Wherever his finger landed, that would be where he travelled next.

As they walked back along the promenade Thomas tried to summon some of his normal excitement when contemplating a new adventure, but this time his heart was not really in it. His mind was preoccupied with thoughts of home: the rolling green hills, the woods he'd played in as a boy, even the peaceful spot right at the edge of the estate where his father and brother were laid to rest.

Chapter Six

Dearest Caroline,

I hope you are keeping well. It seems like a century has passed since we saw each other last winter. I was very saddened to hear the news of Lord Trowridge's passing. Please forgive me for the lateness of my condolences. I have been out of the country for some months, but you are never far from my thoughts.

How is young Rupert? I remember the week I spent with you in January with such fondness. He was such an adorable little baby and I'm sure he's bringing you even more joy as he grows.

I do not know if any gossip has reached your ears down in Dorset, but I am in a little bit of trouble. These last three months I've been exiled from London, sent to stay with my mother's family in northern Italy. I won't bore you with all the sordid details, but I have found myself with child, and you can imagine Mother's reaction to that little scandal.

Her plan was to tell the world I had gone to

nurse my ailing grandmother—who is as strong as an ox and still shows up the young farmhands. I would reappear in society in a year and no one would be the wiser. My child was to be adopted by some Italian family and I would never set eyes on him or her again.

I know I should probably have been grateful, Caroline, but I couldn't bear the thought of my baby calling someone else Mama. Out of everyone I think you would understand the most.

Anyway, I escaped and now I've met an English gentleman who has offered to escort me back to England. He seems very capable and I feel safe in his company, even if he is rather forceful and confident in character.

Now I have the biggest favour to ask of you. I know if I return home my mother will send me back to her family in Italy and if that happens they will take my baby away from me. Caroline, can I come and stay with you whilst I wait out the rest of my pregnancy and work out exactly how to live my life as the mother of an illegitimate child? For I will not give up my baby for anyone, no matter what the future brings.

I remember you saying you have a certain freedom now Lord Trowridge has passed and I wonder if I can impose on you for a short while? I would be happy to be hidden away, or to live a simple life in one of the cottages on your estate.

I have no money and nowhere else to turn. Caroline, I'm sorry to ask so much of you, but I hope one day I will be able to repay you.

We will be leaving Italy any day now. Lord

Hunter is just tying up a few loose ends from his life here and then we will be starting our journey back to England. I am not sure of the exact date we will arrive in Dorset, but perhaps I might call on you when we arrive to hear your answer.

I cannot wait to see you and young Rupert again.
All my love,
Rosa

Rosa sat back, folded the letter in half and slipped it into the envelope. She was asking a lot of her old friend, maybe too much, but she didn't have much choice. Caroline was kind and loyal and wasn't one to worry overly much about what others thought of her. Rosa knew her oldest friend wouldn't hesitate to take her in, but that didn't mean asking was any easier.

'Who are you writing to?' Thomas asked as he sauntered across the terrace, tossing a ripe orange up in the air and catching it with ease.

'Caroline, the Dowager Lady Trowridge,' Rosa corrected herself. 'She's my oldest and dearest friend.'

'She sounds severe.'

Rosa laughed. No one who had ever met Caroline would describe her as severe.

'She's twenty years old, no more than five feet tall and laughs at absolutely everything.'

'Not your average widow, then?'

Thomas was of course right, despite there being many young widows in society, the term often conjured up images of statuesque women in their later years presiding over a large family with an iron will.

'Not your average dowager,' Rosa agreed. 'She married at eighteen, had her son at nineteen and was a widow by the age of twenty.'

'Poor girl.' Then Thomas paused. 'Or maybe very astute.'

Rosa rather thought it was the latter. Caroline hadn't protested when the childless Lord Trowridge had started courting her, she'd actively encouraged it. He was kind, wealthy and willing to give her years of independence in exchange for a short time dedicated to making an old man happy. Rosa thought the union had been a success; Lord Trowridge had got a pretty young bride for the last months of his life and now Caroline was in charge of her son's upbringing and the entire Trowbridge estate until Rupert came of age.

'I've informed her of my plans to return to England and asked for her help when we arrive.' Rosa took a breath, then pressed on. 'I'm sure she would be happy to lend me the money to reimburse you for the travel expenses.'

Thomas shrugged. 'It doesn't cost that much for a passage from Italy to England, I'm sure I can afford it. We can find another way for you to repay me.'

Rosa's eyes widened and she felt the blush begin to creep into her cheeks.

Thomas threw his head back and laughed heartily at her expression. 'I meant you can cook me another one of those delicious meals.'

Rosa's blush deepened, but she resisted the urge to cover her face with her hands. Of course Thomas wasn't proposing she repaid his kindness with intimacy. Throughout the week she had stayed with him there hadn't been even a flicker of flirtation from him. He had meant it when he'd told her that her virtue was safe with him on the first evening of their acquaintance, he hadn't behaved improperly once. Rosa knew she should be thankful, especially after her awful experience with David, but she felt a tiny surge of disappointment every time Thomas didn't take an opportunity to get closer to her.

Gaining back control of herself, Rosa smiled. 'Next time I'll add less garlic.'

It wouldn't be quite so galling if Rosa didn't feel her heart start pounding in her chest every time Thomas stepped in close to her. He was an attractive man, his body toned and muscular from the early morning swims and his eyes full of mischief and laughter. Rosa knew she never wanted to get involved with a man again, but Thomas tested her resolve sometimes. At least when he wasn't ordering her around or teasing her.

'Signora Felcini is coming to cook tonight,' Rosa said. 'So I'm sure I can persuade her to give me one last lesson before we leave.'

The elderly Italian woman who came in to cook and clean for Thomas a few times a week had taken Rosa under her wing. She ordered Rosa around in rapid Italian and expected her to chop and help with the evening meal, but in return Rosa was treated to a lesson in rustic Italian cookery. In Rosa's mind it was a fair exchange.

'I have made arrangements for us to leave first thing tomorrow morning. Your family are causing a bit of a stir searching for you nearby, so I think it would be prudent to leave as soon as possible.'

'Thank you,' Rosa said quietly.

She still wasn't quite sure why Thomas was helping her, it wasn't as though he got much out of their arrangement, just trouble from the Di Mercurios and the expense of transporting her to England. Whatever his motivations Rosa was keen not to examine them too carefully; Thomas was her only hope now she was penniless and stuck so far from home.

Thomas wiped the sweat from his brow, adjusted the bandages on his hands and squared up to the punch-bag hanging from the branches of the sturdy olive tree. Quickly he hooked and jabbed, dancing lightly on his toes around the inanimate opponent.

He'd learned to box at school, along with all the other sons of the gentry, classes where their wiry games master instructed the small group on the basics of boxing. Of course that had been no use for the real world and nearly four years ago, when he'd first been beaten and robbed on his journey through Europe, he'd vowed to learn to defend himself better. The first year of his travels he'd been attacked five times. It was unsurprising really. He was a well-dressed young man who needed to carry money with him—a prime target for any ambitious criminal. After each attack Thomas had retreated for a while, licked his wounds, then restarted his training with renewed vigour. He picked up techniques from the countries he visited, practised his defensive and attacking modes every day, and soon he no longer had to hide his modest purse on his person or avoid the more unsavoury areas of the cities he visited.

Now training every evening had become part of his daily routine, just like the refreshing early morning swim in the lake.

With one last high kick Thomas began unwrapping the bandages from his hands. He loved this feeling just after he'd exercised, the heady mix of exhaustion and exhilaration. Over the years he'd developed a deep-seated respect for his body and worked hard to keep it in top physical shape. Too many people took their physical health for granted, but he'd seen how quickly a man could be robbed of his ability to control his limbs, to walk, to run, to jump. He was determined to enjoy every minute he had conscious control of his muscles so he would regret nothing if and when the Hunter family curse struck.

'Do you think…?' Rosa said as she rounded the corner of the villa and came into view. 'Oh.'

Thomas had to hide a smile. She became so flustered whenever she caught sight of his bare skin, a deep flush spread across her cheeks and she seemed to lose her ability to speak for a few seconds. He liked to watch her rally, to refuse to give in to her embarrassment and try to continue as if nothing was amiss.

Nonchalantly Thomas pulled on his shirt. No need to make the poor girl suffer any more than was necessary.

'Yes?' he asked.

Rosa wasn't an innocent, her growing bump attested to the fact that she'd been intimate with at least one man, but Thomas had the feeling that despite the fact she was soon to be a mother she wasn't actually well acquainted with the pleasures of the flesh. For a moment his body tensed at the idea of being the one to make her moan and sing out with pleasure, but quickly he pushed the thought away. They had a long journey ahead of them together, he needed to be in control of himself and banish these intriguing but unwelcome fantasies.

'Do you think we should eat outside?'

Thomas nodded. It was their last night at the villa and he wanted to watch the sunset over the lake one last time.

Together they set the table and, whilst Thomas poured the wine, Rosa brought out the dish she had prepared with Signora Felcini. As always it looked and smelled delicious; Thomas could detect hints of rosemary and garlic and a garnish of lemon sprinkled over lightly cooked fish.

As he sat down and watched her serve up the fish and accompanying vegetables he was struck by what an idyllic domestic scene this was. For many men this was all they desired: a good-looking woman as a companion, someone to run their household whilst they amused themselves with other pursuits. Even Thomas, with his deep-seated desire to travel, had to admit there was a certain appeal to the idea. Rosa would make an ideal companion. She was interesting to talk to, good-natured and kind. Of course he wasn't looking for someone to settle down with, but he wondered if she might be able to solve another problem for him.

He had just picked up his fork and tasted the first mouthful of the delicious dish in front of him when he heard a commotion coming from the front of his villa. At first, as he listened to the raised voices and clatter of feet on the road, Thomas assumed it was drunken travellers making the racket, but as the voices came nearer he felt his muscles tense and his senses heighten.

There was a hammering at the front door of the villa and Thomas just had time to see Rosa's knuckles turning white as she gripped the table before he was on his feet and moving inside.

'Stay out of sight,' he instructed quietly, in a tone that brooked no argument.

Rosa nodded and wobbled out of her chair before

grasping the cane she was still having to rely on if walking more than a few paces.

'Englishman!' an angry voice called out in English with a thick accent. 'We know you're in there.'

Thomas suppressed the grin that was trying to break out on his face as he strode to the door. Already he could feel the energy coursing through his body, the anticipation of the confrontation making him feel alive. He never went looking for trouble, but Thomas couldn't deny he enjoyed the feeling he got when the odds were stacked against him in an encounter such as this.

Just as the hammering began again Thomas threw open the door with a flourish and flashed his most charming and infuriatingly calm smile.

'What can I help you fine gentlemen with this evening?' he asked, making sure he caught the eye of each man in turn. In total there were five; five small and wiry Italian men who looked as though they'd smelled blood and were eager for some more.

'We know you have her,' the man at the front of the group said.

'Who do I have the pleasure of talking to?' Thomas asked.

'Antonio Di Mercurio.'

'Ah, the lecherous one.' Rosa had told him much about her stay with the Di Mercurio family over the past week and Thomas was intrigued to match the characters to faces. 'That would make you two Piero and Michele.' He gestured to the other two young men roughly the same age as Antonio. 'And you must be Luca and Luigi, these fine gentlemen's fathers.'

'Where is my niece?' one of the older men snarled.

'Rosa? Oh, she left days ago. Decided to take a ship

to India, I think, or was it the Caribbean? I know it was somewhere far from here so she would never have to see the people who had kept her prisoner again.'

'Prisoner? We're her family. You're the one who's abducted her, stolen her from our care. Brought her to live in sin with you.' This was from Antonio again.

'Gentlemen,' Thomas said calmly, his thoughts returning to his dinner cooling on the terrace, 'tell me how you think this little expedition of yours is going to end?'

None of the men spoke and Thomas nodded in satisfaction. Although he'd led a private life here in Italy his reputation was still whispered about by the young men in the taverns. He was not a man to be trifled with, no doubt why the Di Mercurios had taken quite so long to approach his residence and demand Rosa back, and why there were five of them when ordinarily one would do.

'Turn around and return home and we will say nothing more on this matter.' Thomas even managed a friendly smile. One of the younger men recoiled, stepping back on to the foot of another family member.

'We will go to the magistrate,' Luca or Luigi threatened.

'That is not a good idea,' Thomas said slowly and quietly. He had learnt long ago that men responded to a low, quiet threat more than a shouted one and he saw the evidence again today as the Di Mercurio men huddled together for a few minutes, arguing fiercely in hushed voices.

'Rosa,' Antonio shouted eventually, craning to see over Thomas's shoulder. 'You are on your own. The family washes its hands of you. Go gallivanting about Italy with this scoundrel if you like, we no longer care. But just remember you will never again have the protection of the Di Mercurio name.'

Thomas watched as the Di Mercurio men each gave him a particularly dirty look, one of the older ones holding his eye and spitting on the ground by his feet.

'Good evening to you all,' Thomas called cheerily, before turning back into the house and closing the door behind him.

He almost laughed as he caught sight of Rosa in the corner of the room holding her cane aloft as if it were a weapon, but then saw the expression on her face. He crossed over to her with long, quick strides and instinctively took her into his arms, feeling her shudder with relief as he pulled her to him.

As he held her close, inhaling the sweet scent of her hair and feeling the pounding of her heart through both their chests, Thomas felt a momentary pang of desire. Not for Rosa—well, not exactly—but more for this lifestyle, this experience. Part of him longed to have a woman and maybe even a child to look after, someone to put above all else, someone to cherish and protect. He knew that was never in his future; he couldn't bear finding a woman he loved, marrying her and then having to watch her watch him suffer through the illness that might strike at any time. It wasn't fair and he wasn't that cruel.

Not everyone marries for love, the small voice in his head whispered.

It was something he had been contemplating for a while, but up until now it hadn't seemed possible. He could marry, find a kind and patient woman to give his family name to, someone he could take home to his mother and leave as a companion for the lonely older woman. It wasn't a great romance, but many of his contemporaries had married for far worse reasons.

As Rosa's head sunk to his shoulder the idea gripped hold of him and wouldn't let go. He could marry her, protect her and her unborn child, and rid himself of the guilt he felt at leaving his mother behind whilst he travelled the world in one swoop. It was madness, but maybe no more so than any other paths in life.

Chapter Seven

Rosa frowned as Thomas darted forward to take her hand and help her down from the carriage. He was being attentive, too attentive, and it was making her nervous. They had been travelling for three days, long dusty days spent in the carriage watching the scenery pass by, and for those three days Thomas had been the most perfect of travelling companions. He'd held doors for her, assisted her at every opportunity and organised their accommodation without her having to lift a finger.

'We'll rest here for the night,' he said, gesturing to the ramshackle coaching inn by the side of the road.

Rosa nodded, knowing she didn't have much choice in the matter. The whole journey had been taken out of her hands. Thomas had seen to it that she never lacked any possible comfort, but hadn't consulted with her on the details of their route across northern Italy to Venice. She knew she shouldn't complain, that was how things had to happen, but it was beginning to irk her to have all her decisions made for her.

'Have a rest before dinner,' Thomas instructed and Rosa felt herself stiffen.

'I think I'll go for a stroll,' she said, just to be perverse. Truly a lie down sounded heavenly and, despite being cooped up in the carriage for most of the afternoon, Rosa felt weary all the way down to her bones, but she refused to let anyone tell her what to do with her life ever again. For twenty years she had acquiesced to her mother's every wish, followed every rule, only to be thrown out and disowned after one single mistake. Never again would she allow Thomas or anyone else to make her decisions for her.

Thomas looked around sceptically. 'A walk? Here?'

Rosa followed his gaze and had to admit it maybe wasn't the most picturesque of spots. Their journey had taken them through rolling hills and towering mountains, past shimmering lakes and lush fields, but this little spot by the coaching inn was far from pretty. On the edge of a small town, the air was thick with the smell of manure and smoke and the buildings that lined the road were in various stages of disrepair. A stray dog wandered aimlessly down the middle of the road, sniffing at the heaped piles of rubbish and every so often letting out a mournful whimper.

'I need to stretch my legs,' Rosa lied, cursing her stubbornness. She could be heading towards a comfortable bed and a short rest before the evening meal, but instead she was going to have to pretend to want to explore the town.

Thomas regarded her for a moment through narrowed eyes and then shrugged. 'If that is what you desire. I will enquire about rooms for the night and then I will escort you.'

It was too much. Rosa wanted to scream, to grasp him by the shoulders and shake him until he told her why he was being quite so obliging. Before they had set out on their journey he had been kind, certainly, and extremely generous offering to escort her back to England, but he had teased her, joked with her. He would have wheedled out the real reason Rosa had refused to rest within a few minutes of light probing. She didn't know why he had changed, but it was making her feel uncomfortable, as if he wanted something from her.

As Thomas walked away Rosa stifled a sigh. If only it were as simple as him wanting *her*, but there hadn't been any suggestion that he found her remotely attractive. She glanced down at her growing bump and had to smile; she supposed her days of attracting eligible young men were well and truly over. Despite pretending not to care Rosa knew this was more difficult to adjust to than she had initially thought. Sometimes it was nice to be wanted, to be desired. From now on she would be either a fallen woman or a mother, neither of which were thought of as conventionally attractive.

That still left her with the question of what it was exactly that Thomas wanted.

She watched him disappear into the coaching inn and waited for a few minutes, feeling her dissatisfaction grow. She wanted to kick something, vent her frustration, but with her ankle still paining her from time to time she knew it wasn't a very sensible idea.

When Thomas hadn't emerged after five minutes Rosa turned her back to the inn and started to wander away. He could easily catch her up and she was still in view of the inn, it wasn't as though anything untoward would happen to her just a few paces down the road.

'Pretty flower for a pretty lady,' an old woman croaked as Rosa walked past her.

'I'm sorry, I haven't any money,' Rosa replied, smiling kindly at the elderly woman, and started to turn away. She spoke slowly, testing out each word in her head before articulating it.

'Never mind, my dear, it pleases me to brighten up the day of a pretty young thing.'

The old woman levered herself up from the battered chair she'd been sitting in and approached Rosa, taking her firmly by the arm and looking up into her eyes.

Rosa struggled not to squirm under the piercing nature of the stare and gently tried to pull away.

'You're troubled, my dear, it doesn't do for a woman with child to be so worried.'

Rosa glanced down, wondering if her pregnancy had reached the stage where it was obvious to passers-by on the street.

'Come, let us see if we can't relieve you of some of those worries.'

Without really meaning to Rosa felt herself following the elderly lady in through a crooked wooden door and taking a seat on an upturned wooden crate. There was something mesmerising about her companion, almost hypnotic, and Rosa felt herself begin to relax as the woman bustled around preparing a pot of tea.

'I really should be getting back,' Rosa said as the woman poured water into a battered old kettle.

The old woman didn't reply and Rosa wondered if she had even heard her. It would be extremely rude just to get up and leave, but she didn't really know what she was doing in this stranger's house.

'You worry about your future,' the old woman said. 'And the future of your unborn child.'

'Doesn't every woman worry about her future? Every mother worries about her child.'

The old woman pottered about the small room some more before setting a cup of tea in front of her. Rosa hadn't had a decent cup of tea since she'd left England many months ago and she longed to cradle the warm china in her hands, inhale the distinctive scent and take a sip.

'Go ahead,' the old woman said. 'Drink.'

With a backwards glance over her shoulder at the empty doorway Rosa picked up the cup and sipped. It was heavenly and reminded her of home, of long winter afternoons curled up on the window seat in the library reading book after book, watching the rain splatter against the glass, or warm summer afternoons sipping tea in the shade and her father declaring, *'Hot drinks do cool you down in warm weather.'*

'Mothers worry about their children,' the older woman said as Rosa took her first sip. 'But most do not have to worry about the scandal of birthing a bastard.'

Rosa choked on her mouthful of tea, the warm liquid spluttering out of her mouth as she looked up in shock.

'It is written on your face, my dear, but do not fret, I do not mean to announce your secret to the world. I only wish to help.'

'Help?' This was all becoming a little surreal.

'Do you not wish to know what the future holds, how you will live, what dreams for your baby will be realised?'

Suddenly all the pieces slotted into place. This woman was some sort of fortune teller, a wise woman who made her living out of luring weary travellers in from the street, then promising to reveal the mysteries of the future.

'I have to go,' Rosa said, standing up abruptly.

'Go, then.' The woman shrugged.

For some reason Rosa didn't move. She didn't believe in the supernatural, had never queued with the simpering, excited village girls at the fayres to have her palm read, to hear the lies about who she might marry or what she might achieve. She could understand the appeal, having a sliver of hope that the predictions might come true, but she had never wanted to listen to the same words as every girl in front and behind her.

'I have no money,' Rosa repeated.

'I don't ask for any.'

'Then what do you want?'

'To relieve some of your worries, my dear.'

Rosa sank back into her chair.

'Come, give me your hand.'

Rosa stretched out her hand, palm upwards, and felt herself stiffen momentarily as the old woman took hold of it and closed her eyes.

'You've had much suffering in your past. A loss of innocence, a betrayal of trust. You're hurting more than you care to admit.'

The words sliced into her and Rosa had to remind herself it wasn't anything that wasn't obvious from the way she carried herself and the fact she was pregnant and unescorted.

'You carry a broken heart, but don't want anyone else to know how badly you were hurt.'

Rosa squeezed her eyes closed as the memory of David's hot breath against her neck came crashing back. The memory she'd tried so hard to forget, the hot, sharp pain and the stone-cold dread.

'Hush, my dear. We all get hurt in this world, it is what you do afterwards that defines you as a woman.'

Rosa was just about to pull her hand away, to break the connection between her and this strange, observant old woman when the twig-like fingers tightened around hers.

'Now for the future.'

'Rosa.' Thomas's voice came low but insistent from the doorway and Rosa felt herself tensing with guilt. Slowly, with a great effort to remain calm and composed, she turned and faced him. She had nothing to feel ashamed about, no reason she could not go wherever she pleased, talk to whoever she wanted.

'What is going on here?' His voice was severe with a hint of concern and Rosa realised she was pleased to have jolted him from the polite persona he had been hiding behind these last few days.

'Just a cup of tea and a talk with a lonely old woman,' the fortune teller said with a secret smile towards Rosa.

'I was worried about you.'

She should have waited for him as she'd agreed, Rosa knew that, but she found she couldn't apologise for wandering off on her own.

'You're suffocating me,' she said quietly.

'Suffocating you?'

She nodded, not able to explain exactly what she meant, just wanting him to understand she'd noticed the difference in him these last few days.

'Come, we'll talk about this in private.'

Rosa was about to protest, but stopped herself. She didn't really want all the citizens of this small town hearing their argument. Thomas took her arm and just as he was about to lead her out Rosa looked back to thank the woman for her time.

'I don't think I need to tell you your future,' the old woman said, leaning in close so only Rosa could hear, a broad grin on her wrinkled face.

Before she could respond Thomas had guided her back into the street and started marching down the road. Rosa almost had to run to keep up, her body tilting to one side as she tried not to strain her injured ankle.

'Where are we going?' she asked, breathless.

'Somewhere private.'

'Back to the inn?'

'That's not private enough for what I have to say.'

His tone of voice told her all she needed to know. He was angry, although she couldn't quite make out why.

He didn't stop walking until they were well outside the town boundaries and then it was only to vault over a low wall. His hands were surprisingly gentle as he leaned back across the wall, gripped Rosa around the waist and lifted her over.

They were standing in a field of wheat, the green shoots just turning golden at the tips. For a moment Thomas's hands stayed in place, holding her above her hips, and Rosa felt her heart begin to flutter as his eyes met hers. There was something new in his gaze, something that hadn't been there before, and Rosa found she was unable to look away.

'Don't do anything like that again,' he said softly. 'I was worried about you.'

All the rebellion and the fire she had felt when he'd burst into the old woman's house and demanded she leave fizzled out with that one sentence. He was worried about her. He cared for her safety.

'I'm sorry,' Rosa murmured, still not able to look away.

'Why did you go off alone?'

Rosa tried to collate a sentence in her head, but found as soon as she thought of the words they were whisked away. Something strange was happening to her body, a heat was rising from deep inside her and she was unable to think of anything but the man in front of her.

'I wouldn't have been much longer in the coaching inn.'

'It wasn't that…' Rosa began, trying to make him understand it hadn't been impatience that had led her to wander the town unescorted. 'I felt stifled, constrained. I needed some time alone.'

Thomas dropped his hands from her waist and Rosa had to resist the urge to grip them and put them back.

This reaction to Thomas, this stirring inside her, was unnerving to say the least. He was an attractive man, both physically and in so many other ways, but Rosa hadn't expected to ever be attracted to another man again. Not after what David had done to her. It shouldn't matter that Thomas's eyes sparkled in the sunlight, that he had protected her at every opportunity and could make her laugh with a single sentence. Rosa knew she should be wary of all men, no matter their positive attributes, but with Thomas she seemed to want to throw all caution to the wind.

'Stifled?' Thomas repeated, turning half-away from her and looking out over the fields.

'When we were at the villa we laughed all the time. You teased me, challenged me.'

She glanced up at him, wondering if the silence meant he was offended.

Thomas sighed. 'And then suddenly I changed.'

Rosa nodded.

He remained still and quiet for a few minutes, but Rosa could see he was choosing his next words, his next explanation carefully. As she waited she felt her pulse quicken with anticipation. She wasn't sure what she wanted him to say, what reason she wanted him to give, but she did want him to touch her again, to take her hand and look into her eyes as he spoke.

Thomas's mind was reeling. It wasn't working, his policy of polite chivalry. A plan had begun to form in his mind on their last evening at the villa, as the Di Mercurios retreated and Rosa had looked at him with those big, worried eyes. A plan that would protect her from the worst the world had to offer whilst conferring certain advantages for his life as well.

He was considering asking Rosa to marry him, and soon. Of course he hadn't fallen in love with the girl, she was pretty, good company, and rather stoical given all the world had thrown at her, but he wasn't interested in love or romance. Despite this he did think they could be of use to one another.

Thomas kept repeating to himself the advantages Rosa would gain from the marriage: a stable home, a decent future, no fear of raising an illegitimate child, but he knew that was to try to assuage the guilt he would feel for deceiving her. He liked Rosa, respected her, but if he were to propose it would be surrounded with half-truths and lies.

He needed to make a decision. If he were to go ahead with his plan, then ideally they would need to wed before they set sail for England. That way the marriage would be a *fait accompli* when they arrived home, with no way of anyone interfering with the result.

'You look so serious,' Rosa said quietly. She raised her hand and hesitantly touched his forehead, trying to smooth out the frown lines between his eyes. It was an intimate gesture, one that he could see she had made on impulse, but her cool fingers felt soothing on his skin. She'd make a good wife, there was no doubt about it— not that he was planning on sticking around to take advantage of a traditional marriage.

'I'm sorry I've been behaving strangely,' Thomas said. 'I've had a lot on my mind.'

'I'm sorry I wandered off. I never meant to worry you.'

'I'm sorry I reacted so brusquely, I thought you might be in danger.'

'I'm sorry…' Rosa began, but was interrupted by Thomas's raised hands.

'Enough, enough. I think it is safe to say we're both sorry for our recent behaviours.'

Rosa smiled softly at him and Thomas felt something tightening inside him. Quickly he suppressed the feeling. That was the last thing he needed, an unwanted attraction to the woman he was considering marrying.

'Seeing as we're out here in the countryside, and seeing as you've been feeling stifled, why don't we take a walk?' Thomas suggested. He needed some time to think, to mull over his options, to wrestle with his conscience, but he also recognised he needed to keep Rosa agreeable.

He offered her his arm and felt a peculiar contentment as she slipped her hand into the crook of his elbow.

'So what did that old woman want with you?' he asked.

Out of the corner of his eye he saw Rosa blush, a pink glow blossoming on her cheeks. It made her look young and fresh, a healthy glow that he found strangely endearing.

'I think she was going to tell my fortune,' Rosa said eventually.

'You believe in all that?'

Rosa shook her head vehemently.

Thomas stepped quickly in front of her, took her hand and looked down at it, frowning and pretending to concentrate hard on the criss-crossing lines.

'I see a bright future for you, young lady,' he said, doing his best impression of an old crone.

'Stop it,' Rosa said, swatting his arm and pulling her hand away.

They walked on for a few more minutes, enjoying the late afternoon sunshine and revelling in the cool breeze that wafted across the fields.

'What's been on your mind?' Rosa asked eventually.

'Hmmm?'

'You said you'd had a lot on your mind. Are you worried about returning home?'

Thomas shook his head slowly. He couldn't tell her he had been contemplating asking her to marry him, she'd probably expire on the spot. He needed time to phrase the question correctly, show her it was to her advantage. It would be more like a business agreement than a traditional marriage, he would gain a companion for his mother, someone to keep his only living relation company whilst he was free to travel the world. And he'd gain an heir, not his own flesh and blood, but his mother could ensure the child was well brought up and it would stop the home of his ancestors leaving the family altogether.

'Have dinner with me tonight,' Thomas said, side-stepping the question.

'We always have dinner together.' Rosa laughed.

'I don't mean in the coaching inn. Be ready at eight and I'll collect you from your room.'

It was only a few hours away, but it would have to be enough time for him to make a final decision. Tonight he would either propose or discard the idea completely.

Chapter Eight

Thomas paced about the small room, struggling with the knot in his cravat. He hadn't had a valet for a long time, not since soon after he'd left England. The young man he'd employed to accompany him on his travels, to look after his possessions and keep him relatively smart, had wept throughout the crossing from England to France with homesickness and Thomas had promptly bought him a return fare as soon as they'd disembarked the ship. His wardrobe had suffered, but he had much preferred the freedom of travelling alone.

Forcing himself to stand still in front of the small looking glass hung from one of the solid beams, he concentrated on the delicate movements of his fingers. Normally he revelled in tasks such as this, tasks where he could enjoy still being able to complete fine movements with his hands, things that one day he might no longer be capable of doing. Tonight, however, he was distracted and preoccupied.

Still he hadn't made up his mind as to whether he was going to propose to Rosa. The past two hours he had swung from one decision to the other, talking himself round when he had thought his mind was made up.

A quiet tap on the door made him pause. He finished adjusting his cravat in the mirror and when he was satisfied he crossed over to the door and opened it.

'It is five minutes to eight, my lord,' a young maid said, looking down at the floor as she spoke. 'My master said to let you know the time.'

She had scurried off down the dimly lit corridor before Thomas even had the chance to thank her.

He pulled on his boots, straightened his jacket and left the bedroom, stepping across the hallway and knocking on Rosa's door.

As she opened the door Thomas felt his eyes widen a fraction at the sight before him. Before leaving Garda he had loaned her the money to buy some new dresses for the journey. One she had been wearing the past couple of days was practical, made of cotton and a dark shade of blue. This dress he had caught a glimpse of as she'd unpacked her packages, but it looked rather different on.

The dress was white with a bright red ribbon around the waist, but it was more the cut that made him linger over the sight of her. Cut to skim over her hips and pinch in just above her waist, it emphasised her curves and her naturally tanned skin. Rosa had let her dark hair cascade over one shoulder, pinning it loosely. She looked every inch an Italian beauty.

Throughout his years of self-imposed exile, and even during his time studying at university and running the family estate whilst his brother was unwell, Thomas had made a conscious effort to avoid female company. It wasn't that he disliked women, quite the opposite, in fact, but from a young age he had been aware of the disease he might possibly carry in his body, aware of the risk of passing it on to his own offspring. He would not inflict the suffering his family had endured on another generation, so he had avoided any situation where he might be tempted by a woman. Over the years it had been difficult, especially when his friends talked of their mistresses and the merry widows they were pursuing, but Thomas had held firm.

Right now, looking at Rosa as a woman for the first time and not just someone needing his help, Thomas felt his resolve falter a little. He had an unnerving urge to sweep her up into his arms, deposit her on the four-poster bed behind her in the bedroom and kiss every inch of her body. He wanted to peel the dress from her, revealing the silky soft skin underneath.

He had to suppress a groan. This was Rosa he was thinking about, the woman he was hoping to have an entirely platonic marriage with.

'Are you well, Thomas?' Rosa asked, reaching out and touching him on the arm.

The heat of her fingers seemed to burn through his layers of clothing and into his skin.

'Quite well,' he managed to croak.

'You look a little strange.'

Thomas rallied. It had been a long day and he'd made some momentous decisions, that was all there was to it. In five minutes he would be back to his normal self and completely under control.

Rosa stepped forward and turned her face up to his. Her breasts brushed lightly against his arm and her lips parted ever so slightly. Thomas could just imagine himself leaning down and covering her lips with his own, kissing her as she moaned underneath him, possessing her.

'I don't mind waiting a few minutes if you need to rest.'

Rest was the last thing on his mind as he reached out and placed a hand lightly on her back to guide her down the stairs. Thankfully the corridor was dark and allowed Thomas time to regain control of himself and by time his foot hit the bottom step of the staircase he felt much more like his normal self. Just as long as Rosa didn't turn to him with that concerned expression again, her lips pouting into a soft O-shape and her eyes wide with worry.

'Everything is ready for you, my lord, just as you asked,' the landlord said quietly as he sidled up to Thomas.

Leading Rosa out the back door of the inn and into the darkness beyond, Thomas felt the weight of responsibility as she trustingly laid a hand on his arm, allowing him to guide her. It was surprising she trusted him so much, out here alone in the darkness, but Thomas supposed he hadn't given her much choice these last few weeks. It was either trust him or try to forge her way in a foreign country all alone.

Nevertheless, the responsibility for another's well-being was unnerving. For years he'd only had to think of himself, to protect himself. Now there would be someone else to put first, at least until he could deliver her safely into his ancestral home with all the servants poised and ready to cater to her every whim.

'Where are we going?' Rosa asked. In the soft moonlight Thomas could just make out the gleam of her eyes looking up at him.

'Be patient,' he counselled. 'And the surprise will be even better.'

Two minutes later the first of the candles Thomas had ordered to light the way came into sight. From there on the landlord had placed a candle every few feet along the path, to guide them to their final destination.

Rosa gasped with pleasure as they followed the trail of candles to a small table in a clearing. It was surrounded by over fifty flickering candles, set up to make the whole area feel like an intimate grotto.

'Thomas, it's beautiful.'

He glanced at her, watching the pleasure on her face as she realised he'd done this all for her and felt a flash of guilt. He wasn't sure why he had insisted on such a spectacle for his proposal, it wasn't as though he was going to dress it up as a romantic gesture. Far from it— he was going to calmly and precisely set out all the reasons it would be advantageous for them to make a match, but still he had decided to make the evening special.

Deftly he pulled out Rosa's chair and waited for her to sit down before plucking the bottle of wine from the table and pouring out two glasses. He'd asked the landlord for dishes that could be eaten cold so they would have absolute privacy for the evening.

'What is all this in aid of?' Rosa asked, her big dark eyes seeking his own out in the candlelight. There were a hundred questions written on her face, mixed with just a little bit of hope. Thomas had seen how she'd looked at him from time to time, when she'd come across him topless whilst boxing or when he emerged from the lake after his morning swims. He might be sworn to a life of celibacy, but that didn't mean he didn't recognise when a woman's skin flushed and breathing became just that little bit more erratic. He wasn't sure if she just found him physically attractive or if it was the fact he'd swooped to her rescue when she was in need of help the most, but Thomas acknowledged Rosa was a little infatuated with him. What he found slightly worrying was his willingness to play on that attraction to get what he wanted.

'Eat,' Thomas said, gesturing at the plates piled high with brightly coloured salad in front of them.

As Rosa picked up her fork Thomas focused his mind for the task ahead.

'I have a proposition for you,' he said, choosing his words carefully. 'I would like you to listen to what I have to say and think about it very carefully before you give me an answer.'

Rosa smiled at him, but her expression turned serious as she studied him.

'I think we should marry.'

Rosa almost choked as he said the words.

'Don't jest, Thomas,' she said. 'I know I am unmarriageable, but please don't poke fun.'

'I'm completely serious.'

'Why would you want to marry me? You're not in love with me. You barely know me.'

All very good points, but he knew enough.

'You need to marry, and soon, or the child you carry will be illegitimate for ever.'

Rosa waved a hand, realised she was still brandishing her fork, placed it on the table and then resumed her gesticulating.

'That's not what I asked. I know why I'm in desperate need for a husband.' Rosa grimaced. 'But no man in his right mind would take me on.'

'Maybe I'm not in my right mind.' She regarded him

in silence, almost warily, until he spoke again. 'Just listen and I will explain.

'You need a husband, a father in name at least to your child. Just imagine, your son or daughter growing up as my heir, with a good family name and no hint of shame or scandal.'

'It doesn't make sense...' Rosa started to say, but Thomas held up a hand imperiously so she would let him continue.

'We would return to England as husband and wife, at least in name, and I would take you to my home. You would have an income, somewhere safe to live, a good education for your child.'

He saw her eyes widen and her eyebrows raise as he continued talking. Rosa was an intelligent young woman and he was going to need all his guile to convince her it was a good idea without telling her all the sordid family secrets driving his proposition.

'It would be a marriage in name and law only. I am not talking about a romantic union, of course there would not be love between us, but I think we rub along well together and over time a certain companionship develops. You would be mistress of your own home, never having to bow to your mother's tyranny again. I would not interfere in how you led your life or how you raised your child.' He paused, watching Rosa carefully. He could see some of his arguments had appealed at least, but that he was far from convincing her at the moment.

'I don't see why you would do all of this.'

'I wish to continue travelling the world,' Thomas said slowly.

'Then surely it makes no sense to burden yourself with a wife and child.'

'I find myself worrying about leaving my mother with no companion, no one to share her old age with.'

'Then employ someone to be her companion.'

No, he needed someone who would be compelled to keep the family secrets, not someone who had no loyalty beyond the money they were paid. Of course he could tell her the truth, tell her of the awful Hunter family curse that had already claimed his father and his brother and might well claim him, too. One day he would, but right now the idea of reliving the awful years of slow decline was too painful.

'There is a certain expectation for a child to carry on the family name.'

'All the more reason not to marry me. My child would by law be your first born, despite not carrying your blood.'

Thomas shrugged and Rosa frowned at his assumed air of flippancy.

'No man wants that,' she said resolutely. 'Another man's child as their heir.'

'There are worse things.'

Rosa shook her head. 'You wouldn't think so when you decided to settle down and found yourself chained to me, with no hope of your own flesh and blood inheriting. No man wants that.'

'Do not presume to tell me what I would want,' Thomas said, hearing the icy tone to his voice and regretting it immediately. This was not the way to win over any woman.

'Then treat me with at least a modicum of respect and tell me the truth behind your proposition.'

'You are nearly five months pregnant and unmarried. My motivations should not matter.'

He regretted the words as soon as they left his mouth, but she was challenging him, provoking him more than he'd expected or prepared for.

Rosa drew herself up, straightening her back and lifting her chin, looking as though she were about to go into battle.

'I may be pregnant with an illegitimate child. I may have very few prospects and very little hope for a decent life, but that does not mean I will tolerate being lied to and deceived. I deserve more than that.'

He saw the tears in her eyes and the miniscule movements of the muscles in her throat as she swallowed again and again in an effort not to shed them. Up until now he hadn't fully appreciated the strength Rosa must possess to even think about raising an illegitimate child alone in a world that penalised even the most upstanding of women. He'd underestimated her in many ways and now the quick and easy marriage he had been hoping for was out of the question. She might have started the evening trusting him, but she certainly didn't trust him now.

'Rosa, I only meant to point out the advantages you would gain from the marriage.'

'And I ask again: what would you truly gain? You're a shrewd man, Lord Hunter, and you wouldn't be suggesting this match if there wasn't something substantial for you in it.'

'I told you…'

'You told me nothing.'

Rosa stood, the legs of her chair scraping along the ground.

'I may not have much in this world, Lord Hunter, but I do still have my dignity and a little self-respect. I think I will retire before anything further is damaged.'

He watched her go, cursing his brain for not being able to come up with the right words to convince her to stay, to convince her a marriage of convenience was the right thing for both of them, even if she didn't know his true motivations.He wondered if he were doing wrong by Rosa, asking her to marry him without telling her the whole truth, but quickly dismissed the idea. His proposal had made it clear it would be a marriage of convenience, nothing more. She would gain his name and his protection, and some day soon he would disappear from her life. What would it matter to her if he took ill in a few years' time? He had resolved never to be a burden on anyone, so he would suffer through the progression of the disease alone, without Rosa ever even needing to know.

Mumbling a profanity in Italian, Thomas stood and strode out into the darkness, letting out a primal growl of frustration once he was certain he was all alone. It should have been so straightforward, so easy. He'd imagined it a hundred times—outlining his proposition, the advantages for Rosa, her grateful acceptance. Never had he thought she might turn him down because he wasn't telling her the whole truth. His explanation should be enough.

He made to turn and follow Rosa, but his remaining self-control stopped him. He needed a new approach, a new line of reasoning, before he tried again. One thing was for sure, Rosa would marry him. There weren't many things in life Thomas didn't manage to make go his way, even if it took more work than he'd originally thought. Before the week was out Rosa would be his wife.

Chapter Nine

'What a strange night it has been,' Rosa murmured, looking down and placing her hand on the bump that was just visible through her dress. 'I wonder what you would make of Thomas's proposal.'

She should have headed straight back to her room when she'd left Thomas, but Rosa was restless and knew she wouldn't sleep. The last place she wanted to be was tossing and turning in bed on such a balmy night, so instead she had crept through the quiet courtyard, past the stables filled with sleeping horses and found a secluded spot a few hundred yards away from the inn. Her seat was an upturned log, but any discomfort she felt was more than made up for by the view in front of her. Away from the lights of the inn the sky was dark, but that darkness was studded by hundreds upon hundreds of sparkling stars. It made Rosa feel small, sitting here underneath such a sky.

'I'm sure I *should* have accepted his offer,' Rosa continued. It was strangely comforting to speak aloud to the tiny person growing inside her. It made her feel a little less alone, a little more grounded and sure of her place in the world. 'I just don't like being lied to.'

That was the crux of the matter. In truth Rosa could appreciate all the merits of Thomas's proposal from her point of view. How wonderful it would be to have the protection of a strong and powerful gentleman. Not to have to endure a hard life where she never knew where her next meal might be coming from or who might find out her terrible secret. Even just the fact that her child would not be born out of wedlock should have had her dragging Thomas to a church before he could change her mind.

'Maybe your grandmother is right. Maybe I am a foolish, reckless girl with only half a brain.'

Rosa fell silent. She should have given more thought to the offer before turning it down. What did it matter why he was proposing? He was a kind man, she doubted he would ever raise his voice to her, let alone a fist. He was courteous and entertaining, and when he looked at her with those sparkling blue eyes Rosa found the world around them merging into the background.

'Your mama is getting carried away,' she whispered. Thomas had never once mentioned romance. He liked her, Rosa was sure of that, just as people liked their spinster aunt or a younger sister, but he certainly hadn't proposed because he was overcome by love for her, he'd told her that theirs would be a marriage in name and in law only. The unnerving and unwanted attraction she felt towards him was most definitely one-sided.

Sitting back, Rosa considered the reasons Thomas had given for the proposal. He wanted a companion for his mother and an heir to his estate. None of it made sense. There was no guarantee his mother would like her, or vice versa. It would be much more sensible to hire a companion, someone who could be easily replaced if there was a clash of personalities. A wife was much harder to dispose of.

'And men want their own blood for their heirs,' Rosa said. 'As much as I would like you to inherit a grand estate, I cannot see a situation where Thomas would not want a child of his own. I will not have you put aside for another in a few years.'

This was a weaker argument. Even if Thomas did change his mind completely after marriage Rosa's child would still be considered legitimate because it would be born in wedlock. It didn't seem to matter so much the circumstances around conception, as long as the mother was married when the child was born.

She tried to come up with a sensible reason for Thomas's proposal, but nothing came. None of it made sense and that was reason enough to turn down the offer. She would not trap herself and her child in a situation without fully understanding all the angles first.

'Am I making a mistake?' she whispered, more up to the stars now than to the child in her womb.

Of course there was no answer. It wasn't the first time in her life that Rosa wished for a confidant, a sister perhaps or a close friend to talk through the options and puzzle out the conundrums. She had never had anyone like that, her childhood had been lonely and grey, a strict upbringing in a solemn household ruled by her mother's iron will. When Rosa had come out in society she'd had friends for the first time, young women who weren't quite as sheltered as her, people to talk to in the noisy corners of the ballroom or over a hot, sweet cup of tea in the afternoon. She'd been close to Caroline, of course, but most of the other young women had been scared away by her mother's sharp tongue and dragon-like demeanour.

'Soon I'll have you, my little love,' Rosa said, feeling the warm glow she always did when she pictured the small baby she would soon hold in her arms. They would never be starved of love, never have to cower away from her as she had from her own mother. She might not be able to provide much, but she was determined her household would be filled with love and laughter, not dread and misery.

Standing, Rosa stretched and looked about her. She certainly hadn't found any answers to the many questions Thomas had left her with, but she knew even with another few hours of pondering she would not be any further forward. All of a sudden she felt weary, the events of the last few days catching up with her. She wanted her bed and she wanted a deep, dreamless sleep to restore her. Maybe in the morning, after a proper rest, things might be clearer.

Thomas paused outside Rosa's door, listening for any sign that she was awake. Everything was quiet inside, but still he lifted his fist to tap on the wood, only dropping it at the last moment. Now wasn't the right time. He might want to get the matter resolved as quickly as possible, but it wouldn't do to smother the girl. She might have even come round to the idea of marrying him by morning all by herself.

Instead of crossing the corridor to his own room Thomas padded silently back downstairs into the bar below. The landlord was still behind the wooden counter, stacking glasses and wiping surfaces, and gave a nod of acknowledgement to Thomas as he entered.

Without Thomas even having to ask, the landlord set a cup of wine on the counter between them before pouring one for himself.

'The evening did not go as you planned,' the landlord said, studying Thomas.

'How did you guess?' Thomas asked, then immediately regretted the hint of sarcasm in his voice. Signor Granese had been most obliging when Thomas had asked for his assistance in setting up the dinner arrangements that evening, and like landlords the world over had a genuine interest in the people sitting in his bar.

'No. It didn't go as planned.'

'I have four daughters. Good, strong, hard-working country girls. I could introduce you.'

'To all four? I think they'd eat me alive.'

Signor Granese gave out a hearty laugh, throwing his head back and allowing the rumbles of amusement to travel all the way from his expansive belly.

'Tomorrow is a new day,' Signor Granese said as Thomas took a mouthful of wine. 'Maybe your English lady will be more receptive to your advances after a night's sleep.' The Italian man regarded Thomas for a few more seconds. 'Or maybe you just need to try harder.'

'It's not like that,' Thomas said quietly. 'I'm not courting her, there is no need to win her heart over. It's her head I'm appealing to, her reason.'

Signor Granese guffawed with laughter again for a few seconds, his face only turning serious again when he saw Thomas's expression.

'You're serious? And here I was thinking you were an intelligent man. It seems I was mistaken.'

'I'm offering her security, safety, a good home and a future. She should be jumping at the offer.'

'And yet she turned you down,' Signor Granese said quietly. 'Why do you think that was?'

Thomas could still see her confused expression, the hope tinged with mistrust written all over her face. She had wanted to say yes, wanted to take the easy path and forget about all her worries, but she had been too wary, too mistrusting.

'She doesn't trust me.'

'Nonsense,' Signor Granese said. 'She travels with you alone, allows you to take her off into the deserted countryside. The lady trusts you.'

'I don't think she trusts anyone, not really.'

As he took another mouthful of wine he remembered the quizzical look on her face as he'd explained his reasons for proposing. In his head he'd expected her to be so grateful for the opportunity he was willing to give her she wouldn't question his motives too closely, but that had been the real sticking point. She hadn't believed him when he'd said he purely wanted a companion for his mother and a wife in name, to provide an heir and look after his estate.

He sighed. He shouldn't be too surprised—one of the things he liked most about Rosa was her shrewd intelligence, the way her dark eyes bored into you as if she were searching for your very soul. Well, today he'd certainly come up short in her estimation.

'Women are the same the world over. They want flattery, romance. They want to be chased, pursued, made to feel like the most important person in your life.'

'Rosa's not like that.'

Signor Granese shrugged. 'It's your choice, but try it and see. Show her the fantasy, the idea of the romantic life you could lead, and I guarantee she will say yes to you.'

The last thing he wanted was to seduce Rosa with romance. His reaction to her earlier that evening had been uncomfortable: the acute desire, the longing to touch her, to kiss her lips. He'd managed to get himself under control, to convince himself it was only natural for a man to have urges when he spent so long cooped up with an attractive young woman. Nevertheless, he couldn't guarantee he'd be able to keep his desire at bay if he started manufacturing intimate situations. Too long he'd spent celibate to ruin things now.

The landlord moved away, bidding Thomas goodnight and leaving a candle flickering on the counter to help guide him to bed.

Thomas finished the rest of his wine in one gulp and stood. He wasn't sure why he was quite so keen to have this matter resolved so quickly. Part of him wondered if it was the impending sense of something going wrong, the knowledge that he had outlived his older brother already and he was only a few months off the age his father had first noted symptoms of the disease that plagued their family. He had an urge to get things sorted, to tie up any loose ends and ensure everyone he cared for was provided for. Then he would be free to travel again, to set off into the world and pack as many different experiences into his life as possible.

'Romance,' he growled under his breath, as if the idea offended him. He pushed back the high stool he was sitting on and got to his feet. The irksome thing was the landlord was probably right. He'd seen how Rosa blushed when she looked at him, how she relaxed when it was just the two of them. A few days of courting and in all likelihood she would say yes to his proposal. The question was, could he be that ruthless?

Chapter Ten

Rosa paced backwards and forward across the small bedroom, trying to prepare herself for the uncertainties of the morning. Part of her wondered if she had dreamed the surreal events of the evening before. The proposal had been unexpected to say the least and she wondered if in the cold light of day Thomas might want to just forget the idea.

Eventually she could delay her descent downstairs to breakfast no longer and cautiously opened the door leading out to the corridor. It was deserted. Rosa sighed in relief—she had half-expected Thomas to be waiting there ready to pounce on her as soon as she emerged. He was a man used to getting his own way, she didn't expect him to take her refusal without any protestation.

'Good morning, Rosa,' Thomas said in her ear as she stepped outside. He must have been waiting just round the corner, out of view.

She jumped, darting her hand to her mouth to prevent a squeal of shock.

'I trust you slept well.'

She hadn't slept at all, but she felt a strange obstinacy blossoming. She would not let him see how much he'd unsettled her.

'Wonderfully, thank you. The bed was very comfortable.' She smiled as if she didn't have a care in the world, trying not to stiffen as Thomas took her elbow and guided her downstairs.

'I've asked the landlord to lay on a special breakfast. You ate so little last night.'

'There really was no need.'

'Nonsense.' Thomas waved a dismissive hand. 'You're eating for two. I wouldn't want the child you are carrying to go without sustenance because of me.'

Rosa's eyes narrowed.

'I'm sure one evening without food would not make too much of a difference.'

'I want only the best for you, both of you.'

Rosa looked at him with raised eyebrows, trying to convey that she knew what he was doing and she wouldn't fall for it. His concern for the baby she was carrying was genuine, that she knew. Throughout the time they had spent together he had taken the utmost care not to endanger Rosa's unborn child and to ensure she was well provided for at all times. That had been done discreetly and without any need for him to signpost what he was doing.

'I was thinking; we probably should ask a doctor to check you over before we commence our voyage back to England. Ensure you are fit to travel.'

'Is that really necessary?'

Thomas shrugged. 'We won't know until the doctor gives his verdict.'

'And if he says I'm not fit to travel?'

'I know of a wonderful villa on the edge of Lake

Garda. Rumour has it the last tenant left quite abruptly so we may get it at a premium rate.' Thomas's eyes were sparkling as he grinned at her and Rosa couldn't hide her own smile.

Breakfast smelled divine as they entered the small dining room and Rosa felt her stomach gurgle in anticipation. She might have protested an evening without food did not matter, but reality was very different.

'Good morning,' a ruddy-faced young man said in English, rising as they entered. He was seated beside a pretty young woman of about Rosa's age. Both had breakfast laid out before them, but the man only had eyes for his wife.

'Fingers Peterson,' Thomas roared as he regarded the other man.

'Hunter. What on earth are you doing here?'

'Fingers?' the pretty young woman said in a soft, low voice.

'I beg your pardon, madam. Just a nickname from our schooling days.'

'This is Lord Hunter, my dear. Most decent chap at Eton.'

Thomas had been to Eton. Of course he had. Her mother would be fluttering her eyelashes and talking about pure bloodlines right about now.

'Hunter, this is my wife, Francesca. The most beautiful and sweetest woman in the world.'

They were newlyweds. No one who had spent more than a few months together could look that happy. Rosa thought of her parents. After twenty-five years of marriage they barely spoke to one another and when they did it was usually for her mother to admonish her father about something.

'A pleasure to meet you, Mrs Peterson,' Thomas said, taking the young woman's hand and bowing over it.

The Petersons turned expectantly to Rosa and she felt herself begin to fidget.

'I had no idea you were married, Hunter. What a dark horse you are. No one's heard from you for years, travelling the globe, and it turns out you've got yourself hitched to a beautiful Italian mystery woman.'

Rosa opened her mouth to protest, but felt Thomas's hand slip around her waist and squeeze ever so gently.

'And you're expecting a child, how wonderful for you both,' Francesca Peterson chipped in.

The words of protest died in Rosa's throat. This was the first time that anyone had directly mentioned her pregnancy—that anyone had noticed solely from her appearance. She wouldn't be able to hide the growing bump any more. The dresses she had were already stretching over her lower abdomen and she knew her face and figure were filling out as happened to all pregnant women. Now her pregnancy would announce to the world she had lost her virtue and she would have to get used to being shunned by all the decent, godly members of society.

She'd expected to feel stronger, more defiant. She was unmarried and with child, but she'd hoped she would still want to shout it from the rooftops, to hold her head up high and withstand the withering looks and unkind remarks. Instead she wished no one would notice, that she could go back to carrying her child in secret. It was a sobering thought.

'My darling Rosa,' Thomas said, lifting and kissing her hand. 'Although not entirely Italian, she is with child.'

'Congratulations!' Peterson beamed.

Rosa smiled weakly.

'Sit down, my dear,' Thomas instructed, pushing her gently on to the long bench. 'You need to eat something.'

'I don't think I've seen you for, what? Four years. And then we bump into each other in the wilds of Italy,' Peterson was saying. Rosa felt as though the words were washing over her, but not quite penetrating her consciousness. 'The last time we were together must have been your dear brother's funeral.'

Rosa felt Thomas stiffen beside her and frowned. She hadn't known he'd once had a brother.

'Your brother?' Rosa murmured quietly. The look Thomas shot her would have silenced a lion.

'He was such a decent chap.'

'He's sorely missed,' Thomas murmured. 'So what brings you to Italy?' Changing the subject quickly.

'Honeymoon. I never managed to leave the Home Counties as we planned to at school. None of this travelling the world, but once we were married it seemed like the perfect opportunity to see a little of the foreign lands.'

'And how are you enjoying your honeymoon, Mrs Peterson?' Thomas asked.

It was the most innocent of questions, but Rosa would swear the new Mrs Peterson blushed a little under Thomas's gaze.

'It is most satisfactory, thank you, Lord Hunter.'

Not the most ringing endorsement of married life, but her husband didn't seem to notice.

'Are you honeymooning, too?' Peterson asked.

'No. We are travelling to Venice to find a passage home to England.'

Mrs Peterson beamed in delight. 'We are heading to Venice, too. We must join parties.'

'What a fabulous idea,' Mr Peterson agreed.

Rosa felt Thomas stiffen beside her. It would put a stop to any further marriage proposals on his part. She should be encouraging the coupling of their parties, but part of her wanted to push the Petersons away. She enjoyed the moments spent alone with Thomas, much more than an unmarried lady should. And if they travelled together they would have to keep up the charade of being married and of the child she was carrying being of Thomas's blood. It would be exhausting.

'We set out straight after breakfast,' Thomas said eventually.

'Brilliant. No need to dilly-dally in the provinces. We'll be in Venice in no time.' Peterson raised a glass of orange juice in a toast. 'To travelling companions.'

'Travelling companions,' Rosa and Thomas murmured, a little less enthusiastically than their new friends.

'Why on earth did you tell them we are married?' Rosa hissed as she ran across the yard, trying to keep up with Thomas.

'It seemed the most logical thing to do,' he said with a shrug. 'It was either that or explain why I'm travelling with a pregnant, unmarried, unescorted young woman.'

Thomas had to hide a smile at the Italian expletives that coursed from Rosa's mouth. She'd certainly learnt some of the native tongue during her time in the country, although hardly anything that could be used in polite conversation.

'And now we're stuck with this pretence for the rest of our journey.'

'Think of it as a rehearsal,' Thomas said.

'A rehearsal?'

'For when we are married.'

'We are not getting married.'

He turned quickly, causing Rosa to barrel into him, and caught her arms gently.

'We will be married, my sweet.'

He could see the defiance flicker in Rosa's eyes and wondered if this was why he liked her so much. She knew, in her heart, that the right thing to do was marry him, but still she protested. It was thrilling, if a little frustrating.

'I could just tell your friends we are not married. That this is not your child.'

'Go ahead.'

He saw her hesitate, then had to hide a smile as she huffed and stalked away.

It had been a shock to see Peterson as they walked in to breakfast, but now he had reconciled himself to the idea of sharing the journey with his old school friend he thought things had worked out to his advantage. He'd sensed Rosa stiffen besides him as her pregnancy had been noticed, heard her breathing accelerate and felt her agitation increase. For all her desire to not care what the world thought of her, Rosa had been brought up to be a respectable woman with good morals. Admitting to two near-strangers that you were unwed and were expecting an illegitimate child could not be easy.

So he'd given her an escape, a way to preserve her dignity with just a little lie. The timing could not have been better. Hopefully Rosa would realise her entire life would be a series of uncomfortable encounters if she insisted on raising her child alone.

Fifteen minutes later he was sitting across from her in the carriage, waving to the Petersons from the window. They had agreed to stop for lunch in one of the villages about three hours away, but until then he had Rosa to himself.

'Lady Rosa Hunter,' he murmured.

'What was that?'

'Just familiarising myself with your new name. Lady Rosa Hunter.'

'I like my current name, thank you very much.'

'How would you like me to address you in front of the Petersons?' he asked, watching her wriggle in her seat. 'Lady H.? Darling Rosa? Rosie-Posie? Sweetheart? Sugar plum?'

'Just my name will do very well,' Rosa said, trying hard not to rise to his baiting.

'We are meant to be in the first throes of love,' Thomas mused. 'Maybe we should endeavour to be closer to one another.'

Before Rosa could protest he slid in to sit beside her, looping an arm around her waist.

She regarded him with a haughty expression, but through the thin fabric of her dress Thomas could feel the pounding of her heart.

'I'm sure the Petersons will expect us to kiss,' Thomas murmured. 'I'm assured all newlywed couples do.'

They were close, their faces mere inches apart, and as Thomas's gaze flickered down to Rosa's lips he realised he wanted this. Not because it would further his aim, but because he wanted to taste her lips, to run his fingers through her hair and pull her against him. He wanted her.

'I think ours was a more practical marriage, most assuredly not a love match.'

Thomas leaned in closer and could feel her breath dancing across his skin. He reached up and tucked a stray strand of hair behind her ear, letting his fingers linger for a few seconds. Rosa swallowed, her tongue darted out to wet her lips and Thomas felt something tighten deep inside him.

'Well we must have liked each other at least enough to consummate our marriage,' Thomas said, his voice low.

Rosa glanced down, then back up, her eyes meeting Thomas's. He saw confusion in them, tinged with desire, but there was something else as well. She was nervous, he realised, more nervous than she should be.

Slowly, against his better judgement, Thomas sat back, breaking off the intimate connection between them.

'What happened, Rosa?' he asked, the levity gone from his voice.

'Wh-what do you mean?' Rosa stuttered.

'How did you end up being alone and pregnant?' It was blunt, but he knew Rosa wouldn't tell him anything unless he asked directly.

'I'm sure I don't need to tell you what occurs between a man and a woman for a child to be made.'

Thomas levelled his best aristocratic stare at her.

Rosa sighed. 'It's not a particularly interesting story.'

'Like it or not, Rosa, our lives are tied together at least until we reach England. Help me to understand what happened to you.'

'What do you want to know?' Rosa asked, looking

at him with large eyes imploring him to skim over the details.

'How did you meet him?'

'David? I've known him as long as I can remember.' Rosa stared off into the distance as if remembering a time far back in her childhood. 'My family had a country house in Kent and David's family owned the property next door.'

'You were of an age?'

Rosa shrugged. 'He was four years older than me, but he had a younger sister I spent my summers with.'

The allure of a friend's older brother. Thomas had known of a few young women seduced by someone who should have been looking out for their welfare, not exploiting it.

'So what happened?'

'I allowed myself to be seduced.' She paused, her eyes flitting about the carriage as if she weren't sure where to look. 'There wasn't any grand plot on his part, no excessive subterfuge.'

'Did you love him?'

Thomas realised the answer to her question actually mattered to him. He wasn't just asking because he wanted to work out the best way to proceed with her resistance to his proposal, he truly wanted to know if she had been in love with this man.

'I thought I did. I was infatuated, I suppose.'

'Did he love you?'

She snorted and Thomas could see the tears glistening in her defiant eyes.

'No.'

He waited, there was obviously a lot more to the story she wasn't letting on.

'Did he tell you that he loved you?'

'Not in so many words. There were gestures and tokens. But he never actually made me any promises, not explicitly.'

Thomas grimaced. He'd known plenty of his sort, the kind of man who seduces and entraps an innocent young woman, making her think he loved her only to pull away when he grew tired or someone new came along.

'You thought you would be married?' Thomas asked softly.

'The night…' Rosa trailed off, hugging her arms around her chest protectively. 'He gave me a ring, just a tarnished old thing. He didn't say a word when he placed it on my finger.'

'He let you believe it was a proposal.'

Rosa nodded. Reaching out, Thomas took one of Rosa's hands in his own, entwining their fingers before gently resting it down in her lap. 'And afterwards?'

'I didn't see him for a few days, but that wasn't unusual.'

Thomas could imagine Rosa waiting nervously for the man she thought she loved to come and make things right. To save her from scandal, from ruin. Rosa sighed and closed her eyes, and Thomas realised the effort it was taking for her to tell this story without breaking down and losing control of herself.

'Eventually I managed to sneak out one evening. I waited for hours for him to return home from some soirée he'd been attending.' She shivered as if remembering the chill that seeped under her skin as she waited for the father of her child. 'He was drunk when he returned and scornful. He dismissed me almost immediately, called me a harlot and denied the child was his.'

Thomas felt his muscles tense and his jaw clench. It was cowardly behaviour to condemn Rosa like that and completely unforgivable.

'I begged and pleaded with him, promised I had never been intimate with anyone else.' Rosa gave a wry smile, but Thomas could tell it pained her to remember the shame and embarrassment of having to beg the man she loved to acknowledge her. 'He told me never to contact him again.'

'That's when you told your parents.'

Rosa nodded. 'I knew I was with child as soon as I missed my monthly courses. I spoke to David about a week later and my parents as soon as he had rejected me.'

'What did they say?'

'My mother ranted and raved for about half an hour, told me I was a disgrace, a whore, no better than a common prostitute.'

'And your father?'

'He just looked at me, disappointed.'

Thomas could tell it was her father's reaction that had hurt her more. From the snippets of information he had gleaned about Rosa over the last few weeks, it sounded as though she'd had a difficult relationship with her mother at the best of times. It was her father who had read to her at night as a child, who had taken her for trips out into the countryside and discussed books and politics with her over dinner.

'Mother arranged for me to be sent away.'

'And your father didn't object.'

'It is hard to contradict my mother.' Despite Rosa's defence of her father Thomas wondered if she was a little disappointed not to have found someone to stand up for her on that front. 'So there you have it,' Rosa said with a grimace. 'All the sordid details.'

Not all the sordid details, Thomas thought. There was still more she was holding back, something deeper, more painful, that she wasn't quite ready to talk about yet.

'I think you have been very poorly treated,' Thomas said, shifting so he was facing her.

'I think I have been very foolish.'

'And I can see why you find it difficult to trust me,' he pressed on.

'I…' Rosa started to interrupt, but Thomas held up a silencing hand.

'You fear history may repeat itself, that I may promise you the world and then go back on my promise. You are fighting for your future, and the future of your child, and you are reluctant to put that future in anyone's hands but your own.'

He paused, but could see his speech was ringing true at least a little. He always had been eloquent, always won the debates at university and been able to talk round even the most hostile of hosts on his travels.

'I want to marry you, Rosa. And I want to do it here and now, or at least as soon as possible. Once we have said our vows there will be no backing out, no abandoning you.'

'Why?' It was barely more than a whisper, but the single word cut through Thomas and halted the flow of his speech.

'I told you why. I want to protect you and your child, give you a future. I want a companion for my mother, I want a family to enliven the estate.'

Rosa shook her head sadly. 'It still doesn't make

sense, Thomas. You're not telling me something and I will not marry you unless you give me the whole truth.'

He felt his throat tighten, the uneasiness that surrounded him whenever anyone got close to the truth about his family weigh down upon him.

'There is nothing else,' he said, trying to sound light and reassuring, but knowing the words came out stiff and untrue.

Rosa shook her head, disentangled her hand from his and waited for him to meet her eye.

'What about your brother?' Rosa asked.

Thomas felt every muscle in his body tense.

'What about him?'

'You never told me you had a brother, and by the way you reacted when Mr Peterson mentioned him he must have been very dear to you.'

'He was,' Thomas said stiffly. 'He died. It is difficult to talk about.'

Rosa waited, looking up at him with her big, inquisitive eyes.

'I'd rather not talk about it,' Thomas said.

Rosa sighed, leaving a long pause before continuing. 'I do find it hard to trust, after what I've experienced I think that is justifiable. I cannot tie my life to yours, to tie both of our lives to yours, when I know you are lying to me. Please do not ask me again unless you are ready to tell me whatever it is you are hiding.'

Chapter Eleven

Rosa flopped back on the bed and let out a weary groan. It was exhausting, pretending to be married to Thomas. Every time they sat down to eat he would put an arm around her, pull her in close and insist on feeding her morsels from his plate. Every time the carriages stopped to allow them to stretch their legs Thomas would lift her down, kiss her cheek and take her hand before Rosa could even think about making an escape. And every time they were alone together he would regale her of tales from his travels or escapades from his time at university.

It wasn't that she didn't like the attention, far from it. A day spent with Thomas courting her was thrilling and entertaining and pleasurable, but every moment they spent together she felt him chipping away at her resolve to resist him.

Rosa knew that was the point, he was a determined man, someone who wasn't used to being denied anything, and he was approaching her resistance to his proposal with an assault by charm. She was determined she would not falter.

She groaned as there was a soft knock on the door. After a day spent travelling all she wanted was five minutes to lie down before dinner.

She opened the door to find Thomas leaning in a relaxed manner on the doorpost.

'Is it time for dinner already?'

'Not quite. There is a small problem.'

Rosa heard movement in the corridor passage behind Thomas before she saw Mr and Mrs Peterson, followed closely by a worried-looking landlady.

'There aren't enough rooms.'

She frowned, watching Mr and Mrs Peterson open the door to the room across the corridor and enter, only to leave the door open behind them.

Rosa dropped her voice, aware they had an audience. 'Not enough rooms? What do you mean?'

'Very busy time of year... Lots of travellers heading for Venice... Last room available,' the landlady gushed in rapid Italian, but after a few weeks in the country Rosa was skilled enough to get her general meaning.

'It just means we will have to share a room, my dear,' Thomas said, his voice light and jovial.

'No.' Rosa shook her head adamantly. 'There must be another way.'

'No need to be shy, darling, we share a room at home after all.'

'No.' Rosa continued to shake her head.

'I know it is unpleasant when you are travelling,' Mrs Peterson said, her ringlets bobbing up and down earnestly as she spoke, 'You are weary to the bone and confined to such cramped quarters, but needs must, Lady Hunter.'

'I could share with Mrs Peterson,' Rosa whispered

to Thomas. For some reason she hadn't really warmed to their female travelling companion, but she supposed she could endure one night in her company if it meant she wouldn't be sleeping in the same room as Thomas.

'I will be a complete gentleman,' Thomas said, his voice low. Quickly he grasped her hand and planted a kiss in the middle of her palm. Whilst Rosa was distracted by the feel of his soft lips on her skin Thomas turned to the landlady and the Petersons. 'The matter is resolved. My wife and I will share a chamber.'

Before Rosa could protest Thomas swept her into the room and closed the door behind them.

'No,' Rosa said emphatically.

'Many married couples share a bedroom.'

'We're not married.'

'Not yet.'

'My answer is still no.'

'To sharing a bedroom or to marrying me?'

'Sharing a bedroom. Marrying you. Everything.'

'Not everything, surely,' Thomas said, raising an eyebrow suggestively.

'Everything,' Rosa repeated firmly.

'I don't mean to ravish you and then force our marriage,' Thomas said, the smile lingering on his lips, but his voice becoming more serious.

'It wouldn't be appropriate.'

'Who is to know?'

'The Petersons.'

'They believe we are blissfully married. Rosa, you are travelling unchaperoned with a single man through a foreign country. And you are already pregnant. I don't believe spending one night, one *chaste* night, in the same room as me is going to make much difference to your reputation.'

She knew he was correct. Soon she would have to let go of her desire to keep up appearances. She would have to learn to show the world she was a ruined woman, disgraced and abandoned. It just went against everything she had been brought up to believe, although she knew ultimately any humiliation would be worth holding her baby in her arms, nurturing her son or daughter through their childhood. It still didn't make spending the night in the same room as Thomas any easier.

'There is no other option, Rosa. I will sleep in the chair; you may have the bed.'

She knew the matter was resolved in Thomas's eyes. When he spoke in that tone of voice, firm and unwavering, there was no swaying him. He began to unpack their small bags, shaking out the creases from the hastily packed clothes and hanging them in the small wardrobe. Rosa realised he did this out of habit, the movements so natural to him from his years spent travelling, moving on from place to place every few days.

As she watched his fingers danced over the knot of his cravat and for a second she thought he might start to undress right there in front of her. The memory of his taut body, the tanned skin pulled tight over the firm muscles, made her feel hot all over and Rosa felt her fingertips grip the edge of the bed just that little bit harder. After a second Thomas tugged at the cravat, pulling it from his neck and letting it fall to the chair.

'Damn uncomfortable thing,' he murmured.

Rosa already knew he was more comfortable in simple shirtsleeves and trousers—the cravat and jacket were not only impractical in the scorching sun, but just other things to get dusty and dirty on the road. Once the cravat was dealt with he stripped off his jacket, turning quickly to catch Rosa watching him.

'I suppose I'd better stop there,' he said quietly, carefully folding his shirtsleeves over on themselves to reveal his bronzed forearms.

'I doubt they'll serve you dinner if you take any more off.'

'You'll want to get changed, I expect,' Thomas said, studying her intently.

Rosa nodded, waiting for him to take his leave, but he just stood watching her for a few more seconds.

'I can meet you downstairs,' she prompted.

Thomas nodded abruptly, spun on his heel and opened the door. He lingered, looking back over his shoulder as if he wanted to say something, but eventually shook his head and closed the door.

Thomas strode across the courtyard, avoiding the horse dung on the way, making straight for the barn. He needed to do something physical. For days on end he had sat in a coach all day long and barely moved even when they had stopped. He missed his early morning swims, his boxing training, even the exertion of vaulting on to the back of a horse and galloping through the countryside.

Inside the barn, once his eyes had adjusted to the dim light, Thomas saw exactly what he was looking for: somewhere to work up a sweat. The hay loft at one end of the barn was reached by a ladder, which had been fixed to the ground with large metal screws. The ladder was immovable and sturdy, and just the thing he could use to work out some of the tension he felt fighting to be released.

He walked round to the back of the ladder, reached above his head and gripped a rung. Slowly, his muscles protesting, he pulled himself up until his chin was level with the bar. His descent was controlled and steady, and Thomas found himself starting to relax.

No wonder he was tense, the situation with Rosa was enough to drive a man to despair. Still she was refusing him. He understood she was scared, he understood she'd been hurt and betrayed before, but he was offering her a way to save herself from complete ruin. Any other woman would be running to the altar before he could change his mind.

For a second he imagined her up in their room, slipping out of the dress she was wearing, turning to look at him over her shoulder with those big, brown eyes. He'd wanted to stay. When he'd suggested she change for dinner he'd wanted to sit back and watch her as she slowly undressed.

Thomas grunted as he pulled himself up again, trying to focus on the burn of his muscles rather than the picture of Rosa letting her dress pool around her ankles.

Of course he'd been tempted by women before, he could appreciate a curvaceous body or bright smile as much as the next man, but he had always strived to keep women he found attractive at a distance. Ever since he had vowed as a young man the Hunter family curse would stop with him Thomas had known he would have to exercise tight self-control. Just one slip, one night where he gave in to his desires and there was the chance of a child being conceived, a child that might be damned to live their life in fear of the insidious disease that robbed them of control of their muscles. No, he wasn't going to risk that for a night of giving in to his desires.

So he had remained celibate. It had been harder at university, when all of his friends were off bedding women of the town, regaling each other with stories of their prowess in the bedchamber. Thomas had sat back on these occasions, affected a knowing smile, and infuriated his friends by not telling them anything. Of course that had earned him the reputation of being a consummate seducer, one who would keep a woman's secret, and there was all sorts of speculation on who he'd had affairs with.

Whilst he had been travelling things had been a lot easier. He'd avoided spending any amount of time with women he found attractive and thus avoided the problem.

But now there was Rosa. Rosa with her dark eyes that conveyed warmth and laughter. Rosa with her soft, caramel skin. Rosa with the body he wanted to sweep up into his arms and lay on the bed, exploring with his hands, his lips, until they both collapsed with pleasure.

Thomas lowered himself back to the floor and paused to wipe the sweat from his forehead. Rosa was pretty and good-natured and yet had a steely quality to her that he admired greatly. Maybe it was only natural he felt this desire for her as they spent more time together. It wouldn't be a problem if he was just delivering her back to England. He had managed to keep control of himself for many years, he could manage a few more weeks. No, the problem arose now he had decided to court her, to seduce her into marrying him. He wanted to kiss her, to run his hands over the curve of her waist, and it wasn't just so she went along with his plan and agreed to marry him.

With a sharp exhalation Thomas reached for the rung of the ladder and resumed his pull ups. He would just have to be strong, to stay focused on why he was doing this and what he wanted to achieve. Rosa was no seasoned seductress, he should be able to resist her.

'My, my, Lord Hunter, what a strong man you are.'

Thomas lowered himself to the floor before turning the quarter-circle to see who had entered the barn. Mrs Peterson smiled coyly as she walked towards him. There was something slightly predatory in her eyes and Thomas found himself moving a step to the left to keep the ladder between him and his friend's wife.

'I saw you enter the barn from my bedroom window and just had to come and find out what you were up to.'

'Exercising.'

'I can see that. So this is what it takes to maintain a physique like yours.'

Mrs Peterson had reached the ladder now and raised a hand, running her fingers over one of the wooden rungs. Thomas eyed her, trying hard to keep his expression neutral. She had been a quiet travelling companion, saying very little over the meals they had all shared, but nevertheless Thomas had felt her eyes burning into him on a number of occasions, noted the mischievous smile that flickered across her lips when she thought no one else was looking. Thomas knew exactly what sort of woman she was and he knew it would be wise to keep his distance.

'I should be getting back to my wife,' Thomas said, emphasising the last word.

'Surely there is no rush. In her condition Lady Hunter will be glad of a few moments' rest.'

Mrs Peterson took another step towards him, moving around the ladder like a snake slithering effortlessly round an obstacle. Thomas planted his feet firmly on the ground, he refused to retreat any further.

A flash of white caught his eye from the doorway of the barn and Thomas surreptitiously focused his gaze over Mrs Peterson's shoulder.

'We haven't had much chance to get to know each other, just the two of us,' the married woman said. Her hand darted out and brushed an invisible speck of dirt from Thomas's shirt, her fingers lingering on the soft material for far longer than was necessary.

Thomas glimpsed the figure outside the barn freeze and knew immediately it was Rosa. She'd come to find him and now realised he was alone in the barn with Mrs Peterson. If she ran, the speculation on her part would completely ruin his chances of ever convincing her to marry him.

'I really should be getting back,' Thomas repeated, sufficiently loudly for Rosa to hear.

'Come now, don't tease a woman,' Mrs Peterson said.

Rosa hadn't moved from her spot just outside the barn doors. It dawned on him she didn't know he'd spotted her and had decided to see what unfolded between him and Mrs Peterson for herself.

Mrs Peterson raised her other hand and placed it on his upper arm, squeezing the muscle underneath her fingers. She'd taken a step closer to him and now there was only a couple of inches between their bodies. He smelled the sweet scent of lavender radiating from her skin. Despite her proximity, despite what she was offering him, there wasn't even the smallest flicker of desire on his part.

He glanced up again. Rosa was still outside, still watching, thinking she hadn't been spotted. There was the chance he could turn this encounter to his advantage. It would be underhanded and sly, but he hadn't exactly been truthful with Rosa so far, so why worry about it now?

'What are you suggesting, Mrs Peterson?' Thomas asked, his voice completely emotionless.

'I'm suggesting we enjoy each other's company a little more. That you put those big muscles of yours to good use.' Her body was pressed up against his now, her hips moving ever so slightly against his own.

Thomas grasped her by the arms and heard her moan at his touch, before the confusion blossomed in her eyes as he gently but firmly pushed her away from him.

'I am sorry if I have ever given you the wrong impression,' he said. 'But I care only for one woman.'

Hurt and rejection flashed across Mrs Peterson's face, but then she rallied and Thomas realised she hadn't been deterred yet.

'There is no suggestion that you don't love your wife, Lord Hunter. All I'm proposing is a little fun, indulging in a little mutual pleasure between two adults. I'm sure you do not wish to trouble your wife with your desires in her condition.'

'I do not wish to offend you, Mrs Peterson, but Rosa is everything I could ever want. She is beautiful and kind and *loyal*,' he stressed the last word, stepping back from his friend's wife at the same time. 'I would never do anything to jeopardise my relationship with her, whatever her condition and whatever anyone else offers.'

The speech was entirely for Rosa's benefit, listening outside the barn, and Thomas only felt a little guilt at being so underhand. If she would just see sense and agree to his proposal he wouldn't have to sink to these depths.

Mrs Peterson recoiled as if she'd been slapped, an unattractive grimace taking over her delicate features.

'I am sure this was just a momentary lapse in your dedication to your own husband and we will have no need to speak of it again,' Thomas said, brushing past Mrs Peterson and striding down the length of the barn. He had to hide a smile as he caught a glimpse of Rosa retreating back into the inn before she could be found eavesdropping.

Chapter Twelve

'**D**amn shame if you ask me—pardon my language, Lady Hunter.' Mr Peterson gesticulated wildly as he spoke, almost knocking over the bottle of wine that stood on the table.

Rosa wasn't sure what was a *damn shame*, she'd stopped following the conversation a few minutes earlier when it became clear Mr Peterson was completely drunk and not making any sense whatsoever.

'I think it's time we got you to bed,' Thomas said with a grimace.

'Oh, not yet, the night is young,' Mr Peterson protested.

'Your wife will be wondering where you are.'

Rosa thought she saw the inebriated man shrug his shoulders dejectedly.

'I doubt it,' he slurred. 'Has more headaches than a dog that's been kicked by a horse.'

Mrs Peterson had indeed sent her apologies she wouldn't be present at dinner, pleading an awful headache. More like embarrassment, Rosa thought, then chastised herself for being unkind. She wasn't sure exactly what she had witnessed in the barn when she had stepped out into the courtyard, but it had looked very much like Mrs Peterson propositioning Thomas and Thomas turning her down.

She watched as Thomas gripped Mr Peterson by the arms, manoeuvred him from his chair and took most of his weight before moving out of the room. Rosa followed behind, wondering if she should do anything to help, but not wanting to get too close to the stumbling feet and flailing arms.

Once Mr Peterson was safely deposited outside his room Thomas turned his attention to Rosa.

'Shall we retire for the evening?' he asked.

It was an entirely innocent question, asked with no guile or even a hint of ulterior motive, but Rosa felt a shiver run down the length of her spine all the same. This was the moment she had been anticipating and dreading in equal measure; the moment she and Thomas would step over the threshold of their shared room and decide exactly what the night held for them.

Rosa tried to stop the unbidden images that flashed before her eyes. Thomas emerging naked and glistening from the lake, Thomas pulling his shirt slowly over his head, his body slick with sweat after boxing. Thomas moving in closer to her in the carriage, his body flush against hers, his eyes heavy with desire and promise.

Rosa found herself nodding, not trusting herself to speak. Knowing her luck her voice would come out as a high-pitched squeak and Thomas would be fully aware of the trepidation she was feeling.

He held open the door for her, waiting for her to enter the small room before he followed behind her. There was a loud click as the door closed behind them and then silence.

'I can sleep in the barn if this makes you too uncomfortable.'

Damn him for being so chivalrous. She would have no qualms about sending a man to sleep in the barn if he didn't offer to do so with such good grace.

'Would you unlace my dress?' Rosa was gratified to see Thomas's eyes widen. At least she could still surprise him, even if she was probably ten times more nervous than he about their sleeping arrangements.

She turned slowly towards the window, glad the soft candlelight concealed the worst of her blushes. She sensed Thomas step in closer to her before she felt his fingers on her skin. Gently he unclasped the fastening at the top of her dress, before letting his fingers drop to the delicate ties beneath, pulling to loosen and unlace. Again and again Thomas's fingers brushed against her skin, each time sending tiny jolts through her body. His breath was warm against her neck and Rosa felt herself arch her back ever so slightly, letting her head roll back towards him. She swayed, knowing she should step away but not quite able to, and then as she felt his steadying palm against her lower back Rosa stiffened.

Even though her dress was loose and she wore only a cotton chemise underneath, it felt as though her chest was being held in a vice which was tightening second by second. A pain shot through her body and her breath came in short gasps.

'Rosa?' His voice sounded distant and faint in Rosa's ears. 'What's the matter?'

Not now. This couldn't be happening to her now. This wasn't David, pressing her up against the wall, forcing his lips on to hers. This wasn't David, lifting her skirts whilst she desperately tried to hold them down, silencing her protests with a rough hand over her mouth. This was Thomas, kind, patient Thomas. A man innocently unlacing her dress. A man who'd never once even tried to kiss her, not really.

She felt Thomas's strong hands encircling her arms and allowed him to lead her to the bed. Gently he sat her down and rested a hand on her shoulder. Even this platonic touch made Rosa tense and she could only breathe properly again when Thomas retreated to the other side of the room.

After a minute or two Rosa had gained control of herself enough to realise Thomas was watching her warily, but had not tried to approach again.

'I'm sorry,' she mumbled.

'Nothing to apologise for,' he said, giving her a smile that would reassure even the most anxious worrier.

She waited for the inevitable questions. A panic attack was not the usual way to react when a man placed a hand in the small of your back. Especially a man she had spent so much time with.

'I don't know why…' she started, but Thomas shook his head.

'You don't have to tell me anything.'

Rosa frowned. Normally Thomas wanted to know every last detail about everything. He was a man who liked to be in control and for him to hold back from questioning her must mean she had worried him. Or he already thought he knew what had occurred.

'I wouldn't have suggested we share a room if I'd known,' he said after a few minutes.

'Known what?' Rosa was feeling more her normal

self now and his understanding tone was beginning to grate on her.

'What you went through with David.'

'You don't know what I went through with David.'

'You're right, of course.'

He capitulated so easily that Rosa felt her entire face crease into a frown.

'My earlier offer still stands. I am happy to sleep in the barn.'

She was half-tempted to send him off to bed down with the horses just to wipe the understanding, commiserating look from his face.

She sighed. Thomas was being a complete gentleman, giving her space, not pressing to know why a man's hand on her back made her turn into a shuddering idiot, and she wanted to punish him for being so nice.

'No. We are adults and I am quite recovered now, thank you.'

He nodded, not moving from his position leaning against the wall next to the door.

'But perhaps you could step outside whilst I finish undressing,' she suggested.

He was out the door before Rosa had finished the sentence, closing it softly behind him and leaving Rosa to change in private.

As she slipped off her dress and brushed out her hair Rosa cautiously allowed herself to analyse her reaction to Thomas a few minutes earlier. David had done a terrible thing to her, that she knew. She'd known she would be skittish around men, had planned never really to get close to one ever again, but then her life had collided with Thomas's. Thomas with the startlingly blue eyes, Thomas with the taut muscles and the protective nature.

Thomas who seemed intent on rescuing her from every-one and everything, including herself. The number of times she'd wanted him to kiss her, wanted him to take her in his arms and pull her to him. It had surprised her after what had happened with David, but she couldn't deny she was attracted to Thomas.

Then he'd laid a hand on the small of her back, the most innocuous of touches, and it was as though she'd been back in the kitchen of David's family home, petri-fied that someone would discover them, petrified some-one wouldn't before it was too late. Maybe it was because David had always touched her there, his intimate little reminder when they were in public that they were bound together.

Rosa shook her head. She didn't want to think of David or the damage he'd inflicted on her. True, there would always be a reminder, the small life that was growing inside her every day, but Rosa knew that was a positive, something good that would come out of some-thing bad.

She slipped into bed, propping herself up on the fluffy pillows, and waited for Thomas to re-enter the room. She would have to give him some sort of explanation as to what had occurred, but she wasn't sure how much she wanted to tell him.

Thomas paced up and down the corridor outside their room, his fists balling and unballing as images of a face-less scoundrel accosting Rosa hurtled through his mind. He knew exactly what that little episode in the room had been about, exactly what had happened to her.

Over the last few weeks as she'd revealed parts of her story to him Thomas had managed to piece together much of what her life must have been like in England. The overbearing mother, the kind but downtrodden father, the dull existence of a well-bred young lady stagnating in the countryside when the London Season was over. Cue the entrance of a slightly older man. A man who should know better than to dally with a debutante. A man who should be interested in protecting a woman's reputation, not ruining it.

That was where Rosa had always skipped part of the story. He'd heard how she'd waited for a proposal that had never come, how even when presented with a pregnancy the so-called gentleman had not stepped up and married the woman he had ruined. But Rosa had never spoken about what had actually happened between her and this young man.

Now he was wondering if it had been entirely consensual. Given her reaction to his touch he rather thought not.

After ten minutes had passed Thomas knocked quietly on the door and waited for Rosa's command to enter. She was already in bed, the covers pulled up almost to her chin, and Thomas had to stifle a laugh.

'I can close my eyes whilst you undress,' Rosa suggested, her voice a little uncertain.

Thomas shook his head, kicking his boots off and then falling into the very upright and very firm chair that stood on one side of the bed. Rosa had placed a blanket and pillow to one side for him, but even with these he doubted he would sleep much. Maybe he would be better off in the hay with the animals.

'What did you think Mr Peterson meant by his comments at dinner?' Rosa asked, her voice unnaturally shrill.

Thomas could sense her nervousness even from this distance and weighed up how best to put her at her ease.

'I get the sense Mrs Peterson isn't as attentive a wife as my good friend would hope for.'

He smiled at Rosa, seeing her weigh up his answer.

'Why do you think that?'

This was too easy. She was just giving him the opportunity to divulge the little meeting with Mrs Peterson in the barn, the meeting she had witnessed but didn't know he knew that. It was exactly the chance he'd been waiting for—the chance to show he was trustworthy, the sort of man she would want to marry.

Thomas opened his mouth to reply, but found the words catching in his throat. Now didn't seem like the right time to deceive Rosa. After what he'd found out about her relationship with David he couldn't quite palate his underhand plan to get her to agree to marry him.

'I saw you in the barn,' Rosa said softly.

Thomas remained quiet.

'I heard what you said.'

'It was the truth.'

'We're not married. It wouldn't have been a betrayal if you had taken up her offer. She's a very attractive woman.'

Thomas shook his head. 'It would have been a betrayal. Peterson is my friend. And we may not be married, but I hold you in much too high a regard to even contemplate any other woman.'

As the words left his mouth Thomas found he actually believed what he was saying. They weren't just the honeyed words to seduce her into marrying him, he actually did hold her in high regard not to want to hurt her in any way.

'And Mrs Peterson is not an attractive woman. Beauty comes from inside, cruelty and jealousy overshadow any skin-deep prettiness.' He looked at Rosa, took in her soft features and warm smile. 'You glow when you stand next to any other woman, Rosa, you outshine them all.'

He could see the now-familiar blush blossoming on Rosa's cheeks. He loved that blush…that signal that something he'd said or done had affected her in such a primitive way.

She shifted in bed, her hair falling around her shoulders and across the bedclothes, and Thomas found himself wishing he was sitting there next to her, close enough to touch her, to smell her. There was something so strong about Rosa, but tonight he had caught a glimpse of her vulnerable side and he wanted to wrap her in his arms and protect her from the Davids of this world.

Physically shaking himself, Thomas momentarily closed his eyes. This wasn't what all this was supposed to be about. He wasn't actually supposed to be seducing Rosa, for his entire adult life he had managed to resist the allure of attractive women, Rosa should be no different. Why then did his whole body thrum with excitement as he imagined slipping into bed next to her?

'What happened with David?' Thomas asked, surprising himself with the question. He was an inquisitive man, a man who always managed to make people tell him what he wanted to know, but the last thing he wanted was to hurt Rosa by making her retell a painful experience.

She sighed and for a moment Thomas thought that would be the end of the matter, but then she started speaking, her words quiet and measured.

'I suppose you deserve to know,' Rosa said.

He didn't, no one *needed* to know what had gone on between them, but Thomas didn't stop her. He wondered if that made him a bad person.

'We arranged a rendezvous one night. I thought David meant to propose. He hadn't approached my father, but I fooled myself into thinking we were far too modern, far too independent for that.'

Thomas could imagine Rosa creeping out, certain she was going to meet the man of her dreams, the Prince Charming young girls were conditioned to hope for.

'He let me in the kitchen door and kissed me immediately. I could tell there was something different about him, something that I hadn't sensed before.' She shifted in bed, letting the sheets fall a little, but Thomas could see she still clutched them tightly with her fingers. As she tried to speak again her voice caught in her throat and he realised he couldn't let her go on. He might want to hear it, might want to know what she had been through so he could better judge what advances she would respond to now, but he wouldn't be able to live with himself if he made her speak of something she didn't want to relive.

'Shhh,' he said, rising for his chair and taking the two short paces to the bed. He sat down beside her and took her hand in his own. 'You don't have to tell me anything, not if you don't want to.'

She looked at him, eyes wide and frightened, and her lips parted a little. In that instant Thomas knew he had to kiss her. He wanted to fold her in his arms and never let go, but more than that he wanted to kiss her soft lips, hear her moans as he trailed his fingers across her skin.

'Inappropriate,' he murmured. This was not the right moment to start acting on his lust for Rosa.

'What?'

'I can imagine what he did to you, Rosa. And I don't want you to have to think about it again, not for my benefit. If you wish to talk about it then please do, but if you don't then that is your choice as well.'

'He didn't force me. Not exactly.'

The *not exactly* almost broke his heart. The scoundrel had forced himself upon her and then made Rosa feel as though she was the one who'd done wrong.

'Rosa, you are a well-bred young woman, seduced by an older and trusted man. Even without anything else that is a wrongdoing on his part.'

'He gave me a ring,' Rosa said. 'But he never actually said the words, never asked me to marry him.' She closed her eyes and Thomas could see the blood draining slowly from her face at the memory. 'Somehow he manoeuvred me up against the wall and all of a sudden his hands were under my skirts.' She swallowed and Thomas realised he was holding his breath as she spoke. It was devastating to listen to Rosa's ordeal, to see how much she blamed herself for this scoundrel's actions. 'I said no, asked him to stop, but he just ignored me.'

Suppressing the rage he felt for this David, Thomas tried to concentrate on what Rosa was saying instead of the burning fury at how she had been treated.

'But I didn't scream,' Rosa said softly. 'I could have woken that whole household up, put a stop to what David was doing in that way, and I didn't.'

'That doesn't mean what he did was acceptable,' Thomas said. 'He forced you, even if you didn't shout out for help.'

'I thought he loved me.' She said it quietly, as if ashamed she had been fooled so easily.

'I'm sure that was his plan, to make you think he loved you.'

'I used to think girls who were seduced by men who had no intention of marrying them such fools.'

'Not fools. You see the good in people, Rosa. It is a wonderful attribute, but sometimes it means you get hurt.'

'Sometimes I still feel his hands on me, his breath on my neck.'

Thomas closed his eyes for just a second, trying to master the wave of anger that crashed over him. If he ever met this David it would take all of his substantial self-control not to beat the man to a pulp. No one should have to live in such fear.

He looked at Rosa, studying her features, the expressions that flitted across her face. Right now he had to put his own agenda aside. Tomorrow he could re-evaluate the best way to get her to agree to marry him, but tonight he would put her first.

'You're safe now, Rosa,' he said, squeezing her hand. 'And I promise to protect you all the time you remain with me.'

She looked at him, a half-smile playing on her lips.

'If I agree to be your wife?'

'Whether you agree to be my wife or not.'

They sat in silence for a few minutes, then slowly Rosa allowed her head to sink down to Thomas's shoulder. He listened to her breathing, watched the steady rise and fall of her chest. For a long while he could tell she wasn't asleep, but didn't want to shatter the peace by talking any more.

It was strangely comforting to feel the weight of her head on his shoulder. For so long he had made it an aim in life to push everyone else away, that way no one else would suffer if he became ill, but he was slowly realising that in doing so he was missing out on something important. The closeness that had blossomed between him and Rosa over the last few weeks was more than anything he'd experienced in years. Not since university had he encouraged friendships and never had he actually wanted to sit and talk to someone as he did with Rosa. Maybe he should just tell her the awful truth about his family, maybe it would be cathartic to be honest with someone he cared about.

As soon as the idea had occurred to him he dismissed it. Anyone in their right mind would run away screaming if they knew what possible fate would befall them if they tied themselves to him. Years of watching his mind and body decline, the worry about him fathering any children and their possible fate. No, it would be better to stick to his plan—to secure a companion for his mother, a healthy heir for the estate and then distance himself from everyone who cared about him to save them the pain later on.

Chapter Thirteen

'Venice is such a *smelly* city,' Mrs Peterson said, waving a dismissive hand out of the carriage window.

'You've been before?' Rosa asked, trying to keep the irritation from her voice.

'No, but everyone says so.'

Rosa managed to restrain herself from rolling her eyes and leaned forward further to try to catch all of the sights of the city they were entering.

'I think it sounds fascinating. A city built on water.'

'If you like that sort of thing.'

'I do,' Rosa said, a little more abruptly than she'd meant to. Six hours she'd been cooped up in the carriage with the annoying woman and her patience was starting to wear thin.

'So tell me,' Mrs Peterson said, a sly look crossing her face, 'what is the enigmatic Lord Hunter really like?'

Rosa sat back and regarded her companion warily. Over the last few days she'd noticed the sidelong looks, the fluttering of her eyelashes, the pouting lips and seductive smiles Mrs Peterson employed whenever Thomas was around. She didn't flirt overtly, not enough for poor Mr Peterson to complain, but Rosa had noticed how she changed when Thomas was close.

At first she'd felt some unexpected pangs of jealousy. Thomas wasn't hers to be jealous about, not really, but when Mrs Peterson stroked his arm or tilted her face up so the sun made her eyes sparkle Rosa had felt jealous all the same. As time had gone on and Thomas had not reacted even slightly to Mrs Peterson's flirtations Rosa had started to find the other woman's behaviour a little amusing.

'What do you mean?'

'Well is he a kind husband? Is he a bore? Is he wild in the bedroom? Come, Lady Hunter, we're friends and this is what friends talk about.'

The carriage was beginning to slow and Rosa wondered if she could delay enough to avoid having to answer any of Mrs Peterson's questions, but as the silence dragged out Rosa sighed and started talking.

'He is kind, the kindest man I've ever known. Generous, too, although he will not accept thanks for his generosity. He holds everyone to very exacting standards, most especially himself, and I don't think anyone could describe him as a bore.'

'You're ignoring one of my questions, Lady Hunter,' Mrs Peterson teased. 'Perhaps I am to assume therefore Lord Hunter is only mediocre in the bedroom.'

'Assume what you will, Mrs Peterson, but Lord Hunter is not mediocre at anything he turns his hand to.' Rosa said it without blushing, trying to hide her smile as Mrs Peterson's eyes widened.

'You mean…'

'Ladies,' Thomas said, throwing the carriage door open. 'Welcome to Venice.'

Rosa almost leapt into Thomas's arms she was so eager to escape the carriage. She regretted assuring Thomas she would be perfectly happy if he chose to ride into the city, he'd been such an attentive travelling companion sitting in the carriage with her day after day that he deserved one morning of freedom. What she hadn't been prepared for was Mrs Peterson's insistence she travel with her instead.

'Smelly,' Mrs Peterson said, nodding her head in satisfaction.

Rosa looked around her in awe. Although she had caught glimpses of the city on their journey through the outskirts, nothing had prepared her for this. Traders shouted in rapid Italian, enticing customers to buy their wares. Immaculately presented men strolled through the streets, calling words of greeting to the beautifully dressed women regarding the world below from their stone balconies. To one side the canal heaved with small boats, transporting passengers and goods, the men in charge of navigating the small waterways shouting and gesticulating as they bumped and scraped their way towards their destinations.

'Magnificent, isn't it?' Thomas whispered in her ear. 'I think Venice is my favourite city in the entire world.'

She could see why. Everywhere she looked there was life and vitality. Most people looked happy, and the ones that didn't were not afraid to show their emotions, gesticulating wildly and venting their anger or irritation.

'I'm sure our lodgings will have rooms available,' Mr Peterson said, dismounting his horse and taking his wife by the arm, guiding her out of the way of a young woman carrying a basket full of fresh fish.

Rosa held her breath. She wanted Thomas to refuse,

for their party to split and to go back to it just being her
and him. It wasn't that she didn't like the Petersons, or at
least she liked Mr Peterson well enough, but she craved
the private moments she'd shared with Thomas at his
villa and on the first half of their journey.

'I'm afraid this is where we must say our goodbyes,'
Thomas said, clasping his old friend by the hand. 'I have
an apartment prepared for the night and tomorrow we
seek passage to England.'

'Surely not, Lord Hunter. You must dine with us one
last time at the very least.'

'It has been a pleasure, Mrs Peterson, but tonight I
must insist my wife rests before we continue our ardu-
ous journey.'

Rosa watched the other woman pout and felt Thomas
slip his arm around her waist, almost possessively.

'Can we not tempt you to join us, while Lady Hunter
rests?'

'Hush, my dear, leave the poor chap alone. We have
intruded on their company for far too long, Lord and
Lady Hunter will be wanting some time together.' Mr
Peterson smiled apologetically and for an instant Rosa
felt sorry for this sweet man who knew all too well his
wife was flirting with his old friend.

'Look after him,' Mr Peterson said as he kissed
Rosa's hand.

She frowned, surprised by the comment. If ever
there was anyone who didn't need looking after it was
Thomas. He was so strong, so capable.

They finished their goodbyes and watched the Petersons disappear into the crowd. Thomas spent a few
minutes arranging for the groom they had hired to find
a stable for the horses before he was back at her side.

'An apartment?' Rosa asked as he took her by the arm.

'Unless you'd rather spend the night with the Petersons?'

She swatted him lightly on the shoulder.

'It is the apartment of a friend. He is currently out of the country and has kindly offered me the use of it whenever I'm in town.'

'How very convenient.'

'Wait until you see it, my dear.'

Rosa felt herself almost skipping along she felt so light and happy. She had Thomas back to herself, they were in a city she had always dreamed about visiting and the Di Mercurios had been left far behind them.

Thomas led her through the maze of streets, over crumbling stone bridges, across quaint little squares. The entire city was moving and alive, and Rosa felt its vitality energising her as they walked.

After fifteen minutes they stopped outside a plain building with a thick wooden door. Thomas knocked and greeted the short, swarthy man who opened the door like a long-lost friend.

'The rooms we're staying in are upstairs.' Thomas grinned, indicating the sweeping staircase. Before Rosa could react he lifted her into his arms and took the stairs two at a time, following the Italian man up the three flights.

Thomas didn't set her down until they were over the threshold of the most beautiful room Rosa had ever been in. Light filtered in through shuttered windows, which when opened revealed a sumptuous sitting room. Silks and satins covered almost every surface and the floor was layered with thick rugs. A chandelier fit for the grandest ballroom hung from the ceiling and delicate glass lamps filled every recess.

'Do you like it?' Thomas asked.

'It's fit for royalty.'

Thomas grasped her hand and pulled her from room to room, showing her the beds laden with dozens of pillows, a room dedicated solely to bathing and finished with the highlight of the entire residence: the balcony. Out here they had a view over one of the canals. Far below them the boats skimmed across the water, the boatmen shouting at each other in rapid Italian as they passed. Over the rooftops Rosa could make out the tips of churches and bell towers, and far beyond the shimmering of the lagoon.

'Rosa,' Thomas said, his voice low and serious. 'Marry me.'

For an instant she almost agreed. It was a heady combination: a romantic spot and a man she adored asking to tie them together for eternity. She wavered. Still he would not tell her the true reason for his proposal, still she sensed he was holding something back, but as time went on and she found herself falling for the man asking her to marry him Rosa wondered how much that actually mattered. He was offering her a respectable future for her and her child. She knew he was a good man, a man who would never purposefully hurt her, so maybe it didn't matter if he couldn't open up to her fully just yet. There would be time for that when they were married.

'Marry me,' he repeated, looking deep into her eyes.

'Thomas…' she began, but before an answer could form on her lips his mouth was on hers. He kissed her hungrily, as if he'd been waiting for an eternity to kiss her, to taste her. Rosa felt all her protestations die in that moment as his lips met hers.

She stiffened slightly as his hands came up and encircled her back, but then as her body realised it was Thomas kissing her, Thomas holding her, she relaxed. Rosa felt his fingers stroking across her skin even through the cotton of her dress and moaned softly. For weeks she had been dreaming of this moment, craving Thomas's kiss, his touch. Now it was a reality and it was so much better than she'd ever imagined.

His lips danced across the angle of her jaw down on to her neck and Rosa shivered as his breath tickled her skin. A warm glow was building from deep inside her and Rosa felt pure joy as Thomas pulled her even closer to him, whispering her name. No matter what he was hiding from her, this couldn't be faked. He desired her, she'd seen it in his eyes before, just as she desired him.

'Marry me, Rosa,' he murmured into her ear, taking her lobe gently between his teeth as he waited for her answer.

'Yes,' she managed to utter, groaning in protest as Thomas pulled away to study her.

'Yes?'

'Yes, I'll marry you.'

Rosa saw the triumphant look for a second before his lips were back on hers, more frenzied, more passionate even than a few minutes ago. She felt his body press against hers, felt the evidence of his desire as he held her close to him.

'Say it again,' he whispered, as he ran his hands down her back, resting them tantalisingly just above her buttocks.

'I will marry you,' she repeated, loving the fire that

was burning in his eyes for her. She'd never imagined wanting another man after David, but Thomas made her feel as though that was all just a bad dream.

He kissed her one more time, before reluctantly pulling away, holding on to the stone balustrade as if to steady himself.

'Then we have a wedding to organise.'

Rosa wanted to protest, to ask him what the hurry was. She wanted him to scoop her up in his arms and carry her through to one of the luxurious beds and kiss her until she begged for mercy, but something stopped her. She'd never been shy before, never doubted that men might find her attractive. She'd not been conceited enough to think herself the belle of the debutantes, but she knew she had a pretty enough face and no major flaws, but that had been before she was five months pregnant. Now she felt cumbersome and swollen, and wondered that Thomas felt anything resembling desire for her at all. She didn't want to push him, only to be rejected, despite the fire she saw in his eyes.

'You rest, my dear. I will return later with everything organised.'

And without another word he left the room. Rosa remained where she was long after the door had closed behind him, uncertain of what had just occurred. She'd just agreed to marry him and then he'd as good as fled from her presence. Despite this being her first engagement Rosa was pretty sure that wasn't how things were meant to happen.

Slowly she sat down at the dainty writing desk and took a piece of paper, holding the pen for over a minute before beginning to write.

Dear Caroline,
I am to be married. Truly I do not quite know how
this happened, but I am sure Lord Hunter is a
good man who will provide for me and my child.
I'm still in shock after accepting his proposal, but
wanted to pen you this short note so you will not
worry about me.

After our wedding we will return to England,
to his family home. When we are back on English
soil I will write again and hopefully it will not be
too long until we are reunited.

I miss you and your sage wisdom.
All my love,
Rosa

Chapter Fourteen

⌒⌒⌒

Thomas strode up and down outside the bedroom, trying not to look down at his hands. Two minutes ago they had been shaking and he kept telling himself it was just from nerves. It was natural for a man to be a little tense on his wedding day, natural for there to be a minute tremor in his fingers.

He glanced down again, holding his hands out in front of him and frowning as he scrutinised them. Nothing. Not even a hint of movement. With a sigh of relief Thomas allowed himself to sink down into one of the plush chairs and close his eyes for a second.

Soon the wedding would be over and they would be on their way to England. True, they would be thrown in close proximity during the voyage, but once he had delivered Rosa safely into his mother's care he would be able to distance himself.

Again the memory of their kiss resurfaced, rekindling the desire that had been hiding just below the surface these past three days. He wanted Rosa, more than he'd ever wanted another woman in his entire life, and she was so tantalisingly close. Each day since she'd agreed to marry him he'd seen her hurt eyes as he had disappeared for hours on end, pretending there was much to prepare for the simple ceremony and their trip home. The truth was he couldn't bear to be close to her—every moment he could see her, touch her, smell her, he risked giving in to his desire and ruining everything.

'I will not desire her,' he murmured to himself. That was not the point of their marriage. Although in a few hours they would be husband and wife he had never planned for it to be a conventional union. He needed someone who would be grateful for the protection and status he could give them, and not be too upset when he declined to visit her bedchamber. If only he hadn't kissed Rosa. It hadn't been planned or calculated, hadn't been part of his ploy to get her to agree to marry him. He'd just seen her standing on the balcony, her lips pursed as she considered his proposal, and he'd just *had* to kiss her.

'Never again,' he promised himself, feeling the stab of disappointment as he denied his body the one thing it really desired.

He stood abruptly as the door to Rosa's bedroom opened and she stepped out nervously. Immediately all his resolutions were forgotten as Thomas moved towards her and took her hand. He bent over it, kissing the soft skin gently, before raising his head and allowing his eyes to meet hers.

'Are you sure?' Rosa asked simply.

He almost laughed. She probably thought his absence the past few days was from doubting his decision to marry her now she had actually agreed. Little did she know he'd had to put physical distance between them, had to avoid any situation where he might accidentally touch her because one touch would be all it took to shatter his resolve.

'I'm sure.'

They walked in silence down the spirals of the staircase and out into the street below. Thomas could feel Rosa's hand clutching at his arm and for the first time he realised what a momentous day this was for her. All along he'd told himself she was gaining something from this arrangement, but he'd tried to deny all that she was giving up. Once they were married she would no longer be free to do as she desired, she would have a husband, someone else to consider, and whilst he was alive she would not be able to marry another man of her choosing. They would be tied together at least in name for the entirety of whatever future he had.

To make it worse Thomas felt uneasy about walking down the aisle with Rosa with the secret of the disease that ran in his family still unspoken between them. He knew Rosa had a right to know, soon she would be part of the Hunter family, too, but he kept telling himself she would never be directly affected. He would leave long before the disease had a chance to develop in him. Still, the guilt of his secret weighed him down as they crossed the cobbled street.

He led her down to the edge of one of the small canals, helping her down into one of the narrow gondolas awaiting them. He saw her eyes widen and a smile of delight appear on her face and part of him began to relax. This was Rosa he was marrying, not some stranger. He knew what she liked, what she disliked. Theirs might not be the most conventional of marriages, but they could rub along together well enough for the next few months until he set off on his travels again.

'Are you nervous?' he asked her as they settled back on the cushions lining the bench on the small vessel.

Rosa laughed. 'Of course. I'm about to marry a man I barely know. A man my mother would approve of.'

'I feel as though that's a bad thing.'

'It is. She would approve of your title, your family heritage. No doubt you have a large entry in *Debrett's*.'

'But would she approve of me?' Thomas asked, moving in closer so he could drop his voice and whisper in Rosa's ear. He was rewarded by one of her fabulous blushes and a stern, rather matronly look.

'No, probably not,' Rosa conceded. 'You are far too impulsive and spend too little time overseeing your estate.'

Thomas settled back on the cushions and watched the city float past as they skimmed over the water. He felt strangely content sitting here next to Rosa, for a while he could forget he was about to deceive her, trap her in marriage without telling her his awful family secret, instead just enjoying sitting with her by his side in his favourite city in the world.

Too soon the gondola bobbed to a halt and Thomas had to lift Rosa on to dry land. She fidgeted nervously whilst he paid the *gondoliere*, looking about her as if she couldn't decide whether to run whilst she still had the chance or cling to him until they'd said their vows.

He'd found a small chapel a few streets away from St Mark's Square with a priest who had agreed to marry them. For a hefty fee this man had overlooked the fact Thomas wasn't Catholic, their visitor status to the city and the need for an official ceremony quickly without all the usual rules and regulations. Thomas knew it would have been simpler to wait until they were back in England, but now he'd secured Rosa's agreement to marry him he didn't want to waste any time in making things official.

'Thomas,' Rosa said, her voice unusually quiet. 'I'm Catholic.'

He grinned at her, at the worried expression on her face and the momentary panic in her eyes.

'I know, my dear,' he said, patting her on the hand reassuringly.

'No, I mean I may not be a very good Catholic…' she grimaced, one hand floating to her abdomen '…but I cannot get married outside the Catholic faith. The ceremony has to be Catholic for it to be valid.'

'I know, my dear,' Thomas repeated. 'We're in Italy. All the priests are Catholic. All the churches are Catholic. The only thing that isn't Catholic is me and I'm assured that as long as I'm baptised in a Christian faith, which I am, we can still marry in the Catholic Church.'

'Oh.' Rosa considered his words for a moment. 'You really have thought of everything, haven't you?'

'I aim to please.'

He led her through the narrow, winding streets, over a couple of stone bridges and to the Chapel of the Virgin Mother. As they neared the chapel Thomas sensed Rosa slow and her grip on his arm tightened a fraction.

'Is something wrong?'

Rosa shook her head, biting her lip at the same time.

'Rosa, look at me. Look at me.' He waited until she complied. 'You can still back out,' he said softly, hoping he wouldn't regret the words. 'We may not know each other well and it may seem like a rush to get married, but I promise you I will be a good husband to you. I will ensure you and your child want for nothing, that you are housed in comfort and cared for. I will never be cruel or demanding and you will be free to make your own decisions about your future.'

He watched her as she searched his eyes, as if looking for something more. He wondered if she wanted a declaration of love, but dismissed the idea immediately. Rosa was an intelligent and observant woman, she would know any such declaration was a lie. He was fond of her, he enjoyed her company and rather inconveniently he desired her in his bed, but he did not love her. He'd shut his heart off from the idea of love many years ago and even Rosa's plentiful charms could not change his mind on that front.

Eventually she nodded, even managing a weak smile.

'Shall we go in, my lady?'

Thomas pushed open the door to the small chapel and led Rosa down the narrow aisle. There were only five rows of pews, all of which were empty except the very front row.

'Who are they?' Rosa whispered as they walked towards the priest standing at the front of the church.

'Our witnesses.'

She gave them a sidelong look and then leaned her head in to Thomas again.

'But who are they?'

He shrugged. He'd paid the priest extra to provide the witnesses. They were probably devout churchgoers, or maybe the priest's drinking friends. It didn't matter to him, as long as the marriage was legal and witnessed by the correct number of people.

'Signorina Rosa Rothwell?' the priest asked.

Rosa nodded.

'Normally I would conduct a short interview in the

weeks before a wedding to ensure both parties were entering into the union of marriage for the correct reasons,' the priest said quietly. 'I understand there are some time pressures at work which mean the usual formalities need to be dispensed with, but I must ask: is there any reason you would like to postpone the ceremony?'

Thomas found he was holding his breath as he waited for Rosa's response. Eventually she gave a small shake of her head and the priest smiled broadly at them both. Clapping his hands together, he arranged Thomas and Rosa in front of him and addressed the gathered witnesses.

Thirty seconds in to the ceremony and Thomas found himself wondering if the priest was drunk. A minute in he was quite certain of it and was contemplating whether there was a touch of madness about the elderly priest as well.

Rosa sent Thomas a worried glance and he responded with his most reassuring smile. It didn't matter if the old man was drunk or mad, he was an ordained priest, licensed to marry them and he seemed to be saying all the right words.

'Miss Rothwell, Lord Hunter, have you come here freely and without impediment to give yourselves to each other in marriage?'

As Rosa said yes alongside him Thomas felt a swell of triumph. There were more questions to come, and the vows themselves, but he'd had a horrible feeling she might remember all of her reservations about marrying him and ask to postpone. Now she was committed. Only a few more minutes and they would be husband and wife.

'Will you honour each other as husband and wife for the rest of your lives?'

'Yes.'

'Will you accept children lovingly from God and raise them according to the law of Christ and his Church?'

All eyes in the chapel drifted to Rosa's bump as hurriedly he and Rosa agreed.

'Since it is your intention to enter into marriage, join your right hands and declare your consent before God and the Church.'

'I, Thomas William Hunter, take you, Rosa Rothwell, to be my wife. I promise to be true to you in good times and in bad, in sickness and in health. I will love you and honour you all the days of my life.'

He looked up at Rosa as he spoke, saw the nervousness and tentative hope in her eyes. She'd suffered so much, lost so much in such a short space of time. He knew she was trying to curb her hopes, to rein in any dreams of a normal life, but still her natural optimism and excitement were breaking through.

As she met his gaze he felt something stick in his throat. He knew he shouldn't be deceiving her like this, knew he did actually care for Rosa and this wasn't the way to treat someone that you cared about, but also knew there was no going back now. He'd deceived her, kept the illness that ran in his family from her, and consigned her to sharing the dreadful uncertainty of never knowing if or when the disease might strike.

'I, Rosa Rothwell, take you, Thomas William Hunter, to be my husband. I promise to be true to you in good times and in bad, in sickness and in health. I will love you and honour you all the days of my life.'

As she spoke a shiver ran down Thomas's spine and he felt as though his whole world had just altered. Quickly he dismissed the notion. Rosa was nearly his wife in name, but soon he would have escorted her safely to the family home and he would be back to travelling the world on his own. In reality, hardly anything had changed.

'What God has joined, no man must divide,' the priest declared, grasping their joined hands and raising them up for the assembled witnesses to see.

A prayer followed, something long and rambling and spoken in Italian that even Thomas could barely understand, before they exchanged rings. This part of the ceremony passed in a blur for Thomas, he could barely remember a word that had been spoken after the priest's declaration.

What God has joined, no man must divide.

It was so final, so complete. He had a wife. The one thing he had always vowed not to have. Someone else who relied on him, someone else to be hurt by whatever cruelties the future had in store for him.

Quickly Thomas shook his head. This was just the shock talking. Rosa knew this wasn't going to be a conventional marriage, it wasn't as though it was a love match. She would be safe and cared for, along with her child, keeping his mother company and keeping an eye on the estate. He would be her husband by law, but in reality they would lead very separate lives. If he did become ill and die Rosa's life would hardly change.

As they exchanged rings he caught Rosa smiling at him. Her earlier nervousness had disappeared and she'd even warmed to the exuberant and gesticulating priest, the suppressed laughter visible in her eyes as she watched the official enthusiastically instruct Thomas how to place the ring on her finger.

He rallied. This was what he'd wanted. Rosa was his

wife, they were legally bound together and he could ensure she was protected in the future.

'Now the bride and groom often kiss,' the priest whispered, leaning forward. 'I'm sure you two young lovebirds know what to do.'

He treated them to a salacious wink that made Thomas question how rigid the vows of celibacy were being followed in this little corner of Venice.

Rosa turned to him and Thomas knew he would have to kiss her. Part of him rejoiced, shouted and screamed with happiness that one more time it was acceptable to pull her in close to him and cover her lips with his own. The other part of him knew it would make the notion of never touching, never kissing, never even entertaining a single night of intimacy with Rosa even more difficult.

Slowly they came together, stepping closer as if it were part of a much practised and choreographed dance. Thomas's hands raised instinctively to brush away the hair from her eyes, to tilt her face up so she was gazing up at him, waiting for the moment they came together. Savouring every second, he dipped his head and brushed his lips against hers, kissing her gently at first, knowing all the things he wanted to do to her were inappropriate in this religious place, but not being able to stop his imagination anyway.

As he felt Rosa respond to him, rising up on her toes to get closer to him, one delicate hand grasping the back of his neck as though she were clinging on for her life, he groaned and deepened the kiss, almost devouring her before pulling away. Now was not the time or the place, but that didn't make it any easier to step away from his new wife, especially knowing this would be the last time they kissed.

Quickly they signed the register, thanked the witnesses, shook hands with the jubilant priest and made their escape back down the aisle of the chapel.

'Lady Hunter,' Thomas said, as they stepped out into the brilliant sunshine from the dark chapel, 'would you care to accompany me on a little trip?'

Rosa laughed. 'Where are you taking me now, Husband?' She said the last word tentatively, as if she couldn't quite believe it was true.

'Well, we leave for England tomorrow, so I thought we should explore a little more of Venice on our last day.'

'That sounds wonderful.' She paused. 'Although I'd be quite happy returning to our rooms for the rest of the afternoon.'

She blushed a wonderful deep shade of pink as she made the suggestion and Thomas was left in no doubt as to her true meaning. He felt a surge of desire, his body responding to his new wife's suggestion of retiring to bed together until the time they had to board the ship for England. He wanted nothing more than to hurry her back to his bedroom, lock the doors and spend twelve hours exploring every inch of her body.

Thomas clenched his fist, digging his nails into the palm of his hand. He was better at controlling himself than this. Better at doing what was right, not what he wanted. He hadn't spent all those years remaining celibate to cave just when all the aspects of his life were falling into place.

Chapter Fifteen

~⌒∽∽⌒~

Rosa felt her heart begin to pound in her chest as they walked up the sweeping staircase hand in hand. The afternoon had been pleasant—a trip to the island of Murano in the Venice lagoon to watch the traditional glassblowers go about their work and then an hour spent being gently propelled along the canals and waterways—but the entire excursion had been overshadowed by her nerves about this evening.

She'd seen Thomas's reaction when she had suggested they return to their rooms immediately after the wedding, seen the desire overshadowed by something else. Throughout their short relationship he had acted warily around her and she rather supposed it was because of the small life growing inside her, and the manner in which it was conceived.

If she was truthful, Rosa was nervous. She didn't know how she would react to another man's hands on her, but this wasn't any man. This was Thomas. Her husband. The man she wondered if she was falling in love with.

'I'm sure you're weary, my dear,' Thomas said as he unlocked the door and escorted her into the set of rooms.

'It has been a wonderful day,' Rosa said.

'You must rest before our journey to England begins tomorrow.'

Rosa nodded, wondering whether he would take his place in her bedroom immediately or leave her to change first before coming in.

Thomas stopped outside her bedroom door and kissed her gently on the forehead, his hands lingering on her arms as if reluctant to let go. Then all too soon he had turned around and disappeared into his own room.

Rosa darted into her bedroom, closed the door and rested her head on the painted wood. It was cool under her forehead and immediately she found herself calming. She wasn't being asked to do anything she didn't want to do, nothing more than what thousands of women around the world did on their wedding nights every single day.

Slowly she started to loosen her clothing, letting the layers drop to the floor one after another. Once only her chemise remained Rosa diligently tidied her clothes away and stood looking nervously at the door.

She had no nightclothes, nothing special to slip into on her wedding night. For the last few weeks she had slept in a simple chemise, not needing any further layers in the heat of the Italian nights. It hadn't bothered her until now, when she wondered what Thomas would think to his bride greeting him in her cotton undergarments.

Rosa grimaced and then climbed into bed. She felt a fluttering in her stomach, acknowledged the nerves that multiplied by the minute as she waited for her husband.

Ten minutes passed, and then fifteen. Despite reclining on the stack of plush pillows Rosa didn't feel in the least sleepy. There wasn't a chance she would doze off on her wedding night.

* * *

When forty minutes had passed without a peep from Thomas, Rosa got up from the bed and padded over to the door. Maybe he was waiting for her in his bedroom. She had never been married before, didn't know the etiquette. Her mother hadn't deemed it necessary to impart any feminine wisdom to her, so maybe it was usual for the bride to go and seek out her husband on the wedding night.

Feeling a little foolish and uncertain, Rosa opened the door to her room and stepped out. There were no candles burning, suggesting Thomas had indeed retired to his bedroom. No doubt waiting for her and wondering what was taking his new wife so long.

Quietly Rosa tapped on the door and when she didn't receive an answer turned the handle and pushed it open. The room was in darkness, but a soft glow was cast across the bed by the moonlight shining in through the window. Rosa could see Thomas's hair on the pillow, his body beneath the sheets. Summoning up her courage, Rosa stepped into the room and walked over to the bed. Without listening to all the tiny doubts clamouring to be heard in her head, she lifted up the covers and slipped in beside Thomas.

As soon as her body touched his she felt him stiffen. For a few seconds she expected him to touch her, to murmur something to her and then to kiss her until she begged him to do more. That was what she'd been imagining ever since their first kiss on the balcony, what she'd pictured a thousand different ways each more pleasurable than the last.

He didn't move. Rosa lifted her hand, felt it tremble, but continued anyway. Gently she placed it on his chest and felt his heart thumping beneath his skin. With her own breathing becoming shallow Rosa let her fingers trail down Thomas's body, feeling his muscles tense.

'Rosa,' he groaned, sounding almost pained.

She moved in closer to him, aware that as yet he still hadn't touched her, hadn't done anything but accept her caresses. Something felt wrong, but she didn't know what. Maybe it was just her inexperience.

Angling her head upwards she moved in to kiss him, softly brushing her lips against his. For a short moment he kissed her back, went to grasp her and pull her close and Rosa felt herself relax. He wanted her.

Then his hands were on her, but pushing her away. She saw him leap out of bed, wondering how he moved quite so quickly.

'What are you doing?' he asked sharply.

Rosa felt her entire world crumble. She'd done something terribly wrong, broken some rule she didn't even know about. All she'd wanted was to be a good wife, to show Thomas she would not let her past stop her fulfilling any part of her new role.

'I thought...' she stuttered.

'You can't be in here, Rosa.'

'It's our wedding night.' She heard how pathetic and lost her voice sounded, hated the naivety there.

'Go back to bed, Rosa.'

Suddenly she rallied. This was not her fault, this was not normal. Throughout her short time as a debutante all the girls had whispered about what occurred once you were married. Everyone knew intimacy in the bedroom was saved for the wedding night, but then a husband would insist on consummating the union, and often.

They were married, there was absolutely no reason for them not to be intimate. Unless…

Rosa gasped, her hand flying to her mouth and then to her abdomen. He thought of her as sullied goods. She was carrying another man's child, she'd already given herself to someone else. He might care for her enough to marry her to protect her future, or whatever reason he insisted on keeping to himself, but he couldn't bring himself to be intimate with her.

She could feel her thoughts running away from her. A small voice of reason tried to protest, tried to tell her that Thomas did find her attractive, to remind her of the passion she'd felt when they'd kissed, but the horror and the embarrassment were way too much.

'We'll discuss this in the morning.'

Rosa climbed out of the bed, barely able to look Thomas in the eye. Wrapping her arms around her, she cursed her thin chemise, wishing she was wearing something more robust, more conservative.

Quickly she backed away from the bed, watching as Thomas kept as much distance between them as possible as if he was afraid she might attempt to rush at him again.

She'd almost reached the door by the time she'd recovered enough to meet his gaze.

'I don't understand,' she said, forcing her voice to remain firm and hating the slight quiver at the end of the sentence.

'We will talk about it in the morning,' Thomas repeated firmly.

Rosa felt the tears brimming in her eyes and knew she could not let him see her cry. She was confused, shaken by his rigid rejection of her, but she still had a modicum of pride.

Taking a deep breath, Rosa concentrated on holding her head high as she turned and walked from the room. She didn't look back, she couldn't, for as soon as she'd turned around the tears had started to fall down her cheeks and nothing on earth would entice her to let Thomas see how upset she was.

Thomas cursed and threw his boot across the room. It was difficult to get on at the best of times, but this morning, after tossing and turning all night long, the tough leather had got the better of him.

Forcing himself to calm down, Thomas retrieved the boot and tried again. Losing control would not help. He needed a clear head and a silken tongue. Rosa was a sensible woman, last night had just been a simple misunderstanding. Once he had explained things he was sure she would come round.

Thomas knew he was deluding himself. The look of hurt and confusion as he'd jumped out of bed, the sobs he'd heard through the walls despite her attempts to muffle them—all of it confirmed that he was a complete and utter bastard.

He could protest for hours that he hadn't led her on, hadn't let her believe their marriage was anything other than one of convenience, but Thomas knew it wasn't true. Yes, he had told her they were marrying so she would get the protection of his name and he would gain a companion for his mother and someone to oversee the minor estate business whilst he was away, but his actions hadn't backed up that cold reasoning. He'd seduced her, wooed her, courted her and then finally kissed her. Of course Rosa had been expecting a conventional wedding night.

Thomas knocked softly on her door. No response. He paced backwards and forwards for a few minutes before knocking harder. Still no response.

Letting out a low growl, he banged on the door with his fist before realising he was taking out his guilt on the ornately carved inanimate object.

Ten minutes later Rosa still hadn't emerged from the room and Thomas began to feel uneasy. She had every right to avoid him for as long as possible, but their ship left in less than three hours and he hadn't heard even the faintest hint of movement.

'Rosa, can I come in?'

He waited, listening for any sound that might reassure him.

'Rosa? Again nothing. 'Rosa, I'm coming in.'

He waited for another few seconds, half-expecting her to rush at the door to prevent him invading her private space, but there was still no sound. Gently he tried the door. It wasn't locked and opened smoothly.

Inside the room was filled with morning light. And completely empty.

'Rosa?' Thomas shouted, looking round in disbelief before going to search the rest of their rooms. It didn't take very long. With just two bedrooms, a sitting room, a bathroom and the large balcony there weren't many places to hide and Rosa wasn't in any of them.

'Rosa,' he shouted again, just in case he was being completely blind, but the reality of the situation was already sinking in. She'd left. Less than one day into their marriage and she'd left him.

A wave of concern washed over him. Rosa was young and pretty in a city she didn't know. Although in appearance she could pass for an Italian, as soon as she opened her mouth it was obvious she was foreign, which made her even more of a target. With no money of her own she wouldn't last more than a few hours.

Visions of all the awful fates that could befall her flashed across Thomas's mind and quickly he tried to suppress them. Imagining Rosa set upon by thieves or cornered by one of the many rowdy groups of sailors that tore through Venice as the ships docked made him curse out loud.

Quickly he dashed out of their rooms and down the stairs to the street, all the while trying to work out exactly where Rosa might seek solace in this city of strangers.

Chapter Sixteen

Rosa stared out over the rail at the shimmering water and frowned. It was getting late and soon the captain would want to weigh anchor and set sail, with or without his most influential passenger.

When Rosa had first fled their rented rooms not long after the first rays of sunshine had filtered in through the windows to signal a new day she had been so upset and angry that she'd planned on not informing Thomas of her plans at all. He hadn't given her the courtesy of telling her the truth about their marriage so why should she let him know of her plans. She'd boarded the ship, early, been shown to a small but perfectly comfortable cabin, and spent the morning pacing the deck and brooding.

Finally she'd relented and found a boy to take a message to Thomas to tell him of her whereabouts, but that had been well over an hour ago and there was still no sign of her odious husband.

Perhaps it would be better to sail for England alone. The passage had already been paid for and once back on English soil she could just pretend the whole embarrassing affair hadn't happened.

Just then Rosa caught sight of a familiar figure saun-
tering towards the ship as if he had all the time in the
world. She heard herself growling and clamped a hand
over her mouth. It was just like Thomas to expect the
entire world to revolve around him, to be confident a
ship wouldn't leave until he was aboard.

She wondered if she should retire to her cabin, but
dismissed the idea almost immediately. Last night she
had run from Thomas, but today she would not. With
hours to analyse his behaviour, to revisit every little
thing they'd said to each other, every little thing they'd
done, Rosa knew he had been hiding something from
her all along. He'd proposed, and then when she hadn't
fallen into his arms, a twittering mass of gratitude, he'd
courted her and seduced her. She'd even found herself
thinking she might be falling in love with him. Today
she knew he was in the wrong and she wouldn't leave to
save him the embarrassment of having to face her, even
if her actions hurt her as well.

'Rosa,' Thomas said in greeting, obviously aware of
the audience they had on the ship.

'Lord Hunter.'

'I hope you are well.'

'As well as can be expected.'

Thomas stepped closer, his voice dropping low, his
hand reaching out to touch her elbow.

'I was worried about you, Rosa. Don't do anything
like that again.'

'Like what?' Rosa asked sweetly.

'Don't run off.'

'You noticed my absence?'

'Of course I noticed your absence. I was worried out
of my mind.' He ran a hand through tousled hair and

Rosa realised he was speaking the truth. 'I've spent the entire morning chasing around Venice, imagining you dead or robbed or worse.'

'Worse than dead?'

'Don't joke, Rosa. I was worried about you.'

'I sent a message.'

'An hour ago.'

'I didn't expect you to be up any earlier. Not after the exertions of your wedding day.'

'Our wedding day.'

'Of course.'

He was standing close to her and they both spoke in low voices, conscious of the crew preparing the ship to leave around them.

'Rosa,' he said, having the common sense to break off first from their shared gaze. 'What happened last night…' He trailed off.

Rosa waited for the apology she knew would never come. Thomas was too used to getting his own way, too confident in his ability to win people over.

'I thought we had an understanding,' he said eventually.

'And what was that?'

'We both gained something from the marriage. You get the protection of my name for yourself and your child. I get a wife who will look after my family interests and be a companion for my mother.'

She regarded him without answering for over a minute. As the seconds ticked by he began fidgeting, something she'd never seen him do before.

'Lord Hunter, do you have any family interests on this ship?' Rosa asked, satisfied with Thomas's confused expression.

'No.'

'And is your mother currently in the vicinity requiring a companion?'

'No.'

'Then I suggest we talk again when we reach England.'

'Rosa…'

'Lady Hunter,' she corrected icily.

'Rosa…'

The rest of his protestation was lost to her as she spun on her heel and stalked off across the deck and down to her cabin below.

'Don't worry, little one,' Rosa whispered as she bent her neck and looked down at her now sizeable bump. 'Mama is here for you. We don't need anyone else.'

Four and a half weeks. It was ridiculous. Beyond ridiculous. Four and a half weeks they had been on this ship and she hadn't uttered a single word to him. When he greeted her she nodded politely in acknowledgement, but didn't speak. Whenever he approached she neatly extracted herself from whatever conversation she was engaged in with their few fellow passengers or the captain and glided away. He hadn't even had the chance to ask her a direct question and force an answer from her lips.

'Heave!' the first mate shouted from a few feet away.

Thomas watched as the sailors battled with the sail, trying to rein it in and secure it before the wind battered the ship even more. Four and a half weeks they'd enjoyed sunny skies and balmy temperatures and today, within sight of the English coastline, a storm was coming.

'Heave! Heave!'

The order was shouted again and again and Thomas

could see the exertion on the sailors' faces. Suddenly one toppled, letting go of the rope which snaked through his arms, whipping backwards and forward like a wild animal. Quickly the other men braced themselves, but Thomas could see it wouldn't be enough. He jumped forward, caught hold of the rope, clenched his hands into fists and added his weight and strength to the line of men.

'Heave! Heave!'

Feeling his muscles bulge and burn, he heaved alongside the sailors, desperately trying to pull in the sail. Little by little they advanced and by the time it was safely tied down Thomas was sweating despite the bracing wind.

Just as he was rubbing his hands together to get rid of the rope burn Thomas felt the first of the fat raindrops on his face, and within seconds the rain was bouncing off the deck. In the distance the clouds looked ominous and dark and Thomas knew it wouldn't be long before the thunder and lightning hit.

'Lord Hunter,' the captain had to shout to be heard over the crashing of the waves. 'Your wife just headed below deck looking unwell. We're advising all passengers to stay in their cabins until the worst of the storm passes.'

'Will we reach the harbour today?'

They were heading for Portsmouth, the town almost visible on the horizon, but Thomas knew the ship battered by a storm might end up anywhere along the coast.

'It is in God's hands,' the captain said.

Thomas saw the concern on the older man's face and cursed inwardly. He'd sailed on many ships, weathered many storms, but he wasn't more than six months pregnant. Rosa would be uncomfortable and frightened and worried for her unborn child.

With quick strides he crossed the deck and swung himself down the narrow stairs. He wouldn't take no for an answer—today Rosa would let him into her room.

Thomas knocked firmly on the door, needing to hold his ear against it to listen for an answer over the whistling of the wind. Nothing, just silence. Cursing under his breath he rattled the door handle and to his surprise found the door swung inwards with no resistance. The sight that greeted his eyes made his blood chill.

Rosa was curled up on the bed, hugging her knees as best she could with the bump in the way. Her face was drained of blood, completely white surrounded by her tousled dark hair. Petrified eyes stared up at him without really seeing him.

'Rosa, what's wrong?' Thomas asked, rushing to her side. 'Is it the baby?'

He looked for the blood, for a sign that something was wrong with the small life inside her, and felt an immense relief when she shook her head.

He sat down next to her, grasping her hands in his own. They were icy cold and trembling and he could see the dents where her nails had dug into the skin of her hands.

'Rosa, what's wrong?'

Shuddering Rosa manoeuvred herself up into a sitting position and then flung her arms round Thomas's neck and buried her face in the space between his head and shoulder. He felt her warm breath on his skin, felt the fluttering of her heart in her chest and realised she was petrified.

'Is it the storm?'

A miniscule nod.

Slowly Thomas felt the icy dread begin to ebb away. He'd thought something was physically wrong with Rosa, something he wouldn't be able to fix. Fear of the storm was distressing for her, but with soothing words of comfort he could at least ease a little of her terror.

He raised a hand to her head and stroked her hair with long, slow movements.

'Hush,' he said softly. 'There's nothing to be afraid of. I'm here. I've got you.'

With a light touch he traced his fingers down her back, keeping her close to him and trying to draw away the pure fear he'd seen in her eyes.

The ship was rocking now, listing side to side as the waves no doubt battered it outside. The small pieces of furniture in the room were just beginning to slide backwards and forward with the movement and Thomas knew before long they would have to secure anything loose that might cause injury. Luckily Rosa did not have much in the way of belongings, just a small bundle of clothes and a couple of books borrowed from the captain. Apart from the bed there was a small chair and table, a shelf with a mirror above it that he supposed acted as a dressing table, and a ceramic washbowl.

'Rosa, I need to make this room safe for us,' Thomas said softly, eyeing the ceramic washbowl as it teetered precariously on its stand. 'I am going to let go for just a minute, remove the loose furniture from the room and then I will be straight back with you.'

She looked up at him, naked fear still in her eyes, but nodded nervously.

Quickly he stood, grabbed the washbowl and chair, dragged them out of the room and down the narrow corridor. He flung both into his own cabin before returning for the small table and the books and repeating the journey. No doubt things would break and get damaged in the storm, but all he cared about was keeping Rosa safe from flying debris.

Closing the door firmly behind him, Thomas took his place by Rosa's side again. She'd regained a little colour in her cheeks and this time instead of burying her head in his chest she managed to look up at him and give him a weak smile.

'I suppose you think I'm very foolish,' she murmured.

'There's nothing foolish about being scared of a storm,' Thomas replied. Many a good ship had been sunk in storms just like this one and many good men lost their lives. Living by the coast, so close to Portsmouth, had taught Thomas to respect the sea and acknowledge the power of the weather in determining the fate of ships and their sailors.

'I've always been scared of them,' Rosa said, giving a little self-deprecating laugh.

'You were scared as a child?'

'I remember when the storms would come I would hide under my bed, make a fortress with pillows and my favourite doll.' Rosa frowned at the memory. 'And then one day my mother came into the room and dragged me out, told me I was too old to be hiding from the storm. She pulled me all the way downstairs and out into the rain and made me stand there until the thunder was rumbling overhead.'

'That's cruel.'

'I know. I think she meant to cure me of my fear, but ever since then I've been even more afraid.'

'I'm not surprised.' He paused and then decided to go

on. 'When I was a boy if there was a storm my brother would wake me and pull me from my bed. Together we would creep up to one of the attic windows and watch the lightning fork across the sky and try to guess when the thunder would rattle the window frames.'

'I often wished for a brother or sister to share those moments with,' Rosa said.

'I miss him.'

Rosa looked at him and Thomas realised he had not spoken to her about his brother before. When she had questioned him on their journey across northern Italy he had answered abruptly and refused to talk any more of his family. He didn't talk often about his father or his brother, it was too painful to remember them as they had been in the prime of their lives before the illness had struck. Thomas felt an unfamiliar lump growing in his throat as he pictured Michael grinning as he led him into some mischief, laughing as they ran across the fields on the estate and looking after him when Thomas had first been sent to join his brother at school.

'You loved him very much, didn't you?'

He nodded. More than anyone else. He'd mourned his father when he'd died, felt the sadness descending on him and shed tears as he'd realised he would never get to talk to his father, hug his father, ever again, but it had been Michael's illness and death that had felt like a mortal blow. It was so unfair that someone so kind, so full of happiness and light, could be snatched away so cruelly.

'I'm sorry you lost him,' Rosa said, squeezing his hand.

'It was a long time ago.' It still felt like yesterday. Thomas could remember every detail from the day Michael had called him home and sat him down, how he'd tried to explain the disease that had claimed their father was now coming for him. Thomas had seen the naked fear in his brother's eyes and knew this was the worse fate; to know you were slowly going to lose the use of your body and mind and not be able to do a single thing about it.

'It doesn't matter how long ago it was, I don't think losing someone you love ever stops hurting.'

Thomas glanced up, saw Rosa's pale, anxious face and realised in that moment how much he had wronged her. She was kind and gentle and deserved so much more than the deceit and lies he'd built their relationship on.

'I'm sorry, Rosa,' he said.

Her eyes widened with surprise at his words.

'What for?'

'For everything. I've treated you badly.'

The ship lurched to one side, almost hurling them off the bed, and Rosa clutched at his arm so hard it hurt. Quickly Thomas gathered her to him, pulling her on to his lap whilst shuffling further back on the bed.

'I think I have some explaining to do.'

Chapter Seventeen

Rosa eyed Thomas warily. She felt strangely safe gathered up in his arms and sitting on his lap. The lurching of the ship seemed less worrisome with his arms around her, but that didn't mean she wasn't still angry with him.

'I'm not sure where to start,' Thomas said, smiling weakly at her.

'Why did you want to marry me?' Rosa asked.

He sighed, lifted his hand and ran it through his hair before pulling her a little closer to him.

'So many reasons. I like you, Rosa.'

'I like many people, our butler at home, the captain of this ship, the man who serves those wonderful iced buns in Hyde Park. Liking someone is not enough of a reason to marry.'

'I know. I think I need to tell you a little more about my family.'

Rosa saw him look down at her and realised he was nervous. Thomas, the man who fought off armed bandits without breaking a sweat, Thomas, who had scaled the ship's rigging with the crew to help on particularly blustery days, was nervous about revealing the truth about himself.

'When I was born I was my parents' younger son. My brother was already being groomed to take over the running of the estate that he would inherit when he became the next Lord Hunter. I would perhaps go into the army or make myself useful to my brother.'

'Did your parents treat you differently?'

'Not really. We had the same education. The same love and care from our parents. It was more my perception of our roles. Michael had to be serious, to work hard. I could have a little more freedom.'

He paused and smiled softly, as if remembering the good times of his childhood. The smile faltered suddenly as he continued.

'When I was eight my father became unwell. It was gradual—first he started having twitches in his limbs, uncontrollable movements. Then he started forgetting things he would normally have had no trouble remembering. And then his personality, his whole being, changed.'

Rosa held back from asking the question that was on the tip of her tongue. He would tell her if he desired what had caused the disease, whether it was syphilis or some other contagion.

'Over the years he declined, forgetting who we were, forgetting who he was. In the end it was a blessing when he died. At least he wasn't suffering any longer.' Thomas paused as the ship creaked after being buffeted by a particularly large wave. Rosa realised her anxiety over the storm had lessened since becoming so engrossed in Thomas's story.

'How awful,' she murmured, realising how devastated she would be to lose her father.

'It was then Mother sat us down and explained what our father never could.'

Rosa looked up at him as the silence stretched out, wondering what it was that was so awful, what secret their father had been hiding.

'You don't have to tell me,' she said, hating the anguish in his eyes.

'I do. You deserve to know. You're part of this now, part of the family.'

A clash of thunder sounded close by, reverberating around the ship, and making Rosa jump and cling on to Thomas. He waited for her to relax a little, for her breathing to become steady and her fingers to relax their grip, before continuing.

'There is a disease in my father's family, the Hunter family curse they call it,' he said, laughing without any trace of humour. 'It is handed down from generation to generation. Not everyone is affected, but there is no way of knowing why one person may suffer whilst another is spared.'

Rosa felt her eyes widen. Of course she had heard rumours of such things, whispered gossip about the families you didn't want to marry into, those that had an unnaturally high rate of madness or premature death, but she'd never actually met anyone who had confirmed these rumours before.

'My mother sobbed as she told us, knowing she was giving us something worse than a death sentence.'

Rosa felt all the blood drain from her face.

'You're afflicted?' He couldn't be, not Thomas. He was so vivacious, so alive. She couldn't imagine a world where he was struck down with the sort of illness he'd described.

Thomas shrugged. 'Who knows? That's the biggest cruelty. So far I have not exhibited any signs, but some people are affected at the age of twenty, some not until they are sixty. You have an entire lifetime to obsess about whether you will be afflicted.'

'And your brother?' Rosa asked, realising the truth behind his brother's death.

'He first showed symptoms at the age of twenty—he died nearly four years ago now.'

Rosa saw the pain on Thomas's face and felt the tears well up in her eyes. He'd suffered so much, lost so many close to him, and still he had to live with the uncertainty of never knowing if one day he would wake up with the signs of the disease.

'I can't imagine anything worse,' Rosa said, trying to digest everything. It now made sense why he had spent so long travelling the world, his burning desire to do as much as possible right now. Rosa knew anything could happen to anyone, people were struck down with particularly severe chest infections or were thrown from horses, but that was always an abstract threat to your life. She couldn't imagine having something like this hanging over her. She supposed he must feel chased, haunted even, as if he needed to keep moving, keep experiencing new things so he would have no regrets if he did become ill.

'So now you understand why I can never have children of my own.'

Rosa frowned.

'I will not risk passing this on to my own offspring. This curse, this affliction, will stop with me.'

Suddenly a few more pieces of the puzzle fell into place. She'd thought it strange when Thomas had insisted he would not want any children, had dismissed her worries about him claiming her unborn child as his heir only to regret it when wanting a son of his own. Thomas had a very good reason never to want children, not any that might carry this awful affliction into the next generation.

'I never thought I would marry, Rosa,' Thomas said quietly. 'I'd resigned myself to a single life, but I did recognise my decisions had consequences for others. By marrying you I get an heir, one that I can be certain will not have to live his life in fear of this disease. I get a wife to take an interest in my estate whilst I am away and keep my mother company. And I get to protect you and a child who has done nothing wrong but will otherwise be stigmatised their entire life.'

Rosa felt a shiver run through her body. They were all very good reasons, very practical reasons. Everything he was saying made sense, but her brain couldn't help but replay one little phrase: *whilst I am away.* He was planning on delivering her back to England and setting off on his travels again. She would have a husband in name, but nothing more, not really. She would lose Thomas, the man she rather thought she would find it impossible to be without. These last few weeks of ignoring him had been pure hell for her. She'd missed his smile, his witty quips, his sharp observations about the other passengers. Every day she'd wished for his apology so she could go back to enjoying his company.

'When you turned up in my life it seemed like too good an opportunity to miss.'

The ship lurched suddenly and Rosa almost went tumbling off Thomas's lap and on to the floor. He caught her at the last minute, pressing her close to his body. Rosa placed one hand on his chest and looked up into his eyes.

Their faces were close, so close she could have tilted her chin just slightly and their lips would be touching.

'And of course you never wanted our wedding night,' Rosa said softly.

She saw Thomas swallow, saw his lips part and his pupils dilate just a fraction.

'It's not about what I want and what I don't want, Rosa,' he said, his voice low and gruff. 'I cannot risk passing this disease on, cannot risk siring offspring of my own. I will not do it.'

Rosa felt her heart squeeze in her chest. It was admirable, really, his determination to stop anyone else suffering as he had. She couldn't imagine what it was like, losing first your father and then your brother, knowing all the time you might be next.

She sat cradled in Thomas's lap, her heart pounding every time the ship tilted, sending her few loose possessions over the room, and tried not to cry. Thomas's resolve was admirable, but it also meant they would never have a proper marriage. Not the marriage she had fantasised about on her wedding day.

Thomas felt drained. He'd never told anyone about the Hunter family curse before, never put into words his pledges and promises to himself, but Rosa was special. She was his wife. She would share the fear of the future now…she would be affected by the disease almost as much as he.

'If I do begin to exhibit symptoms, I will not ask you to look after me,' he said.

'You wouldn't have to ask. I'm your wife.'

He shook his head. 'I do not wish to burden anyone more than is necessary. In a few weeks I will set off for the Americas or perhaps China. If I become ill I have enough funds to pay for someone to look after me.'

'Of course it is your choice,' Rosa said, a little stiffly. 'But just remember when you care for someone it is no chore looking after them.'

She didn't understand, not really. Didn't grasp the trajectory of the illness, didn't grasp that it wasn't just like nursing someone through a bout of pneumonia, it was years of slow deterioration, with the sufferer slowly becoming more reliant on others to do everything for them.

'You care for me?' he asked, the question drowned out by the creaking of the wood surrounding them.

'What did you say?' Rosa asked, having to raise her voice to be heard.

A loud rumble of thunder made the ship vibrate and Thomas could feel the waves buffeting it from either side. Rosa was clinging on to him tightly again, her fingers pressing in to his neck. Part of him wanted to bend down and kiss her, to make her forget her fear and get lost instead in pleasure.

That thought was cut short as the ship keeled to one side violently, sending them both tumbling across the room. Thomas managed to catch Rosa before she hit anything and struggled back to the bed with her where he pinned her down.

'I may need to bind us to the bed,' he shouted over the creaking ship.

Panic blossomed in Rosa's eyes.

'No,' she said vehemently. 'I can't be trapped.'

'We can't have you thrown across the room again.' As he spoke the ship listed and gave an ear-splitting groan, as if the wood was protesting against the buffeting it was receiving.

Just as Thomas reached down to grab the bed sheet the door to the cabin was thrown open and a worried-looking sailor burst in.

'We're taking on water,' he shouted. 'Captain orders everyone up on deck.'

Thomas felt an icy chill travel down his back. There was only one reason the captain would order the passengers to the deck in a storm—the ship must have been seriously damaged.

Grasping Rosa firmly, he pulled her upright, steadying her as she stumbled before finding her balance. The whole cabin was definitely listing to the left now, even when the ship rocked from the impact of the battering waves.

Quickly he led her into the corridor, knowing their best chance was to get to the deck of the ship ahead of the other passengers so he could assess the situation before general panic endangered them all.

He had to haul Rosa up the narrow stairway and felt her slip almost immediately as they got to the deck.

'I can't swim, Thomas,' Rosa shouted, her eyes wide as they slid on the treacherous wood. Rain buffeted them from every direction and the wind was so strong it was a struggle to stand upright.

'Everything will be fine,' Thomas bellowed, keeping his voice as calm as possible, all the while cursing parents who didn't throw their children in a lake or pond and teach them the very basics of swimming.

They struggled over to the captain who was shouting orders to the crew.

'What's happening?' Thomas asked.

The captain's face was pinched and worried, his normally cheerful manner replaced with an overwhelming despair. He glanced at Rosa and lowered his voice.

'We're going down. It's only a matter of time. We're launching the longboats now.'

Thomas felt time slow as he digested the captain's words. Normally he would be asking what he could do to help, but right now he had one single priority: ensuring Rosa and her child reached land safely and unharmed.

'Captain,' a sailor shouted, his face a picture of alarm.

They all turned to see what he was pointing at. Approaching fast was a huge wall of blackness. A wave bigger than anything Thomas had ever seen. One glance at the captain's face said it all. There was no way the ship was going to survive an impact that big. As the crew noticed the growing wave one by one they fell still. A couple dropped to their knees, clasping their hands together, others stood and gawped at the monstrosity speeding towards them.

'Rosa, listen to me,' Thomas shouted, grabbing her by the arms. 'Hold your breath as we go in, kick for the surface and find something to grab hold of. I promise you I will come for you.'

The pure fear flashed across her face and Thomas wondered if she might freeze in the face of such a danger, but then the courage he knew was inside her broke through and she nodded.

'I promise I will come for you,' he repeated.

The wave was seconds away from them now, all other sound had been drowned out by the roaring of the wall of water. Thomas pulled Rosa to the rail of the ship, gripped her hand so tightly he wondered if he might crush her fingers and pulled her over.

They fell into the darkness. The impact of the water stung even through his clothes and immediately Thomas felt Rosa's hand wrenched out of his grip. For long seconds his body was tossed about in the water, limbs flailing this way and that. As he was buffeted Thomas felt the force of debris sailing through the water around him and knew the ship had been hit.

After what seemed like an eternity he allowed himself to kick, trusting his body's intuition to angle him towards the surface. He broke through, desperately gasping a breath of air, before immediately being thrust under by another wave. When he broke the surface again his eyes began searching for Rosa.

Behind him the ship was at an unnatural angle, half-submerged beneath the water and sinking fast. Broken slats of wood dotted the surface of the sea and to his left a ripped and battered sail flapped impotently. None of that concerned Thomas, he just needed to find Rosa.

Panic started to build and he had to force himself to suppress it. Panic was no use to him. He prized his clear head in a crisis and now was not the time to lose it.

Twice more he was dunked under the water by huge waves, coming up spluttering each time and trying to avoid thinking of Rosa's petrified expression as she'd told him she couldn't swim.

He couldn't lose her. He just couldn't.

Kicking hard, he propelled himself through the water, covering only tiny distances before being thrust this way and that by the sea. Just as the panic was about to seize him Thomas spun in the water. He'd heard something, a faint shout.

There, bobbing a few feet away, was Rosa.

She looked exhausted as he kicked his way over to

her. She was half out of the water, clinging on desperately to a bobbing piece of debris.

As he reached her he gripped on to the wood and kissed her, tasting the salt on her lips and feeling an overwhelming relief that she was alive.

'My baby!' she shouted over the roaring of the wind.

Thomas nodded. He needed to get her out of the water and to safety.

'Can you stay afloat?' he asked.

Rosa looked as though she wanted to cling on to him and never let go, but bravely she nodded. Thomas knew she would do anything to save her child.

As he'd been searching for her he'd noticed one of the longboats bobbing on the waves. It was upside down, but looked more or less intact. If he could get to it and clamber in, he could pull Rosa to safety.

A fork of lightning lit up the sky, followed closely by a loud rumble of thunder. The storm was directly overhead now and for just a moment the wind seemed to drop a little. Thomas used the slight lull to thrash his way towards the longboat, wincing as another flash of lightning illuminated the crashing waves.

He risked a glance behind him, reassured himself that Rosa was still afloat, and pressed on. It seemed to take an eternity to reach the longboat. By the time he was clinging on the side he had to pause to suck in great gasps of breath and to allow his muscles to recover.

Quickly he ducked under the water, swimming just half a stroke and popping up underneath the upturned longboat. Without anything to brace against Thomas knew it was going to be near impossible to flip the boat over, but he had to try. He would not let Rosa drown, would not let her unborn child perish, he would use every reserve of strength to save them.

With his hands pressed against the wood, he waited as the sea swelled around him. Just as a big wave lifted him and the longboat up he pushed with all his strength. There was movement, but not enough. Again he waited, felt the swell of a wave and pushed again. This time he thought he'd done it, thought the boat was going to teeter over, but suddenly it crashed back down on him.

Gritting his teeth, Thomas braced himself again, waiting as some smaller waves buffeted him. As the sea started to draw away, a sure sign a large wave was coming, Thomas tensed and then pushed with every ounce of strength in his body. He roared as the boat lifted, caught the wave and flipped over, crashing into the water and sending a salty spray into his face.

Quickly he glanced towards Rosa. She was still clinging on to the wood, but by now she must be tiring, nearing the point where her strength would leave her.

Ignoring his own protesting muscles, Thomas gripped the side of the boat and hauled himself up, shouting in triumph as he saw the two oars still clipped in place. He gripped the two long poles, put them into position and began to heave the longboat over towards Rosa.

With the waves still crashing around them Thomas was certain the boat would capsize at any moment, but eventually he made it back to Rosa still afloat.

'Give me your hand,' he shouted.

She looked at him warily. 'You'll never be able to lift me.'

True Rosa was not as light as she once had been and Thomas's arms were tired from all the exertion, but he knew nothing would let him fail Rosa now.

'Do you trust me?' he asked.

He waited, realising he was holding his breath.

'Then give me your hand.'

Slowly, the fear etched on her face, Rosa let go of the wooden boards with one hand and reached for Thomas. He grabbed her by the wrist and pulled, knowing he would bruise her delicate skin, but aware it was the price he had to pay to get her out of the water.

Panting, they collapsed tangled together in the bottom of the boat. Immediately Rosa flung her arms around Thomas's neck and he pulled her to him, squeezing her and feeling his heart pounding in his chest.

'You're safe now,' he said, knowing it wasn't quite true, but saying it all the same. 'I've got you. You're safe.'

Chapter Eighteen

❧❧❧❧❧❧

Rosa shivered and huddled in closer to Thomas. She could feel the chill from the water right down to her bones and her sodden dress clung to her body, emphasising the cold, but she was alive. The moments after they had jumped from the boat, hand in hand, Rosa had felt a blind panic take over her. There was no feeling like being plunged into the murky, roiling depths of the freezing sea when you couldn't swim more than a stroke or two. She'd been separated from Thomas immediately, but had followed his instructions, kicking for the surface, and luckily had broken through right next to the broken boards. There she had hung, clinging on with raw fingers, until Thomas had come for her, just as he promised he would.

'We need to get to the shore,' Thomas said, raising his voice over the wind and crashing of the waves.

Rosa wasn't sure if the storm was moving on, or if they were just a little more sheltered, huddled in the longboat, but it felt as though the worst was passing over.

'Where is the shore?' she asked.

They both looked around them, searching the darkness for some clue to the direction of land. Rosa knew they had been mere hours away from the port when the storm had struck, but who knew how far they'd been blown off course in that time.

'This way,' Thomas said decisively. 'Keep alert for any signs of life—we may chance upon one of the sailors or other passengers.'

Rosa looked out to sea, her head twisting this way and that, looking for the slightest movement. She desperately wanted to catch sight of a bobbing head or a waving hand, anything that might tell them they weren't the only ones to survive this terrible storm, but the swell of the waves made it so difficult to see more than a few feet on either side of their small boat.

'We have to get you to dry land. Stay low in the boat, try not to move too much,' Thomas said as he picked up the oars again and started to propel them through the water. Rosa was suddenly very thankful for all the hours Thomas had spent building his physical strength. Although he was wet and dishevelled, he still seemed to have a reserve of energy.

They moved through the water, slowly at first, the small boat rocking violently from side to side as it was battered by the elements. Little by little the storm started to settle, the wind dropped, the sea calmed and the rain that had been pelting down became a fine drizzle until that, too, was gone.

Rosa kept still as the minutes ticked by, all the time letting her eyes roam across the surface of the water, ready to direct Thomas if she saw any signs of life. As they drew further away from the site of the shipwreck Rosa knew it was less likely that they would come across anyone, but still she looked, sometimes twisting to check behind her in the hope that she might detect some movement.

'Thomas, look,' she shouted after a few minutes.

She pointed in front of them to their left. It wasn't another survivor she had seen, but in the distance was a small, flickering light. Most likely from a lantern or a candle left in a window, but whatever it was it meant only one thing: they were heading the right way.

Rosa allowed herself to feel the first tentative stirrings of hope. Maybe they would get out of this, maybe they would survive. One day she might be sitting by the fire telling her child the story of how they had been shipwrecked off the coast of England.

'I see it,' Thomas said, and Rosa detected a new-found enthusiasm in his voice. He pulled at the oars just a little harder, propelled them through the water just a little faster.

It seemed to take for ever to get closer to the light, but as it began to burn brighter Rosa almost shouted in relief as another light joined it and then another. Closer to them she thought they were probably lanterns and where there were lanterns there had to be people.

'Hello, there!' a voice shouted from the shore.

'Hello!' Thomas bellowed back.

Three more pulls of the oars and the boat crunched into the stones of the beach and immediately two men waded into the water and grabbed hold of the side of the longboat to pull it further in. Thomas jumped to his feet, hopped out of the boat and without missing a step swept Rosa into his arms. He sloshed through the water, holding Rosa tight to his chest, and strode up on to the beach. Even when they were on dry land he didn't put her down and Rosa was glad. She rather thought her legs might give way if she tried to stand.

'Lord Hunter?' a man asked, his voice tinged with disbelief.

Thomas turned and looked at one of the men who had pulled the boat up on to the beach.

'Todd Williams, what a sight for sore eyes you are.'

The other men standing round gawped at Thomas as they all recognised who he was. Rosa wondered if this was a surreal dream, some sort of hallucination. Surely Thomas didn't know everyone in England.

'Our ship sank,' Thomas said. 'It was hit by the storm. I would be most obliged if you could gather a rescue party and row out to the wreckage and search for survivors.'

The men on the beach nodded as if they had just been given a direct order.

'Yes, my lord,' Todd Williams said. 'We saw the storm hit, saw the ship listing, but couldn't risk launching our boats until the winds died down.'

'I also must ask for your assistance in getting my wife to safety.'

Rosa smiled weakly as all eyes turned to her. She felt as though she might fall asleep on her feet and her shivers had turned into full body shakes some minutes ago.

'I brought my horse down here, my lord. It would probably be quickest if you rode that home.'

'I'm much obliged,' Thomas said. 'I will see your horse is returned tomorrow.'

Giving a nod of thanks and wishing the men good luck with their rescue mission, Thomas clutched Rosa closer to him and began to stride up the beach. Rosa felt her body being lifted on to the horse and complied with

Thomas's instructions to hold on tight. Immediately he was up behind her, cradling her between his arms and urging the horse on in the same breath.

Rosa thought she must have slept while they rode, despite the coldness and the wind that still whipped at her wet clothes, but it seemed only moments later that Thomas was pulling on the reins and stopping outside a grand doorway.

'Where are we?' Rosa asked. She'd only followed parts of the conversation on the beach, but realised they must be near Thomas's family home for him to know all of the men mounting a rescue party.

'Home, my dear.'

'Surely that's not possible.'

'The ship must have been blown west of Portsmouth,' Thomas said with a shrug. 'We're only ten miles outside the city.'

He helped her down and steadied her as she staggered forward, raising a hand to bang on the huge wooden door in front of them.

'Open up, for the love of God,' he shouted when thirty seconds had passed without an answer. Rosa saw him raise a hand to hammer again, but just as his fist hit the wood the door opened a crack. 'Took you long enough, Timkins,' Thomas said as a surprised butler in a dressing gown opened the door.

'My lord, we weren't expecting you for another few days.'

'Which room is the warmest?' Thomas asked.

'Thomas? Is that you?'

Rosa used the last of her strength to raise her head to look at the figure in white descending the staircase.

'I need to get Rosa warm, Mother. Now.' Rosa heard

the panic in his voice, realised this was the most concerned she'd ever seen him and knew she should be worried, too, but everything seemed too surreal, too other-worldly, and as she felt Thomas slip an arm around her waist she felt her grip on consciousness loosen.

As she felt her body being swept upwards she caught a few odd words—*storm...shipwreck...longboat...chill*—before she slipped into darkness.

Thomas lifted his sodden clothes off his body and moved closer to the fire. He was tempted to throw on a nightshirt and dash back to Rosa, but he knew she was in capable hands, more capable than his own right now. He needed to get properly warm and dry so he could be there for her whatever the next few days would bring.

He thought about the baby inside her, thought about the stress and the cold it had been subjected to, and wondered if Rosa's body had been enough protection. He did know if anything happened to the baby Rosa would be devastated. She'd risked so much to protect her unborn child, it was cruel that fate had thrown so many obstacles in her way.

Rubbing his body dry, he slipped into one of his old nightshirts and wrapped his dressing gown around him. He took another mouthful of the whisky he'd found in his room and relished the burn as he swallowed, feeling the warmth inside his stomach seconds later.

With one last look at the fire that burned steadily in the grate he stepped away, dreading what he might find when he returned to Rosa, but knowing he could not keep away. Whatever she was suffering, whatever happened, he would be there for her. He just wished he could take some of her pain himself, he'd rather suffer than watch her hurt.

Quietly he tapped on the door to his mother's room. She'd insisted Rosa be taken there, it was the warmest room in the house and the bed was made up ready. As Rosa had slipped from consciousness his mother had taken over, summoning servants and ordering him to get changed and get warm before he returned. She hadn't asked a single question as to who Rosa was and all he'd told her was of the ship and the storm.

When there was no answer he opened the door a crack and stepped inside. It was wonderfully toasty in the bedroom and his mother must have ordered all the candles to be lit as the room was illuminated in a soft glow. Thomas looked at the bed. Rosa was lying there, tucked up under the covers, the top blanket pulled right up to her chin. She looked peaceful and innocent like that, as if she didn't have a care in the world.

'How is she?' Thomas asked as he walked over to the bed and looked down at his wife.

'She woke briefly, but the poor girl is exhausted. She asked for you. And about her child.'

Thomas's eyes flickered to the visible bump beneath the sheets.

'I've sent a groom to fetch the doctor, we'll know more then,' his mother said, giving him a weak smile.

He perched on the edge of the bed, stroking the hair from Rosa's forehead and leaning in to place a kiss on the rapidly warming skin.

'Is the child yours?' his mother asked softly.

He went to shake his head but found he couldn't complete the movement. The baby might not be his true baby, his flesh and blood, but Thomas could not deny the growing bond he felt with Rosa's unborn child.

'It's complicated,' he said eventually.

'But you care for her?' his mother asked, glancing at Rosa.

'Rosa is my wife,' he said. 'I can't lose her, not like this.'

His mother nodded and Thomas was grateful she left the questions there. Soon he would tell her everything, but right now he didn't have the energy to explain the ins and outs of their relationship.

'Sit down. I'll have one of the maids bring you some food and then you must rest.'

'I can't leave her,' Thomas said.

'You can rest in the armchair,' his mother instructed. 'And I will stay with Rosa all night. I promise to wake you if anything changes.'

Thomas sank down into the soft armchair, feeling his muscles finally relax after all the exertion during the night. For a few seconds he fought to keep his eyes open, but knew he was fighting a losing battle. Less than a minute later he had fallen into a deep, dreamless sleep.

Chapter Nineteen

Rosa awoke as the light started to filter through the curtains. She stretched, feeling every muscle in her body aching, and burrowed down under the sheets. As she became more aware of her surroundings the events of the last few days filtered back. Warily she opened one eye and then the other. She had absolutely no clue where she was. She remembered the ship sinking, Thomas rescuing her in a longboat and the long slog to shore, but after that her memory blurred.

'Good morning, sleepyhead,' Thomas said as she struggled to sit up.

He looked rested and refreshed and as if he'd spent the last few days relaxing at home, not battling to survive a storm and a shipwreck.

'Where are we?' Rosa asked.

'Home.'

'Home?'

He nodded, grinned, looked around him before flopping on to the bed beside her.

'How can we be home?'

'The storm blew up a little further along the coast, we washed up near my family home, so I brought you here.'

'How long have I been asleep?'

'Over twenty-four hours. We thought it best for you to rest.'

'We?'

Thomas grimaced. 'Dr Pewton. He's been four times to check you over. I'll summon him again in a minute to let him know you are awake.'

Rosa bit her lip. She didn't want to ask the question, but needed desperately to know.

'And the baby?' It came out as nothing more than a whisper.

Thomas's smile froze and Rosa felt her heart squeeze in her chest.

'The doctor said it's too early to say,' he said softly. 'But at the moment he seems to be unperturbed by your spell in the water.'

'Really?'

'Really.'

Rosa felt the tension that had been balling in her stomach ever since waking up start to dissipate and she allowed herself a tentative smile.

'I'm glad you are well, Rosa,' Thomas said, taking her hand. 'I have been worried about you.'

Rosa felt her pulse quicken as he brought his lips to the skin over her knuckles. She hadn't had time to process everything he'd told her in her cabin whilst the storm had raged outside, but she did know the hurt and the anger she'd felt on their wedding night had ebbed away and was being replaced by something new. Something warm and pleasant.

'I haven't thanked you for saving my life,' Rosa said, glad when Thomas didn't relinquish her hand.

'There's no need to thank me.'

'Thank you anyway. I know I would have died without you.'

He smiled at her, his eyes lingering on hers for just a second longer than was necessary.

'You're my wife. It's my duty to protect you, or have you forgotten our vows already?'

Rosa couldn't help but laugh. It felt good to have the old Thomas back, the man who teased her and laughed at every opportunity. She'd missed him on the long voyage back to England.

Resting her head back on the pile of pillows, Rosa closed her eyes momentarily and considered what Thomas had just said. It was his duty to protect her, although she doubted many other husbands would go to the lengths Thomas had to save her life. She wondered if duty was the only thing motivating him, or whether there was something else, some deeper feeling, hidden beneath his impenetrable exterior.

'Thomas,' Rosa said quietly. 'Were there any other survivors from the ship?'

He paused and Rosa knew he felt the same guilt at leaving people behind as she did, although she was certain her baby would have been at higher risk if they had.

'Some of the locals mounted a rescue once the worst of the storm died down. Thirty were saved, but twelve have not been found and assumed perished. The captain is amongst the missing.'

'He was such a kind man.'

Nodding, Thomas squeezed her hand. 'We should

have a memorial service for all those that died once you have recovered,' he suggested.

'That's a lovely idea.'

'I should let you rest. I shall summon the doctor and ask him to check you over. And I must inform my mother you are awake. She's been beside herself with worry.'

Rosa's eyes shot wide open and she felt her breath catch in her throat.

'Your mother?' she asked.

'Yes—middle-aged woman, lives here, raised me from childhood.'

'Yes, yes, yes,' Rosa said with a dismissive wave of the hand—she was too agitated to pay much attention to his words. 'Have you told her we're married?'

'Of course.'

'And what about…?' Rosa trailed off, placing a hand on her abdomen.

'I've told her it is complicated. It is up to you what more you say.'

Thomas bent over and kissed her lightly on the forehead, his lips only just brushing her skin before they were gone all too soon.

'You are a very lucky woman, Lady Hunter,' Dr Pewton said, snapping his doctor's bag closed with one hand before straightening up.

'You truly cannot find anything wrong with the baby?'

'It is difficult to tell, but the movements are usually a good indicator things are progressing as they should. If you do not feel any movements for a long while then please have your husband fetch me.'

'I cannot believe there is no damage after such a lengthy submersion.'

'The female body was built to nurture and protect the unborn child, it would appear your body did just that. I will return to see you tomorrow. Please rest until then, we can talk about getting you out of bed tomorrow.'

'Thank you, Doctor.'

Rosa watched as the elderly man left the room and allowed herself a small smile of relief. She had been convinced the time she'd spent underwater and bobbing around in the cold sea must have damaged the baby, despite feeling the strong kicks she knew so well. It was reassuring to know the doctor was not overly concerned for her baby.

She was just about to close her eyes and rest as the doctor had ordered when there was a quiet knock on the door. A few seconds later it opened and a petite, pretty, middle-aged woman slipped into the room.

'Rosa, my dear, I wanted to pop in and check on you.'

Rosa felt a flutter of nerves in her stomach. This was her mother-in-law, the woman Thomas held in such high regard, the woman she was destined to spend the rest of her life living with. On first glance you couldn't have imagined a more different woman to Rosa's own mother. She was smiling where Rosa's mother was haughty, welcoming where Rosa's mother was stand-offish. Physically, too, the two women were opposites. Thomas's mother was small, with delicate features and blonde hair streaked with a few strands of silver. Rosa's mother was statuesque in her bearing, with dark hair and olive skin.

'I am the Dowager Lady Hunter, but you must call me Sarah.'

'Thank you for taking me into your home,' Rosa said, having to clutch her hands together to stop them from shaking.

'Nonsense, my dear, it is your home too now. My son tells me you two were married a month ago.'

Rosa searched for the reproach, the disapproval, in her mother-in-law's tone, but could find none. There was just genuine interest and happiness.

'I must confide in you, Rosa, I never thought I would have a daughter-in-law, I never dared to hope these last few years. And now to be blessed with a daughter-in-law and a grandchild on the way, I cannot tell you how happy I am.'

Rosa shifted under the bedcovers and immediately Sarah was by her side, adjusting the pillows behind her.

'Thomas tells me I must not wear you out,' she said with a tender smile. 'But I had to come in and meet you properly. We will have plenty of time to get to know one another over the coming weeks.'

Sarah stood, squeezed Rosa's hand and turned to head for the door. Rosa felt a wave of turmoil crash over her. This lovely woman had welcomed her into the family home, provided for her every comfort and was doing her utmost to make Rosa feel comfortable, all the while probably believing Rosa was carrying her flesh and blood. She should say something, explain the truth.

'Lady Hunter...' Rosa started. 'Sarah...' But she could not find the words.

'We can talk more later, my dear. You rest now.'

'If I don't get out of this room I will scream,' Rosa said, plastering her most determined expression across her face.

'I can't see anything wrong with this room,' Thomas said cheerily. 'Beautiful wallpaper, nice airy feel, good view over the lawns.'

Rosa growled. Since returning home, and especially since the doctor had given her the all clear, her husband had regained much of his old carefree nature and sense of humour. Rosa was glad, but sometimes he could be infuriating.

'There's nothing wrong with the room,' Rosa said through gritted teeth. 'That is not what I meant, as you very well know. If I do not move from this bed soon I fear I will become stuck to it for eternity.'

Thomas raised an eyebrow as if he was considering the merits of having her stuck in bed. Rosa thought she saw a flash of desire as he eyed her, but quickly he covered it. Interesting.

'Either you help me to get up and go downstairs or I will do it all by myself.'

'Shall I find you a big old branch to use as a crutch?'

Rosa reached out to swat his arm, but Thomas dodged her efficiently. She struggled upright, swung her legs over the edge of the bed and started to push up. Her bump had become more cumbersome over the course of their voyage to England, and now she had to take a second whenever she changed positions to regain her balance.

Once she was steady on her feet she looked up. Thomas was just staring at her, he'd made no move to take her arm or come to her side as he normally would.

'Rosa,' he said, his voice barely more than a whisper. 'I just saw a movement.'

She glanced down and placed a hand on her belly. It was mid-afternoon, the time the baby was at its most active and she loved it when she could feel the kicks and movements inside her.

'Come here.' Rosa took Thomas's hand and sat back down on the bed, pulling him to sit beside her.

Gently she placed his hand on her belly, feeling his warm fingers through the thin cotton covering. They sat, completely still and completely silent, for thirty seconds until another strong kick came from the baby inside her.

'I felt it,' Thomas exclaimed. 'I felt the baby kick.'

Rosa watched his face as he gazed at her belly, his hand still in place. She saw amazement and awe as well as something else in his eyes, something that looked a little like love.

'Does it do this a lot?' Thomas asked.

'All the time, especially mid-afternoon. Normally in the morning he's quiet.'

'Are you going to be a late riser like your mother?' Thomas asked, directing his question down towards her belly. 'Your mother does like to waste the morning lounging in bed.'

'It's not a waste,' Rosa said with a smile. 'It makes sense to wake up slowly rather than to jump into the day.'

'I think on that matter we will have to agree to disagree.'

Still he hadn't removed his hand from her belly and Rosa felt a peculiar warmth spreading through her. It felt wonderful to be touched like this, to have Thomas's hands on her slowly stroking her skin. For a second she allowed her eyes to close and her head to drop back.

'Mmm…' she moaned involuntarily.

'I think your mama likes being stroked,' Thomas said, bending his neck and speaking softly.

Gently he raised his other hand to join the first, moving both in sweeping circles around her belly, scrunching up the material of her nightgown before smoothing it out again.

She watched him stroke her, watched the rhythmic movements of his hands across her skin, and realised she was happy. True, she'd only just survived the storm and the shipwreck, was married to a man who planned on running away abroad at the first opportunity and would have to make a life for herself in someone else's home, but still she felt happy. She was alive and her baby was well. She was safe, and would be safe for the rest of her life. Although Thomas's mother might not know all the details about their marriage, she seemed lovely and accommodating, and Rosa knew she could make the best of living here.

Glancing at Thomas, Rosa realised she had forgiven him. Forgiven him for deceiving her, forgiven him for his reaction to her on their wedding night. He should have told her before about the illness that ran in his family, but she could understand why he hadn't. Just as she could understand why he had sworn himself to a life of celibacy to stop any future generations from suffering from the disease.

'Thomas,' Rosa said, closing her eyes and letting her head fall back. 'Whilst I am pregnant there is no chance of you fathering a child with me.'

She felt his hands freeze on her belly, but couldn't bring herself to open her eyes to gauge his reaction.

He cleared his throat, made a noise as if he were about to say something and then cleared his throat again.

'It was just a thought,' Rosa said, opening her eyes and pushing herself upright.

She had to take Thomas's arm and tug on it to get him moving, and as she glanced at his face she could see he was still lost in her words.

'Come,' she said. 'I really would like to get some air.'

Chapter Twenty

'Whilst I am pregnant there is no chance of you fathering a child with me.'

How many times in the last two weeks had he repeated that phrase in his head? Rosa's voice, so soft and calm, giving him an invitation to do what he most desired.

He glanced over at his wife as she walked arm in arm with his mother through the gardens. They were fast becoming good friends, as he knew they would. Often he would find them laughing together, walking arm in arm or with their heads bent over a book. Thomas knew he should be pleased, it was just what he'd planned. A safe haven for Rosa to raise her child in and a companion for his mother. Now there should be nothing to stop him from packing his bags and picking a new destination for his adventures.

Except there was. Thomas looked again at Rosa. She still seemed graceful despite being over seven months pregnant. Her feet glided across the ground, her back was straight and the folds of her dress hung flatteringly around her figure.

He wanted her. He wanted to sweep her up into his arms, carry her to the bedroom and spend the next three months making love to her. He wanted to hold her close to him, stroke her skin and run his fingers through her hair.

Thomas groaned. It would be simpler if it was just pure desire that consumed him, but as the days went by he found he was actually happy, he was content to stroll through the gardens with Rosa, to show her the familiar sights from his childhood. He wanted to spend every waking minute with her, listen to her insights and tease her so her cheeks turned pink.

Last night he'd found himself making bargains in his head. He would just stay until the baby was born and then he would go; he would just stay until Rosa was recovered from the birth and then he would go; he would just stay until the baby had smiled or crawled or walked.

'Thomas darling, will you be joining us for tea?' his mother called over.

He started to walk across the lawn, reaching the wrought-iron table just as Rosa did and pulling out her chair for her. She smiled up at him with affection in her eyes.

Thomas felt his heart squeeze. This was all any man could want. A lovely wife, a child on the way, a family who loved him and a comfortable home. Maybe he should allow himself to be content, to enjoy his unexpected good fortune. Surely after the years of uncertainty, after all the people he had lost, he deserved a little slice of happiness.

He shook his head. It would be too selfish. Giving Rosa that hope, that glimpse of a normal life, only to burden her with a rapidly declining husband if and when the disease struck. His aim had always been to protect his loved ones from the illness, he couldn't falter now.

Rosa had just poured the tea and was digging into a large slice of sponge cake when one of the footmen came hurrying across the lawn.

'My lord, a gentleman is here to see Lady Hunter.'

Rosa looked up expectantly, but Thomas could hear the hesitation in the footman's voice.

'Who is it?'

'He wouldn't give his name, my lord, but he insisted Lady Hunter see him. He is a little out of sorts. Indisposed.'

'Drunk?'

'Quite, my lord.'

He saw the colour drain from Rosa's face, just as it had when the Di Mercurios had turned up at his villa demanding she be returned all those months ago.

'I will deal with him.'

'No.' Rosa caught his arm. 'I wish to come with you. I won't hide away in my own home.'

Out of the corner of his eye Thomas saw his mother smile as Rosa described the place as home.

Thomas was about to protest, about to insist she stay safely hidden whilst he dealt with whoever this drunkard turned out to be, but then he saw the determination on her face and knew she would not be deterred. She'd come so far from the scared girl he'd met climbing over the Di Mercurios' wall. He wouldn't deny her the chance at saying her piece to whoever this was from her past.

Hand in hand they followed the footman across the lawn and into the house.

'I have put the gentleman in the green room, my lord. Do you wish for me to come in with you?'

Thomas waved a dismissive hand. There weren't many men he'd met that he couldn't best in a one-on-one fight. Not that this would come to that, hopefully.

'David,' Rosa said, her voice flat and devoid of emotion. 'What are you doing here?'

The man standing by the window staggered as he took a few steps towards them, but then stopped as he caught sight of Rosa's figure.

'It's true,' he slurred. 'You are pregnant. I didn't believe it when you told me.'

Thomas felt Rosa bristle beside him, but allowed her to remain in control. Any sign of violence and he would step in.

'There were rumours you'd been sent to Italy in disgrace.'

Rosa said nothing, just laid a hand protectively on her bump.

'And now you've married this…' he seemed to search for the right word '…libertine.'

As insults went it was rather weak.

'I can't see that is any of your concern, David.'

'Of course it's my concern. You are carrying my child.'

'No, she isn't,' Thomas said calmly.

David spluttered and held up an accusing finger. 'That is my child. I know it is.'

Thomas put a protective arm around Rosa and gave her a little squeeze.

'Rosa is my wife. The child she is carrying is my child. Now please state your business and then leave.'

'Do you know what a whore you married?' David spat, hatred in his eyes.

Thomas dropped a kiss on the top of Rosa's head in a way he knew would just infuriate the man.

'I know exactly the kind of woman I married.'

'She begged me to take her. Couldn't keep her hands off me. Squealed like a whore, too.'

'We both know that isn't true,' Thomas said with a shrug. 'But if you need to tell yourself that to sleep at night then so be it.'

'I bet she said I raped her, forced myself upon her. She was willing, looked up at me with those big eyes and pleaded for me to take her.'

'I thought you loved me, David,' Rosa said sadly. 'I was young and naïve and stupid, but I never asked you to ruin me. I begged you to stop.'

'What do you want?' Thomas asked.

'I could tell the world,' David said, a malicious grin spreading across his face. 'I could tell the world the baby is mine—that you have married a fallen woman and the child is a bastard.'

Thomas took a step closer to David, drawing himself up to his full height. The other man took an involuntary step backwards as he approached and Thomas had to suppress a smile.

'You could tell everyone that, but what would be the point?'

'I want money. Five hundred pounds and I won't say a word.'

'No.'

'No?'

Thomas shrugged. 'There's no scandal here. Rosa is a married woman. She's pregnant with my child. My heir. The baby will be a Hunter.'

'Rumours can cause a lot of damage.'

'I'm sure they can. But you won't be the one spreading them.'

'I will.'

Thomas placed a hand on the other man's shoulder and felt him flinch.

'Your name is David Greenway, is that correct? Son of Mr Peter Greenway.'

David nodded, obviously nonplussed at the change of direction the conversation had taken.

'Your family home is a lovely old Tudor house with seven bedrooms and your father employs four servants. Unfortunately the Greenway family fortunes have taken a turn for the worse in the last few years—do correct me if I'm wrong.'

David mumbled something under his breath.

'As I understand it your father has borrowed a substantial amount of money against the family home. Money that he is struggling to pay back.'

'How…?'

'How do I know? Well, I had a long chat with a new friend who was moaning about a debt that will never be paid. He was loathe to turn the family out of their home, seeing as there are four women in residence to consider, but really couldn't continue as it was. I offered to buy the debt from him and he almost bit off my hand in his eagerness.'

Thomas watched as the blood drained from David's face and smiled in a businesslike manner.

'So I could call in your father's debt at any time. Or not. Tell me, you are the eldest son, are you not? You stand to inherit the house once your father dies.'

There was a minute nod from David.

'Stay away from my wife, stay away from our child.

If I ever hear even a hint of a rumour about the legitimacy of our child then I will call in the debt so fast your mother and sisters won't even have time to pack their bags before they become homeless. Do you understand?'

David nodded.

'Good. Thank you for your visit. This has been most helpful. I hope we never see each other again.'

Thomas stepped back to let David past, watching as he stumbled towards the doorway.

'You were magnificent,' Rosa said. 'And you didn't even hit him.'

'I'm not all about the violence.'

'How did you know about the debt? I didn't even tell you his full name.'

Thomas smiled at her, placed a finger on her chin and tilted it up towards him. He was feeling reckless and a little out of control. Without thinking of the consequences he dipped his head and brushed his lips against hers, lacing his fingers through her hair and pulling her body closer to him.

Rosa melted in his arms and as he deepened the kiss Thomas knew he could lose himself in her for ever.

'I thought he might make trouble for us, so I sent a man to find out who he was, where he lived and any dirty family secrets. When my man uncovered the debt it seemed too good an opportunity to miss.'

'You did all that for me? For us?'

He kissed her again.

'Of course. You are my wife, I will do anything to protect you.'

Including keeping his distance, a voice screamed inside his head, but for once Thomas shut it down and gave in to his desire.

He ran his hands down Rosa's back, caressing her through the thin cotton of her dress, and cupped her buttocks. As he caressed her he felt Rosa stiffen in his arms, and then as if giving in to her own desires she relaxed.

'I've been thinking about what you said,' Thomas whispered in her ear. 'Constantly.'

'I say a lot of things.'

'You know what I mean.'

'I do.'

'I'd like to take you up on that offer.'

Rosa pulled away just a little and smiled up at him. Thomas felt his whole body tighten with desire and knew their whole relationship had been leading up to this moment.

'Come.' Rosa took his hand and pulled him from the room, giggling as they ran up the stairs.

Thomas knew he should say something to dampen her expectations. This didn't change his plans in the long term; he would still have to leave in a few months. Theirs would not be a normal marriage. He knew he should say something but he couldn't, he wanted this too much, couldn't bear the thought of Rosa pulling away from him now.

Upstairs, in Rosa's bedroom, they paused for a second and just looked at one another.

'You're sure?' Thomas asked.

'Can I tell you a secret?' Rosa whispered. 'I've been dreaming of this for a very long time.'

With a groan Thomas kissed her again, pouring all his passion and desire into the meeting of their lips. His tongue flicked out and tasted her, and he knew at that moment one taste would never be enough.

Gently he spun her round and with dextrous fingers

unlaced her dress, pushing it down hastily to reveal the chemise underneath. The thin cotton was almost see-through, and Thomas felt his desire swell and grow as he saw the outline of her body beneath it.

Pulling her in close to him, Thomas peppered kisses all the way down her neck to her collar bone, loving the way her body responded to his caresses.

'I want to see you,' he whispered in her ear, then grasped the hem of her chemise and lifted it up over her head.

Thomas took a step back, but as his eyes slid over her body Rosa raised her arms to cover her belly. He caught them and gently pressed them back to her side.

'You're beautiful,' he said. 'All of you.'

Raising one hand, he trailed his fingers down in between her breasts, over the bump of her belly and down to her most private place below. Rosa gasped as he touched her there and he felt her legs wobble underneath her.

Quickly he gripped his shirt and pulled it off over his head, his trousers following closely behind. Then he led Rosa to the bed and laid her down, sliding in beside her.

Through all his years of celibacy Thomas had imagined how this moment would feel, but never had he imagined anything quite so perfect. He realised he was glad he had waited, glad Rosa was his first, his only. No one else would ever make him feel this good.

He kissed her again, a long, sensuous kiss, and let his hands caress her body. He felt her fingertips on his back, pulling him closer to her. Dipping his head, hearing her moan of protest as he broke the kiss, he captured one of her nipples between his teeth. Rosa groaned, arching her back.

'I need you, Thomas,' she whispered.

And he needed her. Carefully he rolled her on to her side, facing away from him, and pressed his body up against hers. With one arm around her waist, pulling her tighter to him, he pushed forward, entering her and hearing her moan of pleasure as he did so.

Thomas had never felt so alive, so stimulated and slowly he began to rock his hips backwards and forward. He was gentle at first, conscious that he didn't want to hurt Rosa, but as she pressed back into him again and again he picked up speed.

He dropped his hand that had been around her waist down lower and began to stroke, guided by her moans of pleasure as his fingers grazed her.

Thomas felt the climax build inside him, knowing he would not be able to last much longer, but determined to give Rosa her pleasure before he took his. He kissed her neck, thrusting inside her at the same time, and after a few more strokes felt Rosa's body grow taut around him as she let out a low moan. Immediately Thomas felt his own release, pushing into Rosa one last time and hearing his own moan of pleasure.

They lay there, bodies pressed together, skin against skin, for a long time without speaking. Thomas felt a peculiar contentment wash over him. For months he had wanted to take Rosa to his bed and it had been even better than he had imagined. He knew, no matter what he told himself, this could not be a one-off. Their intimacy had just fuelled his desire for his wife rather than slaked it.

Chapter Twenty-One

❧❧❧❧❧

Rosa beamed as she watched Thomas galloping over the fields in the distance. She loved to watch him in action, appreciated the effort that went into keeping his body in prime physical condition. Now, after he'd confided in her about his family secret, she could understand completely why he worked so hard to maintain peak physical fitness. The threat of losing control of his movements and his body made him look after himself more than the average man.

Rosa could appreciate the result as well. For two weeks now Thomas had slipped into her bed, pulled her close to him and worshipped her body every night, and Rosa could picture every groove of muscle, every firm contour of his body.

Each night he whispered it would be their last, that he would not succumb again, but it was as though he were drawn back to her bed as the sun went down.

Rosa didn't complain, she was dreading the day he did stay away, knowing that once he had broken away from her she might never get him back. She cherished the closeness between them, loved those sleepy moments when he held her in his arms before they both drifted into unconsciousness. One day soon the doctor would tell her to cease anything even remotely physical and then Thomas would not dare to touch her until the baby had been born. After that…well, Rosa knew how adamant he was that no future generation should be afflicted with the Hunter family curse.

'Is my son showing off again?' Sarah asked as she joined Rosa on the bench that looked out over the estate.

'He is a very fine horseman.'

The older woman smiled, a hint of pride in her eyes. 'Thomas does many things very well. The trouble is he knows it, too.'

They watched him in silence for a few minutes, enjoying the late morning sun.

'How are you settling in, my dear?' Sarah asked as Thomas disappeared over the brow of a hill.

'I feel so at home,' Rosa said quietly. 'More at home than I ever did in my own house.'

'This is your house now and your home.'

Rosa felt a lump form in her throat. They'd been living at Thomas's family home for a little over a month and she felt more at ease here than she ever had before. Her days were spent reading, strolling through the gardens and taking tea with her mother-in-law. Her nights were even more enjoyable and Rosa felt her cheeks flush at the thought.

'I'm very happy here,' Rosa said and knew it was the truth. For all her hurt and upset when Thomas had revealed his intention to escort her back to England and then leave her to live as mistress of his estate, Rosa now knew it was an enjoyable life.

'I haven't seen Thomas this happy in years. You're good for him. And this baby will be good for him, too.'

Biting her lip, Rosa suppressed a nervous laugh. She did think she was good for Thomas. The last few weeks he'd been happy and relaxed. The haunted look on his face, had disappeared, and the sense of urgency he'd had ever since she'd first met him had mellowed. For once he seemed to be enjoying living a normal, simple life and Rosa knew she'd played a big part in that.

'I wish…' Rosa started, but found herself unable to complete the sentence.

Sarah looked at her with the same dazzling blue eyes as her son and smiled encouragingly.

'I wish I could make Thomas want to stay.'

'He's planning on leaving?'

Rosa immediately regretted voicing her thoughts. The last thing she wanted to do was cause Sarah any unnecessary distress. She was about to open her mouth to try to rescue the situation when the older woman spoke.

'Of course he is. I don't know why I'm surprised. Silly boy.'

An unbidden smile flitted across Rosa's lips and she quickly tried to suppress it.

'Well, he is a silly boy. Look at what he's got: a lovely wife, a child on the way, a beautiful home. Men would kill to have half of what he does and he's determined to run away from it all.'

'I think he doesn't wish to be a burden if he does become unwell.'

Sarah sighed. 'I know. He saw how it hurt me when his father became ill and again with his brother. Thomas lived through the agony of watching someone he loved be slowly stripped away until just a husk was left. He wishes to protect us both from that.'

'But he doesn't even know if he will develop the disease.'

'After his brother died I told him to travel,' Sarah said quietly. 'I saw the fear and the sadness in his eyes and knew he needed something else to focus on, something positive. And I wanted him to have something to remember, something to be proud of, if he did develop the disease.' She stared out into the distance for a few minutes in silence. 'But he's too focused on gaining those new experiences to realise exactly what it is that would make him happy now.'

Rosa felt tears threaten to spill on to her cheeks.

'He could be so happy being a husband and a father, if he just let himself,' Sarah said. Taking Rosa's hand, she patted it softly. 'I'm sure he'll come round with time, realise what he would be giving up if he left.'

Rosa watched as Thomas re-emerged over the brow of the hill, allowing his horse to trot happily back towards them. Maybe he would realise how perfect the life they could have together would be, but she wasn't sure. He was so determined, so stubborn, that she knew once he'd set his mind to a particular course of action not much could sway him away from it.

'Well whatever happens I am thrilled to have you here with me. And I never expected to be a grandmother. I feel doubly blessed.'

Rosa cleared her throat, knowing she had to confess the child was not Thomas's. She couldn't bear to deceive the kindly older woman any longer.

'I'm not sure how much Thomas has told you about

how we met and the circumstances of my being in Italy,' Rosa began nervously.

Sarah looked at her with interest. Rosa felt her mouth go dry and stuttered the next few words. The older woman held up a hand to stop her.

'If you are trying to tell me this child is not of Thomas's blood, I am well aware of that fact,' Sarah said, squeezing Rosa's hand. 'Thomas told me far from everything, but I could fill in the gaps with educated guesses.'

Holding her breath, Rosa waited for her mother-in-law's reaction.

'In a way I'm glad,' Sarah said with a small smile. 'Thomas would never risk passing on the disease to the next generation of Hunters and I have to respect his decision. But this way he gets an heir without having to spend his life worrying about what future the child might have to endure because of his cursed blood.'

'That's exactly what Thomas said.'

'And of course I get a grandchild. I do love children.'

Rosa could tell from the warmth in Sarah's voice that she would shower this child with love and affection, even though it was not her flesh and blood.

'You two look awfully serious,' Thomas said as he reined in his horse and swung down from its back.

'We're discussing you,' his mother said with a smile.

'Surely I don't have so many flaws to warrant such concerned expressions.'

Both Rosa and Sarah remained silent for a few moments and then burst out laughing.

'May I deprive you of Rosa's company for a while?' Thomas asked his mother, holding his hand out to Rosa and helping her from the bench.

He loved watching her move, loved seeing the slow, careful way she manoeuvred herself into a standing position, how she had to steady herself for a few seconds to find her balance and the slight waddle to her gait as she walked.

'Of course. You two go and enjoy yourselves.'

Slowing his pace so Rosa didn't become overtired, Thomas led her away from the house across the lawn.

'Where are we going?'

'Have a little patience and you will see. It's somewhere new. Somewhere secret.'

'Thomas, I've strolled through all the gardens ten times over this past month. I think I would have noticed somewhere secret.'

'That's the beauty of a secret place, you can walk past ten times without even noticing it's there. You need someone to show you the way.'

'I told your mother about the baby,' Rosa said, her eyes fixed to the ground.

He knew she felt awkward discussing the child, awkward talking of the baby from another man she was carrying.

'What did she say?'

'She had guessed that you were not…' Rosa trailed off. Even though the child was not of his blood he would still be its father.

Thomas stopped abruptly and turned to face Rosa. He saw the worry in her eyes and the little pucker between her eyebrows.

'Rosa, I know this child is not of my flesh and blood, and until it is born I suspect I won't truly know how I feel about him or her. But I can promise you I will nurture and cherish this baby as if it were my own.'

He saw the flicker of hope in Rosa's eyes and knew it was the right thing to say, even if he wasn't sure it was the truth. If he was completely honest he had mixed feelings about this child that was about to burst into their lives. He wanted to love the little boy or girl Rosa was carrying, and he thought he might do so already, but he just wasn't sure. Could a man love another man's child as he would his own? Thomas didn't know the answer to that and he rather suspected he wouldn't know until he looked down into the child's eyes and held the little bundle in his arms.

Not that Rosa needed to know all of that. She had enough to worry about with the impending arrival, she didn't need to dwell on whether her husband would love her baby.

'I know it is an impossible situation.'

'I was well aware of your condition and the consequences of that when I married you,' Thomas said with a smile.

'But then you were planning on bringing me back to England and then bidding me farewell.'

Thomas felt his whole body stiffen. These last few weeks had been marvellous. He'd been cocooned in happiness, surrounded by love and joy, but he knew it had to come to an end. He thought Rosa had known that, too.

'Rosa, I want to be here when you give birth,' Thomas said slowly. 'And of course for a few weeks afterwards.'

He watched as she tried to hide the pain as she understood the true meaning of his words. He was still going to leave her, still planning on abandoning her in his country estate whilst he went to travel the world.

'I wish to see you settled with the baby, of course.'

'But then you will leave.' Rosa's voice was completely

flat and devoid of emotion, but her eyes betrayed the true pain she was feeling.

'That was always the plan,' Thomas said.

He'd never deceived her, never lied to her and told her he would stay, but he'd seen the hope blossoming in her as they'd grown closer these last few weeks. Every time he slipped into bed beside her Thomas had known it would make the eventual farewell so much harder, but he just hadn't been able to keep away.

'I know. You will return to travelling the world and I shall be a companion to your mother.'

'Do you not get on well with my mother?'

'That's not the point,' Rosa said, her voice low and overflowing with emotion.

He went to reach out and touch her arm, but Rosa pulled away.

'I can't stay here, Rosa.'

'Why not?'

'You know why.'

'Tell me again. Make me understand.'

'Come with me.' Thomas didn't try to touch her again and was acutely aware of the space between them as reluctantly she followed him. He led her through the formal gardens and off to one side, out into a wooded area. They walked for about ten minutes in silence before Thomas stopped and motioned to the monument in front of them.

It was his brother's grave. Situated in a clearing in the woodland his brother had loved so much as a child, the grave was neat and lovingly tended.

'I wanted to show you this. I come here to talk to my brother sometimes. To ask his advice.'

Rosa carefully knelt in front of the grave and bent

her head for a few moments. Thomas could see her lips moving, but didn't recognise the words.

'I understand you lost two people very dear to you,' Rosa said softly. 'And I understand you live in fear of one day succumbing to the same disease. What I don't understand is why you feel you must push everyone away and face this on your own.'

Thomas stepped forward and placed a hand on the smooth headstone, running his fingers over the inscription.

'I saw the pain my mother had to live through every single day watching my father lose first his physical abilities and then his mental. By the end there wasn't even a trace of the man she had married left.'

'She must have been devastated by the loss,' Rosa said. 'But I know she was glad to be there for your father through those years of decline. To share the good days along with the bad.'

'I don't ever want to be a burden like that.'

Rosa stepped towards him and cupped his face in her hands. Thomas felt her soft skin against his rough stubble.

'If you love someone it isn't a burden. It's just what you do.'

Thomas looked into her eyes and saw the raw emotion and felt his throat begin to constrict. He knew she cared for him, had known it ever since they'd travelled across Italy together, but now he could see pure love in her eyes.

Before he could answer, before he could even begin to formulate a single word, Rosa dropped her hands and turned away. Without looking behind her she walked back through the trees and into the garden and Thomas wondered if he'd lost her for good.

Chapter Twenty-Two

⸙

Dear Caroline,

I must apologise for leaving it so long in between my letters. So much has happened since I last penned you that short note from Venice, letting you know of my pending marriage.

We are now back in England and have been for some weeks, but much of that time I have been recuperating from a shipwreck on our voyage home. It was terrible, Caroline. I've never experienced such fear. Not for myself, as you must understand better than many, but for my child.

The doctor is as confident as he can be that the baby sustained no injury or damage during my time in the water, but I find myself fretting still. The only thing that can reassure me is feeling my little baby's determined kicks and somersaults inside me.

I am now residing at Longcroft Hall, my husband's family home in Hampshire. At present there is me, my husband and his mother in residence, but I fear that soon Thomas might leave England

*again and set off on his travels around the world.
He is determined to go, even though I know he is
happy here with me.*

*The situation is perhaps too complicated to go
into in a letter, but suffice it to say Thomas thinks
he would be protecting me in the long term if he
left now. What he does not seem to understand is
that my heart will break if he leaves me. Every
day I hope he might change his mind, and when I
catch him looking at the child growing inside me
I can see him waver.*

*Is it completely pathetic that I don't care if it is
me he stays for or the baby? As long as he stays
close.*

*Enough about my woes. I know I am very lucky
to have a safe and stable home and a legal father
for my child.*

*Caroline, I yearn for news of you and your dar-
ling son. It will not be long before I give birth myself, but I wish I could see you and confide all of
my hopes and fears. You always did have a level
head and a way of making everything work out
for the best.*

*You are most welcome to come and visit here
at Longcroft Hall, or once I am recovered from
childbirth I could make the trip to you.
With all my love,
Rosa*

Rosa waited for the ink to dry and then folded the sheet
of paper in half, slipping it into an envelope and penning
the address on the front. She wished dearly for her old
friend, Caroline always knew what to do in a difficult

situation and Rosa wanted someone she could tell about every aspect of her life, good and bad.

Rosa looked up as the door opened and Thomas strolled inside.

'I've received a note,' he said and, although his voice was light and untroubled, Rosa could see the concern on his face.

'Who from?'

He cleared his throat. 'Your father.'

'Papa?'

Rosa stood a little too quickly, had to hold out her arms to try to catch her balance and then gave up and fell back on to the sofa.

'It seems he arrived in the village yesterday evening and is currently staying in the inn.'

Rosa felt her heart leap and then sink again immediately.

'And my mother?' she asked.

'He doesn't mention her in his note.'

Rosa had a flashback to the hatred and disgust on her mother's face when she had sent her on her way to Italy.

'Your father has asked if he may call on us, at our convenience.'

Hope and doubt mingled in Rosa's mind. She wanted to see her kind, gentle father so much, but she didn't think she could stomach the upset of listening to her mother rant and rave. She felt Thomas's eyes on her, watching her closely.

'I was planning on taking my horse out for a ride this afternoon,' he said slowly. 'Perhaps I could travel to the village and see whether he came alone. If he has, then I will extend an invitation to dinner tonight.'

'Thank you,' Rosa said softly. He always seemed to

know exactly what she needed, sometimes even before she knew it herself. Except when it came to his plans to abandon her in England, of course.

'Our child should know at least one more grandparent,' Thomas said, taking her hand and placing a kiss on her wrist.

Rosa glanced surreptitiously at his face, wondering if he'd realise what he had just said. *Our child.* Up until this moment Thomas had always referred to the baby growing inside her as *her* child. She wondered if it was just a slip of the tongue or if he was coming to think of the baby as theirs.

Stepping closer, Thomas tilted her face up and kissed her gently on the lips. These last couple of days he'd started being more careful as he touched and kissed her. The caresses were no less in number, but it was as though he was subconsciously aware that soon Rosa would be going through a great ordeal and wanted her to save her strength for that.

She looped her arms up around his neck and pulled him closer to her, giggling as he brushed against her bump. Hearing him whisper her name as he peppered kisses along her jawbone and down her neck made her shudder with delight and Rosa allowed herself to be swept away by the moment.

They were both all too aware that soon they would not be able to share the ultimate act of intimacy, but Rosa was keen to persuade Thomas that they could still have a close and physically loving relationship without risking her getting pregnant with his child.

Running her hands down his body, she grazed her fingers over the toned muscles of his chest and abdomen, smiling as he let out a faint moan as she tucked a finger into his waistband.

'You don't know what you do to me, Rosa,' Thomas whispered.

Deftly she unbuttoned his trousers and sunk to her knees in front of him. She felt his eyes on her, watching with a mixture of disbelief and pleasure as she took him into her mouth. Slowly she began to move backwards and forward, watching his reaction to every flick of her tongue or stroke of her hand. Soon she knew exactly what made him groan in pleasure and what made him clutch at her shoulders in delight.

Rosa looked up at him, saw him looking lovingly down at her, his eyes a little glazed as he stiffened and climaxed.

Dropping lower, Rosa watched as Thomas recovered, stroking her hair and cupping her face until he was composed enough to help her to her feet.

'Where on earth did you learn that?' he asked.

Rosa blushed. It had been a very awkward but very enlightening conversation with one of the housemaids. A couple of days ago Rosa had decided she would fight for Thomas. She loved him, that much she knew, and she wasn't going to let him leave without doing her utmost to persuade him to stay. That included showing him the sort of relationship they could have over the coming years.

'We women discuss these things all the time,' she said, hiding a smile as he looked momentarily alarmed. It wasn't often she was able to ruffle her husband and she appreciated her small victory even if it was short lived.

'We men talk, too,' Thomas said, a mischievous glint in his eyes.

For a second Rosa didn't grasp his meaning, but gentle hands guiding her to the armchair were enough to make her eyes widen.

'Men can't do that to women,' she said, feeling foolish as soon as the words left her mouth. Patricia the housemaid hadn't told her anything about this.

'Oh, yes, we can.'

Deftly Thomas lifted Rosa's skirts and she felt his hand on her thighs. He caressed the smooth skin for a second before grasping hold of the top of one stocking and rolling it down. Quickly he repeated the movement on the other leg. Even though her dress was still covering most of her upper legs she felt exposed and a thrill of excitement ran through her.

'Anyone could come in.'

'Then they should know better than to disturb a man alone with his wife.'

Rosa felt any further protestations die on her lips as he kissed one ankle, moving up her leg ever so slowly, making her enjoy every caress.

Rosa gasped as his lips reached the very top of her thigh and then let out a disappointed sigh as he pulled away and returned to the bottom of her other leg.

'Patience, my dear,' he said with a wicked grin.

Trailing his lips up her leg, he paused again at her thighs and for one frustrating second Rosa thought he would pull away again, but then his mouth was on her and Rosa groaned in pleasure.

Letting her head drop backwards, she closed her eyes as he kissed and caressed her, his touch making her want to scream in delight. Clutching at Thomas's hair, Rosa felt her hips buck up to meet him again and again until something exploded inside her.

It was a full two minutes before she felt ready to open

her eyes and look up at her husband, who was now standing over her looking very pleased with himself.

Thomas pulled at his cravat and sighed. Despite being back in his family home surrounded by servants who were at his beck and call he still didn't have a valet. He didn't want one, didn't want to share his daily rituals with a stranger, but he couldn't deny a valet would come in handy when faced with a cravat.

'Tell me again how he seemed,' Rosa said, slipping up behind him and looping her arms around his waist. Thomas felt a strange contentment as he allowed Rosa to spin him round and felt her dexterous fingers deftly pulling the cravat into shape.

'Nervous,' Thomas said, thinking back to the unassuming, quiet man he had met briefly at the inn.

'Did he look well?'

Thomas hesitated, recalling the dark circles around Rosa's father's eyes and the clothes that didn't seem to fit properly.

'You'll be able to judge for yourself in a few minutes,' he said, inspecting his neatly tied cravat in the mirror in front of him.

He watched as Rosa paced nervously backwards and forward across the room, halting only to peer out of the window every so often.

'And you're sure my mother wasn't with him?'

'Completely sure.'

Thomas could see the anxiety in Rosa's eyes and realised how important this evening was for her. When she'd talked of her parents she'd always recalled her father with love and fondness. He knew she was still hurting from being sent away by her mother and her father not stepping in to put a stop to the plan.

'He's here,' Rosa said, leaning into the window to catch a glimpse of her father.

'Are you ready?' Thomas asked.

She nodded, but didn't look in the least bit ready.

'Remember I am here, no matter what happens this evening.'

Rosa looked up at him with silent gratitude and Thomas felt his heart squeeze in his chest. He hadn't realised quite how much Rosa had burrowed into his heart these last few months. They had gone from unlikely companions to so much more. He knew he couldn't have made a better choice for his wife, although he did worry he was beginning to care for her maybe too much. On occasions like tonight he felt every inch of her anxiety and worry as if it were his own and he wanted to protect her from anything that threatened to hurt her.

They walked down the stairs and heard soft voices coming from the drawing room. Thomas's mother had agreed to take on the official role of hostess for their small dinner party, leaving Rosa free to try to mend the rift between her and her father.

Pushing open the door, Thomas led Rosa inside, noting the increased pressure on his arm as she gripped him a little harder. The conversation between Rosa's father and Thomas's mother petered out as father and daughter laid eyes on each other. For a moment it was as if the whole room was frozen in time and then Rosa slipped from his side and threw herself into her father's arms.

'Papa,' she said as he embraced her, his entire face lighting up with delight.

'My little Rosa. I have missed you terribly.'

He drew back from her, held her at arm's length and regarded her. 'How you've changed these last few months.'

Thomas stiffened, ready to jump to Rosa's defence if her father even thought about uttering a harsh word.

'You look so healthy, and so happy.' There were tears in the old man's eyes as Rosa took both of his hands in her own and squeezed them.

'I am happy, Papa,' Rosa said quietly.

Thomas felt the stab of guilt in his gut. She was happy—they both were. There was no denying it. However much he tried to pretend he wasn't thoroughly enjoying domestic life, he knew it was a lie. He loved being married to Rosa, loved how she offered sage words of wisdom over the running of the estate he was just refamiliarising himself with, loved how they laughed together all day long, and loved the closeness when they fell into bed side by side at night.

He often found himself wishing that this part of their lives could stretch on for ever—that they could continue to live this carefree existence without the ever-present worry of his family illness.

'This is my husband, Papa. Lord Hunter.'

'We had the pleasure of meeting earlier today,' Thomas said, stepping forward to shake his father-in-law's hand.

'Rosa, my dear, before we say anything further there is something I must talk to you about.'

Thomas saw Rosa's face drop and stepped closer, wondering how he might shield her from any potential bad news.

'I have been an awful father to you,' Mr Rothwell said, his face a picture of misery and regret. 'I should never have let your mother send you to Italy to stay with that wretched family of hers. I failed you when you needed me the most.'

'Papa, there's no need…'

'There's every need. I am not a strong man, not forceful in my personality, but I knew you needed me to stand up for you and I cowered away, taking the easy path. I have regretted it for every moment since.'

'I forgive you, Papa,' Rosa said quickly, looking pained by her father's distress.

Thomas saw the tears slip out of the older man's eyes as Rosa embraced him and heard Rosa sniff some back of her own.

'Come,' Thomas's mother said quietly, 'dinner is served. Please take your time and follow when you are ready.'

Thomas waited for Rosa to enter the room on her father's arm, pulled out her chair and ensured she was comfortable before taking his own seat.

'Papa, where is Mother?' Rosa asked softly as the first course was placed in front of them.

Reaching for Rosa's hand under the table, Thomas gave it a quick squeeze.

Mr Rothwell grimaced. 'We have been leading separate lives since you were sent to Italy,' he said. 'Your mother resides in London, I spend most of my time in our country house. I haven't seen her for many weeks now.' He paused as if considering whether to say more. 'And I must say we're both much happier for it. But enough about me and your mother—that is an ongoing saga no one wishes to hear about. Tell me how you two met.'

Thomas sat back and listened as Rosa recounted their

early relationship, laughing as she recalled how she'd flattened him on the road outside the Di Mercurios' villa and been lured into the wise woman's house on their journey to Venice. So much had happened in the four months since he'd first met Rosa, so much in his life had changed, yet one thing, this disease he might or might not have, was still hanging over him.

'I hope I can be a good grandfather to your child, my dear,' Mr Rothwell said as the conversation turned to the baby.

'You should come to stay once Rosa has recovered from the birth. If that is what you wish, Rosa?' Thomas's mother suggested.

'I would love that, Papa.'

Mr Rothwell beamed, pure joy in his eyes, and Thomas realised that whatever the older man's faults he loved his daughter and her unborn child unconditionally.

'Come, Rosa,' Thomas's mother said as they finished their dessert. 'Take a stroll with me along the patio.'

Standing, Thomas watched his wife exit through the doors on to the veranda that they'd thrown open part way through the meal due to the balminess of the evening.

'Whisky?' Thomas offered as he crossed to the side board, picking up two glasses.

'Yes, please.'

Thomas poured two glasses of whisky and led his father-in-law through to his study. In Thomas's mind it was the most comfortable room in the house, with two soft leather armchairs positioned by the fire, which thankfully today did not need to be lit.

'I need to thank you as well, Lord Hunter,' Mr Rothwell said as they both settled back into the armchairs.

He waited for the older man to go on, regarding him with curiosity.

'I know how much you have done for my daughter over the last few months. I dread to think what would have happened to her if you hadn't found her when you did.'

The myriad dangers for a woman travelling alone played out quickly in Thomas's mind. Rosa had been so desperate to escape from the Di Mercurios that she hadn't properly considered the consequences of her running away.

'Any gentleman would have done the same.'

Mr Rothwell shook his head. 'Many gentlemen are scoundrels, or just not interested in anything other than themselves.'

He couldn't argue with that. Thomas had come across many so-called gentlemen in his time. Often the ones with the loftier titles were the most selfish and uninterested in others.

'I also want to thank you for marrying Rosa, you've saved her from a lifetime of hurt and pain. I am well aware I do not know the full circumstances around your marriage, but I thank you for the benefits it confers on my daughter. She has suffered enough.'

Thomas nodded. From the very beginning he had repeated all the advantages their union held for Rosa, it had been his way of convincing himself he was doing it all for her and not himself. He felt strangely comfortable with this kindly older man, as if he could tell him anything, unburden all his secrets and regrets.

'When I first proposed to your daughter I told myself it was to save her from ruin. To protect her from the heartache of being shunned by everyone she had ever known, to protect her child from growing up under the cloud of illegitimacy.'

'That is a very selfless reason to propose.'

'I also wanted a wife to protect my interests at home and a companion for my mother. Someone who I could bring back to England and leave here to oversee the parts of my life I wanted to run away from,' he confessed, swirling his whisky around his glass.

'You weren't planning on staying with her?'

Thomas heard the shock in Mr Rothwell's voice and knew Rosa's father probably wasn't the best man to confide in when it came to his marital dilemmas, despite his kindly demeanour.

Mr Rothwell sighed. 'Do you know I was madly in love with Rosa's mother when we first met? She was so beautiful, so exotic, so different from all the debutantes my parents pushed in front of me. I even thought her disdain for me was exciting, a challenge to be overcome.'

Thomas couldn't imagine pursuing a woman who actively disliked him, but everyone was different.

'When she agreed to marry me I thought the disdain had all been an act, part of her ploy to keep me interested. I thought once we were married things would be different between us.'

From the snippets Rosa had told him Thomas knew this hadn't been the case. It sounded as though Rosa's mother had disliked her father every day they'd been together.

'It wasn't different. She never loved me, never even liked me. At the time her family were in a dire financial situation so she was sent out to marry well. She'd always dreamed of a title, to be Lady Elena, but no one with a title was foolish enough to take her on, so she had to settle for me.'

'Does Rosa know all this?'

'Mostly. Elena has a terrible temper. She says the most hurtful things when in a rage.'

Thomas regarded the man sitting across from him sipping at his whisky. Rosa was certainly not like her mother, her disposition was sweet and kind, but she wasn't entirely like her father either.

'Perhaps our lives would have been better if we'd resided in separate countries,' he mused, smiling softly. 'Anyway, I suppose the point I was trying to make, is that all marriages are complicated.'

They sat in silence for a few minutes, staring at the empty fireplace in the dwindling evening light.

'She loves you, did you know that?' Mr Rothwell said eventually.

Thomas nodded. He did know it. He'd known it ever since she'd been so hurt when he'd rejected her in the bedchamber in Venice. Only a woman in love would be quite so pained by the rejection. And every day since their return to England he'd seen that love blossom and grow, thrilled to be the recipient of that love and petrified that he would break her heart.

'Whatever the reason for wanting to lead a separate life to Rosa, just remember that she loves you. And I'm told the love of a good woman is nothing to be sneered at.'

'I don't want to hurt her.'

'Then don't leave her.'

Thomas shook his head. 'I'm worried I will hurt her more if I stay. If we build a life together, raise our child and allow ourselves to be happy, then it will be all that much worse when something bad happens.'

'What will happen?'

Thomas remained silent. He wasn't quite ready to tell anyone else of the family curse just yet, especially the man whose daughter had just married into the family.

When no reply was forthcoming Mr Rothwell pressed on. 'How certain are you that this awful event is going to happen?' he asked.

'There is no way of knowing.'

'So you are giving up a future of happiness for something that may never occur.'

'But it may do.'

'If it were me,' Mr Rothwell said slowly, as if still pondering his words, 'I would want to do everything in my power to be sure one way or the other before condemning myself to a life of misery.' The older man stood, crossed to his chair and placed a fatherly hand on his shoulder. 'Both you and Rosa deserve that.'

Half an hour later the room was becoming so dark it was getting difficult to see, but still Thomas hadn't moved. He felt paralysed with indecision and it was as uncomfortable as it was unfamiliar.

He didn't want to condemn Rosa to a life of misery, of course he didn't, and he knew after a few months without him she would settle into a comfortable routine, especially with the baby to keep her company. He, on the other hand, would be miserable for ever without her. No matter where he went, which exotic countries he travelled to and which wonders he immersed himself in, he would know what his life could be like with Rosa. Nothing could compare to the simple pleasures of the last few weeks.

Decisively he stood. He still couldn't make the final

commitment to stay here with Rosa just yet, but he would take Mr Rothwell's advice, he would consult a doctor about his family's disease, get a better idea of what might face him and the odds that he would develop it, and then work out if he could follow his heart and stay.

Chapter Twenty-Three

'He's left?' Rosa asked, hating the tremor in her voice.

'He didn't tell you?' Sarah asked, eyes wide with surprise. 'He didn't tell me either.'

'He came and kissed my cheek this morning, but I was half-asleep. I don't *think* he said anything.'

Rosa's mother-in-law took her hand and squeezed it softly. 'I'm sure he isn't gone for good.'

'Last night, after my father left, he was very quiet, very pensive. I asked him what was troubling him, but he didn't really give me an answer.'

Instead he'd pulled her into bed with him, told her not to waste her energy worrying about him and tenderly made love to her. Rosa had fallen into a deep, dreamless sleep afterwards and barely remembered her husband rising and bidding her farewell early in the morning.

'He doesn't seem to have taken much with him,' Rosa added, hopefully.

Surely he wouldn't abandon her like this, without saying goodbye. She knew he was still planning on leaving one day, but he'd given no indication that day was drawing near.

* * *

Rosa spent the rest of the morning curled up on one of the armchairs in Thomas's study with a book. She had less than a month to go in her pregnancy now and even the exertion of getting up and getting dressed each morning took its toll. Each time the baby inside her kicked Rosa smiled, loving the little signs of life.

After a couple of hours in the study Rosa felt much more relaxed, but sitting in one position had made her back ache more than normal. Hauling herself to her feet, Rosa started to stroll through the hallways, taking time to admire the paintings on the walls. She laughed at the stern visages of Thomas's ancestors and delighted in the beautiful landscapes, all the time, using one hand to massage her lower back.

A sharp pain made her stop and hang on to the back of a conveniently positioned chair just as Thomas's mother emerged from the drawing room.

Immediately the older woman was at her side, guiding her down into the chair and calling for one of the maids.

'What is wrong my dear?' Sarah asked, her face clouded with concern.

'I'm sure I've just twisted awkwardly,' Rosa said, sure of no such thing. 'I've got an aching pain in my back and sharper pains coming round the front.'

'Betty, go and fetch two of the footmen and ask Mr Timkins to come here, too.'

The young maid scurried off to find the footmen and the butler as Rosa felt Sarah's hands rest softly on her bump.

A few seconds later the pain started again, a faint tightening sensation accompanying it.

'I am no doctor, but I think it may be time.'

Rosa shook her head. The baby couldn't be coming yet—she wasn't ready.

Two footmen emerged into the hallway and quickly Sarah instructed them to carry Rosa upstairs.

'I'm sure I can walk,' Rosa protested, trying to stand.

Another pain gripped her as she moved and Rosa fell back into the chair, closing her eyes as if trying to block out the discomfort.

'Upstairs,' Sarah ordered.

Rosa felt the chair being lifted slowly and then the soft rocking as the two footmen carried her through the hall and up the stairs. Clutching the seat with both hands, Rosa gripped so hard her knuckles turned white, only letting go as the chair was placed gently on the floor in her bedroom.

'I want Thomas,' Rosa whispered. It was all she wanted right now, her husband's reassuring voice telling her everything would be fine, his arms wrapped around her giving her strength and his lips pressed against her skin.

'Fetch the doctor,' Sarah ordered. 'And send for Emma.' Emma was the young housemaid currently acting as Rosa's lady's maid.

Rosa heaved herself up from the chair, ignoring the ache in her back and the taut muscles in her stomach. She suddenly felt constricted, as if all her clothes were shrinking as she stood up in them, and she grappled with the ties on the back of her dress.

'I need to get out of this,' Rosa panted, pulling at the material when it wouldn't come loose.

Immediately Sarah was by her side, quickly unlacing the fabric and lifting it up over Rosa's head. By the time

Rosa's maid Emma had entered the room Rosa was clad only in her long chemise.

'Let's get you to the bed,' Sarah instructed.

'No, I need to move. It feels better when I move.'

Rosa clutched at her bump, holding it gently as she waddled across the room. She paused at the window, looking longingly out to see if Thomas happened to be galloping down the driveway.

No one appeared, and Rosa felt the tears threatening to spill out of her eyes. He couldn't have left her, not like this, not when she needed him the most. Over the last few weeks she'd really felt as though she were getting through to him, really believed that he had started to see the benefits of them enjoying a conventional married life. She'd noticed the affection in his eyes when he looked at her. It wasn't love, he'd never mentioned love, but it was affection, and for now that would have to be enough.

She didn't want to cope with this on her own.

Rosa swung her legs on to the bed and grimaced as the doctor placed his cold hands on her belly.

'Do you feel a tightening now?' he asked, frowning as he concentrated.

'Yes,' Rosa panted, breathing hard as the pain built to a crescendo.

'Good. Your body is getting ready to deliver this baby. It shouldn't be too long now.'

'How long?' Rosa asked, her grip on the bedsheets relaxing as the pain began to subside.

'Difficult to say, but I should think you will have your son or daughter by tomorrow morning at the latest.'

Tomorrow morning was a long time away, especially

when she was in so much pain. Every hour the pains worsened, so much so that each time she told herself this must be as bad as they got, knowing full well it was a lie.

'I will come and check on your progress in a few hours' time,' the doctor said. 'In the meantime you know where I am if there are any problems.'

'He's leaving?' Rosa asked, her voice laced with panic.

'Hush, my dear,' Sarah said. 'It's better that way. Men, even medical men, get in the way during childbirth. We women have been doing this on our own for generations.'

'You won't leave me?'

'I won't leave you.'

Rosa looked up into her mother-in-law's eyes. 'I wish Thomas was here.'

'I do, too, Rosa.'

'I think I love him.'

Sarah squeezed her hand and Rosa closed her eyes, letting out a loud, guttural groan as the pain began to build again.

Chapter Twenty-Four

Thomas looked down, wondering how many pages of the newspaper he'd flicked through without taking any of it in.

'Dr Jones will see you now,' a young and eager assistant said as he emerged from the consulting room.

'Lord Hunter, it is a pleasure to see you.'

'Have we met before?' Thomas asked. He didn't recall the man, but over the years his father and brother had consulted many doctors.

'I knew your father well, but I think you were always away at school when I visited. How is your mother?'

'Still grieving, but she has found a way to start living her life again.'

The doctor smiled, leaned back in his chair and adjusted his glasses.

'So tell me, Lord Hunter, what brings you to see me today?'

Thomas hesitated. The questions he'd come to ask were difficult to formulate.

'I wish to know more about the disease that afflicted my father and brother. And my risk of developing it.'

Dr Jones steepled his fingers together, contemplating Thomas's request before he started speaking.

'Your father and brother suffered from an inherited condition that affected both their movement and their memory. We know it was of gradual onset and it was progressive. They both became worse with each passing month.'

Thomas nodded, remembering coming home from school at the end of term and not knowing what state his father would be in, dreading what he would find.

'When I first met your father we spent quite some time tracing this disease back through the family. Your father had known many of his relatives had died an unnaturally early death, but there was a lot of secrecy surrounding the illness and those who suffered from it.'

Thomas realised he was holding his breath as he waited for the doctor to continue.

'Not everyone in the family was afflicted. Both men and women suffered from the disease, but only about half of the family members developed it. It was difficult to be sure as in some generations people had died young of other causes.'

'So there is a chance...' Thomas trailed off, unable to complete the sentence.

'There is a good chance you are not affected.'

'How can I be sure, one way or the other?'

Dr Jones shook his head. 'Unfortunately it is impossible to be sure. The disease seems to develop at different ages in different people. Do you have any symptoms?'

'Sometimes I think I have a tremor in my hands.'

'Let me examine you.'

Thomas obligingly removed his jacket, feeling the tremor in his hands as he did so.

'You are nervous,' Dr Jones stated. 'Understandably.'

'My hands are shaking.'

Slowly, as if he had all the time in the world, the doctor inspected Thomas's hands, turning them over and watching the minute movements.

'Make a fist,' he instructed. 'Now relax. Pick up the pen on my desk and write your name. Good.'

Thomas complied with all the instructions, writing his name, turning the key in the lock on the door and untying a knot the doctor presented to him.

'I now need to see you walk.'

Trying to walk normally, Thomas paced backwards and forward across the consulting room, changing his gait as the doctor asked him to walk first on his toes and then as if on a tightrope.

'Good.' The doctor's face was serious and his tone of voice didn't give anything away. 'Come and stand in front of me. Now, I need you to follow my finger with your eyes, keeping your head still.'

Half an hour later, once Thomas had been prodded and poked and undergone a rigorous examination, the doctor sat back in his chair and motioned for Thomas to have a seat.

'You're as healthy as an ox,' he declared.

'And the tremor?'

'Anxiety. You believe you will one day develop a movement disorder, so you are more aware of the smallest movements in your hands than the general population.'

'You can find no sign of the disease?'

'None.'

'But you can't tell me I will not ever develop it?'

'Lord Hunter,' Dr Jones said with a heartfelt sigh, 'I could be trampled by a horse on my walk home to-night. Does that mean I should hide away in my house and never leave it again?'

Thomas shook his head. He knew exactly the point the doctor was making, but his situation was different.

'The likelihood of you being trampled by a horse is much less than me developing my father's disease.'

'Very true,' the doctor said, but didn't appear as though he thought he had lost the argument. 'And it is entirely your choice if you wish to squander your life worrying about something that may or may not ever happen.'

The illness had been a black cloud following him around for so many years the idea of trying not to worry about it was almost inconceivable.

'It is not an active choice I make.'

'And I do understand that, Lord Hunter. Just as I ac-knowledge I have no real idea how it must feel to have this disease, the very disease that killed your father and brother, hanging over you. But you came to me for ad-vice and my advice to you would be to live your life, whether you have five years or fifty. Cherish every sin-gle moment *because* you may have less time than the average man. Find what makes you happy and keep on doing it again and again.'

Rosa. The thought flew unbidden into his mind. *Rosa made him happy.*

'Stop letting this disease ruin your life before you have developed a single symptom.'

Thomas stood abruptly, the doctor's words hitting him and making him feel as though he were seeing the world for the first time.

'Thank you, Doctor.'

'One more thing, Lord Hunter,' the doctor said as Thomas shook his hand vigorously. 'You may consider whether you wish to father any children.'

Thomas smiled. 'This disease stops with me, Dr Jones.'

Leaving the doctor's office Thomas felt lighter than he had for years. He knew he had been consumed by grief after his brother's death, and that had clouded his judgement in many matters. He'd fled the country, telling himself he had to squeeze as many experiences into his life as possible as he didn't know when it would end. Thomas didn't regret that, he'd seen so much, experienced so many different cultures these last few years. What he did regret was his insistence that he must face the future on his own. He'd pushed away the people who loved him, first his mother and then Rosa.

Still, the idea of subjecting Rosa to the pain of watching him suffer through the terrible disease made him uncomfortable, but he knew if he abandoned her now, fled the country and continued his travels around the world, that would hurt her even more. He would be choosing to leave her.

Quickly he pushed his way through the crowds towards the inn he had left his horse at earlier that morning. It would take him nearly two hours to ride home from Portsmouth even if he pushed his horse hard. Suddenly he just needed to be home, needed to hold Rosa in her arms, kiss her lips and tell her what a fool he'd been.

A cold shiver shot down his spine as he wondered if she would forgive him his folly. Ever since he'd proposed he'd treated her badly. He'd seen her growing affection for him and tried to ignore it. He'd allowed the love between them to blossom, but at the same time told Rosa it could not last. He had treated her appallingly.

With a shake of his head he dismissed the notion. Rosa loved him, any fool could see that. She would forgive him and if she didn't he had a whole lifetime to make it up to her.

Two hours later Thomas pushed open the front door, wondering where all the servants were. Normally a footman would be positioned in the entrance hall, ready to receive any visitors, but today there was no one to be seen.

A bloodcurdling scream shot down the stairs and stopped Thomas in his tracks for a second. Then he was running, taking the stairs three at a time. He reached Rosa's bedroom door in less than ten seconds and threw himself inside.

Another scream nearly deafened him before he could take in exactly what he was seeing.

'Rosa…' he whispered, trying to make sense of the scene in the room.

Rosa was half-sitting, half-lying on the blood-soaked sheets covering the bed. His mother was standing by her side, squeezing Rosa's hand and murmuring words of encouragement, whilst two maids hovered nervously in the background. A motherly-looking older woman stood at the foot of the bed, waiting with outstretched arms and a frown of concentration.

Thomas heard Rosa panting, then came another scream that seemed to last for eternity, followed by total silence.

A small cry pierced the silence, more of a gurgle than anything else.

For two seconds no one moved, then Thomas dashed forward. Rosa smiled up at him weakly and then looked hopefully at the bundle the older woman was scooping up.

'Your son,' she pronounced and Thomas felt as though the ground had shifted beneath him.

He leaned in, pausing to kiss Rosa on the forehead, and look down at the pink little face wrapped tightly in a blanket.

Thomas had been both waiting for and dreading this moment. This was the moment when he would know if he could truly love another man's child as his own.

The baby opened his eyes and looked up at him.

'Our son,' Thomas whispered.

There was no doubt, no second guessing. Thomas felt an overwhelming surge of love and happiness looking down into the innocent child's face.

'Our son,' Rosa repeated, tears spilling from her eyes.

Chapter Twenty-Five

Thomas stroked the silky soft hair on his son's head and wondered if Rosa would be offended if he compared it to moleskin. It wasn't that he thought their son looked like a mole…although sometimes when he first woke up from one of his numerous naps…

'Edward?' Rosa suggested.

'I knew an Edward with a squint once,' Thomas said, shuddering.

'Lionel?'

'Scrawny child in the year below me at Eton. Think he wet his trousers during games once.'

'Oliver?'

'Had a dog called Oliver when I was young.'

Rosa took a deep breath. 'Are there *any* names you consider acceptable?'

'Thomas is a good strong name.'

Rosa laughed. 'You would never know who I was referring to.'

'There's another benefit I hadn't thought of.'

Rosa leant out of bed and swiped at him, missing and almost falling in the process.

'Your mama didn't mean to hit us,' Thomas whispered.

'I wasn't aiming at our son.'

For a second Thomas stared down into the child's face, mesmerised by the dark eyes and tiny features.

'Michael,' Rosa said quietly.

Thomas looked up, saw Rosa biting her lip, waiting for his response.

'Michael,' he repeated. 'It suits him.'

Leaning in over the bed, Thomas kissed Rosa, smiling as he felt her arms clutching at his neck as if willing him never to leave her. In the excitement of the birth he hadn't had time to tell her about his trip to the doctor's office in Portsmouth or of the decisions he'd made whilst he was there. Now didn't seem to be the right time. He had treated Rosa so badly, toyed with her heart, he felt as though he needed a big declaration, something that would make Rosa realise he meant what he said and he was here to stay.

'Are you sure you don't wish me to find a wet nurse?' Thomas asked as baby Michael looked up at him and started smacking his little lips.

'Quite sure. Did you know the children of the nobility are more likely to be undernourished than the children of the common people in the first six months?'

'That can't be true.'

'Many wet nurses will feed their own infants first, meaning the children they take in often go hungry.'

'Well, we wouldn't want you to go hungry,' Thomas said, bending down to kiss his son on the tip of his nose. 'Your mother turns into a wild beast when she needs her food.'

'I do not,' Rosa said indignantly.

He looked at her with a raised eyebrow until she glanced down, muttering under her breath.

'Anyway, Michael is my child and I will feed him.'

Thomas stood and passed her the baby, helping her to position him against her breast.

'I will be back soon, my love,' Thomas said as he leant down and kissed her forehead. 'Get some rest once Michael has finished feeding.'

Quickly he made his way downstairs to his study. He was loathe to leave Rosa and their baby, but mother and child needed to sleep and he had an important event to organise. With a steady hand he penned three letters, summoning a footman to take them once he was finished. Rosa would likely be back on her feet in a few days and mostly recovered in a couple of weeks. He would plan his surprise for two weeks' time, to ensure she could enjoy it properly.

'We are very lucky,' Rosa said softly, looking down at her lovely son cradled in her arms. His nose was pressed against her breast and he was suckling loudly, a dreamy, faraway look in his eyes. 'We have your father to look after us.'

Even in the midst of childbirth Rosa had noticed when Thomas had entered the room. She'd felt pure relief, his presence was the one thing that could reassure her through the haze of the pain and the ordeal of giving birth.

She'd watched warily as Thomas had approached their son, seen the uncertainty on his face as he stepped forward to see the child who would bear his name, but not his blood. There was no doubt in Rosa's mind that Thomas had felt instantaneous love for the small child, the love of a parent for their baby, that indescribable rush you felt when you held your little bundle for the first time.

'I think he cares about us both very much,' Rosa continued. 'And I think you've made it much harder for him to leave us both behind.'

'Am I disturbing you?' Sarah asked as she poked her head through the gap between the door and the doorframe.

'Not at all. Thomas has given me strict instructions to rest, but I feel so happy I don't think I could sleep now anyway.'

'I won't stay long. I just wanted to see my grandchild again.'

'We have decided on a name,' Rosa said softly. 'But if you don't like it then we would be quite happy to come up with something different.'

'Your child's name is your decision, my dear.'

'We would like to call him Michael.'

Rosa saw the tears fill the older woman's eyes and run down over her cheeks.

'If it is too painful…'

'No,' Sarah said firmly. 'It is one of the loveliest things anyone has ever done.'

They sat side by side for a few minutes, staring down at Michael's angelic face and drooping eyelids.

'A child unites people like nothing else.'

'I was so scared when I first found out I was pregnant,' Rosa said quietly. 'This pregnancy threatened to tear my whole life apart, and in a way it did, but something much better was built from the wreckage. I feel very lucky.'

'Do you think you will attempt a reconciliation with your mother?' Sarah asked.

Rosa shrugged. She had suffered through so many years of her mother's harsh judgements and cold demeanours that she wasn't sure how much more she could take.

'I think I will focus on my life here for a while. If she wishes to reconcile then I would welcome her, but I don't think my heart could take another rejection from her.'

Sarah stood, leaned over and kissed first baby Michael and then Rosa on the forehead. 'This is your home now and you will always be welcome here.'

Chapter Twenty-Six

Rosa opened the door a crack and heard the furious whispering outside. Straining to catch the words in between the giggles of the excited maids, Rosa grimaced as the door creaked and gave her away.

'It's not time yet, my lady,' the older of the two maids said, her voice uncertain.

'Lord Hunter said you must stay put until he comes to fetch you.'

Rosa sighed and closed the door again. There was no point arguing, the poor maids were only following orders, but she wished Thomas would hurry up. Twenty minutes ago Sarah had come to take Michael downstairs, and it was the longest time Rosa had spent apart from her baby since giving birth.

She wasn't entirely sure what Thomas had planned, but her sharp ears had picked up the sounds of doors opening and closing multiple times and hushed voices whispering in the hall down below.

Flopping back on the bed, Rosa was startled by a knock on the door and was still reclining when Thomas flung it open and strode in.

'It's time,' he declared.

'Time for what?'

'Your surprise.'

'What is my surprise?'

He grinned. 'Just a little something I've organised. Come downstairs and you will see.'

Rosa smoothed her dress—a new gown Thomas had ordered for her especially for this occasion—and slipped her hand into the crook of her husband's elbow.

'Is that music I can hear?'

Soft notes were beginning to float up the stairs as they left the bedroom and walked along the landing.

'Yes. It's your favourite piece.'

He was right, it *was* her favourite piece, but she had never told him that.

Thomas grinned again at her expression. 'Your father told me.'

'Father is here?' Rosa asked, looking around as if expecting him to spring out from behind one of the paintings.

'Enough questions. You'll spoil the surprise.'

Rosa found herself smiling. These past couple of weeks Thomas had seemed lighter in mood, more carefree. He thrived as a father, responding to Michael's needs as if he had been trained for the role, and he and Rosa had been closer than ever before. Not physically, not yet, Rosa was still recuperating from the birth, but he'd hinted that he wanted to be when she was ready.

Time and time again Rosa had to tell herself not to read too much into his words, not to get carried away with the dreams of a perfect life with her perfect family. Thomas still hadn't confirmed whether he was planning on staying or going, although every morning when she woke in his arms she allowed herself to hope just a little bit more.

They reached the closed doors into the drawing room and Thomas squeezed her hand before flinging them open. The music became louder all of a sudden and Rosa saw a dozen heads turn to look at them.

'Thomas, what is happening?' Rosa whispered.

She could see her father, sitting in the front row next to Thomas's mother, head bent over his grandchild. Behind them sat her dear friend Caroline and her son Rupert. On the other side of the room were a couple of elderly women that Rosa took to be Thomas's relatives and two young men accompanied by their wives.

He didn't answer for a few seconds, first leading her to the front of the room down the aisle in between the chairs. A smartly dressed man smiled indulgently at them both before taking a step back.

'Thank you for coming today,' Thomas said, turning to face their intimate audience. 'As you may know, Rosa and I wed in a hurried ceremony whilst we were still in Venice. None of our family or friends were present and I did not mark the occasion with the celebration it deserves.' He paused, turning to Rosa. 'Fortunately my beautiful wife has forgiven me for that, and many more omissions, and has given me the chance to improve upon that behaviour.'

Rosa saw their gathered guests smile as Thomas spoke. For her part she felt as though she were in a dream. She could hear the words coming from Thomas's mouth, but seemed unable to process them.

'Rosa, my darling, my love. I know I have wronged you in so many ways both before and after our wedding. Can you forgive me?'

'What is all this?' Rosa whispered so only her husband could hear.

'A fresh start.'

'Do we need a fresh start?'

'Most decidedly. Rosa, I know I badgered you into marrying me, but I honestly feel it was the best decision of my life. You've made me realise what is important.'

Rosa felt her heart soar and struggled to listen to Thomas's next words.

'Before I met you I thought the most important thing was seeing and experiencing as much of the world as possible, just in case I became unwell and couldn't do the things I wanted to. I was restless, but largely directionless. These last few months you've made me see what really makes me happy.' He turned and smiled at Michael who was cooing and gurgling softly. 'You and our son. That is what makes me happy.'

'And the disease?' Rosa whispered.

She'd seen something change in Thomas around the time of the birth of their son, but she hadn't been able to work out exactly what. He'd become more positive, as if he'd decided not to let the terrible disease that one day might affect him spoil the here and now.

He shrugged. 'Maybe one day I will develop symptoms, maybe I won't, but I realise I cannot let the possibility of what might happen in the future ruin my life now. I'm a lucky man, I have a beautiful wife, a lovely home and a perfect son. I need to start appreciating my blessing rather than worrying about the future.'

Rosa beamed. It was all she had ever wanted for him. She knew the shadow of his brother's and father's deaths would always hang over him, as would the disease that might one day claim his body and mind, too, but he really was trying to appreciate all the good in his life right now.

'I love you, Rosa,' Thomas said softly. 'I've loved you for a long time, I was just too caught up in my worries to realise it.'

'You love me?'

'Do you doubt it?'

Rosa realised she was shaking her head. She didn't doubt it. Their married life might have been far from ideal initially, but once Thomas had allowed himself to enjoy her company she had seen the pleasure and happiness bloom.

'I love you, too.'

'I know,' he said with a mischievous grin.

Rolling her eyes at his confidence, she allowed him to pull her in closer to his side.

'Marry me?'

'We're already married, Thomas.'

'I know, but it was such a rushed affair, so impersonal, I thought we could have the marriage blessed.'

'Is that possible?'

'Father Young, here, assures me it is allowed.' Thomas dropped his voice. 'And he was particularly keen to bless the marriage seeing as the initial ceremony was not in his beloved Church of England.'

Rosa glanced up at the vicar and saw him smiling benevolently at her.

'Shall we begin?' Father Young asked.

After a short prayer Rosa and Thomas repeated their marriage vows and then Father Young uttered a blessing over their union.

'Congratulations,' he said quietly once he was finished with the blessing.

The assembled guests stood and clapped as Thomas led Rosa down the short aisle, before turning back and retracing their steps so Rosa could take baby Michael from her mother-in-law's arms.

'Where would you like to go for our honeymoon?' Thomas asked as they led their guests through to the dining room where a mouth-watering selection of food had been laid out.

'I know of a beautiful villa on the edge of Lake Garda that might be available,' Rosa said.

'You little minx,' Thomas whispered. 'You just want to see me swimming naked again.'

'The thought had crossed my mind. It would almost be worth braving the voyage again.'

'Only almost?'

'Well, it's not as though you need much of an excuse to take your clothes off, is it?'

Thomas threw his head back and laughed, before slipping a hand around Rosa's waist and making her shudder with anticipation by trailing his fingers over her lower back.

'Do you know, I never imagined I could be this happy?' Thomas said as he pulled out her seat, watched her as she cradled Michael into a more upright position in her arms and then pushed her chair in towards the table. 'I never dared to hope.'

Quickly, before their guests entered the room, Thomas bent his neck and kissed Rosa softly on the lips, pulling away only to drop a kiss on Michael's forehead.

'My perfect little family,' he murmured.

Epilogue

Rosa glanced impatiently to where Thomas was talking quietly with his solicitor, Mr Biggins. She knew the words of advice the elderly man was bestowing on her husband were important, but she wouldn't be able to contain her excitement and anticipation much longer.

'This institution holds over a hundred children at any one time,' Mr Pitt, the governor of the orphanage droned in her direction. 'Over a hundred children to house, feed and clothe.' He shook his head as if he couldn't believe the expense was justifiable.

'The children provide an income too, though,' Rosa said sweetly. 'They work.'

Mr Pitt scoffed and shook his head. 'Barely enough to provide one meal a day. The rest of the money comes from charitable donations.'

'Shall we go upstairs?' Thomas said, stepping away from the solicitor and taking Rosa's hand.

Rosa watched with a smile as Thomas scooped their son on to his shoulders and dashed up the stairs, making Michael scream with delight. Mr Pitt grimaced at this outward display of merriment, but held his tongue.

'Tell your mama to hurry up,' Thomas said as Rosa approached the top of the sweeping staircase.

'You're too slow, Mama,' Michael giggled, squirming as Rosa bent and placed a kiss on the top of his head.

'The girls have a dormitory to your left, the boys on the right. The nursery is at the end of the corridor.'

Rosa and Thomas had visited the orphanage before, but never had they ventured upstairs to the nursery.

'Tell us more about the child,' Thomas said, his face suddenly serious.

'Elizabeth is two months old and came to us two weeks ago,' Mr Pitt informed them. 'Her father was a sailor, he perished at sea before Elizabeth was born. Her mother died of a bad chest. She has no other relatives to take her in and look after her, hence she came to us.'

As he spoke Mr Pitt led them through the nursery, past row after row of cribs, some with tiny crying babies inside. The two young girls, neither much older than twelve themselves, ran backwards and forward, trying to comfort the squalling infants without much success.

They stopped and Rosa looked down into the crib, squeezing Thomas's hand as she did so.

'She's not got any hair,' Michael observed from his position on his father's shoulders.

'Some babies don't have any hair for the first few months.'

'Why not?'

Rosa blinked, then smiled at her son, 'Because everyone is different. Some babies have hair, some don't. Just like some have blue eyes and some brown.'

'I've got your eyes,' Michael said, then frowned in a way that made Rosa's heart swell with love. 'But you've got your eyes, too.'

'That's right, darling.' Turning to Mr, Pitt Rosa asked, 'Can I hold her?'

The governor of the orphanage shrugged and stepped back, as if he didn't want to get too close to an actual child.

Rosa leaned over the small baby, taking a minute to stroke her head and feel the silky smooth skin.

'Would you like a little sister?' Thomas crouched down so he was level with Michael.

'Will I have to share my toys?'

'Yes.'

'Even Ted-Ted?'

'Ted-Ted is just for you.'

Rosa cradled the little girl gently, feeling a warm gush of happiness as her eyes flickered open and focused on Rosa's.

'I wouldn't *mind* a little sister,' Michael said. 'As long as I'm the big brother.'

'Always.' Thomas stood, ruffling their son's hair before moving closer to Rosa. 'What do you think?' he asked.

'She's perfect.'

Six months ago Rosa had been watching Thomas and Michael chase each other across the lawn when she'd been struck by the desire to add to their family. She'd nurtured this wish in private for a few weeks before Thomas had wheedled it out of her. Rosa had always known their family would be limited to three and she knew she was blessed to have such a wonderful husband and son, but sometimes she yearned for a little baby to take care of, another child to raise through infancy and beyond.

Despite her desire for another child, Rosa had tried

to put the idea from her mind. Thomas had remained healthy in the five years since their marriage, but still they were both very aware the Hunter family curse could strike at any time. He would not risk fathering any children, and as such Rosa had attempted, albeit unsuccessfully, to put aside her broodiness.

When Thomas had suggested adopting an orphan Rosa had almost cried with happiness. She longed for a little brother or sister for Michael, someone for him to play with and protect, and now it looked as though they'd found just the child.

'Biggins is satisfied the adoption will be legal,' Thomas murmured quietly.

The first time they had visited the orphanage she'd wanted to take Elizabeth home with them straight away. The thought of the little girl suffering in the cold, starved of affection, was distressing, but Thomas had insisted they make everything legal first. He didn't want them to get hurt, to attach their affections to a child who one day might be claimed by an errant parent or relative. Once Elizabeth left the orphanage with them he wanted it all to be final.

'If you are happy we can sign the papers today,' Mr Pitt said. 'Then, of course, there is the matter of the fee…'

Biggins had waved his hand dismissively when Rosa had questioned the legality of this fee Mr Pitts was asking for. 'Think of it as a donation to the orphanage,' he had said. 'Or a bribe to the governor to let things run smoothly.'

Rosa knew all too well that the money they paid would not be spent on the struggling orphans, but would instead line Mr Pitt's own pocket, and reluctantly she had agreed not to make a fuss. Only her desire not to jeopardise the adoption made her keep quiet.

'Let us complete the formalities,' Thomas suggested. 'My wife will dress the child for outside and follow in a few minutes.'

With a wink Thomas led the governor back through the nursery, leaving Rosa alone with her son and his new baby sister.

Carefully Rosa stripped Elizabeth down, removing the rough, abrasive smock she was dressed in and replacing it with three layers of soft cotton. All the time Michael stood watching his new sister intently.

'Now you are a big brother you will need to look after your sister,' Rosa said.

Michael nodded, his expression serious. He looked as though he were standing guard over the crib, protecting the baby girl inside.

'She will need you to show her how to do things as she grows up and to protect her from harm. Can you do that for me?'

'Yes, Mama.'

Rosa pulled Michael into a cuddle and kissed the top of his head. 'You're my special little man. I'm so proud of you.'

Cradling Elizabeth in one arm and holding Michael's hand with the other, Rosa made her way through the nursery and back downstairs. They'd just reached the bottom step when a bundle of pure angry energy came running at them.

'You can't take her! She's not yours!'

Rosa swept Michael behind her protectively as a small girl, red-faced with anger, shot out of a side room and started pummelling Rosa's knees.

'Stop hitting my mummy,' Michael bellowed, refusing to stay behind Rosa and charging at the little girl.

Conscious of the delicate little baby in her arms Rosa crouched down and did her best to separate the two small children.

'What's the commotion?' Thomas asked, striding from Mr Pitt's office, closely followed by the governor himself.

'Emily, stop that at once,' Mr Pitt shouted.

The little girl fell still and looked up pitifully at Rosa.

'Get back to your lessons.'

Her bottom lip began to tremble, but she stood her ground.

'Why don't you tell me what is the matter?' Rosa asked softly.

'You're stealing my sister.'

Ten seconds of silence followed the statement as Rosa and Thomas glanced at the orphanage governor before looking at each other.

'She's *my* sister,' Michael piped up.

Before the two young children could launch themselves at each other again Rosa held up a warning hand.

'Elizabeth is your sister?' she asked the little girl.

A nod. Followed by a few tears rolling down her cheeks.

'Mr Pitt?' Thomas asked, his voice strained.

'Ah, well. The thing is, you see…'

'*Is* this Elizabeth's sister?' As the governor opened his mouth again Thomas fixed him with a hard stare.

'Yes,' he mumbled eventually.

'Older sister,' Emily clarified.

Rosa looked down at the bundle in her arms and felt the tears building in her eyes. They had been so close, so close to completing their family, so close to finding the perfect little addition, but she knew she couldn't take away this poor little girl's only living relative. Sisters needed each other.

'Emily,' Thomas said, crouching down so he was on the little girl's level. 'Is it just you and your sister now?'

Emily nodded. 'Mama made me promise to look after her.'

Rosa felt a lump in her throat as Emily looked earnestly at her little sister.

'How old are you?'

'Four and a half.'

'I'm five,' Michael piped up.

'But girls grow up quicker than boys,' Emily said with a sage wisdom beyond her years.

'Do not.'

'Do so.'

'How do you like it here, Emily?' Thomas interrupted.

She shrugged. 'It's horrible.'

'I can't see—' Mr Pitt began to speak, but Thomas held up an imperious hand.

'But I've gotta learn to live with it because older children never get adopted. That's what *he* said.' She pointed to Mr Pitt.

'Well, it—it *is* the truth,' Mr Pitt stammered, 'The babies often catch a childless couple's eye, but older children…' He let the rest of the sentence hang in the air.

'But I promised Mama I'd look after Elizabeth.'

'Then you can come and be my sister, too,' Michael said simply.

Everyone froze.

Rosa saw Thomas recover first and glance quickly at her.

'Emily, we were hoping to take Elizabeth home with us, to look after her as part of our family,' Thomas said, speaking slowly but seriously, as if he were conversing with an adult. 'If you would like, you could come and stay for a little while, too—see how you and your sister like it at our house.'

'And if we don't we can just come back?'

'If you don't you can just come back.'

'We'd be together?'

'Always. We're not trying to take your sister away from you.'

The serious little four-year-old bit her lip and considered the offer, then held out her hand for Thomas to shake.

Thomas stood up, slipped an arm around Rosa's waist, and quickly kissed her on the cheek.

'So now I have two sisters?' Michael asked.

Rosa opened her mouth to reply, but her son continued.

'Maybe we could choose a brother next?'

Thomas flung his head back and laughed, and Rosa couldn't help but join in with him.

'What are they laughing about?' Emily whispered to Michael.

'I don't know. Sometimes they're strange,' Michael replied, shaking his head.

'This really isn't what we agreed,' Mr Pitt said, stepping forward.

'You never told us Elizabeth has a sister.'

'An oversight…'

'Mr Biggins, here, will sort out the paperwork,'

Thomas said, dismissing the orphanage governor with a look. 'And I'm sure a further donation to the orphanage will help smooth the way.'

That night in bed Thomas pulled Rosa close to his body and began planting kisses along the nape of her neck.

'What have we done?' Rosa asked. 'Are we mad?'

'Most probably. You, at least.'

'We never even talked about adopting *two* children.'

Thomas gently turned her over so she was looking into his eyes.

'But we have enough love for two,' he said softly. 'Surely that's what matters.'

Rosa smiled. Whenever she was doubting herself, whenever she felt unsure of what to do or what to think, Thomas would look at her in that loving way and make everything seem simple.

'Michael seemed to like them.'

'He likes being a big brother.'

'And your mother is spoiling them already.'

'There's no harm in that. Those little girls won't have had much chance to be spoiled up until now.'

'It'll be harder to travel with three.'

Thomas shrugged. 'We managed it with Michael. We can manage it with two more.'

When Michael had turned two Thomas had declared it was high time they saw a bit more of the world and the three of them had set off on an eight month adventure to India. They'd vowed to do the same every couple of years, to choose a destination and travel. It had never been explicitly said, but Rosa knew Thomas still had some of his wanderlust from all the time he spent travelling before he'd met her.

'I can't help thinking of all the other children left behind in that horrible place,' Rosa said quietly.

'Three children I can cope with, but I'm not sure I have it in me to adopt over a hundred.'

'There must be some other way we can help,' Rosa said, looking up at her husband hopefully.

'I'll talk to Biggins, see whether we can find a way to support the orphanage.'

'It's such a grey and miserable place. I don't like to think of the children growing up there.'

'Then we shall not rest until those children are happy and smiling and laughing.'

'Don't tease me. I know you feel the same way.'

Thomas grinned at her. 'I'd have them all here in an instant if I could, but maybe it's better to make the orphanage a better place for those there now, as well as those who will arrive in years to come.'

'I love you,' Rosa said. 'I can't believe we left the house today with one child and returned with three.'

'We can do this,' Thomas said, running his fingers across her forehead and tucking her hair behind one ear. 'You, me, Michael and those two beautiful girls. It sounds like everything we've ever wished for.'

* * * * *